FORGOTTEN REALMS

ELMINSTER
IN MYTH DRANNOR

Ed Greenwood

Wizards
OF THE COAST

ELMINSTER IN MYTH DRANNOR

©1998 TSR, Inc.
©2000 Wizards of the Coast, Inc.

Distributed in the United States by Holtzbrinck Publishing. Distributed in Canada by Fenn Ltd.

Distributed to the hobby, toy, and comic trade in the United States and Canada by regional distributors.

Distributed worldwide by Wizards of the Coast, Inc. and regional distributors.

Printed in the U.S.A.

Cover art by Ciruelo Cabral
First Printing: November 1997
First paperback edition: December 1998
Library of Congress Catalog Card Number: 96-60803

9 8 7 6 5 4 3
ISBN: 0-7869-1190-5
620-08575P-001-EN

U.S., CANADA,
ASIA, PACIFIC, & LATIN AMERICA
Wizards of the Coast, Inc.
P.O. Box 707
Renton, WA 98057-0707
+1-800-324-6496

EUROPEAN HEADQUARTERS
Wizards of the Coast, Belgium
T Hofveld 6d
1702 Groot-Bijgaarden
Belgium
+322 467 3360

Visit our web site at http://www.wizards.com

Novels by Ed Greenwood

The Elminster Series
Elminster: The Making of a Mage
Elminster in Myth Drannor
The Temptation of Elminster

Elminster in Hell
Elminster's Daughter
(May 2004)

The Cormyr Saga
Cormyr: A Novel (with Jeff Grubb)
Death of the Dragon (with Troy Denning)

The Shandril Saga
Spellfire
Crown of Fire
Hand of Fire

The Shadow of the Avatar Trilogy
Shadows of Doom
Cloak of Shadows
All Shadows Fled

Stormlight
Silverfall: Stories of the Seven Sisters

For
Cheryl Freedman
and
Merle von Thorn

two ladies Elminster wanted at his side
(blades, good humor, and all)
when he was in Myth Drannor

Prologue

It was a time of mounting strife in the fair realm of Cormanthor, when the lords and ladies of the oldest, proudest houses felt a threat to their glittering pride. A threat thrust forward by the very throne above them; a threat from their most darkling youthful nightmares. The Stinking Beast That Comes In The Night, the Hairy Lurker who waits his best chance to slay, despoil, violate, and pillage. The monster whose grasp clutches at more realms with each passing day: the terror known as Man.

Shalheira Talandren, High Elven Bard of Summerstar
from **Silver Blades And Summer Nights:
An Informal But True History of Cormanthor**
published in The Year of the Harp

"I did indeed promise the prince something in return for the crown," said the king, drawing himself up to his full height and inhaling until his chest trembled. He adjusted the glittering circlet of gems and golden spires that adorned his brows a trifle self-consciously, smiled at his own cleverness in providing himself with this dramatic pause, and added, voice dropping to underline the nobility of his words, "I promised I'd grant his greatest desire."

Those gathered to watch drew in awed breaths in a chorus that was mockingly loud.

The fat monarch paid them no heed, but turned away in a gaudy swirl of cloth of gold and struck a grandly conquering pose, one foot planted on an obviously false dragonskull. The light of the purple-white driftglobes that accompanied him gleamed back from plainly visible wire, where it coiled up through the patchwork skull to hold the royal sword that had supposedly transfixed bone in a mighty, fatal blow.

Every inch the wise old ruler, the king looked out over vast distances for a moment, eyes flashing gravely at things only he could see. Then, almost coyly, he looked back over his shoulder at the kneeling servant.

"And what, pray tell," he purred, "does he most want? Hmmm?"

The steward flung himself full length onto the carpet, striking his head on the stone pave in the process. He rolled his eyes and writhed briefly in pain—as the watchers tittered—ere he dared to lift his gaze for the first time. "Sire," he said at last, in tones of wondering doom, "he wishes to die rich."

The king whirled about again and strode forward. The servant scrambled up on one knee and cowered back from the purposeful monarch—only to freeze, dumbfounded, at the sight of a merry smile upon the regal face.

The king bent to take his hand and raised him up from the carpet, slapping something that jingled into the steward's palm as he did so.

The servant stared down. It was a purse bulging with coins. He looked at the king again, in disbelief, and swallowed.

The royal smile broadened. "Die rich? And so he shall—put that into his hands and then slide your sword through him. Several times is the current fashion, I believe."

The titters of the audience broke into hoots and roars of mirth, laughter that quickly turned to applause as the costume spells cloaking the actors expired in the traditional puffs of red smoke, signaling the end of the scene.

The watchers exploded into motion, swooping and darting away. Some of the older revelers drifted off more sedately, but the young went racing through the night like furious fish chasing each other to eat—or be eaten. They exploded through groups of languid gossipers and danced in the air, flashing along the edge of the perfumed spell field. Only a few remained behind to watch the next coarse scene of *The Fitting End of the Human King Halthor*; such parodies of the low and grasping ways of the Hairy Ones were amusing at first, but very 'one note,' and above all elves of Cormanthor hated to be bored—or at least, to admit their boredom.

Not that this wasn't a grand revel. The Ereladden had spared no expense in the weaving of the fieldspells. A constant array of conjured sounds, smells, and images swirled and wafted over the revelers, and the power of the conjured field allowed everyone to fly, moving through the air to wherever they gazed, and desired to be. Most of the revelers were floating aloft now, drifting down occasionally to take in refreshments.

This night the usually bare garden walls bristled with carved unicorns, pegasi, dancing elven maidens, and rearing stags this night. Every statuette touched by a reveler split apart and drifted open, to reveal teardrop decanters of sparkling moonwine or any one of a dozen ruby-hued Erladden vintages. Amid the spires of the decanters were the shorter spikes of crystal galauntra whose domes covered figurines sculpted of choice cheese, roasted nuts, or sugarstars.

Amid the rainbow-hued lights drifting among the merry elves were vapors that would make any true-blood light-hearted, restless, and full of life. Some abandoned, giggling Cormyth were dodging through the air from cloud to cloud, their eyes gleaming too brightly to see the world around them. Half a hundred giggles rolled amid the branches of the towering trees that rose over all, twinkling magestars winking and slithering here and there among their leaves. As the moon rose to overwhelm such tiny radiances, it shone down on a scene of wild and joyful celebration. Half of Cormanthor was dancing tonight.

* * * * *

"Surprisingly, I still remembered the words that would bring me here."

The voice came out of the night without warning. Its welcoming tone dared him to recall earlier days.

He'd been expecting it, and was even unsurprised to hear its low, melodious tones issuing from the shadows in the deepest part of the bower, where the bed stood.

A bed he still found most restful, even with age beginning to creep into his bones. The Coronal of all Cormanthor turned his head in the moonlight, looking away from the mirror-smooth waters that surrounded this garden isle, and said with a smile that managed to be happier than his heart felt, "Be welcome, Great Lady of the Starym."

There was silence for a moment in the shadows before the voice came again. "I was once more than that," it said, almost wistful.

Eltargrim rose and held out his hand to where his truesight told him she stood. "Come to me, my friend." He stretched out his other hand, almost beseechingly. "My Lyntra."

Shadows shifted, and Ildilyntra Starym came out into the moonlight, her eyes still the dark pools of promise that he recalled so vividly in his dreams. Dreams that had visited him down all the long years to this very night. Dreams built on memories that could still unsettle him. . . .

The Coronal's mouth was suddenly dry, and his tongue felt thick and clumsy. "Will you—?" he mumbled, gesturing toward the Living Seat.

The Starym held themselves to be the eldest and most pure of the families of the One True Realm—and were certainly the proudest. Their matriarch glided toward him, those dark eyes never leaving his.

The Coronal did not have to look to know that the years had not yet touched her flawless white skin, the figure so perfect that it still took his breath away. Her blue tresses were almost black, as always, and Ildilyntra still wore them unbound, falling at her heels to the ground. She was barefoot, the spells of her girdle keeping both hair and feet inches above the dirt of the ground. She wore the full, formal gown of her house, the twin falling dragons of the Starym arms bold in glittering gems upon her stomach, their sculpted wings cupping her breasts in a toothed surround of gold.

Her thighs, revealed through the waist-high slits in the gown as she came, were girt in the black-and-gold spirals of a mantle of honor. The ends of the mantle drew together to support the intricately carved dragontooth scabbard of her honor blade, bobbing like a small lamp, wrapped in the deep, solemn red glow of its awakened power. The Ring of the Watchful Wyvern gleamed upon her hand. This was not an informal visit.

The moon was right for a chat between old friends, but no matriarch comes aglow in all her power for such things. Sadness grew in the Coronal. He knew what must lie ahead.

And so, of course, she surprised him. Ildilyntra came to a halt before him, as he'd known she must. She drew apart her gown, hands on hips, to let him see the light of the full, gathered power of her honor blade. This also he expected, and likewise the deep, shuddering intake of breath that followed.

Now the storm would come, the snarled words of sarcastic fire or cold, biting venom for which she was famous throughout Cormanthor. The twisted words of harmful spells would lurk among them, to be sure, and he'd hav—

In smooth silence, the matriarch of the Starym knelt before him. Her eyes never left his.

Eltargrim swallowed again, looking down at her knees, white tinged with the slightest shade of blue, where they were sunk into the circle of moss at his feet. "Ildilyntra," he said softly. "Lady, I—"

Flecks of gold had always surfaced in her dark eyes when she was moved to strong emotion. Gold glinted in them now.

"I am not one used to begging," that melodious voice came again, bringing back a flood of memories in the Coronal, of other, more tender moonlit nights in this bower, "and yet I've come here to beg you, exalted lord. Reconsider this Opening you speak of. Let no being who is not a trueblood of the People walk in Cormanthor save by our leave. Let that leave be near-never given, that our People endure!"

"Ildilyntra, rise. Please," Eltargrim said firmly, stepping back. "And give me some reasons why I should embrace your plea." His mouth curved into the ghost of a smile. "You can't be unaware that I've heard such words before."

The High Lady of the Starym remained on her

knees, cloaked in her hair, and looked into his eyes.

The Coronal smiled openly this time. "Yes, Lyntra, that still works on me. But give me reasons to weigh and work with . . . or speak of lighter things."

Anger snapped in those dark eyes for the first time. "Lighter things? Empty-headed revelry, like those fools indulging themselves over at Erladden Towers?" She rose then, as swift as a coiling serpent, and pulled open her gown. The blue-white sleekness of her bared body was as much a challenge as her level gaze. Ildilyntra added coldly, "Or did you think I'd come for dalliance, lord? Unable to keep myself one night longer from the charms of the ruler of us all, risen to such aged wisdom from the strong and ardent youth I knew?"

Eltargrim let her words fall into silence, as hurled daggers that miss their target spin into empty air. He ended it calmly. "This spitting fury is the High Lady of the Starym I have grown familiar with these past centuries. I admire your taste in undergarments, but I had hoped that you'd set aside some of what your junior kin call your 'cutting bluster' here; there *are* only the two of us on this isle. Let us speak candidly, as befits two elder Cormyth. It saves so much . . . empty courtesy."

Ildilyntra's mouth tightened. "Very well," she said, planting her hands on her hips in a manner he well remembered. "Hear me then, Lord Eltargrim: I, my senior kin, and many other families and folk of Cormanthor besides—I can name the principals if you wish, Lord, but be assured they are neither few nor easily discredited as youths or touch-headed—think that this notion of Opening the realm will doom us all, if it is ever made reality."

She paused, eyes blazing into his, but the Coronal silently beckoned at her to give him more words. She

continued, "If you follow your mad dreams of amend-
ing the law of Cormanthor to all non-elves into the
realm, our long friendship must end."

"With the taking of my life?" he asked quietly.

Again silence fell, as Ildilyntra drew breath, opened
her mouth, and then closed it. She strode angrily away
across the moon-drenched moss and flagstones before
whirling around to face him once more.

"All of House Starym," she said firmly, "must needs
take up arms against a ruler so twisted in his head
and heart—so tainted in his elven bloodlines—as to
preside over, nay, eagerly *embrace* the destruction of
the fair realm of Cormanthor."

Their gazes met in silence, but the Coronal seemed
carved of patiently smiling marble. Ildilyntra Starym
drew in a deep breath and went on, her voice now as
imperious as that of any ruling queen. "For make no
mistake, Lord: your Opening, if it befalls, will destroy
this mightiest realm of the People."

She stalked impatiently across the garden, flinging
her hands up at the trees, shrubs, and sculpted banks
of flowers. "Where we have dwelt, loved, and nurtured,
the beauties of the forests *we* have tended will know
the brutal boots and dirty, careless touch of humans."
The Starym matriarch turned and pointed at the Coronal, almost spitting in her fury as she advanced upon
him, adding a race with each step. "And halflings." She
came on, face blazing. "And gnomes." Her voice sank
with anger, trembling into a harsh whisper as she delivered the gasp of ultimate outrage: "Even . . .
dwarves!"

The Coronal opened his mouth to speak, as she
thrust her face forward almost to touch his, but she
whirled away again, snapping her fingers, and turned
back immediately to confront him again, hair swirling.
"All we have striven for, all we have fought the beast-

men and the orcs and the great wyrms to keep, will be diluted—nay, *polluted*—and in the end swept away, our glory drowned out in the clamoring ambitions, greater numbers, and cunning schemes of the hairy *humans!*"

That last word rose into a ringing shout that tore around their ears, setting the blue glass chimes in the trees around the distant Heartpool singing in response.

As their faint clamor drifted past the Living Seat, Ildilyntra stood facing the Coronal in silence, breast heaving with emotion, eyes blazing. Out of the night a sudden shaft of moonlight struck her shoulders, setting her agleam with cold white light like a vengeful banner.

Eltargrim bowed his head for a moment, as if in respect to her passion, and took a slow step toward her. "I once spoke similar words," he said, "and thought even darker things. Yet I have come to see in our brethren races—the humans, in particular—the life, verve, and energy we lack. Heart and drive we once had; we can only see now in the brief glimpses afforded by visions of days long gone sent by our forebears. Even the proud House of Starym, if all of its tongues spoke bare truth, would be forced to admit that we have lost something—something within ourselves, not merely lives, riches, and forest domains lost to the spreading ambition of others."

The Coronal broke into restless pacing as Ildilyntra had done before him, his white robe swirling as he turned to her in the moonlight and said almost pleadingly, "This may be a way to win back what we have lost. A way where for so long there has been nothing but posturing, denial, and slow decline. I believe true glory can be ours once again, not merely the proud, gilded shell of assumed greatness we cling to now.

More than that: the dream of peace between men and elves and dwarves can at last be upon us! Maeral's dream, fulfilled at last!"

The lady with blue-black hair and darker blazing eyes moved from her stillness like a goaded beast, striding past him as a forest cat encircles a foe it remains wary of . . . for a little while yet. Her voice, when it came, was no longer melodious, but instead cut like a lustily waved razor.

"Like all who fall into the grip of elder years, Eltargrim," she snarled, "you begin to long for the world as you want it to be, and not as it is. Maeral's dream is just that—a dream! Only fools could think it might become real, in this savage Faerûn we see around us. The humans rise in magecraft—brutal, grasping, realm-burning magecraft—with each passing year! And you would invite these—these *snakes* into our very bosoms, within our armor . . . into our *homes!*"

Sadness made the Coronal's eyes a little bleak as he looked at what she'd become, revealed now in her fury—far and very far from the gentle elven maid he'd once stroked and comforted, in the shy tears of her youth.

He stepped into the path of her raging stride and asked gently, "And is it not better to invite them in, win friendship and through it some influence to guide, than it would be to fight them, fall, and have them stalk into our homes as smashing, trampling conquerors, striding amid the streaming blood of all our people? Where is the glory in that? What is it you are striving to keep so sacred, if all our people perish? Twisted legends in the minds of the humans and our half-kin? Of a strange, decadent people with pointed ears and upturned noses, whose blinding pride was their fatal folly?"

Ildilyntra had been forced to halt, or her angry

progress would have carried her into him. She stood listening to his rain of questions almost nose to nose, white-clenched fists at her sides.

"Will you be the one to let these—these *beast*-races into our secret places and the very seat of our power?" she asked now, her voice suddenly harsh. "To be remembered with hatred by what few of our People will survive your folly, as the traitor who led the citizens he was pledged to serve . . . our very race . . . into ruin?"

Eltargrim shook his head. "I have no choice; I can see only the Opening as a way in which our People may *have* a future. All other roads I've looked down, and even taken this realm a little way along, lead—and speedily, in the seasons just ahead—to red war. War that can only lead to death and defeat for fair Cormanthor, as all the races but the dwarves and gnomes outnumber us twenty to one and more. Humans and orcs overmuster us by thousands to one. If pride leads us to war, it leads us also to the grave—and that is a choice I've no right to make, on behalf of our children, whose lives I'll be crushing before they can fend, and choose, for themselves."

Ildilyntra spat, "That fear-ladling argument can be made from now until forever grows old. There'll *always* be babes too young to choose their own ways!"

She moved again, stepping around him, turning her head to always face him as she went, and added almost casually, "There is an old song that says there is no reasoning with a Coronal of firm purpose . . . and I see the truth of it now. There is nothing I can say that will convince you."

There was something old and very tired in Eltargrim's face as his eyes met hers. "I fear not, Ildilyntra . . . loved and honored Ildilyntra," he said. "A Coronal must do what is right, whate'er the cost."

She gave an exasperated hiss, as he spread his hands

a little and told her, "That is what it means to be Coronal—not the pomp and the regalia and the bowing."

Ildilyntra walked away from him across the moss, to where a thrusting shoulder of stone barred her way and gave a home to lavender creepers. She folded her arms with savage grace, and looked south out over the placid water. It was a smooth sheet of white now in the moonlight. The silence she left in her wake grew deep and deafening.

The Coronal let his hands fall and watched her, waiting patiently. In this realm of warring prides and dark, never-forgotten memories, much of a Coronal's work consisted of waiting patiently. Younger elves never realized that.

The High Lady of the Starym looked out into the night for what seemed a very long time, her arms trembling slightly. Her voice was as high and as soft as a sudden breeze when she spoke next. "Then I know what I must do."

Eltargrim raised his hand to let his power lash out and trammel her freedom—the gravest insult one could give to the head of an elven House.

Yet he was too late. Sudden fire blossomed in the night, a line of sparks where his power met hers and wrestled just long enough to let her turn. Her honor blade was in her hand as her eyes met his.

"Oh, that I once loved you," she hissed. "For the Starym! For *Cormanthor!*"

Moongleam flashed once along the keen edge of her blade as she buried it hilt-deep in her breast, and with her other hand thrust its dragon tooth scabbard into the bright fountaining blood there. The carved fang seemed to flicker for a moment, and then, slowly, melted away into the river of gore. More blood was pouring from her than that curvaceous body should have been able to hold.

"Eltar . . ." she gasped then, almost beseechingly, her eyes growing dark as she swayed. The Coronal took a swift step forward and raised his hands, the glow of healing magic blazing along his fingers—but at the sight of it she snatched forth the glistening blade and drove it hard into her throat.

He was running now, across the little space that remained between them, as she choked, stumbled forward—and swept her gore-soaked arm up once more to drive the blade of her honor deep into her own right eye.

She fell into his arms, then, lips frozen trying to whisper his name again, and the Coronal let her down gently onto the moss, despite the growing roar of magic tearing past him, streaming up into the night sky like bloody smoke from where the dragon tooth had been. Magic that he knew sought to claim his life.

"Oh, Lyntra," he murmured. "Was any dispute worth your final death?" He rose from her then, looking at the blood glistening on his hands, and gathered his will.

Her gore was a weakness, a route the magic mustering above him could take past his gathered power if he banished it too late.

As he stared at his spread hands, the dark wetness faded from them, until they blazed blue-white with risen magic, racing along his skin like fire. The Coronal looked up, then, at the sudden darkness above him—and found himself gazing straight into the open, dripping jaws of a blood dragon.

It was the most deadly spell of the elder Houses, a revenge magic that took the life of its awakener. The Doom of the Purebloods, some called it. The dragon towered above him, dark, wet, and terrible in the night, as silent as a breeze and as deadly as a rain of enchanted venom. Living flesh would melt before it, twisting, withering, and shriveling into grey rot and tangled bones and sinew.

The ruler of all Cormanthor stood robed in his aroused power, and watched the dragon strike.

It crashed down around him, in a rain that shook the entire island, setting leaves to rustling all around and shattering the stillness of the lake into a hundred racing wavelets. Rocks rolled and moss scorched away into smoking ash where it touched. Thwarted in its strike by the dome of empty air his risen power guarded, it swirled and roared, flowing in a hungry circle around the elven ruler.

Eltargrim stood unmoving, untouched in the circle his power protected, and watched it run into oblivion. Once more it raised its head to menace him, a tattered shadow of its former self. He stood his ground grimly, and it fell away to drifting smoke against the blue-white fire of the Coronal.

When it was all gone, the old elf ran a trembling hand through his white hair and knelt again at the side of the sprawled lady. "Lyntra," he said sadly, bending to kiss lips where dark blood still bubbled forth. "Oh, Lyntra."

Blood spat into smoke on her throat then, touched by his power just as the slaying spell she'd called up had been. More smokes rose, as his tears began to fall in earnest.

He struggled against them, as the glass chimes sounded again, and the faltering of his shielding spells let in a burst of distant laughter and wild, high music from the Erladden revel. He struggled because he was the Coronal of Cormanthor, and his duty meant he had one more thing to say before the blood stopped flowing, and she grew cold.

Eltargrim threw back his head to look once at the moon, choked back a sob, and managed to say huskily, looking into the one staring eye that remained, "You shall be remembered with honor."

And if his grief overmastered him thereafter, as he cradled the body of the one who was still his beloved, there was no one else on the island to hear.

PART I

HUMAN

One

SAVAGE TRAILS AND SCEPTERS

*Nothing is recorded of the journey of Elminster from his
native Athalantar across half a world of wild forests to
the fabled elven realm of Cormanthor, and it can only be
assumed to have been uneventful.*

Antarn the Sage
from **The High History of Faerûnian Archmages Mighty**
published circa The Year of the Staff

The young man was busy pondering the last words
a goddess had said to him—so the arrow that burst
from the trees took him completely by surprise.

It hummed past his nose, trailing leaves, and
Elminster peered after it, blinking in surprise. When
he looked along the road in front of him again, men in
worn and filthy leathers were scrambling down onto it
to bar his way, swords and daggers in their hands.
There were six or more of them, and none looked
kindly.

"Get down or die," one of them announced, almost
pleasantly. El cast quick glances right and left, saw no
one charging him from behind, and murmured a quick
word.

When he flicked his fingers, an instant later, three
of the brigands facing him were hurled away as if
they'd been struck hard by the empty air. Blades flew

spinning aloft, and startled, winded men crashed into
brambles and rolled to slow, cursing halts.

"I believe a more traditional greeting consists of the
words 'well met,' " Elminster told the man who'd spoken, adding a dry smile to his dignified observation.

The brigand leader's face went white, and he
sprinted for the trees. "Algan!" he bellowed. "Drace! A
rescue!"

In answer, more arrows came humming out of the
deep green forest like angry wasps.

El dove out of his saddle a scant instant before two
of them met in his mount's head. The faithful gray
horse made an incredulous choking sound, threw up
its forelegs as if to challenge an unseen foe, and then
rolled over onto its side to kick and die.

It came within a fingerlength of crushing its rider,
who rolled away as fast as he could, hissing curses as
he tried to think which of his spells would best serve a
lone man scrambling through ferns and brambles, surrounded by brigands hiding behind trees with ready
bows.

Not that he wanted to leave his saddlebag, anyway.
Panting in his frantic haste, El reached the far side of
a stout old tree. He noticed in passing that its leaves
were beginning to turn, touched gold and brown by the
first daring frosts of the Year of the Chosen, and
clawed his way up its mossy bark to stand gasping and
peering around through the trees.

Crashings marked the routes of the hurrying outlaws as they ran to surround him. Elminster sighed
and leaned against his tree, murmuring an incantation he'd been saving for a time when he might be
faced with hungry beasts on a night he'd have to spend
in the open. Such a night would never come, now, if he
didn't put the spell to more immediate use. He finished
the casting, smiled at the first brigand to peer warily

around a nearby tree at him—and stepped into the duskwood he was leaning against.

The brigand's startled curse was cut off abruptly as El melded into the old, patient silence of the forest giant, and threw his thoughts along its spreading roots to the next tree that was large enough. A shadowtop, in that direction. Well, 'twould have to do.

He sent his shadowy body flowing along the taproot, trying not to feel choked and trapped. The closed-in, buried feeling drove some mages mad when they tried this spell—but Myrjala had considered it one of the most important things for him to master.

Could she have foreseen this day, years later?

That thought sent a chill through the prince of Athalantar as he rose inside the shadowtop. Was everything that happened to him Mystra's will?

And if it was, what would happen when her will clashed with the will of another god, who was guiding someone else?

He'd have been flying in falcon-shape over this forest, after all, if she'd not commanded him to "ride" to the fabled elven realm of Cormanthor. A bird of prey would have been too high for the arrows of these brigands to reach even if they'd felt like wasting shafts.

That thought carried Elminster out into the bright world again. He melted out of the dark, warm wood into the bright sunlight with the Skuldask Road a muddy ribbon on his left—and the dusty leather of a brigand not two paces away to his right. Elminster could not resist doing something he'd once delighted in, years ago, in the streets of Hastarl: he plucked the man's belt dagger out of its sheath so softly and deftly that the brigand didn't notice. Its pommel bore the scratched outline of a serpent, rising to strike.

Then he froze, not daring to take a step for fear of crushing dead leaves underfoot, and betraying his presence. He stood as still as a stone as the man stalked away, moving cautiously toward where the young mage had run to.

Could he get his saddlebag and flee without being noticed? Even if they hadn't had arrows and some skill in firing them, he really didn't want to waste spells on a handful of desperate men, here in the heart of the Skuldaskar. He'd seen bears and great forest cats and sleep-spiders already on his journey, and heard tales of far more fearsome beasts that hunted men along this road. He'd even found the gnawed bones and rotting, overturned wagons of a caravan that had met death along the road, some time ago . . . and he didn't want to become just one more grisly trailside warning.

As he stood, undecided, another brigand strode around the tree, head down and hurrying, and walked right into him.

They fell to the leaves in startled unison—but the young Athalantan already had a blade in his hand, and he used it.

The dagger was sharp, and his slash laid open the man's forehead with a single stroke as El rolled to his feet and sprinted away, making sure that he stomped on the bow that the man had dropped. It snapped under his boots, and then he was running hard for the road, startled shouts following him.

The man he'd cut would be blinded by the streaming blood until someone helped him, and that made one less brigand to chase Elminster of Athalantar. The Berduskan Rapids were still days away—longer, now that he had to walk—and Elturel was an even longer trip back. He didn't relish going either way with a band of cutthroats hunting him, day and night.

He reached his horse, scrambling back down onto the road, and used his borrowed dagger to cut free his saddlebag and the loop that held his scabbard.

Snatching up both of them, he ran hard along the road, seeking to win a little distance before he'd have to try some other trick.

Another arrow hummed past his shoulder, and he swerved abruptly into the forest on the far side of the road. So much for that brilliant tactic.

He was going to have to stand and fight. Unless . . .

In frenzied haste he dropped his burden and snatched out his sword, the daggers from both boots, and the knife sheathed down his back, its hilt hidden under his hair at the nape of his neck. They joined the borrowed dagger on a clump of moss, clattering into a heap—and he added his fire-blackened cooking fork and broad-bladed skinning knife to them even as he began the chant.

Men were leaping and running through the trees, fast approaching, as Elminster muttered his way through the spell, taking each blade in turn and carefully nicking himself so that drops of his blood fell on the steel. He touched each blade to the tangle of feathers and spiderweb strands he'd scooped out of his pouch-lined baldric, thanking Mystra that she'd whispered to him to mark each pouch so he knew their contents at a glance, and then clapped his hands.

The spell was done. Elminster snatched up his saddlebag to use as a shield against any swift arrows that might come his way, and crouched low behind it as the seven weapons he'd enchanted rose restlessly into the air, skirled against each other for a moment as they drifted about as if sniffing for prey—and then leapt away, racing points-first through the forest air.

The first brigand shrieked moments later, and El saw the man spin around, clutching at one eyeball, and fall down the bank onto the road. A second man spat out a curse and swung his blade in frantic haste; there was a ringing of steel on steel, and then the man reeled and fell, blood spurting from his opened throat.

Another man grunted and clutched at his side, snatching out the cooking fork and flinging it down with a groan. Then he joined the frantic retreat, outpaced by some of his fellows who were sprinting desperately to stay ahead of blades that were rushing hungrily after them.

Whenever steel drew blood, his enchantment fled from it. Elminster dropped his saddlebag and went forward cautiously to retrieve his daggers and fork from the men who'd fallen. It would be easy to slip away now, but then he'd never know how many survived to stalk him—and he'd never get his blades back.

The two El had seen fall were both dead, and a heavy trail of blood told him that a third man wouldn't run much farther before the gods gathered him in. A fourth man made it back to Elminster's horse before the young Athalantan's sword plunged itself into his back, and he fell over it onto his face and lay still.

Elminster retrieved all but his borrowed dagger and one of his belt knives, finding two more bodies, before he gave up the grim task and resumed his journey. Both of the dead men had weapons marked with the crudely scratched serpent symbol. El scratched his jaw, where his unshaven stubble was beginning to itch, and then shrugged. He had to go on; what did it matter which gang or fellowship claimed these woods as its own? He was careful to take all the bows he saw with him, and thrust them inside a hollow log a little farther on, startling a young rabbit out of its far end into bounding flight through the trees.

El looked down at the cluster of bloody blades in his hand and shook his head in regret. He never liked to slay, whatever the need. He cleaned the blades on the first thick moss he found and went on, south and east, through the darkening wood.

The skies soon turned gray, and a chill breeze blew, but the rain that smelled near never came, and Elminster trudged on with his saddlebag growing heavier on his shoulder.

* * * * *

It was with weary relief that he came down into a little hollow just before dusk, and saw chimney smoke and a stockade wall and open fields ahead.

A signboard high on the cornerpost of what looked like a paddock, though it held only mud and trampled grass just now, read: "Be Welcome At The Herald's Horn." Underneath was a bad painting of an almost circular silver trumpet. Elminster smiled at it in relief and walked along the stockade, past several stone buildings that reeked of hops, and in through a gate that was overhung with someone's badly forged iron replica of the looped herald's horn.

This looked to be where he'd be spending the night. El strode across a muddy yard to a door where a bored-looking boy was peeling and trimming radishes and peppers, tossing his work into water-filled barrels, and keeping watch for guests at the same time.

The boy's face sharpened with interest as he surveyed Elminster, but he made no move to strike the gong by his elbow, merely giving the weary, hawk-nosed youth an expressionless nod of acknowledgment. El returned it and went inside.

The place smelled of cedar, and there was a hearth-fire somewhere ahead to the left, and voices. Elminster peered about, his shoulder-borne saddlebag swinging, and saw that he stood in the midst of yet another forest—this one a crowded tangle of treetrunk pillars, dim rooms, and flagstones strewn with sawdust, complete with scurrying beetles. Many of the planks around him bore the scars of old fires that had been put out in time, long ago.

And by the smell of things, the place was a brewery. Not just the sour small beer that everyone made, but the source of enough brew to fill the small mountain of barrels El could see through a window whose shutters had been fastened back to let in a little light and air— and a face that stared in at him, wrinkled bushy brows, and growled, "Alone? Afoot? Want a meal and a bed?"

Elminster nodded a silent reply and was rewarded with the gruff addition, "Then be at home. Two silver a bed, two silver for meals, extra tankards a copper apiece, and baths extra. Taproom's on the left, there; keep your bag with you—but be warned: I throw out all who draw steel in my house . . . straightaway, into the night, without their weapons. Got it?"

"Understood," El replied with some dignity.

"Got a name?" the stout owner of the face demanded, resting one fat and hairy arm on the windowsill.

For a brief moment El was moved to reply merely "Aye," but prudence made him say instead, "El, out of Athalantar, and bound for the Rapids."

The face bobbed in a nod. "Mine's Drelden. Built this place myself. Bread, dripping, and cheese on the mantel. Draw yourself a tankard and tell Rose your wants. She's got soup ready."

The face vanished, and as the grunts and thuds of barrels being wrestled about floated in through the window, Elminster did as he'd been bid.

A forest of wary faces looked up as he entered the taproom, and watched in silent interest as the youth quietly adorned his cheese with mustard and settled into a corner seat with his tankard. Elminster gave the room at large a polite nod and Rose an enthusiastic one, and devoted himself to filling his groaning belly and looking back at the folk who were studying him.

In the back corner were a dozen burly, sweaty men and women who wore smocks, big shapeless boots, a lot of dirt, and weary expressions. Local farmers, come for a meal before bed.

There was a table of men who wore leather armor, and were strapped about with weapons. They all sported badges of a scarlet sword laid across a white shield; one of them saw Elminster looking at his and grunted, "We're the Red Blade, bound for the Calishar to find caravan-escort work."

Elminster gave his own name and destination in reply, took a swig from his tankard, and then held silence until folk lost interest in him.

The conversation that had been going on in a desultory way before his entrance resumed. It seemed to be a "have ye heard?" top-this contest between the last two guests: bearded, boisterous men in tattered clothes, who wore stout, well-used swords and small arsenals of clanging cups, knives, mallets, and other small tools.

One, Karlmuth Hauntokh, was hairier, fatter, and more arrogant than the other. As the young prince of Athalantar watched and listened, he waxed eloquent about the "opportunities that be boilin' up right now—just boilin', I tell thee—for prospectors like meself—and Surgath here."

He leaned forward to fix the Red Blades with wise old eyes, and added in a hoarse, confidential whisper that must have carried clear out back to the stables, "It's on account o' the elves, see? They're moving away—no one knows where—jus' gone. They cleared out o' what they called Elanvae . . . that's the woods what the River Reaching runs through, nor'east o' here . . . last winter. Now all that land's ours for the picking. Why, not a tenday back I found a bauble there—gold, and jools stuck in it, clear through—in a house that had fallen in!"

"Aye," one of the farmers said in a voice flat with disbelief, "and how big was it, Hauntokh? Bigger'n my head, this time?"

The prospector scowled, his black brows drawing together into a fierce wall. "Less o' that lip, Naglarn," he growled. "When I'm out there, swingin' m'blade to drive off the wolves, it's right seldom I see *thee* stridin' boldly into the woods!"

"Some of us," Naglarn replied in a voice that dripped scorn, "have honest work to do, Hauntokh . . . but then, y'wouldn't know what that was, now would you?" Many of the farmers chuckled or grinned in tired silence.

"I'll let that pass, farmer," the prospector replied coldly, "seein' as I like the Horn so well, an' plan to be drinkin' here long after they look at thy weed fields an' use thy own plow to put thee under, in a corner somewheres. But I'll show thee not to scoff at them as dares to go where thee won't."

One hairy hand darted into Hauntokh's open shirt-front with snakelike speed, and out of the gray-white hair there drew forth a fist-sized cloth bag. Strong, stubby fingers thrust its drawstrings open, and plucked into view all it held: a sphere of shining gold, inset with sparkling gems. An involuntary gasp of awe came from every throat in the room as the prospector proudly held it up.

It was a beautiful thing, as old and as exquisite as any elven work Elminster had ever seen. It was probably worth a dozen Herald's Horns, or more. Much more, if that glow betokened magics that did more than merely adorn. El watched its inner light play on the ring the prospector wore—a ring that bore the scratched device of a serpent rising to strike.

"Have ye ever seen the like?" Hauntokh gloated. "Aye, Naglarn?" He turned his head, gaze sweeping across the Red Blade adventurers, who were leaning forward so far in their hunger and wonder that they were almost out of their chairs, and looked at his rival prospector.

"And thee, Surgath?" he charged. "Have ye brought back anything to match half o' this, hey?"

"Well, now," the other bearded, weatherbeaten man said, scratching his head. "Well, now." He shifted in his seat, bringing one booted foot up onto the table, while Karlmuth Hauntokh chuckled, enjoying his moment of clear superiority.

And then the ragtag prospector drew something long and thin out of his raised boot, and grew a grin to match Karlmuth's own. He hadn't many teeth left, El noticed.

"I wasn't goin' to lord it over thee, Hauntokh," he said jauntily. "No, that's not Surgath Ilder's road. Quiet and sure, that's my way . . . quiet and sure." He held up the long, thin cylinder, and laid his hand on the crumpled black silk that shrouded it. "'I've been in the Elanvae too," he drawled, "seein' what pelts—an' treasure— might come my way. Now years ago—probably afore you were born, Hauntokh, I wouldn't doubt—"

The larger prospector snarled, but his eyes never left the silk-shrouded object.

"—I learned that when you're in a hurry, and in elven woods, you can generally find both those things, beasts and loot together, in one place: a tomb."

If the room had been hushed before, that last word made it strainingly silent.

"It's the one place that hunting elves tend to leave be, y'see," Surgath continued. "So if y'don't mind fighting for your life every so often, you might—just

might—be lucky enough to find something like *this*."
He jerked the silk away.

There was a murmur, and then silence again. The
prospector was holding a chased and fluted silver rod.
One of its ends tapered into a wavering tongue like a
stylized flame, and the other ended in a sky-blue gem
as large as the gaping mouth of the nearest Red Blade
adventurer. In between, a slender, almost lifelike
dragon curled around the barrel of the scepter, its eyes
two glowing gems. One was green, and one amber—
and at the tip of its curling tail was yet another gem-
stone, this one ale-brown in hue.

Elminster stared at it for some seconds before remembering to raise his tankard and cover the eager-
ness in his face. Something like that, now, if he had to
duel with elven guards, would come in very handy indeed . . . It was elven work, had to be, that smooth and
beautiful. What powers did it have, now?

"This here scepter," Surgath said, waving it—there
was a gasp and a clatter, then, as Rose came into the
room with a platter of hot tarts, and dropped them on
her own toes in startled amazement—"was laid to rest
with a lord of the elves, I'm thinking, two thousand
summers ago, or more. Now, he liked to play at impressing folk—just like certain lazy, loose-tongued re-
tired prospectors I can rest my eyes on, right now! So
he could make this here rod do things. Watch."

His awed audience saw him touch one of the
dragon's eyes at the same time as he touched the large
gem in the butt of the scepter. A light flashed as he
pointed it at Karlmuth Hauntokh—who whimpered
and dove for the floor, shivering in fear.

Surgath threw back his head and guffawed. "Less
fear, Hauntokh," he laughed. "Stop your groveling.
That's all it does, y'see: throw off that light."

Elminster shook his head slightly, knowing the

scepter must be doing more than that—but only one pair of eyes in that room noticed the unshaven youth's reaction.

As the rival prospector rose into view again, mounting anger in his eyes, Surgath added grandly, "Ah, but there's more."

He pressed the dragon's other eye and the butt-gem in unison—and a beam leapt across the taproom and sent Elminster's tankard spinning. The young man watched it clatter along the wall, smoking, and his eyes narrowed.

"We're not done yet," Surgath said gaily, as the beam died out and the tankard rolled out of the room. "There's this, yet!"

He touched the tail-gem and the butt-gem, this time, and the result was a humming sphere of blue radiance in which small sparks danced and spun.

Elminster's face tightened, and his fingers danced behind his cheese. He looked down, as if peering for his tankard, so that the others wouldn't see him muttering phrases. He had to quell this last unleashing quickly, before real harm was done.

His spell took effect, apparently unnoticed by the other occupants of the taproom, and Elminster sank back in his seat in relief, sweat gathering at his temples. He wasn't done yet; there remained the small matter of somehow getting the scepter away from this old man, too. He *had* to have that scepter.

"Now," Surgath crooned, "I'm thinking that this little toy wouldn't look out of place in a king's fist—and I'm tryin' to decide which one to offer it to, right now. I've got to get there, do the dickering, and get out again without being killed or thrown in a dungeon. I've got to choose me the right king first off, y'see . . . because it's got to be one that can pay me at least fifty rubies, and all of them bigger'n'my thumb!"

The prospector looked smugly around at them, and added, "Oh, and a warning: I also found some useful magic that will take care of anyone who tries to snatch this off me. Permanently take care of 'em, if y'take my meaning."

"Fifty rubies," one of the adventurers echoed, in awed disbelief.

"D'ye mean that?" Elminster blurted out, and something in his tone drew every eye in the room. "Ye'd sell that, right now, for fifty rubies?"

"Well, ah—" Surgath sputtered, and his eyes narrowed. "Why, lad? You have that saddlesack o' yours stuffed with rubies?"

"Perhaps," Elminster said, nervously nibbling on a piece of cheese and almost biting off the tips of his own fingers in the process. "I ask again: is thy offer serious?"

"Well, p'raps I spoke a mite hastily," the prospector said slowly. "I was thinkin' more of a hundred rubies."

"Ye were indeed," Elminster said, his tone dry. "I could feel it, clear over here. Well, Surgath Ilder, I'll buy that scepter from ye, here and now, for a hundred rubies—and all of them bigger than thy thumb."

"Hah!" The prospector leaned back in his chair. "Where would a lad like you get a hundred rubies?"

Elminster shrugged. "Ye know—other people's tombs, places like that."

"No one gets buried with a hundred rubies," Surgath scoffed. "Tell me another, lad."

"Well, I'm the only living prince of a rich kingdom . . ." Elminster began.

Hauntokh's eyes narrowed, but Surgath laughed derisively. Elminster rose, shrugged, and reached into his saddlebag. When his hand came out, he was holding a wadded-up cloak—to conceal the fact that his hand was in fact empty—and to hide the single gesture that would release his waiting, "hanging" spell.

As the adventurers leaned forward, watching him closely, Elminster unrolled the cloth with a flourish—and gems, cherry-red, afire with the reflected flames of the hearth, spilled out across the table before him.

"Pick one up, Surgath," Elminster said gently. "See for thyself that it's real."

Dumbfounded, Surgath did so, holding it up to the light of the whirling scepter. His hands began to shake. Karlmuth Hauntokh snatched one, too, and squinted at it.

Then, very slowly, he set it back on the table in front of the hawk-nosed youth, and turned to look around the taproom.

El dropped his gaze to the man's hairy hands. Yes, his ring definitely matched the symbol borne by the brigands.

"They're real," Hauntokh said hoarsely. "They're more real'n'that." He jerked his thumb at the scepter, looked down at his own golden bauble, and shook his head slowly.

"Boy," Surgath said, "if you're serious . . . this scepter is yours."

Men and women were on their feet all over the room, goggling at the table strewn with sparkling gems. One of the Red Blades strode forward until he loomed above Elminster.

"I wonder where a youngling gets such riches," he said with slow menace. "Have you any more such baubles, to see you down the long, perilous road to the Rapids?"

Elminster smiled slowly, and put something into the warrior's hand.

The man looked down at it. A single coin glimmered in his palm. A large, olden coin of pure platinum.

Elminster took the scepter from its soft midair

twirling, and waved his other hand in invitation at the table of gems. Surgath scrambled for it.

The hawk-nosed youth watched him feverishly raking rubies together and leaned forward to speak to the adventurer, in a soft whisper that carried to every corner of the taproom. "There's just one thing to beware of, good sir—and that's coming to look for more."

"Oh?" the man asked, as menacingly as before.

Elminster pointed at the coin—and suddenly it stirred, rising as a hissing serpent in the man's hand. With a curse the man hurled it away. It struck a wall with a metallic ring, dropped, and rolled away, a coin once more.

"They're cursed, ye see," Elminster said sweetly. "All of them. Stolen from a tomb, they were, and that awakened it. And without my magic to keep the curse under control . . ."

"Wait a bit," Surgath said, face darkening. "How do I know these rubies're real, hey?"

"You don't," Elminster told him. "Yet they are, and will remain rubies in the morning. Every morning after that, too. If you want the scepter back—I'll be in the room Rose has ready for me."

He gave them all a polite smile and went out, wondering how many folk, whether they wore serpent rings or not, would try to slay the spell image that would be the only thing sleeping in El's bed tonight, or turn the room inside out searching for a scepter that was not there. The turf-and-tile roof of the Herald's Horn would do well enough for the repose of the last prince of Athalantar.

Of all the eyes in that taproom that wonderingly watched the young man from Athalantar leave, one pair, in a far corner, harbored black, smoldering murder. They did not belong to the man who wore the serpent ring.

* * * * *

"A hundred rubies," Surgath said hoarsely, spilling a small red rain of glittering gems from one hand to the other. "And all of them real." He glanced up at the reassuring glow of the wards, smiled, and stirred his bowl full of rubies once more. It had cost him the same worth as two of these jewels to buy the wardstone, years ago—but it was worth every last copper tonight.

Still smiling, he never saw the wardstone flash once, as a silent spell turned its fiery defenses on its owner.

There was a muted roar, and then the prospector's skeleton toppled slowly sideways onto the bed. Surgath Ilder would grin forever now.

A few rubies, shattered by the heat, tinkled to the floor in blackened fragments. The eyes that watched them fall held a certain satisfaction—but still smoldered with murder yet to be done. Revenge could sometimes reach from beyond the grave.

After a moment, the owner of those eyes smiled, shrugged, and wove the spell that would bring a fistful of those rubies hence.

We must all die in the end—but why not die rich?

Two

DEATH AND GEMS

The passing of the Mage of Many Gems might have doomed the House of Alastrarra, had it not been for the sacrifice of a passing human. Many elves of the realm soon wished the man in question had sacrificed everything instead. Others point out that in more than one sense—he did.

Shalheira Talandren, High Elven Bard of Summerstar
from **Silver Blades And Summer Nights:
An Informal But True History of Cormanthor**
published in The Year of the Harp

As he went on through the endless wood, the land began to rise again, sprouting crags and huge mossy overhangs of rock amid the ever-present trees. There was no trail to follow, but now that Elminster was past the line of mountains that marked the eastern boundary of the human realm of Cormyr, wherever south and east the trees rose tallest must be the right direction to head for Cormanthor. The hawk-nosed youth with the saddlebag on his shoulder walked steadily toward that unseen destination, knowing he must be getting close by now. The trees were older and larger, hung with vines and mosses. He'd long since left all traces of woodsmen's axes behind.

He'd been walking for days—months—but in a way

he was glad brigand arrows had deprived him of his mount. Even in the lands claimed by the men of Cormyr, now behind him, the hills had been so trackless and heavily wooded that he'd have had to let his horse go, thus willfully breaking Mystra's directive.

Long before the terrain would've forced that disobedience on him, he'd have been coinless from buying hay for the beast to eat, and weary-armed from hacking at tree-limbs to cut a way large enough for the horse to squeeze onwards—presuming, of course, that the horse would've been willing to be ridden into woods too thick to move about in. Woods roamed by things that snarled and howled at night, and caused many unseen things to scream and wail as they were slain.

El hoped not to join their ranks overly soon.

He kept holding spells handy; they allowed him to freeze rabbits and sometimes deer where they stood, and get close enough to them to use his knife. He was getting tired of the bloody, messy butcherings that followed, the constant rustlings and calls that meant he was himself being watched, the loneliness, and of feeling lost. Sometimes he felt more like a badly aimed arrow rushing blindly off to nowhere, rather than a powerful, anointed Chosen of Mystra. Occasionally he hit something, but all too often—though things *seemed* easy and straightforward enough—he plunged right into one blunder after another. Hmm. No wonder Chosen were rare beasts.

No doubt there were rarer beasts lurking somewhere in all these trees right now, hunting *him*. Why couldn't Mystra have given him a spell that would whisk him right to the streets of the elven city? The Moonsea lay somewhere ahead and to his left, ending these trees that were elven territory—and if his memory of overheard merchant chatter and glimpses of

maps in Hastarl served him rightly, it was linked by a
river to an arm of the vast and sprawling Sea of Fallen
Stars, which formed the eastern boundary of the elven
realm he sought. The mountains behind him were the
western edge of Cormanthor—so if he kept walking,
and turned right whenever he found a river, he'd stay
in elven lands. Whether or not he'd ever find the fabled
city at its heart was another matter. El sighed; there'd
been no glows of torchlight or the like at night to mark
a distant city—and he'd not seen an elf since leaving
Athalantar, let alone found one since passing the line
of mountains. Something as simple as a fall over a tree
root out here could kill him, with no one but the wolves
and buzzards to know about it. If Mystra attached
such importance to his getting himself to the city,
couldn't she guide him somehow? Winter could find
him still wandering—or long dead, his bones cracked
and forgotten by some owlbear or peryton or skulking
giant spider!

Elminster sighed and walked on. His feet were beginning to ache so much—a deep bone-ache, that made
him feel sick—that the pain overwhelmed the ever-
present sting of broken blisters and raw skin. His
boots weren't in good shape now, either. In tales heroes
just got to wherever the excitement was without delay
or hardship—and if he was a Chosen of Mystra, surely
he qualified as a hero!

Why couldn't all of this be *easier?* He sighed again.
As the wood went on around him, footfall after weary
footfall, mushroom-cloaked roots rose out of the earth
everywhere, like contorted walls, and full sunlight became rare. Deer were a common sight now, lifting their
heads to watch him warily from afar, and rustlings and
flutterings in the ever-present shade around told him
that other game was growing more plentiful, too.

Elminster ignored most snags and shrubs and

clinging creepers, for fear of lurking danger; not wanting to be hunted by anything hungry that had a nose,
he'd long ago cast a spell that left him treading air a
foot or so clear of the ground. He left no trace of his
passage, keeping to where gnarled forest giants
choked out saplings and thorn-thickets, and the way
was relatively clear. He was making good progress;
when he grew weary he rested in the shape of a cloud
of mist clinging to high branches in the night. Someone or something was following him, of course.

Something too wary, or cunning, to let him get a look
at it. Once he'd even cloaked himself in a spell of invisibility and doubled back on his route. He found the
tracks of his pursuer hastily turning aside to end in a
stream. All the last prince of Athalantar learned was
that the being shadowing him was a lone human—or
some other sort of being that wore hard-soled boots.
On two feet.

So he'd shrugged and pressed on, heading for the
fabled Towers of Song. The elves suffered no human to
see their great city and live, but a goddess had commanded El to go thence, in his first service to her. If
elves clinging fiercely to their privacy didn't approve,
that was just too bad.

Too bad for him, if his alertness or spells failed him.
Once already there had been a burst of blue light in
the dusk off to his left one evening, as a trap spell
claimed the life of an owlbear. Elminster hoped such
magics were specific in their triggerings . . . and
weren't waiting for humans who used spells to keep
clear of the ground.

One thing was increasingly clear to him, now: even
elves eager to be friendly, if Cormanthor boasted any
such, weren't likely to welcome an intruding human
with smiles if that lone visitor was carrying a scepter
of power looted from an elven tomb.

The attention he'd attracted back at the Horn had been a mistake, whatever danger that prospector's ignorance of magic had posed. He'd lost a night's sleep, and had to use hasty spells to snatch himself clear, when at least four folk with spells and daggers had separately attacked his sleeping chamber. The last one had come creeping across the roof, blade in hand, right to where El was listening to the sounds of two of the others knifing each other to death in the darkness below.

Now he was carrying a beautiful—and no doubt very recognizable—thing of gems and chased silver that an elf who saw it might be able to awaken from a distance to turn its powers on Elminster . . . a scepter that might bear a curse or spit magics that harmed anyone arousing them. A scepter that had belonged to an elf whose surviving kin might slay any human who dared to touch it. A scepter someone might be tracing even now.

How could he have been so *stupid?* El sighed again. Somewhere on this journey he had to hide the scepter, in a place where he—and, barring tracing spells, only he, not some mysterious follower or elven patrol— could find it again. And that meant a distinctive landmark; in this endless wood, something of the land beneath the trees, not a tree itself. He kept a watch for something suitable.

Soon after sunrise, on the day after Elminster walked above the dark waters of his twelfth swamp, he found it. The land rose sharply in a line of pointed crags, the last one a bare stone needle like the prow of some gigantic ship eager to sail up to the sun.

Elminster chose the crag next to the prow. It was a lower, tree-girt height, with a duskwood tree he liked the look of clinging to one of its edges. 'Twould do. In among its roots he knelt, scooping up a handful of

earth and crumbling it in his fingers until it fell away
to leave him holding a few stones.

Out of his bag he took the silver scepter, glancing at
it briefly as he laid it on his palm amid the stones. It
was a beautiful thing, one end tapering into the shape
of a tongue of flame. Elminster shook his head in admiration, and whispered a certain spell over his hand.
Then he thrust the scepter into the hole he'd created,
smoothed dirt over it, and plucked up a nearby clump
of moss to lay atop the disturbed earth. A handful of
leaves and twigs completed the concealment, and he
hurried to the next crag along the line. There he
dropped one of the stones, and went on to another
three of the tree-clad heights, to leave a stone at each.
Pausing at the last, he murmured another spell that
left him feeling weak and sick inside, as his limbs tingled with blue-white fire for the space of a long,
leisurely breath.

He took that breath, and another, before he felt
strong enough to make the second casting. It was a
simple thing of gestures, a single phrase, and the melting away of a hair from behind his ear. Done.

The Athalantan kept still for a moment, listening,
and peered back the way he'd come for any signs of
movement. Nothing met his ears and eyes but the
scuttlings of small forest creatures . . . moving in various wrong directions, and ignoring him. El turned and
went on with his journey. He didn't feel like waiting for
hours just to see who was following him.

Mystra had sent him to Cormanthor on a mission.
Just what he was supposed to do there she hadn't revealed yet, but he'd be needed there, she'd said, "in time
to come." It didn't sound like anything one had to hurry
to, but El wanted to see the legendary ciy of the elves.
It was the most beautiful place in all Faerûn, the minstrels said, full of wonders and elven folk so handsome

that looking upon them took one's breath away. A place of revels and magical marvels and singing, where fantastic mansions thrust spires to the stars, and the forest and the city grew around each other in a vast, rolling garden. A place where they killed non-elves on sight.

Well, there was a line in an old ballad about stupid brigands that had become a wry saying among Athalantans: "We'll just have to burn that treasure when we get our hands on it." It would have to serve him in the days ahead. El rather suspected that he'd be spending a lot of time drifting around Cormanthor as a watching, listening mist.

Better that, he supposed, than spending the eternal oblivion of death by spells, to sink forgotten into the earth of an elven garden somewhere, his service to Mystra unfulfilled.

The young man paused at the base of a shadowtop as large around as a cottage, swung his saddlebag from one shoulder to another, stretched like a cat, and set off south and east again, walking fast. His boots made no sound as he trod the empty air. He glanced at the still waters of a little pool as he passed, and they reflected back the image of an unshaven, stragglebearded youth with keen blue eyes, black tangled hair, a sharp beak of a nose, and a long, gangly build. Not unhandsome, but not particularly trustworthy in appearance, either. Well, he was going to have to impress *some* elf, sometime. . . .

Had he looked back at the right moment, El would have seen a cloud of clinging mushrooms rise from the damp forest floor as something unseen disturbed them, and settle softly again as whatever it was whispered a curse and turned hastily aside. Was the young man ahead going to blunder straight into the guarded heart of Cormanthor?

Then the forest gloom to the south and east gave sudden birth to spreading rings of fire, and the ground shook. Yes, it seemed he was.

Elminster hurried forward, running on the air, swinging his saddlebag fore and aft in one hand to give him the momentum to surge forward in earnest. That had been a battle spell, hurled in haste.

Leaves were still flaming in dancing branches ahead, and a tree crashed down somewhere to the west, in answer to the deep, rolling force of the explosion that had shuddered past him moments before.

Elminster dodged around a long side-limb and over a rise, descending into a rocky, fern-filled dell beyond. At its bottom, a spring welled up between old and mossy boulders—one of which was just tumbling back to earth, trailing flames and the spinning bones of something torn apart.

Figures were trotting and scrambling and hacking among those boulders. Elves, El saw, who were fighting burly red-skinned warriors whose mouths jutted tusks, and whose black leather armor bristled with daggers and axes and maces.

Hobgoblins had surprised the elves at the stream and slain most of them. As El raced closer above the ferns, his bag sending them dancing and waving in his wake, an elven sword flashed with spell light as it rose and fell. Its quarry fell away, snarling in pain and clutching at a ravaged neck, as an iron bar wielded by another hobgoblin came down on the head of the elven swordsman with a solid thud that echoed across the dell, sickeningly loud.

The elf's head collapsed in a spray of gore, and his twitching body fell against his companion. This last survivor of the elven patrol, it seemed, was a tall elf who wore a shoulder mantle adorned with rows of oval, gem-adorned pendants that flashed and sparkled as he dodged. A mage, El guessed, raising a hand to hurl a spell.

The elf was faster. One of his hands blossomed into a ball of fire, which he thrust into the face of the staff-wielding hobgoblin. As his foe staggered backwards, roaring in anger and pain, the fire sprouted two long tongues of flame, like the horns of a bull. The flames stabbed out at the red-skinned ruukha, searing away leather armor to lay bare scorched grey hide. The iron staff clanged to the rocks as the hobgoblin spun away, howling in earnest—and the elven mage swept his horns of flame across the face of another assailant.

Too late. The fire was still sizzling across the bat-eared, snarling face of one ruukha when another reached over it to thrust the dark and wicked tines of a longfork clear through the elven mage's upper body.

The seeking bolts Elminster had hurled were still streaking through the air as the transfixed elf struggled his way clear of the bloody tines, shrieking in agony, and slumped into the stream. Hobgoblins were swarming down around the rocks now, stabbing at the writhing elven mage. El saw his fine-boned face thrown back in agony as he gasped out something—and the air above the stream was suddenly full of countless streaking silver sparks.

Hobgoblins jerked and spasmed, arching in agony, as the elf sank back into the roiling waters. Fallen ruukha weapons crashed down around him as his magic raged. Their former owners were still reeling as Elminster's bolts tore into them, spinning them around and filling them with blue-white fire.

Spellflames roared out from hobgoblin mouths and noses, and the eyes above them bulged and then burst into blue-white, spattering mists. The scorched corpses staggered aimlessly into rocks and trampled ferns until they fell—leaving a moaning elf lying in the waters, and more angry ruukha crashing down the far side of the dell with axes, longforks, and blades in their hands.

Elven bodies lay arched and sprawled around Elminster as he came to a halt above the mage. Pain-wracked emerald eyes blinked up at him through sweat-tangled white hair, and widened in astonishment at seeing a human.

"I'll stand with ye," the Athalantan told the elf, lifting his head clear of the blood-darkened water. That deed caused his airstriding spell to fail, and he promptly discovered that one of his boots leaked, as they settled into the cold, rushing waters.

He also discovered that he really didn't have time to care, as ferns rustled around him and more ruukha rose into view, wearing nasty grins of triumph at their deception. The elven patrol had camped in the midst of a hobgoblin haven, or more likely been carefully and completely surrounded as they slept.

The entire dell, it seemed, was full of yellow-tusked, menacing ruukha, raising shields before them as they crouched low and stumped cautiously forward. They seemed to have already learned that mages are always dangerous . . . and to have survived that lesson. Which meant they'd killed mages before.

Elminster stood over the weakly coughing elf and darted a quick glance behind him. Aye, they were there, closing in slowly, faces grinning in anticipation. There must be seventy or more. And the spells he had left were few enough for that to be a real problem.

The prince cast the only magic that might buy him time to think of a proper way out of this. He tore aside a leathern flap of his saddlebag, plucked forth all six of the revealed daggers in an untidy cluster, and hissed the words he needed as he tossed them into the air, snapping his fingers. They took wing like aroused wasps, darting away in unison to circle the young prince, slashing and spinning across the face of a ruukha who was too close.

That awoke a general yell of rage, and the hobgoblins surged down at Elminster, coming from all sides. The daggers whistled and bit at all who intruded into their tight circle, but there were only five of them, against many burly ruukha shouldering to get at the young mage.

A hurled spear struck El numbingly on the shoulder as it tumbled past, and a stone grazed his nose as he staggered back. The unfortunate thing about the flying blades spell was that its rushing daggers gave the ruukha ideas. Why brave that wall of steel when you can just bury its creator under a hail of hurled weapons?

Another stone hit his forehead, hard. Elminster staggered, dazed. An exultant roar rose from all around him, as the ruukha charged. Shaking his head to drive away the pain, El sank down over the elf and spat out the words of a spell he hadn't expected he'd have to use yet. He hoped he'd be in time.

* * * * *

Eyes that glowed with mage sight looked at the tree-clad crag before it, and then at the next one. And the next. Gods curse the usurper! He'd been to all of them!

Had he left the scepter at the first one, and set the others as decoys? Or did it lie in the second crag, or—?

The owner of those smoldering eyes lost faith in the will of the silent gods to curse the young mage-prince properly, and embarked on a thorough and heartfelt job of personally cursing Elminster.

When the snarling was done, a spell was cast. As expected, it revealed a humming web of force lines linking all the crags, but didn't lay clear the location of the scepter. Breaking the web needed Elminster's assenting will . . . or his death.

Well, if the one was impossible, the other would just have to serve. Hands moved again to weave another enchantment. Something rose like heavy smoke from the forest floor, something that hissed and whispered softly and unceasingly as it took shape. Something whose every movement was a menace that bespoke hunger.

Something that suddenly grew solid, rearing upright as it slithered, and flailing the air before it with dozens of raking claws. A magekiller.

Murderous eyes watched it go forth, seeking the last prince of Athalantar. As it whispered its way out of view through the trees, a smile grew beneath those watching eyes . . . from a mouth that did not often smile. Then the mouth moved again, bestowing more curses on Elminster's head. Had they been listening, the gods would have been pleased at some of the more inventive phrasing.

* * * * *

There was an instant of swirling blue mists, and the sensation of falling—and then Elminster's boots scraped on broken rock, and a limp, lolling elven body was in his hands.

They stood on a flat rock partway up the dell, with bent and broken ferns all around, and startled shouts behind them as the ruukha peered this way and that, seeking them—or were sliced by the ring of daggers taking sudden and urgent flight to El's new locale, to take up their protective circling again.

Walking into Cormanthor with a dead or dying elf in his arms might not be such a good idea, either, but right now he had little choice. The prince of Athalantar swung the slim, light body over his shoulder with a grunt and began to walk up out of the dell, trudging carefully amid the ferns to avoid a fall on the uneven ground. There were more shouts from behind him, and Elminster smiled thinly and turned around.

Stones crashed and rolled short, and one spear hissed through the ferns well off to one side, as the ruukha came after him. El chose his spot and made the second journey of his five-jump spell.

Suddenly he was in the very midst of grunting, hurrying hobgoblins, with the elf weighing on his shoulder. Ignoring the sudden oaths and grunts of amazement, El stood tall, turning on one heel to find the next clear spot for the magic to take him to, over—there!

Blades slashed out too late, and he was gone again.

When the swirling mists fell away this time, there were screams from behind him. The whistling daggers had cut a bloody swath through the hobgoblins to reach and encircle El where he'd just been—and now they were trying to reach him again, slashing through the main group of ruukha. The Chosen of Mystra watched hobgoblins see him, turn, and roar out fresh fury as they charged anew—and he awaited them patiently.

None of the ruukha were throwing things now. Their blades and axes were out, each hobgoblin hungry to personally chop and hack this infuriating human. El shifted the elven mage on his shoulder, found the right moment, and jumped again—back to the other side of the rushing ruukha.

There were fresh screams as the daggers swerved to follow him, slicing through the hobgoblins once more. El watched one lumbering warrior lose his throat and spin to the ground not knowing what had slain him, hacking vainly and feebly at an unseen enemy as blood spurted. Many were staggering or limping, now, as they turned to follow their elusive foe. One last jump remained, and Elminster saved it, turning instead to trudge up out of the dell with his dangling burden. Only a few grim ruukha followed.

El went on walking, seeking some vantage point where he could see a distant feature. The ruukha still on his trail were growling back and forth now, reassuring each other that humans tire quickly, and they'd slay this one after dark if he didn't fall earlier.

Elminster ignored them, seeking a long view. It seemed an endless, staggering time before he found one—a thick stand of shadowtop trees across another dell. He made the last jump and left the hobgoblins behind, hoping they'd not care to follow.

His daggers would soon melt away, and when they were gone, he'd little left to fight with.

It was then that a high, faint voice by his ear said in broken Common, "Down. Put—down. Please."

Elminster made sure of his footing in the gloom under the shadowtops, and swung the elf gently down onto a bed of moss. "I speak your tongue," he said in elvish. "I am Elminster of Athalantar, on my way to Cormanthor."

Astonishment touched those green eyes again. "My people will kill you," the elf mage replied, his voice fainter. "There's only one way for you to . . ."

His voice trailed away, and Elminster thrust his hand to the laboring throat and hastily murmured the words of his only healing spell.

The response was a smile. "The pain is less; have my thanks," the mage said with more vigor, "but I am dying. Iymbryl Alastrarra am I, of . . ." His eyes darkened, and he caught at Elminster's arm.

El bent over the elf, helpless to do more healing, and watched long, slim fingers crawl like a shaking spider up his arm, to his shoulder, and thence to touch his cheek.

A sudden vision burst into Elminster's mind. He saw himself on his knees, here under the shadowtops where he knelt now. There was no Iymbryl dying under him, but only dust, and a black gem glistening among it. In the vision, El took it up and touched it to his forehead.

Then the vision was gone, and El was blinking down at the pain-wracked face of Iymbryl Alastrarra, purple at his lips and temples. His hand fell back to twitch like a restless thing on the dead leaves. "You—saw?" the elf gasped.

Trying to catch his breath, Elminster nodded. The elven mage nodded back, and whispered, "On your honor, Elminster of Athalantar, do not fail me." A sudden spasm took him, and he quivered like a dry, curled leaf rocks in winds that will whip it away in a moment. "Oh, Ayaeqlarune!" Iymbryl cried then, no longer seeing the human above him. "Beloved! I come to you at last! Ayaeqlarrr . . ."

The voice trailed away into a long, deep rattle, like the echo of a distant flute. The thin body shook once, and then was still.

Elminster bent nearer—and then recoiled in horror as the flesh under his hands gave forth a queer sigh, and slumped into dust.

It curled and drifted, there in the shade, and at its heart lay a black gem. Just as in the vision. Elminster looked down at it for a long moment, wondering what he was getting himself into, then glanced up and looked at the trees all around. No hobgoblins, no watching eyes. He was alone.

He sighed, shrugged, and picked up the gem.

It was warm, and smooth, altogether pleasant to the touch, and gave off a faint sound, like an echo of harp strings, as he raised it. El looked into its depths, saw nothing—and pressed it to his forehead.

The world exploded into a whirling chaos of sounds and smells and scenes. El was laughing with an elven maiden in a mossy bower; then he *was* the elven maiden, or another one, dancing around a fire whose flames sparkled with swirling gems. Then somehow he was wearing fluted armor and riding a pegasus, swooping down through the trees to drive a lance through a snarling orc . . . its blood blossomed across his view, and then flickered and shifted, becoming the rose-red light of dawn, gleaming from the slender spires of a proud and beautiful castle. . . . Then he was speaking an elder elven tongue, thick and stilted, in a court where the male elves knelt in silks before warrior-maidens clad in armor that glowed with strange magics, and he heard himself decreeing a war of extermination on humankind . . .

Mystra, aid me! What is this?

His despairing cry seemed to bring back the memory of his name; he was Elminster of Athalantar, Chosen of the goddess, and he was riding through a whirling storm of images. Memories, they were, of the House of Alastrarra. Thinking of that name snatched him back down into the maelstrom of a thousand thousand years, of decrees, family sayings, and beloved places. The faces of a hundred beautiful elven maids—mothers, sisters, daughters, Alastrarrans all—smiled or shouted at him, their deep blue eyes swimming up to his like so many waiting pools . . . Elminster was swept into them and down, down, names and dates and drawn swords flashing like striking whips into his mind.

Why? he cried, and his voice seemed to echo through the chaos until it broke like a wave crashing over rocks on something familiar: the face of vanished Iymbryl, regarding him calmly, a hauntingly beautiful elven maiden at his shoulder.

"Duty," Iymbryl replied. "The gem is the kiira of House Alastrarra, the lore and wisdom held by its heirs down the years. As I was, so Ornthalas of my blood is now. He waits in Cormanthor. Take the gem to him."

"Take the gem—?" Elminster cried, and both the elven heads smiled at him and chanted in unison, "Take the gem to him."

Then Iymbryl said, "Elminster of Athalantar, may I make known to you the Lady Ayaeqlarune of—"

Whatever else he said was swept away, along with his face and hers, under a fresh flood of loud and bright memories—scenes of love, war, and pleasant tree-girt lands. Elminster struggled to remember who he was, and to picture himself on his knees under the shadowtops, here and now—the ground his knees could feel.

He slapped at the ground, and tried to see what his hands felt, but his mind was full of shouting voices, unicorns dancing, and war-horns glinting in the moonlight of other times and distant places. He rose, and staggered blindly with arms outstretched until he ran into a tree trunk.

Clinging to its solid bulk, he tried to see it, but it and the other trunks, so tall and dark around it, felt sickeningly *wrong*. He stared at them, trying to speak, and found himself looking at Iymbryl, who was shrieking as the black tines of the longfork burst through him again—and then he *was* Imbryl, riding a red tide of pain, as ruukha laughed harshly all around and raised cruel blades he could not stop. . . .

They swept down, and he tried to twist away, and—struck something very hard, that drove the breath out of him. Elminster rolled on it, and realized dimly that he was on the ground, amid the treeroots, though he couldn't see the dirt his face was pressed against.

His mind was showing him Iymbryl again, and a young, handsome, haughty-looking elf in rich robes rising from a floating, teardrop-shaped chair that hung in a room where blue webs chimed with music. The young elf was rising with a smile to greet Iymbryl, and into El's mind came the name *Ornthalas*. Of course. He was to make haste to Ornthalas and surrender the gem. Along with his life?

Or would it tear his mind out of his skull, flesh and all, when he pulled on the gem?

Writhing in the dirt, Elminster tried to pry the gem from his forehead, but it seemed part of him, warm, solid, and attached.

He must get up. Hobgoblins could still find him here. He must go on, before a tree spider or owlbear or stirge found him, a helpless and easy meal, and . . . he must . . . Elminster clawed feebly at the forest floor, trying to remember the name of the goddess he wanted to cry out to. All that came into his head was the name Iymbryl.

Iymbryl Alastrarra. But how could that be? *He* was Iymbryl Alastrarra. Heir of the House, the Mage of Many Gems, leader of the White Raven Patrol, and this fern dell looked like a good place to camp . . .

Elminster screamed, and screamed again, but there was no one else in his mind to hear. No one but thousands of Alastrarrans.

Three

FELL MAGIC AND A FAIR CITY

*It is rare for any man to make many foes, and strive
against them, only to find a victory so clear and mighty
that he vanquishes them forever, and is shut of them
cleanly, at a single stroke. Indeed, one may say that such
clarity of resolution is found only in the tales of minstrels. In the endlessly unfolding tapestry that is real life
in Faerûn, the gods plague folk with far more loose
ends—and all too many of these prove as deadly as the
decisive battles that preceded them.*

Antarn the Sage
from **The High History of Faerûnian Archmages Mighty**
published circa The Year of the Staff

"You'd challenge the power of the elves? That is
hardly . . . prudent, my lord." The moon elven face
that spoke those words was calm inside its dragon
helm, but the tone made them a sharp and biting
warning.

"And why not?" the man in gilded armor snarled, his
eyes flashing in the shadow of his raised lion-head
visor as his gauntlets tightened on the hilt of a sword
that was longer than the elf he confronted. "Have elves
stopped me yet?"

The vision of two armored war captains facing each
other on that windswept mountaintop faded, and

Elminster moaned. He was so *tired* of this. Each dark or furious or merry scene gave way to the next, exhausting him with the ongoing tide of emotions. His mind felt like it was afire. How by all the gods' mercy did the heir of House Alastrarra stay sane?

Or *did* the heir of House Alastrarra stay sane?

It began then as a gentle whisper; for a moment El thought it was another of the innumerable, softly speaking, caressing elven maidens the visions had brought to him. *Call on me.*

Who, now? El slapped at his own face, or tried to, striving to bring himself back to Faerûn in the present. The present that had hobgoblins, mysterious followers, and magelords and other perils that could so easily slay him.

Call on me; use me. The young mage-prince almost laughed; the seductive whisper reminded him of a certain fat lady night-escort in Hastarl, whose voice was the only thing alluring she had left. She'd sounded like that, whispering huskily out of darkened doorways.

Call on me, use me. Feel my power. Where was the voice coming from?

And then it began; a warm throbbing above his eyes. He probed at it with tentative fingers. The gem was pulsing . . . *Call on me.* The voice was coming from the gem.

"Mystra?" Elminster called aloud, requesting guidance. He felt nothing but warmth. Speaking to it, at least, wasn't forbidden . . . it seemed. He cleared his throat.

Call on me.

"How?" As if in response to his exasperated query, fresh visions uncoiled in El's mind. Energies flowed endlessly within the gem, stored magics that served to heal and shapeshift and change the heir's body, from weightless to able to see in the dark, to . . .

The visions were tugging him away from such revelations now, leading him through scenes of various Alastrarran heirs calling on the gem to shift their shapes. Some merely changed their faces and heights to elude foes; others assumed different genders to lure or eavesdrop; one or two took beast-shape to escape rivals who had blades ready to slay elven heirs with, but no interest in hacking at timid hares or curious cats. El saw how the shift was done, and shown how it could be undone—or would undo itself, regardless of his will. Right, then; he knew how to change shape by calling on the powers of the gem. Why was it showing him this?

Suddenly he was staring at Iymbryl Alastrarra, standing smiling at him in the deep shade under the shadowtops. The face wavered, and became his own— and then shivered again, and was once more the heir of House Alastrarra, emerald eyes under the white hair all Alastrarran heirs had, or quickly acquired. The vision changed again, showing him a rather familiar lanky, raven-haired youth with a hawk-sharp nose and blue eyes, naked above a bathing pool—a body that flowed and sank into the similarly nude body of an elf, all slender hairless sleekness. By its face, Iymbryl. Right; the gem wanted him to change.

With an inward sigh, Elminster called on the powers of the gem to summon up the likeness of Iymbryl. A peculiar surging feeling washed over him, and he *was* Iymbryl, in hopes and memories and . . . he looked down at his hands—the rather battered hands of a man who'd lived and fought hard, recently—and willed them to become the long, slim, blue-white, smooth hands that had crawled so laboriously up his arms to touch his cheek, not long ago.

And the hands dwindled, *twisted*, and . . . became slim, and delicate, and blue-white in hue. He wiggled them experimentally, and they tingled.

El drew in a deep, shuddering breath, called Iymbryl's face firmly to mind, and willed his body to change. A slow, creeping feeling rose in him, in his back and up his spine. He shivered involuntarily, and grunted in disgust. The visions fell away and he was blinking around at the unchanging, patient trunks of shadowtops that had stood here for centuries.

He looked down. His clothes were hanging from him; he was smaller and slimmer, his smooth skin now blue-white. He was a moon elf. He was Iymbryl Alastrarra.

That had been useful enough. Now was there a teleport or homecalling spell in the gem, perhaps, that could take him right to Cormanthor? He slid into the whirling memories once more, seeking. It was like rushing through a busy battlefield peering for just one familiar face among all the hacking, rushing swordsmen . . . no, it didn't seem that there was. El sighed, shook himself, and looked at the ever-present trees. His clothes flapped loosely as he turned, and that reminded him of his saddlebag.

Looking around for it, he suddenly recalled that he'd left it somewhere back in the dell of countless ferns and even more hobgoblins. El shrugged and turned to walk south and east. If the ruukha didn't tear it apart or scatter the contents completely, he'd be able to find it later with a spell; not that he expected to have the leisure for that sort of thing again this year. Nor, perhaps, next season, either. He shrugged again; if that was what service to Mystra meant—well, others endured far worse.

Wearing the shape of an elf would certainly get him into the city of Cormanthor with more ease than he'd taste if he charged in as a human. Elminster sniffed the air; to an elven nose, the woods smelled . . . stronger; his nose took in, or noticed, many more scents. Hmm. Best to think on such things while moving. He set off through the trees, touching the gem on his forehead once to be sure his shifting hadn't loosened or harmed it.

Upon his touch, the kiira made him aware of two things: only braggarts displayed House lore-gems openly—a simple calling on the stone would hide it; and now that he wore Iymbryl's shape, the memories in the gem still awaited him, but no longer overwhelmed.

He hid the kiira first, and then turned to the doorway in his mind that streamed with the vivid lights and colors of waiting memories. This time, they seemed like a sluggish stream through which he waded, going where he desired, and letting the rest slide past. El sought through them for the most recent remembrances of Cormanthor, and for the first time saw its soaring spires, the fluted balconies of homes built in the hearts of living trees, the ornate, free-floating lanterns that drifted about the city, and the bridges that soared from tree to tree, crisscrossing the air. Those spans were arched, and some of them curved as they went. None of them had side railings. El swallowed; it would take some time before he'd feel comfortable strolling along such bold contrivances.

Who ruled this city? The Coronal, the gem showed him—someone chosen rather than born to the office. An 'old wise one' and chief judge in all disputes, it seemed, who held sway not only over Cormanthor the city, but its entire deep woods realm. The office carried magical powers, and the current Coronal was one Eltargrim Irithyl—old and overly kindly, in Iymbryl's view, though the Alastrarran heir knew that some of the older, prouder families held far poorer views of their ruler.

Those proud old Houses, in particular the Starym and Echorn, held much of the real power in Cormanthor, and considered themselves the embodiment and guardians of "true" elven character. In their view, a "true" elf was . . .

Elminster broke off that thought as the idea reminded him uncomfortably of what he'd just done. He'd had no choice—unless he'd been a man utterly without mercy. Yet should he have touched the gem at all, since he'd pledged his service to Mystra?

He came to an abrupt halt beside a particularly gigantic shadowtop, drew in a deep breath, and called aloud, "Mystra?"

Then he added in a whisper, "Lady, hear me. Please."

Into his mind he brought his most striking memory of Myrjala, laughing in aroused delight as they soared through the air together, and of the subtle changes in her eyes that betrayed her divinity as her passion rose . . . seizing on that image, he held it, breathed her name again, and bent his will to calling on her.

There came a coldness at the edges of his mind—a thrilling, verge-of-a-shiver tingling—and he asked, "Lady, is this right for me to do? Have I . . . your blessing?"

A surge of loving warmth rolled into his mind, bringing with it a scene of Ornthalas Alastrarra, standing in a fair, sun-dappled chamber whose pillars were living, flower-bedecked trees. The view was out of the eyes of someone approaching the heir—and when they'd drawn very close to the elf, who was looking slightly puzzled, the viewer's hand rose into the image, reaching for an unseen forehead, above.

The eyes of Ornthalas sharpened in astonishment, and the viewer moved closer, and closer still. To . . . kiss? Touch noses? No, to touch foreheads, of course. The eyes of Ornthalas, so close and wide, wavered like a reflection in water disrupted by ripples. When the disturbance passed, the face had become that of the kindly old Coronal, and the viewpoint drew back from him to show Elminster himself, bowing. Somehow, El knew that he was invoking the Coronal's protection against those of the People who were horrified to discover that a human had penetrated into the very heart of their city, wearing the shape of an elf they knew. An elf he might well have murd—

A sudden wash of warning fire blazed across his mind, sweeping the visions away, and Elminster found himself under the trees, being spun around—by Mystra's grace, he supposed—to face . . . something that was sweeping around roots and gliding among the trees like a large and eager snake. Something that hissed bubblingly and tirelessly as it came, whispering what might have been words. Whispering . . . snatches of spell incantations? The body of this strange beast or conjured apparition was sometimes translucent and always indistinct, unfocused. It veered toward him with a triumphant chuckle, raking the empty air with dozens of claws as it came. It was clearly seeking him.

Was this some elven guardian? Or some fell beast-lich kept alive by ancient magic? Whatever its nature, its intent was clear, and those claws looked deadly enough.

El almost retreated, but the thing was so fascinating to watch—one part of it awkward but tirelessly slithering, the other an endless swirling of what looked like the torn, tattered remnants of spells. Eyes in plenty swam and circled in that shifting and reforming body. It had to be a thing of magic. Mystra would take care of it, surely. After all, she was goddess of magic, and he was her Ch—

Claws stabbed out, and though they fell far short of striking, they left in their wake an eerie tingling. His mind felt a little numbed; he couldn't seem to focus his will on his spells.

What spells did he have left, anyway?

Oh, Mystra. *He couldn't remember.*

As those claws swept at him again, closer now, sudden panic blazed up in his mind like a bright bolt of fire. Run! El turned and darted away through the trees, stumbling as shorter legs than he was used to carried along a body that was far lighter than it should be. Gods, but elves could run fast!

He could sprint with ease around and around this slithering whatever-it-was. On impulse he dodged back toward the way he'd come. The monster followed.

He turned around again, risking the time to cast a simple dispel. Almost the last magic of any consequence he had, though the gem seemed to hold much more. A beast so chaotic, so made of tumbling magics, would surely fall apart at the touch of . . .

His magic blazed forth. The many-clawed, slithering thing flickered once, shook itself, and kept coming.

El ducked his head and started to run in earnest, sprinting through the trees, ducking around mossy rock outcrops and leaping over roots and suspicious-looking mushrooms. The hissing and burbling never ceased behind him.

The last prince of Athalantar felt a little chill as he realized how much faster it was than he'd thought it could be.

Well, he had one little weapon of magic left—a spell that sent a jet of flame leaping from the caster's hand. It was a thing for starting fires or singeing beasts into retreating, not a battle magic, but . . .

El stepped behind a tree, caught his breath, and started to climb it. His new longer, slender fingers found fissures in the bark his human hands couldn't have entered, and his lighter body clung to holds that could not have held Elminster the human. The hissing, slithering thing was close behind, now, as El reached a bough he judged large enough.

When the thing came around the tree, it seemed to

sense him, looking up without hesitation. Elminster put his little jet of flame right into its many eyes, and swung back up out of the way of any leaps.

He expected a squalling and thrashing, or at least a recoiling—but the thing never hesitated, snapping at his hand right through the flame. If anything, it seemed *larger* and more vigorous, not harmed or in any sort of pain.

Claws cut the air in a whistling frenzy; El took one look and decided a higher branch would be prudent. He'd barely begun to climb when the tree quivered beneath him. The thing had slashed through bark and wood beneath as easily as it had cut the air, carving out a claw-hold. A single raking blow cut another as he watched, and without pause the thing hauled itself up the trunk to cut more. El watched in fascination; it was slashing its way up the tree as fast as an armored man could climb a rope!

It would reach him in a few breaths. In the meantime, it was right under him, and would have to take whatever he dropped on it. Not that he had anything left but a few odd spells not concerned with matters of war at all, nor time to learn what the gem could do.

It looked like he'd be jumping soon. On impulse he dodged around the trunk. The many-clawed thing followed rather clumsily, gouging its way around the curve of the tree. Good; he'd not have to worry about it scrambling across the trunk in time to catch him as he fell past. El went back to his former branch—a better perch—and held tight. When the thing clawed its way back into view around his side of the tree, he hurled a light spell right into its eyes.

Light blazed forth, and then faded instantly. The clawed thing never hesitated, and El's eyes narrowed. Yes, it *did* seem even larger, and somehow more . . . solid.

As it climbed toward him, he cast a minor detection

spell at it—to gain lore he did not need.

The spell reached it . . . and faded away, granting him none of the information it was supposed to. The clawed thing grew slightly larger.

It fed on spells! This thing must be a magekiller, something he'd heard of long ago, in his days with the Brave Blades adventuring band. Magekillers were creations of magic, wrought by rare, suppressed spells. Their purpose was to slay wizards who only knew one way to do battle—hurl spells at things.

His magic, no matter how desperate, could only make it stronger, not harm it. Slayer of Magelords and Chosen of Mystra he might be—but he was also unable to stop making mistakes, it seemed, one piled atop another with all-too-fervent energy.

Enough analysis; such thinking was a luxury for mages . . . and just now, he'd best forget about being a mage. He had only a few breaths left to experiment before he'd have to leap down, or die. Carefully El drew one of his belt daggers, and dropped it, point-first, into the many staring eyes of that hissing, burbling head.

It fell freely to the earth far below with a solid thump, leaving a shaft of dark emptiness in its wake right through the heart of the many-clawed thing. The magekiller shuddered and squalled, its tone high and fearful and furious, but somehow fainter than before.

Now it was done keening and was moving again, climbing after Elminster with murder in its eyes. The hole through it had gone, but the entire beast was visibly smaller. The last prince of Athalantar nodded calmly, planted one boot against the trunk below him, and kicked off.

The air whistled past him for a moment before his hands crashed through branchlets, snapping them in a swirling of leaves, and caught hold of the bough he'd aimed for. He clung there for a moment, hearing that urgent squalling sound ringing out again, close above, and then swung out and down, twisting to snatch at a lower branch.

It seemed he wasn't much of a minstrels' hero, either. Instead of the branch they were seeking, his hands found only leaves this time, and tore through them.

An instant later, the Chosen of Mystra hit the ground hard on his behind, rolled over into an unintentional backflip, and found his feet with an involuntary groan. His rear was going to be sore for days.

And his running was going to be an ungainly limp now. Elminster sighed as he watched the slithering thing racing back down the tree in a giddy spiral, to come and kill him.

If he used the lone spell he'd left ready, he'd be whisked back to the scepter . . . but that would leave him with all the walking through the woods to do over again, with this hissing monster and perhaps his mysterious follower lurking between him and Cormanthor.

He plucked up his dagger. He had another at his belt, a third sheathed up one sleeve, and one in each boot—but was that enough to do more than annoy this thing?

Spitting out a very human curse, the elf who was not Iymbryl Alastrarra stumbled southward, dagger in hand, wondering how far he could get before the magekiller caught up with him.

If he could only win himself time enough, perhaps there was something the gem could do . . .

Preoccupied with his haste and wild plans, Elminster almost ran right out over the edge of the cliff.

It was cloaked in bushes: the crumbling edge of an ancient rockface, where the land dropped away into a tree-filled gorge. A tiny rivulet chuckled over rocks far below. El looked along it and then back at the magekiller—which was coming for him as fast as ever, slithering around trees and their sprawling roots with its tireless claws raking the air.

The prince glanced along the lip of the cliff, and chose a tree that leaned a little way out into space, but seemed large and solid. He ran for it, one hand outspread to test it—and only the whispering warned him.

The magekiller could burst into a charge of astonishing speed when it desired to, it seemed. El looked back in time to see the foremost, lunging claws reaching for his head. He ducked, slipped on the loose stones, and made a desperate grab for a root as he went over the edge.

In a bruising clatter of rolling stones he swung against the cliff, slammed hard into it, and got his other hand onto the root, just as the long, serpentine body hissed past him into the gorge below.

There was a jutting rock some forty feet down, and the magekiller made a twisting grab for it. Claws squealed briefly on rock, trailing sparks, and then the jutting rock pulled free of its ancient berth and fell, its unwilling passenger flailing the air beneath it.

Together boulder and spectral beast crashed into the rocks below. They did not bounce or roll; only the dust they hurled up did that. El watched, eyes narrowed.

When the dust settled again, he saw what he'd been waiting for: a few claws, flailing away tirelessly around the edge of the boulder that had pinned the magekiller against the rocks.

So it was solid enough to slash with its claws, and to be pinned down by rocks—but all that harmed it was metal. Or more probably, just cold iron.

Elminster looked down at the crumbling cliff below him, sighed, and started trotting along it, looking for a way down.

About twenty paces along, the way found him. The ground under his boots muttered, like a man talking in his sleep, and slid sideways. El leapt frantically away from the gorge, and then slid helplessly down into it, bumping along atop a river of moving earth and rolling, bouncing rocks.

When he could see and hear again, he'd been coughing on dust for what seemed like hours, and he hurt all over.

He was back in his own form again. Had he lost the gem?

A quick touch reassured him that it was still there, and its powers were still waiting for him. He must have changed back without thinking, to get more reach and try to ride the moving rocks. Or something.

Elminster got up gingerly, winced at the pain of putting his weight squarely on a foot that seemed to have been hit by several hundred rolling stones during his unintentional journey, and started to pick his way along the rocky bottom of the gorge to where the magekiller had been.

It might, of course, have clawed its way through the rock to freedom by now. It might be waiting for him somewhere among all these rocks, very near. In that case, he'd just have to use that spell, and start off through this dangerous part of the woods all over again . . .

Then he saw it: a forest of spectral claws waving awkwardly around the edge of that massive boulder, in a tumbled forest of rocks ahead. He still—somehow—had his dagger in his hand, and he went to work cautiously, stabbing over the edge of the rocks at one claw and then another, watching them melt away like smoke under his blade.

When they were all gone, he ventured past them, to lie atop the boulder that pinned the strange monster, reaching down again and again to stab at the helpless body beneath. His blade never felt anything, but the frantic whispering from beneath him grew slowly fainter and fainter, until at last it stopped, and the boulder settled against the rocks beneath with a clacking sound.

Elminster straightened slowly, bruised but satisfied, and looked back up at the lip of the gorge.

A man was standing there. A man in robes whom he'd never seen before—but who seemed to know him. He was smiling as he looked down at Elminster of Athalantar, as he raised his hands and made the first careful gestures of what Elminster recognized as a meteor swarm. But the smile wasn't friendly at all.

El sighed, waved to the man in sardonic greeting— and with that gesture released his waiting spell.

When the four balls of raging fire raced down into the gorge and burst, the last prince of Athalantar was gone.

The wizard who'd followed Elminster so far clenched his fists as he watched the fire he'd wrought roar away down the gorge, and cursed bitterly. Now he'd have to spend days over his books, casting tracing spells, and trying to find the young fool again. You'd think the gods themselves watched over him, the way luck seemed to cloak him like a mage-mantle. He'd avoided that slaying spell at the inn . . . old Surgath Ilder had hardly been a fitting alternative. Then he'd somehow trapped the magekiller—and *that* spell had taken days to find components for.

"Gods, look down and curse with me," he muttered, his eyes still murderous, as he turned away from the gorge.

Behind him, unseen, pale shapes rose from half a dozen places in the gorge—stone cairns that the fire had scorched in its passing.

They drifted in eerie silence to where a certain massive boulder lay among the stones, and moved their hands in gestures of spellcasting, though they uttered not a word. The boulder rose unsteadily. The wraithlike, floating forms thrust impossibly long tendrils of themselves into the revealed darkness beneath the lifted stone, and plucked forth a many-eyed something that still clawed at the air with feeble talons.

The muttering wizard heard the boulder thunder back into place, and lifted an eyebrow. Had the Athalantan managed only a short jump spell and now set off something nearby in the gorge? Or had the magekiller finally won free?

He turned around, pushing back his sleeves. He still had a chain lightning spell, if the need arose . . .

Something was rising out of the gorge—or rather, several somethings. Wraiths—ghostly remnants of men, their legs trailing away into wisps of white mist, their bodies mere white shadows in the shade.

They could slay, yes, but he had the right spell to . . . he peered at them again. Elves? *Were* there elven wraiths? And held between them, still waving its talons as they dragged it along—his magekiller!

It was at that moment that Heldebran, last surviving apprentice to the Magelords of Athalantar, felt the first touch of fear.

"And you are?" one of the spectral elves asked, as they swept toward him.

"Keep your distance!" the wizard Heldebran snapped, raising his hands. They did not slow in the slightest, so he hastily spun the spell that would blast all undead to harmless dust, forever, and watched it flash out to enfold them like a web.

And fade away, unheeded.

"Stylish," another of the wraithlike elves commented,

as they settled down to the earth in a ring around him. Their feet remained indistinct, and their bodies seemed to pulse, shifting continuously in and out of brightness.

"Oh, I don't know," said a third spectral elf, in heavily accented Common. "These humans always make such a noise and show of things. A simple word and a look would have been enough. They always *exult* so, in the unleashings of their power—like children."

"They *are* children," a fourth replied. "Why, look at this one."

"I don't know who you are," Heldebran of Athalantar snapped, "but I—"

"See? All threats and bluster!" the fourth elf added.

"Well, enough of it," the first elf said commandingly. "Human, fire magics are not tolerated here. You have roused the unsleeping guardians of the Sacred Vale, and must pay the price."

Nervously Heldebran glanced around. The ring did seem tighter, now, though the elves still regarded him calmly, and made no move to lift their arms from their sides. He spat out the words he'd need and raised his hands in hasty claws.

Lightning crackled from the tips of his fingers, dancing bright lines of hungry sparks into the spectral elves. It shot through them, to claw vainly among the trees beyond. Smoke curled up from bark here and there.

One elf turned his head to regard it, and the lightning abruptly vanished, leaving only a few wisps of smoke behind.

The ring stood unchanged. The elves looked, if anything, slightly amused.

"Worse than that," the first elf said sternly, as if the interruption had never occurred, "you created something that feeds on magic and sent it to the very heart of our oldest castings. *This.*"

The ghostly guardian's tone was one of utter disgust. His chest bulged, gave off small streams of bright radiance, and then burst as the magekiller drifted into view through it, claws waving feebly at the elves all around. Heldebran felt a sudden, wild surge of hope. Perhaps his creature could be set against these elf-wraiths, and he might yet defeat them, or . . .

"Let the punishment be fitting and final, nameless human," the stern elf added, as the magekiller turned its head, and saw its creator.

Darkness swam in the many orbs Heldebran stared into, and claws scratched the air with sudden vigor. Whispering faintly, the tattered remnant of his creature drifted forward purposefully.

"No!" the apprentice Magelord shrieked, as those feeble claws cut at his eyes. "Noooo!"

The ring of elven guardians was solid around him now, and their eyes were cold. The human wizard rushed at them, and found himself striking a solid, very hard wall of unseen force. He threw himself along it, sobbing. Then the seeking claws reached him, and dragged him down.

"Anyone important?" one of the elves asked, as the sounds died and they stretched out their hands to drain the magekiller away to nothingness.

"No," another replied simply. "One who might have become a magelord of Athalantar, had their rule not been broken. His name was Heldebran. He knew nothing of interest."

"Was there not another intruder, fighting this hungry thing?" the third guardian asked.

"One of our folk; one who wore a lore-gem."

"And this human was *hunting* such a one, in our vale?" The spectral elf looked down, eyes sudden flames in the ever-present tree gloom, and said, "Call him back to life, that he can be slain again. More slowly."

"Elaethan," the stern elf said, in shocked reproof. "I shall do the reading spells next time. In touching the mind of this human, you become too much like him."

"It's something we all had to guard against, Norlorn, when first they came to the forests where I first saw the sun. Humans always corrupt us; that is their true danger to the People."

"Then perhaps we should destroy any human who passes this way," Norlorn said, drawing himself up into a tower of cold white flame. "That other, who used a spell to escape the flames; he may have borne a lore-gem, but he was human, or seemed so."

"And that is the true danger of such beasts, to themselves," Elaethan said softly. "Many of them seem human, but never manage to become so."

* * * * *

He stood in front of the familiar root. The scepter was beneath it, invisible under the earth and its scattering of twigs, leaves, and clumps of moss he'd arranged so hastily. Elminster peered along the line of crags for nearby danger, found nothing, and used the powers of the lore-gem to check on his spell. Memories swirled briefly, but he wrestled them back from his mind and stood shaking his head to clear it.

He could come back here—or rather, to the scepter—twice more. Not that he wanted to . . . so how to avoid attacks that would drive him here?

The mysterious wizard, or any magekillers he chose to send would be bound to find a certain Chosen of Mystra stupid enough to follow the same route he'd originally taken from this place. So his way from here now would lie east along the crags, then south along the first creek he found heading in that general direction, until it strayed too far from where the trees grew tallest.

In the woods, the light tread and heightened senses of an elf outstripped those of a human, and any elven patrols he encountered would be less likely to attack Iymbryl Alastrarra than an intruding human . . . unless Iymbryl was some personal foe of theirs. Yet he'd seen no trace in the lore-memories, thus far, of Iymbryl being a particular foe of anyone.

It was the work of but a moment to slide into Iymbryl's shape, this time. Elminster thought briefly of the spellbook lost in his saddlebag, and sighed. He was going to have to get used to the lesser, often odd elven spells stored in the gem, which had evidently served the Alastrarran heir as a personal spellbook. He hadn't time to study them now; 'twas best to get well and promptly away from the scepter, in case his wizardly foe came seeking him here.

Elminster sighed again and set out. Would it be best to travel by night, in mist form, and use the daylight hours to study spells? Hmm . . . something to think on as he walked. It could be days before he saw Cormanthor. Did he have days to spend, or did this gem eat at the vitality or mind of its wearer?

If it was eating away at him . . . He smote his elven forehead. "Mystra defend me!" he groaned.

Of course. The unexpected voice in his mind sent him to his knees in thankful awe, but the goddess spoke only eight words more: *The gem is safe. Get on with it.*

After a moment of shocked silence and then a few more spent chuckling weakly, Elminster did so.

* * * * *

The strange purplish light of the musky grove of giant mushrooms gave way to rising ground at last, and Elminster trudged up it with a full load of spells and a weary heart. He'd been walking for days, and met with no one more exciting than a giant stag, with whom he'd been eyeball-to-eyeball at dusk two days ago. He'd come a long, long way from the modest wharves and towers of Hastarl, and even from holds where farm folk had heard of the realm of Athalantar, but he was getting close to the elven city now, judging by the tinglings of warding spells and the occasional glimpses of elven knights in the sky. Splendid they were, in fluted armor that gleamed purple, blue, and emerald as they swooped past in the saddles of flying unicorns whose hides were blue, and who had no wings nor reins to guide them.

Several such patrols banked close to the lone walking elf, staring closely at him, and El got a good look at their ready javelins and small hand-crossbows. Unsure of what to do, he gave them silent, respectful nods without slowing his travel. All of them nodded back and soared away.

Ahead now, in these trees, there were open clearings cloaked in moss and ferns. Rising silently up from concealment among them, was the first foot patrol he'd seen. Their armor was magnificent, and every one of them held a ready longbow as he stepped toward them, not changing his pace. What else could he do?

One, who was taller than the rest, let go of his bow as El approached. It stayed where he'd released it, floating in the air. The elf stepped forward to meet Elminster, hand lifting in a 'stop' gesture.

Elminster stopped and blinked at him. Best to seem weary and dazed, lest his ignorance put his tongue wrong.

"For some days you've been walking this way," the elven patrol leader said, his voice gentle and melodious, "and yet you give no call of passage to patrols . . .

as you have offered none to us. Who are you, and why do you journey?"

"I . . ." Elminster faltered, swaying slightly. "I am Iymbryl Alastrarra, heir of my House. I must return to the city. While on patrol, we were beset by ruukha, and I alone survived—but my spells attracted a human wizard. He set a magekiller on me, and I am . . . not well. I seek my kin, and healing."

"A human mage?" the elven officer snapped. "Where did you meet with such vermin?"

Elminster waved his arm, gesturing back to the northwest. "Many days back, where the land rises and falls much. I . . . I have walked too long to recall clearly."

The elves exchanged glances. "And what if something came upon Iymbryl Alastrarra as he walked, and devoured him, and took his shape?" one of them asked softly. "We've met with such shapeshifters before. They come to prowl in our midst, and feed."

Elminster stared at him with eyes that he hoped looked dull and tired, and raised his hand very slowly to his forehead. "Could one who was not of the People wear this?" he asked, letting weary exasperation sharpen his voice, as the lore-gem faded into view on his brow.

A murmur passed around the patrol, and the elves stepped back without a word from their leader, making way for him to pass. El gave them a weary nod and stumbled forward, trying to look exhausted.

He did not see the patrol leader, behind him, look hard at one of the elven warriors and nod deliberately. The warrior nodded back, knelt in the ferns, touched his hand to the breast of his armor—and faded away.

Now that he was among elves who were afoot, unhurt, and not rushing about in battle, El thought with a shiver, he'd best see how they moved. Did he stand out as an impostor? Or do all who walk upright stagger alike, when weary?

Adding a stumble or two, lest the patrol be watching him, El went on through the trees; huge forest giants soared to the sky, their canopy a hundred feet above him, or more. The ground was rising, and there was an open, sunlit area beyond.

Perhaps here he could . . .

And then he stopped, dumbfounded, and stared. The sun was bright on the fair towers of Cormanthor before him. Their slender spires rose wherever no gigantic tree stood—and there were many such—and stretched away farther than he could see, in a splendor of leaping bridges, hanging gardens, and elves on flying steeds. The blue glows of mighty magic shone everywhere, even in the brightness of full day, and gentle music wafted to him.

El let out a deep sigh of admiration as the music swelled around him, and started walking again. He'd have to be on his guard every moment that he walked amid the Towers of Song.

Now *that* was a change, eh?

Four

HOME AGAIN THE HUNTER

*More than one ballad of our People tells of Elminster
Aumar of Athalantar gawking at the splendors of beautiful Cormanthor upon his first sight of them, and how
he was so breathtaken that he spent an entire day just
walking the streets, drinking in the glories of the Cormanthor that was. Sometimes 'tis a pity that ballads lie
a lot.*

Shalheira Talandren, High Elven Bard of Summerstar
from **Silver Blades And Summer Nights:
An Informal But True History of Cormanthor**
published in The Year of the Harp

In the floating dome of varicolored glass, sunlight
shot the air through with beams of rose-red, emerald,
and blue. A helmed head, turning, flashed back purple,
and that burst of light was enough; its wearer did not
have to speak to bid his comrade come and look.

Together the two elven guards peered down at the
northern edge of the city, beneath their floating post. A
lone figure trudged into the streets with the air of
dazed weariness usually displayed by captives or exhausted messengers who'd lost their winged steeds
days ago, and been forced to continue afoot.

Or rather, not so "lone;" not far behind the staggering elf came a second figure, following the first. This

one was a patrol warrior cloaked in magical invisibility that might well serve to fool the eyes of anyone not wearing helms like those of the two watching guards.

Guards who now exchanged meaningful glances waved together at a crystal sphere that floated near at hand, and leaned forward to listen.

The crystal chimed softly, and there was suddenly noise in the dome: a hubbub of various musical airs, soft voices chattering, and the rumble and clatter of a distant cart. The guards inclined their heads intently for a time, and then shrugged in unison. The weary elf wasn't talking to any of the folk hurrying past him. And neither was his shadow.

The guards exchanged glances again. One of them spread his hands in a "what can we do?" gesture. The intruder—if it was someone not of Cormanthor—had an escort already. That meant some patrol leader who'd had a chance to speak with the lone elf, and see him more clearly, had been suspicious. Perhaps two senior members of the Watchful and Vigilant should be too.

Yet this could be no more than a private intrigue, and the lone elf had walked straight through the veil of revelation spell without it reacting in the slightest.

The other guard answered the spread-hands gesture with a dismissive wave, and turned to the querph tree behind him, plucking some of the succulent sapphire-hued berries. The first guard held out his open hand for some, and passed over the duty-bowl of mint water. A moment later, the elf with the invisible escort was forgotten.

* * * * *

He knew what he was looking for. The lore-gem showed it to him: a mansion cloaked in dark pines

("broody affectations," according to the maids of some
rival houses, Iymbryl knew), whose tall, narrow windows were masterpieces of sculpted and dyed glass,
girt with enchantments that periodically spun ghostly
images of minstrelry, dancing unicorns, and rearing
stags across the moss-carpeted chambers within.
Those casements were the work of Althidon Alastrarra, gone to Sehanine some two centuries and more,
and there were no finer in all Cormanthor.

The grounds of House Alastrarra had no walls, but
its hedges and plantings spun themselves out to form
a continuous barrier along paths marked by irndar
trees that bore the falcon sigil of the House. After
dusk, these living blazons glowed blue, clear to the
eye—there were many such across the proud city—but
by day a certain disguised human mage would just
have to wander until he found a place that matched
the image in his mind.

Most folk thought the servants of gods knew everything and could see all that went on, regardless of how
many walls or night glooms were in the way. El smiled
wryly at the thought. Mystra herself, perhaps, but not
her Chosen.

He stood and marveled amid trees that seemed to
have grown into fantastic spired castles of spidery grace.
The kiira told him of spells that could combine live trees
and shape their growth, though neither Iymbryl nor his
forebears knew much of how such magics were worked,
or who in the city today was capable of them.

Amid the tree castles were lesser mansions of spired
stone and what looked like blown, sculpted glass. However it seemed by the hanging gardens that sprawled
over such edifices that elves could not bear to live unless growing plants or trees shared the same space
with them. Elminster tried not to stare at the circular
windows, the carefully crafted views, and the leaping

curves of wood and stone all around him, but he'd never seen anything built for folk to live in that was so beautiful. Not just this building here, or that, but street upon street upon winding lane, a city of growing trees linked overhead, and a lush splendor of plantings and vistas and magically animated sculptures that casually outstripped the most exquisite human-work El had seen, even in the private gardens of the mage-king Ilhundyl.

Gods. With every step he could see new wonders. Over here was a house crafted like a breaking wave, with a glass-bottomed room hanging beneath the overarching curve—itself a garden of carefully shaped shrubs. Over there was a cascade of water plucked up tower-high by magic, so that it could plunge down, laughing, from chamber to chamber of a house whose rooms were all ovoids of tinted glass; within, the elven inhabitants strolled about, glasses in their hands. Down that lane of duskwoods wound a little path, to an ending at a small round pool. Seats circled the water in a gentle, hovering dance, their enchantments making them bob and rise as they went.

El shuffled on, remembering to stagger from time to time. How was he ever going to find House Alastrarra in all this?

Cormanthor was busy this bright afternoon. Its streets of trodden moss and the bridges, aloft, that leapt from tree to tree, held many elves—but none of the dirt and real crowding of human cities . . . and no creature more intelligent than cats and their winged cousins, the tressym, who was not an elf.

It hardly seemed a city. But then, to El, cities meant stone and humans, crammed together in their filth and shouting and seriousnesses, with a scattering of halflings and half-elves and a dwarf or two among the crowd.

Here were only the blue tresses and blue-white, sleek skins of proud elves who glided along in splendid gowns; or in cloaks that seemed entirely fashioned of the quivering green leaves of live plants; or in clinging leathers enspelled so that shifting rainbow hues drifted slowly around wearers' bodies; or in costumes that seemed to be no more than coyly cloaking clouds of lace and baubles drifting around elven forms. These latter were called driftrobes, the kiira let him know, as El tried not to stare at the slender bodies revealed by their circling movements. Driftrobes emitted a constant song of chimings whose descending runs sounded like many tiny, skillfully struck bells falling down the same staircase.

Elminster tried not to stare at anything, or even to look up much, and sighed dolefully from time to time whenever he sensed someone staring at him. This melancholy manner seemed to satisfy the few passersby who spared him much attention. Most seemed lost in their own thoughts or shared enthusiasms. Though the voices tended to be higher, lighter, and more pleasant on the ears, the elves of Cormanthor chattered every bit as much as humans at a market. El was able to covertly watch what he wanted most to see as he went along: how elves walked, so he could imitate them.

Most seemed to have a lilt and swing, like dancers. Ah, that was it—none strode flat-footed; even the tallest and most hurried of the citizenry danced forward on their toes. In his borrowed shape, El did likewise, and wondered when his sense of unease would lighten just a trifle.

It refused to, and as he went on, turning this way and that among the gigantic trees that rose like castle towers from the mossy ways, it began to dawn on him: he was being watched.

Not the countless casual inspections, the glances of laughing elves and sprawled cats and even winged steeds wheeling overhead, but by a single pair of eyes that was always on him, following him.

El began to double back on his route, hoping to catch a glimpse of whoever was following him, but the feeling grew more intense, as if the source of the scrutiny was drawing closer. Once or twice he stopped and wheeled around, as if to take in the view back along a sweeping avenue—but really to see who shared the path under the arching trees with him, trying to notice any face that was there more than once.

Some elves looked at him oddly, and El turned quickly away. Odd looks meant the lookers thought he was behaving oddly. He mustn't earn attention, at all costs. He'd just have to go on as before, trying to shrug off the odd prickling feeling between his shoulder blades that warned him of the ongoing scrutiny.

Did this open city have some sinister means of identifying intruders not of the People? They must, El supposed, or they'd soon be awash in the shapeshifters men called alunsree, or dopplegangers . . . hmm, but wasn't "alunsree" an elven word? The elves must have faced such problems when humans were still grunting at each other in caves and mud huts.

So he'd been spotted by someone. Someone concerned enough to stalk after him all this time, as he wandered down almost every street and lane of Cormanthor. What could he do?

Nothing but what he was doing—seeking House Alastrarra without seeming to be anxiously looking for anything. He dared not ask anyone where it was, or attract enough attention by his manner that someone might ask him if he needed aid . . . and he dared not call on the magic in the lore-gem unless he was desperate.

Desperate: surrounded by angry elven mages, all seeking his death with risen magic blazing in their hands. El glanced around the street as if such perils might come drifting toward him from all sides in a breath or two, but the scene remained almost like the revels of a feast-day. Folk were dancing in small groups or declaiming grandly as they swept along wrapped in their own self-importance. The fluting calls of horns heralded fresh songs, and off to the east a pair of pegasi riders chased each other across the sky in loops, rolls, and dartings that often sent leaves swirling in their wakes.

If he'd dared to, El would have sat on one of the many benches and floating highseats that flanked the mossy ways, and watched Cormanthor's comings and goings, openly fascinated. Yet if his true form were revealed, he might well be slain on the spot, and he had a mission to fulfill for Iymbryl. Where in all these endless trees *was* House Alastrarra, anyway? He'd been walking for hours, it seemed, and the light told him that the sun was sliding down the western sky. With its descent, the feeling grew in El that his mysterious shadow would attack.

After darkness fell? Or whenever things grew private enough? Where he stood now, the network of crossing trails was growing sparse, and the lights, bridges, and sounds were becoming fewer. If he continued on, he'd probably be heading into the deep green heart of the woods beyond the city, to the . . . southwest. Aye, southwest. He peered that way, and saw hanging creepers, and thick stands of gnarled trees, and a dell full of ferns. That decided him. Fern dells weren't high in his personal ranking of scenic beauty spots just now.

El turned around and picked up his pace, dancing softly forward on his toes as it seemed all Cormanthan elves did. He was moving purposefully now, as if heading for a known destination. His hand wasn't far from the hilt of the dagger that rode hidden in his sleeve. Was he charging straight toward an invisible, waiting foe? One who could draw a blade and hold it out, so that a hurrying false Iymbryl Alastrarra impaled himself on it?

The delicate strikings of a harp arose from a garden of hanging plants to his left as he went on. He had to go on; what else could he do?

After the mission the dying Iymbryl had set him stood his first task for Mystra. El shook his head in exasperation. This place was so beautiful; he wanted so much to just stroll and enjoy it.

Just as he'd wanted to grow up in Athalantar with his mother and father, not shiver in the wilds as an orphan outlaw, hunted by magelords. Aye, there was always *someone* with magic lurking about to ruin things. El set his jaw and went northeast. He'd strike clear across the city, and then try to circle around its outermost trails from there—he reckoned he'd trudged most of its labyrinthine heart already, with nary a sign of the falcon sigil of Alastrarra.

No unseen blade felled him, but the feeling of being watched didn't fade, either. The glows of enchanted symbols were growing stronger around El, now, as he walked. The gleam of the setting sun touched the treetops into golden flame, but down here in the dappled gloom its lances never penetrated.

The elven games and music went on unabated as twilight came down over Cormanthor. El walked on, trying not to show how anxious he was becoming. Could the lore-gem have played him false? Had it shown him an older House Alastrarra, or was the mansion well outside the city? Yet it held no scenes of another family holding, nor any sense that it was elsewhere in Cormanthor. *Surely* Iymbryl had known where he lived.

Aye, known too well for it to matter and be set forth clearly in the gem's stored memories. The whereabouts of House Alastrarra were a known, everyday thing to the bearers of the gems, not something . . .

But wait! Wasn't that a—no, *the* falcon symbol he was seeking?

El turned aside, pace quickening. It was!

His call of thanks to Mystra was no less fervent because of its silence.

The arched gate stood open, blue and green spell-glows winking and crawling up and down its filigree of living vines. El stepped inside, took two paces into the gloom of the twilit garden beyond, and then turned to survey the street behind him.

No elf stood there, but the unseen gaze remained unbroken. Slowly El turned around again.

Something gleamed in the air ahead of him, floating above the winding garden path. Something that hadn't been there moments before. It was the gleaming helm, arms, and shoulders of an elf in armor.

Or the semblance of such a guard—because those arms and shoulders and head were all he faced. The body that should have been beneath them was missing, the dark, gleaming armor trailing away like smoke below the breast of the silent apparition. As El stared at it, something rose menacingly from behind a bush off to the left: another armored form, just like the first.

El swallowed. So he'd awakened the magical defenses of this place. Blasting them with spells was probably not the wisest choice. So he turned slowly on his heels as guardian after guardian rose silently out of the dusk-cloaked garden, to ring him in on all sides.

Fire kindled then, behind the eye slits of one helm,

as El found himself facing the one who'd first blocked his way. The mansion rose beyond it, just as in the scene the gem had shown him. The soft glows of moving lights showed from the tall, narrow windows the Alastrarrans were so proud of.

Right now, some of them might be glancing out those windows to see what manner of creature their guardians were slaying.

As El stood quietly, wondering what to do, and searching frantically through the gem's visions in search of some guidance, thin beams of amber fire suddenly reached out from the fire raging within the helm before him to touch the disguised prince of Athalantar.

El felt no pain; the beams were sweeping *through* him, leaving behind a tingling, rather than burning or tearing. There was a sudden warmth on his brow and a burst of light that almost blinded him. He narrowed his eyes until he could see again.

The lore-gem had blazed into life, glowing like a leaping flame in the darkness of the garden. Its eruption seemed to satisfy the guardians. The searching beams winked out, and the menacing helms began to sink into the darkness on all sides, until El faced only the first one. It hung, helm dark now, in his way.

Elminster made himself walk calmly toward it, until the smokelike trail that marked where its body faded should have been tickling his nose.

But it wasn't. As he took the step that would have brought him into collision with the silent sentinel, it vanished, winking out of existence and leaving him staring at the front door of House Alastrarra. Music came faintly to him through that portal, and tiny traceries of golden light formed endless and intricate patterns on one of its panels.

The lore-gem told him nothing about traps or door gongs or even servants of the portal, so El strode toward the doors and extended a hand to the crescent-shaped handle that hung like a bar in the air before them. Mystra grant that they be unlocked, he thought.

As he took that last step and laid his hand on the bar, El realized that something felt different. For the first time in hours, the ever-present pressure of those unseen, watching eyes was gone.

A feeling of cool relief washed over him—relief that lasted almost an entire breath before the handle under his hand glowed with sudden savage blue fire, and the doors rolled soundlessly open, to leave him staring into the startled eyes of several elves in the hall beyond.

"Oho," Elminster whispered, almost audibly. "Mother Mystra, if ye love me at all, *be with me now.*"

* * * * *

An old trick practiced by thieves in the city of Hastarl is to act with cool condescension when caught where one has no business being. Lacking time to think, El used it now.

The five elves had frozen in the midst of opening fluted bottles of wine and pouring them over heaps of diced nuts and greens on several platters that seemed content to float in the absence of any table. El stepped around them with a calm, superior nod of recognition—something he was very far from feeling, for the gem held no images of servants; Iymbryl had evidently spent little time noticing underlings—and swept on into the back of the hall, where small indoor gardens sprouted. Behind him, the servants hastily sketched salutes and murmured greetings that he did not stop to acknowledge.

A sudden burst of laughter from an open doorway on the right made the servants hasten in their tasks and forget him. El smiled with relief and at the good fortune Mystra had sent him. Along the passage he hadn't chosen, an array of unattended bottles was flying, approaching at chest height and spectacular speed, in obvious answer to a servant's summons.

His smile froze on his face when an elven maid danced out of a crescentiform archway ahead along the right-hand wall and looked him full in the face. Her large, dark eyes filled with surprise as she gasped, "My lord! We did not expect you home for another three dawns!"

Her tone was eager, and her arms were rising to embrace him. Oh, Mystra.

Again El did what his time in the backstreets of Hastarl bid him. He winked, spun away from her on down the hall, and raised a finger to his lips in a sly "silent, now" gesture.

It worked. The lass chuckled in delight, waved to him in a way that promised future ecstasies, and danced away down the passage toward the front hall. The sash of her brief garment swirled behind her for a moment, displaying its glowing falcon sigil.

Of course. That sigil, like those the five by the doors were wearing, was the livery of the staff; they otherwise wore whatever befitted the situation, not any sort of uniform.

And from the memories he was borrowing swam up the face of the lass who'd now danced out of sight around the corner, and her name: Yalanilue. In Iymbryl's remembrance, she'd been chuckling just like that, face close to his. But she hadn't been wearing any clothes at the time.

El drew in a deep breath, and released it slowly and ruefully. At least the lore-gem steered him through the nuances of elven speech.

He went on down the passage, finding an archway to the left leading into a room where reflected stars glimmered in the deserted waters of a pool, and another to the right opening into a darkened room that seemed to house a sculpture collection. Thereafter the passage displayed closed doors down both walls on its run to an ending in a round room where glowing spheres of light floated, drifting gently about like sleepy fireflies as they lit a slender spiral stair.

El took it, wanting very much to be out of the passage before one of the Alastrarras found him. He ascended past a chamber where dancers were stretching into and out of twists and backflips, obviously warming up for a performance to come. Of both sexes, they wore only their long hair, flowing free. Tiny bells were woven into some of the locks, and their bodies were painted with intricate and obviously fresh designs.

One of them glanced at the elf hurrying past on the stair, but El put a finger to his chin as if in deep thought and hastened on, pretending not to have noticed the arching bodies of the dancers at all.

The stair took him then to a landing festooned with hanging plants—or rather, with spire-bottomed bowls enspelled so as to float at varying heights above the landing, to let the trailing leaves of their living burdens just brush the iridescent tiles underfoot.

El ducked between them toward an archway visible in the dimness beyond, still affecting his "lost in thought" pose. Then he came to an abrupt halt as something barred his way.

It blossomed into cold, white brightness, curling up to illuminate the chamber from its source: the naked edge of a leveled sword blade.

The blade hung by itself in midair, but a few drifting motes of magical radiance drew El's eye from it to an elven hand—an upraised right hand in a back corner, near the archway.

It belonged to a handsome, almost burly elf who

must be accounted a muscle-bound giant among Cormanthans. The elf rose with easy grace from the gleaming black gaming board on the floor at which he'd been playing spellcircles, here in the darkness, against a frail-seeming servant—a maid who'd have been beautiful if there hadn't been so much fear in her eyes. She was losing, badly, and no doubt saw ahead the whipping or other punishment her burly opponent had promised her. El wondered for a moment if winning or losing would grant her the greater pain.

The lore-gem told El that the burly elf facing him was Riluaneth, a cousin taken in by the Alastrarras after his parents died, and a source of trouble ever since. Resentful and with a cruel streak that was seldom far from governing him, Ril had delighted in teasing and occasionally tormenting the two young Alastrarran brothers, Iymbryl and Ornthalas.

"Riluaneth," El greeted him now, voice level. The glowing blade turned slowly in the air to point at him; Elminster ignored it.

There was a spell the kiira urgently wanted him to examine; a spell Iymbryl had linked with his image of Riluaneth, binding the two together with a surge of anger. El followed its bidding, standing motionless as his burly cousin glided toward him. "As always, Iym," purred Riluaneth, "you blunder in where you aren't wanted, and see too much. That'll get you hurt some day . . . possibly sooner."

The glow around the blade faded abruptly, and out of the sudden darkness the blade hissed right at El's face.

He ducked aside, followed by Riluaneth's quiet laughter. The sword swooped overhead and raced off into the gloom, seeking its true quarry. The servant sobbed once, utter terror making her too breathless to do more, as the blade raced at her mouth.

Grimly El bought her life at the possible cost of his own. A quick spell plucked the blade out of its flight and wrestled it around to fly away from the elven maiden. Riluaneth grunted in amazement. His hand swept to his belt, to the hilt of the knife he wore there.

Well, a human intruder could do at least one good deed for House Alastrarra this day. El set his teeth and fought off the burly elf's clawing, clumsy mental attempt to regain control of the blade. The attempt ended abruptly as El lifted the streaking blade a little, over Riluaneth's drawn dagger, and let it slide through the elf's midriff.

Riluaneth staggered, doubled over the hilt lodged against his convulsing belly, and clutched at the hilt of his dagger, trying to snarl out some words. The dagger winked as he began the unleashing of whatever fell magic it held. El, not wanting to be caught in something as deadly as it was likely to be, used the spell Iymbryl had intended for Riluaneth the next time there was "trouble."

The burly elf let out all his breath in a gasp of white smoke, and reeled. More white vapors billowed out of his ears, nose, and eyeballs. Riluaneth's brain was afire inside his head, something that Iymbryl had predicted, with uncharacteristic dark humor, would be "a swiftly ended blaze, to be sure."

It was. Elminster barely got out of the way in time as the big, sleek body toppled past him, starting its headlong plunge down the stair. It bounced twice, wetly, on the way down.

Someone screamed at the bottom of the stair. El sorted impatiently through the magics that the gem was proudly displaying, brushing aside images of the deft castings of elves who wore superior smiles, and found what he needed.

A bloodfire spell, to burn away a burly troublemaker

to nothing. A pyre without a barge might be the dwarven way, but Elminster had no time to be fussy about such things; already a triple-chiming gong had struck forth a strident chord on the floor below.

Brief brightness told him Riluaneth's remains had caught fire. El glanced over at the gaming board and found it gone—servant, pieces, and all. He wasn't the only one in this house who could move swiftly.

He might have been the only human ever to slay an elf here, though. Curses upon all cruel and arrogant bloods. Why couldn't he have run into Ornthalas in this corridor, and not into more trouble?

Below, the fire died and the blade clanged to the floor. There must be nothing left of Riluaneth now but trailing smoke and ash.

Time for him to be away from here, elsewhere in this grand house. Word of his part in Riluaneth's passing would spread soon enough. If he could somehow get to the heir first, and pass on the gem . . .

El bounded through the archway and down the passage beyond, sprinting with a lack of grace that would have raised elven eyebrows, but which certainly covered ground faster than they would have cared to. He snatched open a door and leapt into the high-ceilinged chamber beyond, finding himself in a place of floor-to-ceiling screens of filigree-work and lecterns with animated hands sprouting from their tops—hands that proffered open books to him as he darted past.

The Alastrarran library? Or reading room? He'd have liked to spend a winter here, or more, not dash past things without even looking at th—

But there was another door. El dodged around a floating, reclining chair that looked more comfortable than any other seating he'd ever seen and made a dive for the door handle.

He was still two speeding paces away when the door

suddenly swung away from him, opening to reveal a
startled elven face now inches from his own! He could-
n't stop or swerve in time . . .

* * * * *

"He fell right here, Revered Lady!" the dancer
gasped, pointing. His oiled body glistened in the flickering light of the brazier-bowls that circled around
them both in obedience to the will of the matriarch of
House Alastrarra.

The plum-hued gown she wore displayed every tall,
curvaceous inch of Namyriitha Alastrarra from time to
time, as portions of it flowed like smoke to wreath this
part of her or that part of her in glistening rainbow
droplets, and left other parts bare. An expert eye could
tell she had no longer been young for many centuries,
but few eyes bothered to practice any expertise when
faced with such smooth-flowing beauty.

Fewer dared to look her way at all, when her face
was as dark with fury as it was right now. "Keep
back!" she snarled, sweeping an arm out to reinforce
her order. Her gown rose into an elaborate sculpture of
rising, interlaced spines standing up from her shoulders, but her hair burst through them now, a sure sign
of unbridled rage. A servant whimpered softly, somewhere nearby. They'd only seen her thus thrice before—and each time, some part of the mansion had
paid dearly to win her calm.

She wove her magic this time, though, with a few
curt words. The sword rose obediently, quivering with
the power racing through it, and then set off through
the air, point first, up the stair. It would lead her, like
a sure-strike hunting arrow, to Riluaneth's slayer. No
doubt his gambling, dark schemes, or philandering
had earned him his fate, but no one entered House

Alastrarra and struck down one of her own without paying the price, twice over and speedily.

The Lady Namyriitha undid something as she hastened to the stairs, and the lower half of her gown fell away; she kicked it aside and set off up the stairs, bare legs flashing among wisps of patterned lace. Halfway up, her fingers, gliding along the rail, slid through something dark and sticky.

She looked back at the dark blood on the rail without slowing, and then lifted her dripping fingers and looked at them expressionlessly. She made no move to wipe them clean, or to slow her pursuit of the blade cutting through the air before her.

Below, the dancer picked up the discarded skirt uncertainly, and then handed it to a servant and whirled back to the stair to follow the Lady of the House. In his wake, hesitantly, several servants followed.

By the time they reached the landing at the top of the stair there was no sign of Namyriitha or the sword. The dancer began to run in earnest.

* * * * *

El dropped one arm to touch his knee at the last instant, and so it was his rolling shoulder that smashed into the elven servant and the door. Both flew back against the wall of the passage beyond with a mighty crash and rebounded into the passage in Elminster's wake. The elf sprawled on the furs underfoot in a tangle of limbs and did not move again.

Panting, El caught his balance again and ran on. Somewhere beneath him, the gong chimed its chord again. The passage forked ahead—this mansion was *big*—and El turned left this time. Perhaps he could double back.

A poor choice, it seemed. Two elves in glowing

aquamarine armor were hastening down the passage toward him, buckling on their swords as they came. "Intruders!" El called, hoping his shout was close enough to Iymbryl's voice to serve. He pointed back the way the guards had come. "Thieves! They ran thence!"

The guards wheeled around, though one gave El a hard, head-to-toe look, and ran back the way they'd come. "At least it wasn't Lady Herself just making sure we were awake," El heard one of them mutter, as they raced along the passage together. Ahead was a chamber dominated by a life-sized statue of a gowned elven lady, arms lifted in exultation. On its far side was another stair, curving down. A cross-corridor ran out of it, flanked by lounges on which the guards had obviously been reclining. Ornate double doors were along this passage; Elminster chose one he liked the look of, and veered toward it. He was into the passage and only a few running steps from its handles when shouts from the stair told him the two guards had noticed he was no longer with them.

He yanked on the ring handles, and twisted. The doors clicked open, and he whirled inside, drawing them closed as swiftly and as quietly as he could.

When he turned to see what manner of peril he'd hurled himself into this time, he found himself staring at an oval bed floating in midair in the middle of a dark, domed chamber. A leafy canopy floated above it, flanked by several platters carrying an array of fluted bottles and glasses, and a soft emerald glow was spreading across those leaves as the occupant of the bed sat bolt upright and stared at the intruder in her bedchamber.

She was slim and exquisitely beautiful, blue-black hair tumbling freely about her. She wore a night shift consisting of a collar and a thin strip of sheer, gauzy blue-green silk that fell from it down her front—and presumably down her back, too. Bare flanks and shoulders gleamed in the growing light as her large eyes changed from alarm to delight, and she somersaulted from the bed in a graceful sweep of bare limbs to bound forward and fling her arms around El.

"Oh, dearest brother!" she breathed, staring up into his eyes. "You're back, and whole! I had the most *terrible* dream about you dying!" She bit at her lip, and tightened her arms around him as if she'd never let him go. Oh, *Mystra*.

"Well," Elminster began awkwardly, "there's something I must tell you. . . ."

With a boom, a door on the far side of the room burst inward, and a tall, angry-eyed elven maiden clad in a similar night shift stood in the doorway, conjured fire blazing around her wrists. Behind her crowded guards in glowing armor, the falcon sigil of Alastrarra on their breasts, and the winking lights of ready magic flickering and racing up and down the bared blades in their hands.

"Filaurel!" she cried. "Stand away from yon imposter! He but wears our brother's shape!"

The elven maiden stiffened in El's arms, and tried to draw back. El clung to her as tightly as she'd clutched him, uncomfortably aware of the sleek softness of the body pressed against his, and murmured, "Wait— please!" With one sister held against him, the other might not be so quick to blast him with spells.

Her arms quivered with rage as she lifted them to do just that. She paused, seeing that she'd endanger Filaurel. But if she dared not hurl magic just yet, there was no such constraint on her tongue. "*Murderer!*"

"Melarue," Filaurel said in a small voice, trembling against Elminster's chest, "what shall I do?"

"Bite him! Kick him! Let him have no time to work spells, while we come at him!" Melarue snarled, striding forward.

Another door boomed, and its thunder was out-shouted by a magically augmented voice uttering a clear, crisp command. "Be *still*, all!"

The room fell silent and motionless, but for the heaving bosom of Filaurel, pressed against the one who held her.

And for the sword, gliding smoothly through the air at Elminster. It rose, above the head of the elf maiden, until all it could imperil was the tense face of the false elf, who watched it slide straight for his mouth, nearer . . . and nearer . . .

Beyond it stood an elven matriarch in the upper half of a courtly gown, her face calm. Only her snapping eyes betrayed her outrage, as she stood with her hands raised in the gesture that had accompanied her order. A lady used to her will being absolutely obeyed within this House. This must be the Lady Namyriitha, Iymbryl's mother.

El had no choice—call on the gem, or die. With an inward sigh he awakened the power that would turn the sword to flakes of rust, and then dust ere it hit the floor.

"You are not my son," the matriarch said coldly, her eyes like the points of two daggers as she locked gazes with Elminster.

"But he wears the kiira," Filaurel said, almost pleadingly, staring up at where it glowed on the brow of the one who held her—the one who felt like her brother.

Namyriitha ignored her younger daughter. "Who *are* you?" she demanded, gliding forward.

"Ornthalas," Elminster said wearily. "Bring Ornthalas to me, and ye shall have the answer ye seek."

The lady matriarch stared at him, eyes narrow, for a long, silent time. Then she whirled, exposed lace swirling about her legs, and muttered orders. Two of the guards bent their heads and turned, holding their blades high to ensure they harmed no one in the crowd of bodies, and slipped out the door. Though he could see little of their departure, El did not think they were heading for the same destination.

The tense silence that followed did not last long. As the guards behind Lady Namyriitha spread out into an arc on both sides of her and put away their swords to pluck out hand darts instead, Melarue led her own guards forward to ring Elminster about completely.

"Revered mother," she said, spellflames still chasing each other in circles about her wrists, "what danger do we now dance with? This impostor could be spellbound to slay at all costs—a sacrifice whose body holds magics mighty enough to blast us all, and this house asunder around us! Dare we bring the heir of Alastrarra here, into the very presence of this–this shapeshifter?"

"I am *always* aware of the perils awaiting us all, Melarue," her mother said coldly, not turning her head to take her eyes off Elminster for a second, "and have spent centuries honing my judgment. Never forget that I am head of this house."

"Yes, mother," Melarue replied, in a respectful tone that twisted just enough in weary exasperation that El almost smiled. It seemed humans and elves were not so very different at heart after all.

"Please believe," El said to the elf maid in his arms, "that I mean no harm to you, or to House Alastrarra. I am here because of a promise I made, upon my honor."

"What promise?" Lady Namyriitha asked sharply.

"Revered Lady," El replied, turning his head to her, "I shall reveal all when what I must do is done—it is too precious a thing to endanger with dispute. I assure you that I mean no harm to anyone in this house."

"Surrender unto me your *name!*" the matriarch cried, using magic on the last word to compel him. El

shook like a leaf in the thrall of her power, but the gem
steadied him, and Mystra's grace kept him standing.
He blinked at her, and shook his head. There was a
murmur of respect from the ring of warriors, and
Namyriitha's face tightened in fresh anger as she
heard it.

"I am come," a deep yet musical voice said from the
doorway. An old elf stood there, clad in the cape and
robes usually affected by human archwizards. The falcon device of the house was worked into the sash he
wore, repeated many times, yet El knew this was no
servant. Rings gleamed on his ancient fingers, and he
bore a short wooden scepter in his hands, its sides
carved with spiral grooves.

"Naeryndam," the matriarch said curtly, nodding
her head in Elminster's direction, "deal with this."

The old elf met El's gaze, and his eyes were keen
and searching. "Unknown one," the elven mage said
slowly, "I can tell ye are not Iymbryl, of this House. Yet
ye wear the gem that was his. Think ye that possession
of it gives ye rightful command over the kin of Alastrarra?"

"Revered elder," El replied, bowing his head, "I have
no desire to command anyone in this fair city, or do any
harm to ye or thy kin. I am here because of a promise
I made to one who was dying."

In his arms, Filaurel started to shake. El knew she
was weeping silently, and automatically stroked her
hair and shoulders in futile soothings. The Lady
Namyriitha's mouth tightened again, but Melarue and
some of the warriors looked more kindly upon the intruder in their midst.

The old elf nodded. "Thy words ring true. Know,
then, that I am going to cast a spell that is not an attack, and conduct thyself accordingly."

He lifted his hand, made a circling motion, spread

and crooked two fingers, and blew some dust or pow-
der over his wrist. There was a singing in the air, and
the warriors on all sides hastily fell back. The singing
air—some sort of spell-barrier, El guessed—ringed
him around closely.

He merely nodded to the old elf mage, and stood
waiting. Filaurel was crying openly now, and he swung
her fully against his chest and murmured, "Lady, let
me tell ye how thy brother died."

There was suddenly utter stillness in the room. "By
chance I came upon a patrol Iymbryl was part of, in
the deep wood—"

"A patrol he *led*," Lady Namyriitha almost spat.

El inclined his head gravely. "Lady, indeed; I
meant no slight. I saw the last few of his fellows fall,
until only he was left, beset on all sides by ruukha,
in numbers enough to overwhelm his spells, and
mine own."

"*Your* spells?" she sneered, her tone making it clear
she doubted his words. Filaurel's face, however, wet
with tears, was raised and intent on his every word.

"As I fought my way to him, he was pierced through
by a ruukha longfork, and fell into a stream there. My
spells took us both away from our foes, but he was
dying. Had he lived longer, he could have been my
guide to bring him hence. But he had time only to
show me that I should put the kiira to my brow before
he failed . . . and was gone to dust."

"Did he say anything?" Filaurel sobbed. "His last
words: *do you remember them?*" Her voice rose in an-
guish, to ring in the far corners of her bedchamber.

"He did, Lady," El told her gently. "He cried out a
name, and that he was coming at last to its owner.
That name was . . . Ayaeqlarune."

There was a general groan, and both Melarue and
Filaurel hid their faces. Their mother, however, stood

like white-faced stone, and the old elf mage only nodded sadly.

Into this grieving swept new arrivals, slim and
straight-backed and proud. Rich were their costumes,
and haughty their manner, as they came in at the door
and stood staring: four she-elves and two much
younger maids, with a proud, youthful elven lord at
their head. El recognized him from the gem-visions,
though there was no floating chair nor tree-pillars and
sun-dappling here. This was Ornthalas, now heir—
though he did not yet know it—of House Alastrarra.

Ornthalas looked at El in some puzzlement.
"Brother," he asked, one elegant brow lowering in a
frown, "what means this?"

He glanced about the chamber. "The House is yours;
there's no need to challenge our kin about anything."
His gaze fell to Filaurel, and darkened. "Or have you
taken our sist—"

"Hold peace, youngling," Naeryndam said sternly.
"Such thoughts demean us all. See yon gem upon thy
brother's brow?"

Ornthalas looked at his uncle as if the old mage had
lost his senses. "Of course," he said. "Is this some sort
of game? Be—"

"Still for once," the Lady Namyriitha said crisply,
and someone among the ring of warriors chuckled.

At that sound, the young elven lord drew himself up,
looked around the room in an attempt at dignified silence
(El thought he looked like a fat merchant in the streets of
Hastarl who has slipped in horse-droppings and fallen
hard on his behind on the cobbles; he has scrambled up,
and is now looking around to see if anyone witnessed his
pratfall, pretending all the while that there is no horse-
dung on his backside—no, none at all, as all well-bred
people can plainly see . . .), and announced to his uncle,
"Yes, Revered Uncle, I see the kiira."

"Good," the old elf said dryly, and there was another chuckle from the warriors, this one better suppressed. Naeryndam let it die away, and then said, "Ye are sworn to obey the bearer of the kiira, as are we all."

"Yes," Ornthalas nodded, his puzzled frown returning. "I have known this since I was a child, Uncle."

"And remember it yet? Good, good," the old mage replied softly, evoking several chuckles this time. Both Lady Namyriitha and Melarue stirred, exasperation plain on their faces, but said nothing.

"Then do ye swear by the kiira of our House, and all our forebears who live within it, to lift no hand, and cast no spell, upon thy brother as he approaches ye?" Naeryndam asked, his voice suddenly as hard and ringing as a sword blade striking metal.

"I do," Ornthalas said shortly.

The old elf-mage took hold of the young elf's arm, towed him forward through the singing barrier, and then turned to El and said, "Here be he. Do what ye've come to do, sir, before one of my hot-blooded kin does something foolish."

El inclined his head in thanks, took Filaurel gently by the elbows, and said, "My humble apologies, lady, for trammeling thy freedom. It was needful. May the gods grant that it never be so, upon thee, ever again in all thy long days."

Filaurel shrank away from him, eyes very large, and put her knuckles to her lips. Yet as he turned away, she blurted out, "Your honor goes unblemished with you, unknown lord."

El took two quick steps toward Naeryndam, stepped smoothly around him, and bore down upon Ornthalas with a polite smile.

The young elf looked at him. "Brother, are you renouncing—?"

"Sad news, Ornthalas," said Elminster, as their

noses crashed together, and then their brows. As the tingling and flashing begun, he held like grim death to the elf's shoulders, and added, "I'm not thy brother."

The memories were surging around him, then, in a maelstrom that was sweeping him away, and Ornthalas was screaming in shock and pain. A white, roaring surge of magic was tugging at him as it rose, and El couldn't hold on any longer.

"May the law of the realm protect me!" he cried, and then gasped in a hoarse whisper, "Mystra, stand by me!"

The room spun around him then, and he had no breath left to cry anything. His body was stretching, everyone was shouting in anger and alarm, and the last thing the prince of Athalantar saw, as he spun down into tentacles of darkness that came sweeping greedily up to take him, was the furious face of the Lady Namyriitha, dwindling away behind the one solid thing in all this: the leveled wooden scepter, held firmly in Naeryndam's old hand. He clung to that image as utter darkness claimed him.

Five

TO CALL ON THE CORONAL

And so it befell that Elminster of Athalantar found the elven family he had so inadvertently joined and did that which he was sworn to do. Like many who fulfill an unusual and dangerous duty, he received scant thanks for it. Had it not been for the grace of Mystra, he might easily have died in the Coronal's garden that night.

Antarn the Sage
from **The High History of Faerûnian Archmages Mighty**
published circa The Year of the Staff

Ornthalas Alastrarra stumbled across the chamber, clutching his head and screaming, his voice raw and ugly. Crackling lightnings of magic trailed from the gem that shone like a new star upon his brow, back to the one from whom it had come: the sprawled body on the floor, so young, and ugly—and *human*.

Filaurel's bedchamber was in an uproar. Warriors hacked at the barrier that repelled their armor and their blades, and were repulsed. They clawed their way along it, shouting in pain amid bright clouds of sparks, only to stagger back, master their trembling limbs, and try again. Under their high-booted feet Melarue lay sprawled, her hair outflung like a fan around her, stunned from her own attempt to burst through Naeryndam's barrier. She'd forgotten the manyfold enchantments upon her jewelry.

Not so her mother. Lady Namyriitha was standing well clear of the singing air and grimly bringing down the barrier with spell after spell of her own, melting away its essence layer by layer. As those magics crashed and swirled, Filaurel and most of the other women screamed at the sight of Elminster's true nature and at the agony of Ornthalas. Servants crowded in at every door to see what was befalling.

The old elf-mage calmly stepped over the motionless body of the hawk-nosed human and stood astride it, drawing a sword seemingly out of the empty air. Magic winked and chased itself up and down that rune-marked blade as he raised and shook it a little doubtfully, as many an old warrior readies a weapon he finds heavier than he remembered. He raised his scepter in the other hand. When the barrier failed in a wash of white sparks an instant later, and the warriors of House Alastrarra surged forward with an exultant shout, he was ready.

Blue fire swirled out from the tip of Naeryndam's blade, so hot and quick that warriors bent over backward in mid-charge, and fell in awkward, sliding heaps. A sweep of that same blue fire along the furs underfoot, a sweep that left the furs unscorched, sent them rolling and scrambling away again, back to where they'd stood before. One elf flung his blade as he fled, spinning hard and fast through the air at the motionless human. The scepter spat forth its own fire, a stabbing, silvery needle of force, and the thrown blade exploded into a rainbow of snapping sparks that spun and flew until they were no more. One or two of them bounced almost at Naeryndam's feet.

"What treachery is this?" Lady Namyriitha spat at the old mage. "Are you crazed, aged brother? Has the human some sort of spellhold over you?"

"Be still," the old mage replied in calm and pleasant tones—but as she had done earlier, he put his risen power behind his words. The only sounds that followed their rolling, imperious thunder were faint groans from where Ornthalas lay in a corner, his head against the wall, and sobbings here and there where women who'd been screaming struggled to catch their breaths again.

"There's entirely too much shouting and spellhurling in this House, these days," Naeryndam observed, "and not nearly enough listening, caring, and thinking. In a few generations more, we'll be as bad as the Starym."

The warriors and servants stared at the old mage in genuine astonishment; the Starym held themselves to be the pinnacle of all that is noble and fine among the People, and even their age-old rivals acknowledged them first among all the proud Houses of Cormanthor.

The corners of Naeryndam's mouth crooked in what might almost have been a smile as he looked around the room at all the astonished faces. With blade in hand he motioned his kin and the servants all to stand before him, on one side of the room. When no one moved, he let fire roll forth from the blade again, in long, snarling arcs of clear warning. Slowly, almost dazedly, they obeyed.

"Now," the old mage told them, "just for this once, and for a short enough time, ye'll listen—ye too, Ornthalas, risen Heir of House Alastrarra."

A groan was his only reply, but those who turned to look saw Ornthalas nodding, his white face still held in his hands.

"This human youngling," Naeryndam said, pointing down at the body beneath him with his scepter, "invoked the law of the realm. And yet all of ye—save Filaurel and Sheedra and young Nanthleene—attacked him, or tried to. Ye disgust me."

There were murmurs of protest. He quelled them with fire leaping in his old eyes and continued, "Yes, disgust me. This House has an heir right now because this man risked his life, and kept to his honor. He made his way into our city, past a hundred elves or more who might have killed him—would have slain him, had they known his true nature—because Iymbryl asked him to. And because he keeps his word to those not of his kin nor race, those he barely knows, and dared this task, the memories of this House, the thoughts of our forebears, are not lost, and we can keep our rightful place in the realm as a first House. All because of this human, whose name we don't even know."

"Nevertheless," his sister Namyriitha began, "w—"

"*I'm not finished*," her brother said, in tones that cut like steel. "*Thou* listen even less well than the young ones, sister."

Had the moment been less important, the air less full of tension and awe, the gathered House might have enjoyed the sight of the sharp-tongued matriarch opening and closing her mouth like a gasping fish in silence, as her face flooded crimson and purple. No one, though, so much as looked at her; their eyes were all on Naeryndam, the oldest living Alastrarran.

"The human invoked our law," the old mage said flatly. "Younglings, heed well: the law is just that—the *law*, a thing not permitting of our tampering or setting aside. If we do, we are no better than the most brutal ruukha or the most dishonest human. I will not stand idle and see ye of the blood of Thurruvyn fail the rightful honor of our House . . . and of our race. If ye would attack the human, ye must first defeat *me*."

The silence that followed was broken by a groan from beneath the old mage; the raven-haired, hawk-nosed human youth gave an involuntary cry of pain as he stirred. One tanned and rather dirty hand closed blindly on the booted elven ankle hard by it. At the sight a warrior of House Alastrarra cried out and threw his blade.

End over end it flashed, straight at the tousled head of the human, as he started to claw his way up the leg of the elf who stood over him.

Naeryndam calmly watched it come, and at precisely the right moment swept his own blade down to strike the whirling steel aside into a corner of the room. "Thou listen but poorly, do thou not?" he asked with soft sadness, as the warrior who'd thrown the blade cowered away from him. "When is this House going to start using its wits?"

"*My* wits tell me that Alastrarra shall be forever stained and belittled by Cormanthans from end to end of our fair realm, as the House that harbored a human," the Lady Namyriitha said bitterly, raising her hands dramatically.

"Yes," Melarue chimed in, rising from the floor with the pain of her striving against the barrier still etched on her face. "You've lost *your* wits, Uncle!"

"What say ye, Ornthalas?" the old mage asked, looking past them. "What say—our ancestors?"

The haughty young elf looked sadder and more serious than any in the room remembered him ever seeming. His brow was still pinched with pain, and strange shadows yet swirled in his eyes, as memories that were not his own plunged past them in the endless, bewildering flood. Slowly, reluctantly, he said, "Prudence bids us conduct the human to the Coronal, that no stain be upon us." He looked from one Alastrarran to another. "Yet if we harm so much as a hair upon his head, our honor is bereft. This man has done us more service than any elf living, save you, noble Naeryndam."

"Ah," the old mage said, satisfied. "Ah, now. See, Namyriitha, what a treasure the kiira is? Ornthalas wears it for but moments and gains good sense."

His sister stiffened in fresh annoyance, but Ornthalas smiled ruefully, and said, "I fear you speak bald truth, Uncle. Let us quit this field before battle comes to it, and return to our singing. Let the songs be of our remembrances of Iymbryl my brother, until dawn or slumber. Sisters, will you join me?"

He held out his arms, and after a moment of hesitation Melarue and Filaurel took them, and the three siblings swept out of the chamber together.

As they went out, Filaurel looked back at the human, just as the strange man found his feet, and shook her head. Fresh tears glistened in her eyes as she called, "Have my thanks, human sir."

"Elminster am I," the hawk-nosed man replied, lifting his head, his elvish now strangely accented. "Prince of Athalantar."

He turned his head to look at Naeryndam. "I stand in thy debt, revered lord. I am ready, if ye'd take me to the Coronal."

"Yes, brother," the Lady Namyriitha snarled, face pinched in disgust, "remove *that* from our halls—and stop staring at him, Nanthee; you demean us before an unwashed beast!"

The young lass thus addressed was staring in open awe at the human, with his stubbled face, and stubby ears, and—*otherness*. El winked at her.

That brought gasps of outrage from both Lady Namyriitha and Sheedra, the mother of Nanthleene, who snatched at her daughter's hand, and practically dragged her from the chamber.

"Come, Prince Elminster," the old mage said dryly. "The impressionable young ladies of this House are not for thee. Though 'tis to thy credit that thou're not disgusted when faced with folk of other races than thine own. Many of my kin are not so large of mind and heart, and so there is danger for thee here." He held out his winking sword, hilt first. "Carry my blade, will thou?"

Wondering, Elminster took hold of the enspelled sword, feeling the tingling of strong magics as he hefted the light, supple blade. It was magnificent. He raised it, staring in admiration at its feel and at the way its steel—if it *was* steel—shone bright and blue in the light of the bedchamber. More than one of the warriors gasped in alarm at the sight of the mage arming this human intruder, but Naeryndam paid them no heed.

"There is also a danger to us, if a human should see the glories and defenses of our realm, which is why we suffer few of thy blood to catch even a glimpse of our city, and live. Wherefore my blade will cloud thy sight, even as it binds thee to accompany me."

"It is not needful, Lord Mage. I have no mind to cross thee, or escape thee," El told him truthfully, as mists rose to enclose them both in a world of swirling blueness. "And even less of a mind to storm this fair city, alone, in time to come."

"I know those things, but others of my kind do not," Naeryndam replied calmly, "and some of them are *very* swift with their bows and blades." He took a step forward, and the blue mists rolled away behind them, dwindling to nothingness.

El looked around in wonder; they were now standing not in a crowded bedchamber, but under the night sky in the green heart of a garden. Stars glittered overhead. Beneath their feet two paths of soft, lush moss met beside the statue of a large, winged panther that glowed a vivid blue in the night. Will o'wisps danced and drifted here and there above the beautiful

plants around them, swaying above luminous night-
flowers to the accompaniment of faint strains of unseen harps.

"The Coronal's garden?" El asked in a soft whisper.
The old mage smiled at the wonder in the human's eyes.

"The Coronal's garden," he confirmed, his voice a
soft rumble. The words were barely said when something rose out of the ground at their very feet—spectral, and graceful, and yet deadly in appearance.

Blue-white it glowed, all sleek nude curves and long
flowing hair, but its eyes were two dark holes against
the stars as it said in their minds, *Who comes?*

"Naeryndam, eldest of the House of Alastrarra, and
guest," the old mage said firmly.

The watchnorn swayed to meet his gaze, and then
back to look into the eyes of Elminster, from only
inches away.

A chill crackled between living flesh and undead
essence as those dark eyes stared into his, and El swallowed. He'd not want to see that serenely beautiful
face angry.

This is a human. Blue-white hair swirled severely.

"Aye," the old elf told the watchnorn in dry tones. "I
can recognize them too."

*Why bring you a forbidden one where the Coronal
walks this night?*

"To see the Coronal, of course," Naeryndam told the
undead maiden. "This human brought the kiira of my
House from our dying heir to his successor, alone and
on foot through the deep heart of the forest."

The swirling spirit seemed to look at Elminster with
new respect. *That is something a Coronal should see;
there can never be too many wonders in the world.* The
blue-white, ghostly face came close enough to brush
against Elminster's once more. *Can you not speak,
human?*

"I did not want to insult a lady," El said carefully, "and know not how to properly address thee. Yet I think now we are well met." He threw back one booted foot and sketched a sweeping bow. "I am Elminster, of the land of Athalantar. Who art thou, Lady of Moonlight?"

Wonder upon wonder, the ghostly thing said, brightening. *A mortal who desires to know my name. I like that "Lady of Moonlight" you entitle me; it is fair upon the ears. Yet know, man called Elminster, that I was in life Braerindra of the House of Calauth, last of my House.*

Her voice began astonished and pleased, yet ended with such sadness that Elminster found tears welling up in him. Roughly, he said, "Yet, Lady Braerindra, look ye: while ye abide here, the House of Calauth yet stands, and is not forgotten."

Ah, but who is to remember it? The voice in their heads was a sad sigh. *The forest grows through roofless chambers that once were fair, and scatter the bones and dust that were my kin, while I am here, far distant. A watchnorn, now. Cormanthans term us "ghosts," and fear us, and keep away. Hence our guardianships here be lonely, and bid fair to remain so.*

"I shall remember the House of Calauth," Elminster said quietly, his tone firm. "And if I live and am allowed to walk fair Cormanthor freely, I will return to talk with thee, Lady Braerindra. Ye shall not be forgotten."

Blue-white hair swirled up around Elminster, and a chill prickled through him. *I never thought to hear a mortal do me honor in the world again,* the voice in his head replied, full of wonder. *Still less a human, to speak so fair. Be welcome whenever ye can find the time to come hence.* Elminster felt a sudden wrenching cold on his cheek, and he shivered involuntarily. Naeryndam caught hold of his shoulder as he reeled.

My thanks to thee also, wise mage, the spirit added,

as Elminster struggled to smile. *Truly, you bring wonders to show our Coronal.*

"Aye, and so we must pass on. Fare thee well, Braerindra, until next our paths cross," the old elf replied.

Until next, the voice replied faintly, as blue-white wisps sank into the ground and were gone.

Naeryndam hurried Elminster along one of the mossy paths. "Truly, ye impress me, man, by the way ye take on the weight of others' cares. I begin to hope for the human race yet."

"I—I can scarce speak," El told him, teeth chattering. "Her kiss was so . . . cold."

"Indeed—had she meant it to do so, 'twould have driven the life from thy body, lad," the old elf told him. "It is why she serves thus, she and those of her kind. Yet be of heart; the chill will pass, and ye need not fear the touch of any undead of Cormanthor, forevermore. Or rather, for as long as thy 'forevermore' lasts."

"Our lives must seem fleeting to elves," El murmured, as the path took them up into small bowers of curved seats amid shrubs, and past trickling streamlets and little pools.

"Aye," the elven mage told him, "but I meant rather the peril ye stand in. Speak as fairly in the time just ahead as ye did to the watchnorn, lad, or death may yet find thee this night."

The young man beside him was silent for some time. "Is the Coronal one I should kneel to?" he asked finally, as they came up some stone steps and between two strange, spiral-barked trees out onto a broad patio lit by luminous plants.

"Be guided by his face," the mage replied smoothly as they advanced, not hurrying.

An elf sat on nothing at the center of the paved space, with an open book, a tray of tall, thin bottles, and a footrest floating in the air around him. Two cloaked elves who wore power as if it crowned them stood on either side of him; at the sight of the human they glided swiftly forward to bar Elminster's path to the Coronal, slowing only slightly at the sight of Naeryndam Alastrarra behind the human.

"*You* must have helped this forbidden one win past the watchnorns," one of the elven mages said to the old elf-mage, ignoring Elminster as if he were no more than a post or bird-spotted stone sculpture. His voice was cold with anger. "Why? What treachery, reveal unto us, could reach the heart of one who has served the realm so long? Have your kin sent you hither for punishment?"

"No treachery, Earynspieir," Naeryndam replied calmly, "nor punishment, but a matter of state requiring the judgment of the Coronal. This human invoked our law, and survives to stand here because of it."

"No *human* can claim rights under the laws of Cormanthor," the other mage snapped. "Only those of our People can be citizens of the realm: elves, and elf-kin."

"And how would ye judge a human who has in all honor, and not through battle-spoil, worn a kiira of an elder House of Cormanthor, and walked the streets of our city until he found the rightful heir to surrender it to?"

"I'd believe that tale only when it could be proven to me, beyond doubt," Earynspieir replied. "What House?"

"Mine own," Naeryndam replied.

Into the little silence that his soft words made, the old elf in the chair said, "Enough tongue-fencing, lords. This man is here, that I may judge; bring him to me."

Elminster ducked around the mage who stood nearest and strode boldly toward the Coronal. He never saw the mage wheel and cast a deadly spell at him, or Naeryndam nullify it with a scepter held ready for just such an occurrence.

The second mage was hurling another dark magic when Elminster knelt before the ruler of all Cormanthor. The Coronal raised a hand, and that magic, rushing toward his face like a dark roiling in the air, ceased to be. "Enough spell-hurling, lords all," he commanded gently. "Let us see this man." He looked into Elminster's eyes.

El's mouth was suddenly dry. The eyes of the elven king were like holes opening into the night sky. Stars swam and twinkled in their depths, and one could fall into those dark pools and be dragged down, down, and away . . .

He shook his head to clear it, clenched his teeth at the effort required, and set one booted foot on the pave. It seemed as if he were lifting a castle tower on his shoulders when he tried to straighten that leg, and surge to his feet. He growled, and set about doing so.

Behind him, the three elven mages exchanged looks. Not even they could forge on against the Coronal's will, when mindlocked with the ruler of all Cormanthor.

White-faced and trembling, sweat running in rivers down his cheeks and chin, the raven-haired young man rose slowly, gaze still locked with the Coronal, until he was standing beside the seated elf.

"Do you resist me yet?" the old elf whispered.

The young man's lips moved with agonizing slowness as he tried to shape words. "No," he said at last, slowly and deliberately. "Ye are welcome in my thoughts. Were ye not trying to make me rise?"

"No," the Coronal said, turning his head so that the link between their gazes was cut off, as if by a knife. "I strove to keep you on your knees, to master your will." He frowned, eyes narrowing. "Perhaps another works through you."

"My lord!" the mage Earynspieir cried, thrusting

himself between Elminster and the Coronal. "This is precisely the peril you must be shielded against! Who knows what deadly spell could be worked upon you, through this lad?"

"Hold him in thrall, then, if you must," the Coronal said wearily. "All three of you—and Earynspieir, let there be no 'accidentally' broken necks, or frozen lungs, or the like. I shall reveal whom he serves with the scepter, and read his memories of the matter of the kiira thereafter."

From one of the trays floating near at hand the white-robed elf took up what looked like a long claret-hued glass rod, smooth and straight, no thicker than his smallest finger. It seemed almost too delicate to hold together.

El found himself lifted off his feet to hang motionless in the air, hands spread out stiffly from his sides. He could move his eyes, his throat, and his chest; all else was gripped as if by unyielding iron.

A light grew in the glass rod, and raced along its length. The old elf calmly pointed it at Elminster's head, and they both watched the thin ray of radiance slide out of the rod and move through the air, with almost lazy slowness, to touch El's forehead.

A great coldness crashed through the Athalantan, shaking him to his very fingertips. As he quivered there in midair he could hear the clatter of his teeth chattering uncontrollably, and then gasps of amazement from all four elves.

"What is it?" he tried to say, but all that came out through his frozen lips was a confused gurgling. Abruptly he found that his mouth was freed, and that he was turning—being turned—in the air, around to face a ghostly image that was towering over the patio. The spectral outlines of a face he knew.

A calm, serene face regarding them all with mild

interest. Its eyes lit upon Elminster, and brightened.

"Is that who I think it is, man?" the Coronal asked gently.

"It is Holy Mystra," El told him simply. "I am her servant."

"So much I had come to suspect," the old elf told him a trifle grimly. A moment later, he and the young human melted away together, leaving the floating chair, and the air above and before it, empty.

The three mages stared at those emptinesses, and then at each other. Earynspieir whirled around to look up into the sky again. The huge human face was fading, the ghostly tresses curling and whipping like restless snakes as it seemed to draw slightly away from the Coronal's garden.

But what made the elf-mages cower and stammer out the names of their gods was the way the beautiful female face looked at each of them in turn, as a broad and satisfied smile grew across it.

A few moments later, the face could no longer be seen at all.

"Some trick of the young human, no doubt," Earynspieir hissed, visibly shaken. Naeryndam only shook his head in silence, but the other court mage plucked at Earynspieir's arm to get his attention, and pointed.

That vast smile had suddenly reappeared. There was no face around it this time, but all three mages knew what it was. They would see it in their memories until their dying days.

As they turned their backs on the stars and hastened toward the nearest doors that led into the palace, another sight made them all pause and stare in silence once more.

All over the gardens, the watchnorns were rising silently to watch that smile fade.

Six

THE VAULT OF AGES

Beneath the fair city of Cormanthor, in some hidden place, lies the Vault of Ages, sacred storehouse of the lore of our People. 'Let Mythal rise and Myth Drannor fall,' says one ballad, 'and still the Vault remembreth all.' Some say the Vault lies there yet, unplundered and as splendid as before, though few now know the way to it. Some say 'tis the Srinshee's tomb. Some say she has become a terrible mad thing of clawing magics, and has made the Vault her lair. And there are even some who admit that they do not know.

Shalheira Talandren, High Elven Bard of Summerstar
from **Silver Blades And Summer Nights:
An Informal But True History of Cormanthor**
published in The Year of the Harp

There were no mists, this time, only a soft moment of purple-black velvet darkness, and then Elminster was elsewhere.

The white-robed elven ruler stood with him, in a cool, damp stone room whose ceiling arched low overhead. Luminous crystals were set in the places where the crisscrossing stone ribs of its vaults met, one with the next.

The elf and the human stood in the brightest spot, a clear space at the center of the domed chamber. In four

places around its circular arc the wall was pierced by
ornate arches that gave onto long vaulted passages
running—El peered down one, and then another—to
other domed chambers.

A narrow, winding path had been left clear down the
center of each passage, but all of the rest of the space
was crammed with treasure: a spreading sea of gold
coins and bars and statuary, holding in its frozen
waves ivory coffers that spilled pearls and rainbows of
glittering gems.

Chests were stacked six high along the walls, and
chased and worked metal banner-poles leaned against
them like fallen trees. Nearer at hand, a dragon as tall
as Elminster, carved from a single gigantic emerald,
leaned amid the branches of a tree of solid sardonyx;
its leaves were of electrum covered with tiny cut gems.
The prince of Athalantar turned slowly on his heel to
survey this treasure, trying to look expressionless and
very much aware that the Coronal was watching his
face.

There were more riches here, in this one chamber,
than he'd ever seen before in all his life. The wealth
here was truly staggering. The entire treasury of Athalantar was outshone by what would lie beneath him,
were he to simply fall on his face in the nearest heap
of coins. Right by his foot gleamed a cut ruby as large
as his head.

El dragged his gaze up from all the wealth to meet
the searching, starry eyes of the Coronal. "What is all
this?" he asked. "I—that is, I know what I'm looking at,
but why keep it here, underground? The gems would
dazzle far more in sunlight."

The old elf smiled. "My People dislike cold metal,
and keep little of it to look at and touch on a daily
basis; something gnomes and dwarves and humans
never seem able to grasp. The gems we need to serve

us as homes for magic, yes, those we keep about us; the remainder rests in various vaults. That which belongs to the Coronal—or rather, to the court, and thus, all Cormanthor—comes here." He looked down one of the passages. "Some call this the Vault of Ages."

"Because ye've been piling up riches here for so long?"

"No. Because of the one who dwells here, guarding it all." The Coronal raised a hand in greeting, and El stared down the passage that the old elf was facing.

There *was* a figure there, tiny in the dim distance, and as thin as a post. A very graceful post, swaying as it came toward them.

"Look at me," the Coronal said suddenly. When Elminster turned, he found himself looking into the full, awakened might of the ruler of Cormanthor. Once again his boots rose helplessly from the floor, and he hung in the air above the old elf as irresistable probes raced through him, calling up memories of a ferny dell, his spellbook left behind, Iymbryl gasping, and a certain scepter.

The Coronal stopped at that, and then sent El's mind racing back, through brigand battles and The Herald's Horn, to a certain encounter outside the city of Hastarl, where— Now the smiling face of Mystra was back again, blocking the Coronal's probings. She raised a reproving eyebrow at the elf, and smiled to soften her rebuke as the elven ruler reeled and shook his head, grunting in mindshock and pain.

El found himself abruptly back on the floor, dumped like a sack of grain.

When he looked up, he found himself staring into the tiny, shrunken face of the oldest elf he'd ever seen. Her long silver-white hair brushed the tiles below her slippered feet—feet that trod air, inches above the smooth-worn paving stones underfoot—and her skin seemed draped over her bones . . . bones so petite and shapely that she looked exquisite rather than grotesque, despite the fact that except where her diaphanous gown intervened, El could almost see her skeleton.

"Seen enough?" she asked impishly, caressing her hips and turning alluringly, like a tavern dancer.

El dropped his eyes. "I—my apologies for staring," he said quickly. "I've never seen one of the People who looked so old before."

"There are few of us as old as the Srinshee," the Coronal said.

"The Srinshee?"

The old elven lady inclined her head in regal greeting. Then she turned, held out her hand over some empty air, and sat on that air, reclining as if she was lying in a pillow-padded lounge. Another sorceress.

"Her tale is her own to tell you," the Coronal said, holding up a hand to stay further words from Elminster. "First must come my judgment."

He walked a little away from the young man, treading the air above the floor. Then he turned back to face the Athalantan and said, "Your honesty and honor I have never doubted. Your aid to House Alastrarra, without thought of reward or rank, alone is worthy of an armathor—in human words, a knighthood, with citizenship—in Cormanthor. So much I freely grant, and bid you welcome."

"Yet—?" El asked ruefully, at the old elf's guarded tone.

"Yet I cannot help but conclude that you were sent to Cormanthor by the divine one you serve. Whenever I try to learn why, she blocks my inquiries."

Elminster took step toward the old elf, and looked into his eyes. "Read me now, pray ye, and know that I speak truth, Revered Lord," he said. "I am sent here by

Great Mystra to 'learn the rudiments of magic,' as she put it, and because she foresaw that I'd be needed here 'in time to come.' She did not reveal to me just when, and how, and needed by whom or what cause."

The white-robed elf nodded. "I doubt not your belief, man; 'tis the goddess I cannot fathom. I well believe she said just those words to you; yet she bars me from learning your true powers, and her true designs . . . and I have a realm to protect. So, a test."

He smiled. "Think you I show every outland intruder riches that could well bring every hungry human from here to the western sea clamoring through the trees of Cormanthor?"

The Srinshee chuckled, and put in, "Elven ways may outstrip the comprehension of men, but that does not make them the ways of fools."

El looked from one of them to the other. "What testing do you plan? I've little stomach left for more spell duels or wrestlings mind-to-mind."

The Coronal nodded. "This I already know; were you such a one, you'd never have been brought here. To risk myself in your presence is to imperil a strong weapon of Cormanthor; to endanger the Srinshee needlessly is to toy with a treasure of the realm."

"Enough flattery, Eltargrim," the sorceress said primly. "You'll have the lad thinking you a poet, and not the rough warrior you are."

El blinked at the old Coronal. "A warrior?"

The white-haired elf sighed. "I did in my time down some orcs—"

"And a hundred thousand men or so, and a dragon or two," the Srinshee put in. The Coronal waved a dismissive hand.

"Speak of such things when I am gone, for if we tarry overlong we'll have the court mages blasting apart half the palace seeking me."

The Srinshee winced. "Those young dolts?"

The Coronal sighed in exasperation. "Oluevaera, how can I pass judgment on this man if you shatter our every attempt at dignity?"

The ancient sorceress shrugged in her airy ease. "Even humans deserve the truth."

"Indeed." The Coronal's tone was dry as he turned to Elminster, assumed a stern face, and said, "Hear, then, the judgment of Cormanthor: that you remain in these vaults for a moon, and search and converse with their guardian as you will; she will feed you and see to your needs. Folk of the court, myself among them, will come for you at the end of that time, and bid you take but one thing out of these vaults to keep."

El inclined his head. "And the dangerous part?"

The Srinshee chuckled at the young human's tone.

"This is hardly the time for levity, young Prince," the Coronal said severely. "If you choose the wrong thing to bring forth—that is, something we judge to be wrong—the penalty will be your death."

In the silence that followed he added, "Think, young human, on what the most fitting thing you can acquire here might be. Think well."

Winking lights were suddenly occurring about the Coronal's body. He raised his hand to the Srinshee in salute, turned within the rising lights, and was gone. The radiances streamed toward the ceiling for a moment more, and then silently faded away.

"Before you ask, young sir, a moon is a human month," the Srinshee said in dry tones, "and no, I'm not his mother."

El chuckled. "Ye tell me what ye are not—tell me, I pray, what ye are."

She adjusted the air until she was sitting upright, facing him. "I am the councilor of Coronals, the secret wisdom at the heart of the realm."

El glanced at her, and decided to dare it. "And are you wise?"

The old sorceress chuckled. "Ah, a sharp-witted human at last!" She drew herself up grandly, eyes flashing, conjured a scepter out of nowhere into her hand, and snarled, "No."

She joined in El's startled shout of laughter, and let herself down to walk toward him, seeming so frail that El found himself reaching out to offer her a steadying arm.

She gave him a look. "I'm not so feeble as all that, lad. Don't overreach yourself, or you'll end up like yonder worm."

El looked about. " 'Yonder worm'?" he asked hesitantly, seeing no beast or trophy of one, but only rooms of treasure.

"That passage," the Srinshee told him, "is vaulted with the bones of a deep-worm that rose up from gnawing in the deep places and came tunneling in here, hungry for treasure. They eat metal, you know."

El stared at the vaulting along the indicated passage. It *did* look like bone, come to think of it, but . . . He looked back at the sorceress with new respect. "So if I offer you violence, or try to leave this place, you can slay me by lifting one finger."

The old elf shrugged. "Probably. I don't see it happening, unless you're far more foolish—or brutish—than you look."

El nodded. "I don't think I am. My name is Elminster . . . Elminster Aumar, son of Elthryn. I am—or was—a prince of Athalantar, a small human kingdom that lies—"

The old sorceress nodded. "I know it. Uthgrael must be long dead by now."

El nodded. "He was my grandsire."

The Srinshee tilted her head consideringly. "Hmmm."

El stared at her. "You *knew* the Stag King?"

The Srinshee nodded. "A . . . man of vigor," she said, smiling.

Elminster raised an incredulous eyebrow.

The old sorceress burst out laughing. "No, no, nothing like that . . . though with some of the maids I danced with, such could have befallen. In those days, we amused ourselves by peering at the doings of humans. When we saw someone interesting—a bold warrior, say, or a grasping mageling—we'd show ourselves to him by moonlight, and then lead him on a merry chase through the woods. Some of those chases ended in broken necks; some of us let ourselves be caught. I led Uthgrael through half the southern High Forest until he fell exhausted, at dawn. I did show myself to him once later, when he was wed, just to see his jaw drop."

El shook his head. "I can see that it's going to be a long moon down here," he observed to the ceiling.

"Well!" The Srinshee affected outrage, and then chuckled. "Your turn; what pranks have you played, Elminster?"

"I don't know that we need to go into that, just now . . ." Elminster said in dignified tones.

She caught his eye.

"Well," he added, "I survived for some years by thieving in Hastarl, and there was this . . ."

* * * * *

Elminster was hoarse. They'd been talking for hours. After the second coughing fit took him, the Srinshee waved her hand and said, "Enough. You must be getting tired. Lift the lid of that platter over there." She indicated a silver-domed tray that rested atop a heap of armor, amid a spill of octagonal coins stamped from some bluish metal Elminster had never seen before.

El did so. Beneath the lid was steaming stag meat, in a nut-and-leek gravy. "How came this here?" he asked in astonishment.

"Magic," she replied impishly, plucking a half-buried gilded decanter from the heart of a heap of coins at her elbow. "Drink?" Shaking his head in wonder, El extended his hand for it. She tossed the decanter carelessly in his direction. It spun toward the floor, and then swooped smoothly up into his hand.

"My thanks," El said, taking firm hold of it with both hands. The Srinshee shrugged, and the young man suddenly felt something cold atop his head. Reaching up, he found a crystal glass there.

"Your hands were both full," the sorceress explained mildly.

As El snorted in amusement, a bowl of grapes appeared in his lap. He laughed helplessly, and found himself sliding down the coins he'd been leaning against, as they slumped onto the floor. One rolled away, and he smashed it to the floor with his boot heel, to stop it.

"You're going to get awfully sick of those," the elven sorceress told him.

"I don't want coins," El told her. "Where would I spend them, anyway?"

"Yes, but you'll have to shift them all to get at what's buried," the Srinshee said. "I keep the best stuff packed about with coins, you see."

El stared at her, and then shook his head, smiled wordlessly, and applied himself to eating.

* * * * *

"So what brings an elven sorceress who can advise Coronals and blow away deep-worms and lead crowned kings on wild wood chases to some vaults underground no one ever sees?" he asked, when he'd eaten all he could.

The old sorceress had eaten even more, gorging herself on platter after platter of fried mushrooms and lemon clams without seeming discomfort. She leaned back on empty air again, crossed her legs on some invisible floating footstool, and replied, "A sense of belonging, at last."

"Belonging? With cold coins and the jewels of the dead?"

She regarded him with some respect. "Shrewdly said, man." She set her glass on empty air at her elbow and leaned forward. "Yet you say that because you don't see what is here as I do."

She plucked up a tarnished silver bracelet, chased about with the body of a serpent. "Pay heed, Elminster. This is what you need me for: to make the choice the Coronal charged you to, and win your life. This arm ring is all Cormanthor has left of Princess Elvandaruil, lost in the waves of the Fallen Stars three thousand summers ago, when her flight spell failed. It washed up on Ambral Isle when Waterdeep was yet unborn."

Elminster fished a gleaming piece of shell out of the heap beside him. It was pierced at all four corners, and from there fine chains led to silver medallions set with sea-horses picked out in emeralds, with amethyst eyes. "And this?"

"The pectoral of Chathanglas Siltral, who styled himself Lord of the Rivers And Bays before the founding of your realm of Cormyr. He unwittingly took to wife a shapechanger, and the monstrous descendants of their offspring lurk yet, tentacled and deadly, in the waterways of Marsember and what humans call the Vast Swamp."

El leaned forward. "Ye know the provenance of every last bauble in these vaults?"

The Srinshee shrugged. "Of course. What good is a long life and an adequate memory if you don't *use* them?"

El shook his head in wonder. After a moment, he said, "Yet forgive me . . . the folk who wore or fashioned these can't all be kin to ye—if this Siltral fathered no elves, for instance. Yet you feel you belong . . . to what?"

"To the realm of my kin, and others of the People," the sorceress said calmly. "I am Oluevaera Estelda, the last of my line. Yet I rise above the family rivalries of House against House, and consider all Cormanthans my kin. It gives me a reason for having lived so long, and another to go on living, after those I first loved are gone."

"How lonely is it, at the worst?" El asked quietly, rolling forward to look deep into her eyes.

The withered old elf met his gaze. Her eyes were like blue flames against a storm sky. "You are far kinder, and see far clearer, than any human I've ever met before," she said quietly. "I begin to wish the Coronal's judgment did not hang over you."

El spread his hands. "I'd rather not be here, either," he said with a smile.

The Srinshee answered it with one of her own, and said briskly, "Well, we'd best be getting on with it. Dig out that sword by your knee, there, and I'll tell you of the line of elven lords who bore it . . ."

* * * * *

Some hours later, she said, "Would you like some nightglade tea?"

El looked up. "I've never had such a drink, but if it isn't all mushrooms, aye."

"No, there are other things in it, too," she replied smoothly, and they chuckled together.

"Yes, there are mushrooms in it, and no, it's not harmful, or that different from what haughty ladies drink in Cormyr and Chondath," she added.

"Oh, you mean it's like brandy?" El asked innocently, and she pursed her lips and chuckled again.

"I'll make some for us both," she said, rising. Then she looked back over her shoulder at Elminster, who was patiently digging a breastplate out from yet another pile of coins. It was fashioned of a single piece of copper as thick as his thumb, and sculpted into a pair of fine female breasts with a snarling lion's jaws below them. "Don't you ever sleep, man?" she asked curiously.

El looked up. "I get weary, aye, but I no longer need to sleep."

"Something your goddess did?"

El nodded, and frowned down at the breastplate. "This lion," he said. "It has eyes set into its tongue, here, and—"

The bust of the long-lost Queen Eldratha of the vanished elven realm of Larlotha was of solid marble, and as tall as the length of Elminster's arm. It came flying at him at just the right angle, and struck him almost gently behind his right ear. He never even knew it had hit him.

* * * * *

He awoke with a splitting headache. It felt as if someone were jabbing a dagger into his right ear, pulling it out, and then thrusting it home once more. In. Out. In. Out. Arrrgh.

He rolled around, groaning, hearing coins slither as his boots raked across them. *What* had happened?

His eyes settled on the soft, unchanging lights above him. Gems, set in a vaulted ceiling. Oh, aye—he was in the Vault of Ages. With the Srinshee, until the Coronal came to test him on his choice of what to take out of here.

"Lady? Lady—uh—Srinshee?" he asked, and followed his words with another groan. Speaking had awakened a fresh throbbing in his head. "Lady . . . ah, Oluevaera?"

"Over here," a weak, ragged whisper answered him, and he turned toward the sound.

The old sorceress was lying spreadeagled on a heap of treasure, her gown in tatters and smoke rising lazily from her body. A body, largely bared now, that featured many wrinkles and age-spots, but seemed unmarked by recent violence. El crawled toward her, holding his head.

"Lady?" he asked. "Are ye hurt? What befell?"

"I attacked you," she said ruefully, "and paid the price."

El stared at her, bewildered. "Ye—?"

"Man, I am ashamed," she said, lips quivering. "To find a friend, after so long, and throw friendship aside for loyalty to the realm . . . I did what I thought right—and find my choice was wrong."

El laid his pounding head on the coins beside the Srinshee so that he could look into her eyes. They were full of tears. "Lady," he said gently, stricken by the sadness in her voice, "for the love of thy gods and mine, tell me what happened."

She stared into his eyes, forlorn. "I have done the unforgiveable."

"And that was?" El almost pleaded, gesturing wearily at her to let words pour from her mouth.

She almost smiled at that as she replied sadly, "Eltargrim asked me to try where he failed; to learn all

I could from your mind while you slept. But time passed, a day and a night, and still you were sorting through the treasures, with nary a sign of sliding into slumber. So I asked you, and you said you never slept."

El nodded, coins shifting under his cheek. "What did you hit me with?"

"A bust of Eldratha of Larlotha," she muttered. "Elminster, I'm so sorry."

"So am I," he told her feelingly. "Can elven magic banish headaches?"

"Oh," she gasped, putting a hand to her mouth in chagrin. "Here." she reached out with two fingertips, touched the side of his head, and murmured something.

And like cool water lapping down his neck, the pain washed away.

El gasped his thanks, and slid down the coins until he was sitting on the floor again. "So ye set to work on my mind once I was stunned, and—"

Remembering, he whirled and rose to bend anxiously over her. "Lady, there was smoke coming from ye! Were ye hurt?"

"Mystra was waiting for me, just as she waited for the Coronal," the Srinshee told him with the ghost of a smile on her lips. "She cares for you, young man. She thrust me right out of your mind, and told me she'd placed a spell in your mind that could blast me to dust."

El stared at her, and then let his mind sink down to where, for so long, no spells had lain ready. He was going to have to do something about that. Without even a single spell to hurl, and no gem to call on, he was defenseless in the midst of all these proud elves.

Aye, there it was. A deadly magic he'd never known before—so mighty, and so simple. One touch, and elven blood would boil in the body he'd chosen, melting it to dust in a few breaths regardless of armor and defensive magics, and . . .

He shivered. *That* was a slaying spell.

When his senses returned to the here and now, cool fingers as small as a child's were tugging at his wrist, towing his hand to rest on smooth, cool flesh. Flesh that felt like—

He stared down. The Srinshee had bared her breast and placed his hand firmly upon it.

"Lady," he asked, staring into the sad blue flames of her eyes, "what—?"

"Use the spell," she told him. "I deserve no less."

El gently shook his hand free, and lifted what was left of her gown back into place. "And what would the Coronal do to me *then?*" he asked her, in mock despair. "That's the trouble with ye tragic types—no thought for what happens next!"

He smiled, and saw her struggling to give him one in return. After a moment, he saw that she was crying, silent tears welling from her old eyes.

Impulsively he bent and kissed her cheek. "Ye did the unforgiveable, aye," he growled in her ear. "Ye promised me nightglade tea—and I'm *still* waiting!"

She tried to laugh, and burst into sobs. El dragged her up into his arms to comfort her, and found that it was like cradling a crying child. She weighed *nothing*.

She was still sobbing, arms around his neck, when two steaming cups of nightglade tea appeared in the air in front of his nose.

* * * * *

Elminster had long since lost count of the things that he thought most clever. There was a crown that let its wearers appear as they had done when younger, and a glove that could resculpt the skin of battered or marred faces with its fingertips. The Srinshee had set these, and other things he most fancied, aside in a chest in the domed central chamber, but he'd seen less than a twentieth of the treasures held here, and the Srinshee's eyes were growing sad again.

"El," she said, as he tossed aside a flute that had belonged to the elven hero Erglareo of the Long Arrow, "your time grows short."

"I know," he said shortly. "What is this?"

"A cloak that banishes blight from trees whose trunks it is wrapped around, or plants it is draped over, left to us by the elven mage Raeranthur of—"

He was already trudging away from her, toward the chest for things he fancied. The Lady Estelda fell silent and sadly watched him walk away from her. She dared not aid him even by shifting coins, for fear one of the court mages, eager for this human intruder's death, was scrying her from afar.

Elminster returned, looking weary about the eyes. "How much longer?" he asked.

"Perhaps ten breaths," she said softly, "perhaps twenty. It depends on how eager they are."

"For my death," El growled, leaning past her. Was it an accident that she'd rested her hand on this crystal sphere thrice in the last little while?

"What's this?" he asked, scooping it up.

"A crystal through which one can see the course of waterflows through the realm, on the surface or underground; every handspan of their travel, clearly lit for your eye to see beaver dams, snags, and sources of foulness," the Srinshee told him, quickly, almost breathlessly, "crafted for the House of Clatharla, now fallen, by the—"

"I'll take it," El growled, starting past her. He stopped in midstride and kicked at the hilt of a blade buried under the coins. "This?"

"A sword that cuts darkness, and the undead things called shadows—though I believe wraiths and ghosts also—"

He waved a dismissive hand and set off back down the passage toward the chest. The Srinshee adjusted the jeweled gown he'd unearthed and insisted she put on—it persisted in sliding off one aged shoulder—and sighed. They'd be here at any moment, and they—

Were here now. There was a soundless flash of light in the domed central chamber, and El stiffened, finding himself suddenly ringed with unfriendly looking elven sorceresses. Six of them there were, all holding scepters trained at him. Tiny sparks winked and flowed along those deadly things. Along the passage El saw the Srinshee coming up behind him. She snapped her fingers as she came, and a seventh scepter was suddenly in that hand, leveled and ready.

He turned his back on her slowly, knowing who'd be awaiting him in the other direction. Rulers always liked to make entrances. Behind two of the sorceresses was an old elf in white robes, with eyes like two pools of stars. The women slid sideways smoothly to make a place for him in the ring of death. The Coronal.

"Well met, Revered Lord," Elminster said, and gently set the crystal sphere he held down into the open chest.

The elf looked down at the treasures it held, and raised an approving eyebrow. Things of nurturing, not things of battle. His voice when it rolled forth, however, was stern. "I bade you choose one thing only, to take forth from these vaults. Let us all now witness that choice."

Elminster bowed, and then walked to the Coronal, hands spread and empty.

"Well?" the elven ruler demanded.

"I have made my choice," El said quietly.

"You choose to take nothing?" the Coronal asked, frowning. " 'Tis a coward's way of trying to evade death."

"Nay," Elminster replied, voice just as stern. "I've chosen the most precious thing in thy vaults."

Scepters hung quivering in midair all around him, abandoned by sorceresses who were now weaving magics for all they were worth. El turned slowly, one eyebrow raised, as they whispered incantations in a murmuring chorus. Only the Srinshee's hands were still. She held her scepter tipped back so that its point touched her own breast, and her eyes were anxious.

Spells fell upon Elminster Aumar then, spells that searched and proved and scryed, vainly seeking hidden items or disguising magics on the young man's body. One by one they looked to the Coronal and gave small shakes of their heads; they'd found nothing.

"And what is that most precious thing?" the Coronal asked finally, as two of the sorceresses slowly drew in front of him to form a shield, raised scepters in their hands once more.

"Friendship," Elminster replied. "Shared regard, and my fondness for a wise and gracious lady." He turned to face the Srinshee and made a deep bow, such as envoys did to kings they truly respected, in the kingdoms of men.

After a long moment, as the other elves stared at her, the old sorceress smiled and echoed his bow. Her eyes were very bright, with what might be tears.

The Coronal's eyebrows rose. "You've chosen more wisely even than I might have done," he said. More than one of the six court sorceresses looked stunned. There were open gasps of astonished horror around their circle when the ruler of all Cormanthor bowed deeply to Elminster. "I am honored by your presence in this fairest of realms; you are welcome here, as deserving of residence as any of the People. Be one with Cormanthor."

"And Cormanthor shall be one with thee," the sorceresses chanted in unison. There was dumbfounded awe in more than one of those voices. Elminster smiled at the Coronal, but turned to embrace the Srinshee. Tears were shining on her withered cheeks as she looked up at him, so he kissed them away.

As the velvet darkness came down again, and rolled away to reveal a huge and shining hall crowded with elves in their splendor, the Coronal's magic made the chant roll forth again.

Amid the astonished faces of the Court of Cormanthor, all heard it ring clear: "And Cormanthor shall be one with thee."

PART II

ARMATHOR

Seven

EVERY POOL ITS PARTY

When Elminster first saw it, Cormanthor was a city of haughty pretence, intrigue, strife, and decadence. A place, in fact, very like the proudest human cities of today.

Antarn the Sage
from **The High History of Faerûnian Archmages Mighty**
published circa The Year of the Staff

By the time Ithrythra had clicked her way unsteadily up the wooded path to the pool in her new boots, the party was well under way.

"Frankly, gentlest," Duilya Evendusk confided to someone, loud enough to shake leaves off the moonbark trees overhead, "I don't care *what* your elders say! The Coronal is mad! *Completely* mad!"

"You'd know madness better than the rest of us," Ithrythra muttered under her breath, setting her own glass on a float-platter to unlace her thigh-high silver boots. It was a relief to step out of them. The spiked heels made her tower over the servants, yes, but ohh, how they hurt. Human fashions were as crazed as they were brazen.

Ithrythra hung her lacy gown over a branch and shook out the ruffles of her undergown until they hung as they were supposed to. She checked her reflection in the hanging glass under the shadowtop tree, an oval mirror taller than she was.

As she stared into its depths and saw just a hint of swirling things there, she recalled that some Cormanth ladies whispered that this mirror sometimes served the Tornglaras as a portal into dark and dirty streets in the cities of men. The Tornglara lords went to do business that Cormanthor frowned upon, trading with humans. The Tornglara ladies, now . . .

She clucked her lips at those thoughts and set them firmly aside. Fashions were what Alaglossa Tornglara went seeking; fashions, and no more.

Ithrythra gave the legendary mirror a little smile. Her new hairdo had held its sideswirl, firmly woven about the hand lyre, sigil of her House. Her ears stood up proudly, their rouged tips unmarred by over-gaudy jewelry. She turned, so as to survey one side of her body, and then the other. The gems glued down her flanks were all in place. She struck a pose, and blew the mirror a pouting kiss. Not bad.

After the highsun meal of every fourth day, the ladies of five Houses gathered at Satyrdance Pool in the private gardens behind the many-towered mansion that was House Tornglara. There they bathed in the warmest of the pools, in which spiced rosewater had been poured for the occasion, and sipped summermint wine from tall, green fluted glasses. The platters of sugared confections and the justly famous Tornglara vintages flowed freely, and so did the real reason the ladies came back to the same place time and time again: the gossip.

Ithrythra Mornmist joined her chattering companions, making her greetings with her usual silent smiles. As she slipped her long legs into the pool, sighing with pleasure at the soothing warmth of the waters, she noted that her glass was the only one not yet empty. Where were the servants?

Her hostess noticed Ithrythra's glances, and halted in midchatter to lean forward conspiratorially and say, "Oh, I've sent them away, dear. We'll have to fill our own glasses this time—but then, 'tisn't every day one discusses *crown treason!*"

"Crown treason? What treachery can the Coronal have practiced? That elf's too old to have any wits left, or stamina either!" Ithrythra exclaimed, evoking shrieks of laughter from the ladies already in the pool.

"Oh, you're *out* of *touch*, dearest Ithrythra! It must be all that time you spend in your cellars grubbing up mushrooms to earn a living!" Duilya Evendusk said cuttingly; Alaglossa Tornglara had the grace to roll her eyes at this rudeness.

"Well, at least it proves to my elders that I *can* work if I have to," Ithrythra replied, "and so escape being a complete loss to my House—you should try it, dear . . . or, well, no, I suppose not. . . ."

Cilivren Doedance, the quietest and most polite of them all, sputtered briefly over the glass she was filling, and decided the prudent thing to do was to put it down. Setting the glass back on its float-platter, she stoppered the decanter and slid it back into its usual recess in the little stream in the bushes beside her.

"The word's all over the city," she explained calmly. "The Coronal has named some *human* an armathor of the realm! And a *man* human at that! A thief who stole the kiira of a First House, and broke into their city residence to steal spells and despoil their ladies!"

"It wasn't House Starym, was it?" Ithrythra asked dryly. "There's never been much love lost between old Eltargrim and our haughtiest of Houses."

"House Starym has served Cormanthor a thousand summers longer than a certain House I could name," Phuingara Lhoril said stiffly. "Those Cormanthans of truly noble spirit do not find their pride excessive."

"Cormanthans of truly noble spirit do not indulge in prideful behavior at all," Ithrythra replied silkily.

"Oh, Ithrythra! Always *cutting* at us, as if that tongue of yours was a sword! I don't know why your lord puts up with you!" Duilya Evendusk said pettishly, annoyed at having the center of attention wrenched from her grasp.

"I've heard why," Alaglossa Tornglara observed quietly to the leaves overhead. Ithrythra blushed as the other ladies in the pool tittered. Duilya added her own grating guffaw and then hastened to seize center stage once more. The tips of her ears were almost drooping today under the weight of all the gems dangling from their rows of studs.

"Pride or no pride, 'twasn't the Starym," she said excitedly, "but House Alastrarra. They're saying at court that both the court mages would like to challenge the Eltargrim with blades before the altar of Corellon, rather than let a human walk among us and live—let alone be named armathor! Some of the younger armathors, those not lords of Houses, mind, and with little to lose, have been to the palace already to break their blades and hurl the pieces at the Coronal's feet! One even threw his blade right *at* Eltargrim!"

"So how long will it be, I wonder," Ithrythra pondered aloud, "before this human meets with an . . . accident."

"Not long at all, if the looks of the court elders are anything to go by," Duilya gushed on, eyes bright. "If we're very lucky, they'll challenge him at court—or have seeing-spells cast beforehand, so we can all see him torn apart!"

"How very civilized," Cilivren murmured, her voice just audible to Alaglossa and Ithrythra. Duilya, deafened by her own gleeful words, didn't hear.

"And then," she continued, still in full flood, "the

First Houses might call a Hunt, for the first time in centuries, and they'll force old Eltargrim into stag shape and hunt him down! Then we'll have a new Coronal! Oh, what excitement!" In her exuberance, she snatched up a decanter and drained it without benefit of a glass.

Reeling, she promptly slumped back in the pool, shuddering and gagging. "Gods above, dear, don't drown *here*," Phuingara growled, holding her above the waters, "or all our lords'll be at us about talking to those of rival Houses without their leave!"

Ithrythra took great delight in thumping the coughing Duilya solidly in the back. Gems flew across the pool and tinkled against a float-platter.

Alaglossa gave the reigning lady of House Mornmist a tight smile that told Ithrythra her hostess knew quite well that the force of her helpful blow had been quite deliberate—and that silence on that matter might carry a price, later.

"There, there, gentle doe," Alaglossa said solicitously, putting an arm around the shuddering Lady Evendusk. "Better now? The sweetness of our wine often misleads folk into thinking it has no fire—but it's stronger even than that, ah, 'tripleshroom sherry' our lords're always roaring at each other about!"

"Oh," Phuingara purred, "So you've had some of that, have you?"

Alaglossa turned her head and favoured the lady of House Lhoril with a look that had silent daggers in it; Phuingara merely smiled and asked, "Well? How was it?"

"You mean, you want to know what leaves our lords falling into pillars, giggling like younglings and hooting as they lie on the floor and try to shake hands with themselves?" Cilivren said suddenly, laughter in her voice. "Well, it tastes terrible!"

"You've drunk tripleshroom?" Phuingara asked, her voice incredulous.

Cilivren gave the Lady Lhoril a catlike smile and said, *"Some* lords don't leave their ladies out of all the fun."

All of the others, even the still-coughing Duilya, looked at the Lady Doedance as if she'd suddenly grown several extra heads.

"Cilivren," Duilya said in shocked tones, when she could speak again. "I would never have thought . . ."

"That's just the problem," snarled Ithrythra, "you never think!"

Mouths opened in shock all around the pool, but before Duilya could erupt in rage at this insult, the Lady Mornmist leaned forward, her eyes serious, and said into Duilya's face, *"Listen*, Lady Evendusk. How do you think Cormanthor chooses a Coronal? You can't wait for the excitement, you say? Would you feel that way if I told you that naming a new Coronal is likely to mean poisonings, duels in the streets, and mages working nights in their towers to send slaying spells at their rivals all over the city? Human or no human, Eltargrim an addle-brained idiot or not, do you want to die—or see your children slain, and feuds begun that will rend Cormanthor forever, and let *all* the humans into our city over our warring *bones?"*

She gasped for breath, fists clenched in aroused fear and rage, glaring at the four faces that were staring back at her. Couldn't they *see?*

"Gods watch over us all," the Lady Mornmist went on, in a voice that trembled, "I find the idea of a human walking our fair realm revolting. But I'd take that human for a mate if need be, and kiss and serve him day and night, to keep our realm from tearing itself apart!"

She clenched her fists, breast heaving, and almost

shouted, "You think Cormanthor stands so splendid and mighty that none can touch us? How so? Our lords strut and sneer and tell tales of what heroics their fathers' fathers did, when the world was young and we fought dragons barehanded moon in and moon out. And our sons boast of how much bolder they'll be, and can't even down a flagon of tripleshroom without falling over! Every year the axes of the humans nibble at the edges of our fair forests, and their mages grow stronger. Every year their adventurers grow bolder, and fewer of our patrols pass through a season without losing blood!"

Alaglossa Tornglara nodded slowly, face white, as Ithrythra caught her breath, swallowed, and added in a whisper, "I don't expect to see the fair towers of our city still standing when I die. Don't any of you ever worry about that?"

In the silence that followed, she defiantly snatched up a full decanter of summermint and drained it, slowly and deliberately, while they all stared at her.

"Really," Duilya said, laughing uneasily, as they watched Ithrythra Mornmist, apparently unaffected by the wine, set aside the empty decanter and pick up another one to delicately refill her glass, "I think you indulge in wild fancies overmuch, Ithrythra—as usual. Cormanthor endangered? Come, now. Who can threaten us? We have the spells to turn any number of barbarians into—into more mushrooms for the making of sherry!"

She laughed merrily at her own jest, but her mirth fell away into thoughtful silence. She whirled around to confront Phuingara for support. "Don't you think so?"

"I think," Phuingara said slowly, "that we gossip and prattle the days away because we don't like to talk of such things. Duilya, listen to me now: I don't agree with everything Ithrythra fears, but just because no one speaks so openly, or we don't like to hear it, doesn't make her *wrong*. If you didn't hear truth in her words, I suggest you kiss her and ask her very nicely to repeat them again . . . and listen harder this time."

And with those words, the Lady Lhoril turned and began to climb out of the pool, leaving a sombre silence in her wake.

"Wait!" Alaglossa said, catching at one of Phuingara's wet wrists. "Stay!"

The Lady Lhoril turned blazing eyes upon her hostess, and said softly, "Lady, by all you hold dear, pray make your case for *handling* me good."

The Lady Tornglara nodded curtly. "Ithrythra's right," she said earnestly, leaning forward. "This is too important to just pass off as an awkward moment, and go on joking and sparring and watching as the city comes to blows over this human. We must work on our lords to keep the peace, telling them over and over again that a mere human isn't worth unseating the Coronal, and drawing blades, and starting feuds."

"My lord never listens to me," Duilya Evendusk said in a tragic whisper. "What can I do?"

"*Make* him listen," Cilivren told her. "Make him notice you, and pay heed."

"He only does that when we're . . ."

"Then, dearest," Phuingara told her in a voice that cut like a whip, "it's time you got a little better at turning your lord to your will. Alaglossa, you were right to keep me from storming off; we've work to do right here. Do you have any tripleshroom sherry?"

The Lady Tornglara stared at her in surprise. "Why, yes," she said, "but why?"

"One of the few ways I can think of that would win the respect of Lord Evendusk," the Lady Lhoril said crisply, "when he's groaning of a forenoon because of what he's drunk the night before—and cursing at his sons because of what they broke the night before, raging and giggling; you did have to choose a prize oaf, didn't you, Duilya?—is to snatch up a full bottle of that sherry, drink it down in front of him, and then sit there *not* roaring or staggering about. While he's gaping at his gentle lady turned lion, you can tell him off good and proper, and announce that you see no need for all the roistering."

"And then what?" Duilya said, face white at the very thought of facing down her lord.

"And then you could drag him off to bed in front of the whole household," Phuingara said firmly, "and tell him that drinking every night's no excuse for stumbling about like an idiot, making a mockery of the honor of the House, while you're neglected."

There was a moment of silence, and then laughter began around the pool—low at first, but then rising swiftly as the full import of Phuingara's words hit home.

It was Cilivren who stopped first. "You want us to practice drinking tripleshroom sherry until we can drain a bottle without showing it? Phuingara, we'll *die*." She winced. "I mean it; that stuff burns the insides like fire!"

The Lady Lhoril shrugged. "So we'll master it enough to down a few glasses without tears or trembling, and work up a spell, just for ourselves, that'll turn what passes our lips to water as we down it. It's the respect we're after, not to drown our worries about the realm the way our lords do. Why d'you think they drink the way they do? They've seen what Ithrythra has, and just don't want to face it."

"So I get my Ihimbraskar up to the bedchamber, after humiliating him in front of the entire household," Duilya said in a small voice, "and what then? He'll strike me silly, toss my bones out the window, and go seeking a new and younger lady in the morn!"

"Not if you sit him down and give him the same blazing words Ithrythra gave us," Alaglossa told her. "Even if he doesn't agree, he'll be so astonished at your thinking about such things, that he'll probably argue with you like an equal—whereupon you tell him that such disputes are precisely what you're *for*, and then take him to bed."

Duilya stared at her for a moment, and then started to laugh wildly. "Oh, Hanali bless us all! If I thought I had the strength to carry it through . . ."

"Lady Evendusk," Ithrythra said formally, "would you mind terribly if the four of us were linked to you with a spell or two, to—ah, assist with the words you need, at the awkward moments?"

Duilya gaped at her, and then looked slowly around the pool. "You'd do that?"

"We all might benefit from such a spell," Phuingara said slowly. "Clever, Ithrythra." She turned to Alaglossa. "Get that sherry, Lady Tórnglara; I can feel a toast coming on."

* * * * *

"Though in time to come I and others shall teach you some of the spells of our People," the Srinshee said, "a time of great danger awaits you now, Elminster." She smiled. "You didn't need me to tell you that."

El nodded. "That's why ye brought me here." He looked around at the dark and dusty walls and asked, "But what is this place?"

"A sacred tomb of our people—a haunted tower, once the home of the first proud and noble House to try to make themselves greater than the rest of us. The Dlardrageth."

"What happened to them?"

"They courted incubi and succubi, seeking to breed a stronger race. Few survived such dealings, fewer still the birthings that followed, and all elven peoples turned against them. The few survivors were walled in here by our strongest spells, until the end of their days." The Srinshee dusted her hand across a pillar thoughtfully, uncovering a relief carving of a leering face. "Some of those spells still linger, though daring young Cormanthan lords broke in more than a thousand years ago to despoil this castle of the riches of House Dlardrageth. They found little of value, and took away what they did find. They also took back word of the ghosts that linger here."

"Ghosts?" Elminster asked calmly. The Srinshee nodded.

"Oh, there are a few, but nothing that need be feared. What matters most is that we won't be disturbed."

"Ye're going to teach me magic?"

"No," the Srinshee said, drawing close so that she stood looking up at him. "You're going to teach *me* magic."

El raised both brows. "I—?"

"With this," she said calmly, as she spread her empty hands and they suddenly filled with—his spellbook.

She staggered a trifle, under its weight, and he automatically took it from her, peering at it. Aye, it was his. Left in a saddlebag, back in a fern-filled dell in the trackless forest where the White Raven Patrol had met with far too many ruukha.

"My deepest thanks, Lady," Elminster said to her, going to one knee so that he was below her and not towering over her. "Yet at the risk of sounding ungrateful, won't those of the People who are upset by one of my race being named armathor be turning Cormanthor over stone by tree, looking for me? And won't the other elves of thy realm expect me to take up some duties to go with my rank . . . in other words, to be seen?"

"Seen you will be, soon enough," the Srinshee said grimly. "The center of plots and schemes aplenty, even by those who do not wish you ill. We are jaded, in the fair city of Cormanthor, and each new interest becomes something to be sported over by the great Houses. All too often, their sport mars or destroys that which they toy with."

"Elves begin to seem more and more like men," El told her, sitting down on the broken stump of a pillar.

"How dare you!" the old sorceress snarled. He looked up in time to see her smile and reach out to tousle his hair. "How dare you speak truth to me," she murmured. "So few of my race ever do . . . or have done. 'Tis a rare pleasure, to deal in honesty for a change."

"How, now? Are not elves honest?" El asked teasingly, for there was a brightness that might have been rising tears in her old eyes again.

"Let us say that some of us are too worldly for our own good," she said with a smile, strolling away from him on air. She whirled about and added, "And the others are too world-weary."

At her words, a darkness rose behind her, and sudden claws flashed down. El started up with a cry, but the claws flashed through her and raced on through the gloom between them, trailing a thin, high wailing that faded away as if into vast distances.

El watched where it had gone, and then turned back to the small sorceress. "One of the ghosts?" he asked, brow raised.

She nodded. "They want to learn your magic too."

He smiled, and then, seeing her expression, let the grin slowly fade from his lips. "Ye're not jesting," he said roughly.

She shook her head. The sadness was back in her eyes. "You begin to see, I hope, just how much my People need you, and others like you, to breathe new ideas into us and awaken the flame of spirit that once made us soar above all others in Faerûn. Consorting with humans, with our half-kin and the little folk, and even with dwarves is the Coronal's dream. He can see so clearly what we must do—and the great Houses refuse so adamantly to see anything except the dreaming days stretching on forever, with themselves at the pinnacle of all."

El shook his head, acquiring a very thin smile. "I seem to bear a heavy burden," he said.

"You can carry it," the Srinshee told him, and winked at him impishly. " 'Tis why Mystra chose you."

* * * * *

"Are we not met to decide what best to do?" Sylmae asked coldly. She looked around the circle of solemn faces that hovered above the balefire; her own and the other five sorceresses who'd accompanied the Coronal to the Vault of Ages after the High Court Mages, Earynspieir and Ilimitar, had refused to do so.

Holone shook her head. "No sister; that is the mistake we must leave to the Houses and the other folk of the court. We must wait, and watch, and act for the good of the realm when the rash acts of others make it needful to do so."

"So which rash act requires that we take action in our turn?" Sylmae asked. "The appointment of a human to standing in the realm as an armathor—or the responses that will inevitably follow?"

"Those responses will tell us who stands where," the sorceress Ajhalanda put in. "The next set of actions on the part of those players, as this unfolds, may well require that we act."

"Strike out, you mean," Sylmae said, her voice rising. "Against the Coronal, or one of the great Houses of the realm, or—"

"Or against all of the Houses, or the High Court Mages, or even such as the Srinshee," Holone said calmly. "We know not what, yet—only that it is our duty and desire to meet, and confer, and act as one."

"It is our hope, you mean," the sorceress Yathlanae said, speaking for the first time that night, "that we work together, and not be split asunder, hand against hand and will against will, as we all fear the realm will be."

Holone nodded grimly. "And so we must choose carefully, sisters, very carefully, not to fall into dispute among ourselves."

More than one face above the flames sighed, knowing how difficult that alone was going to be.

Ajhalanda broke the lengthening silence. "Sylmae, you walk among all folk, high and low, more than the rest of us. Which Houses must we watch—who will lead where others follow?"

Sylmae sighed gustily, so that the balefire quivered beneath their chins, and said, "The spine of the old Houses—those who despise and stand against the Coronal, and lady sorceresses, and anything that is new these past three thousand years—are the Starym, of course, and Houses Echorn and Waelvor. The path they cleave, the old Houses and all of the timid new ones will follow. They are the tide: slow, mighty, and predictable."

"Why watch the tide?" Yathlanae asked. "However hard you scrutinize it, it changes not—you only invent new motives and meanings for it, as your watching grows longer."

"Well said," Sylmae replied, "and yet the tide aren't those we must watch. They are the powerful newer proud ones, the rich Houses, led by Maendellyn and Nlossae."

"Are not they just as predictable, in their way?" Holone put in. "They stand for anything new that might break the power of the old Houses, to let them supplant or at least stand as equals. As all elves do, they grow tired of being sneered at."

"There is a third group," Sylmae said, "who bear the closest watching of all. They are a group only in my speaking of them; in Cormanthor they hew their own roads, and walk to differing stars. The reckless upstarts, some term them; they are the Houses who will try anything, merely for the joy of being part of something new. They are Auglamyr and Ealoeth, and lesser families such as the Falanae and Uirthur."

"You and I are Auglamyr, sister," Holone stated calmly. "Are you then telling us we six should or will try anything new?"

"We are already doing so," Sylmae replied, "by meeting thus, and striving to act in concert. It is not something the proud lords of any House but those I've named last would tolerate, if they knew about it. She-elves are only for dancing, bedecking with gems, and begetting young on, know you not?"

"Cooking," Ajhalanda said. "You forgot cooking."

Sylmae shrugged and smiled. "I was ever a poor dutiful she-elf."

Yathlanae shrugged. "There are males in this land who are poor dutiful lords, if it comes to that."

"Aye, too many of them," Holone said, "or making one human an armathor would be no more than idle news."

"I see Cormanthor in peril of destruction, if we act not wisely and swiftly, when the time comes," Sylmae told them.

"Then let us do so," Holone replied, and the others all echoed, "Aye, let us do so."

As if that had been a cue, the balefire went out; someone had sent scrying magic their way. Without another word or light, they parted and slipped away, leaving the air high above the palace to the bats and the glittering stars . . . who seemed quite comfortable there until morning.

Eight

THE USES OF A HUMAN

The elves of Cormanthor have always been known for their calm, measured responses to perceived threats. They often consider for half a day or more before going out and killing them.

Shalheira Talandren, High Elven Bard of Summerstar
from **Silver Blades And Summer Nights:
An Informal But True History of Cormanthor**
published in The Year of the Harp

"They're so beautiful," Symrustar murmured. "See, coz?"

Amaranthae bent to look at the silktails, circling and wriggling in the glass cylinder as they danced for the best position below Symrustar's fingers, from which they knew food would soon fall. "I love the way the sun turns their scales into tiny rainbows," she replied diplomatically, having resolved long since that whatever it took, her cousin would never learn just how much Amaranthae hated fish.

Symrustar had over a thousand finned and scaled pets here. From the crowning bowl where she now scattered morsels of the secret food she mixed herself (Amaranthae had heard it said that its chief ingredients were the ground flesh, blood, and bones of unsuccessful suitors), Symrustar's glass fish tank descended more than a hundred feet to the ground, in a fantastic sculpture of pipes, spheres, and larger chambers of hollow glass shaped like dragons and other beasts. Amaranthae wanted to be around—but not too close— on the day Symrustar's father discovered that a certain large tank, out near the end of the branch, resembled him in all-too-unflattering detail.

Lord Auglamyr was not known for his gentle temper. "A thundercloud of towering pride, sweeping all before it" was the way one senior lady of the court had once described him, and her words had been overgentle.

Perhaps that was where Symrustar had acquired her utterly amoral ruthlessness. Amaranthae was very careful to remain supportive and helpful to her ambitious cousin at all times, for she had no doubt that Symrustar Auglamyr would betray her in a twinkling instant, best friends notwithstanding, if Amaranthae ever got in her way in even the smallest degree.

I'm no more free than all these fish, Amaranthae thought, leaning out from the bowl-shaped bower where they sat, at the base of the longest branch left in this westernmost shadowtop of House Auglamyr. Pipe after column after sphere of glass gleamed back the morning light, in the fantastic assemblage that housed Symrustar's finned pets. The servants knew better than to disturb them—or rather, Symrustar— here, and used the speaking chimes instead.

Morning after morning they spent here, reclining on cushions and sipping cool fermented forest fruit juices, while the Auglamyr heiress schemed and plotted aloud how to further her every ambition—and some of them seemed to heart-weary Amaranthae to be no more than manipulating acquaintances for the sake of deft manipulation—and her cousin listened and said supportive things at the right moments.

This morning Symrustar was truly excited, her eyes flashing as she set aside the food, waving a dismissive hand at the tiny gasping mouths in the bowl as she turned away. *By all the gods, but she's beautiful*, Amaranthae thought, staring at her cousin's fine shoulders and the long, smoothly curving lines of her body in its silk robe. A striking eyes and face, even among the beauties of the court. No wonder so many elven lords straightened their ears at the sight of her.

Symrustar lifted one perfect eyebrow and asked, "Are you thinking along the same lines as I am, coz?"

Amaranthae shrugged, smiled, and said the safe thing. "I was thinking about this human male our Coronal has named armathor . . . and wondering what you'd do with this most unlikely of surprises, most sprightly of ladies!"

Symrustar winked. "You know me well, 'Ranthae. What do you think a human would be like to dally with? Hmmm?"

Amaranthae shuddered. "A man? Ughhh. As heavy and lumbering as a stag, with the stink to match . . . and all that *hair!*"

Her cousin nodded, eyes far away. "True. Yet I hear this unwashed brute has magic—human magic, far inferior to our own, of course, but different. With a little of that in my hands, I could surprise a few of our overproud young mages. Even if the human's spells are but little wisps of things suitable for impressing gullible younglings, I've one such who could use a little impressing: Lord Heir Most High Elandorr Waelvor."

Amaranthae shook her head in rueful amusement. "Haven't you tormented him enough?"

Symrustar raised one shapely brow again, and her eyes flashed. "Enough? There *is* no 'enough' for Elandorr the Buffoon! When he's not grandly proclaiming to all the city that this or that spell he's created is greater than anything that bad-tempered maid Symrustar Auglamyr can craft, he's crawling in my bedchamber window with fresh blandishments! No matter how firmly—"

"Rudely," Amaranthae corrected with a smile.

"—I refuse him," her cousin continued, "he's back a few nights later trying again! In between, he hints to his drinking companions about the unmatched sweetness of my charms, remarks to ladies in passing that I worship him in secret, and flits about the libraries of men—*men*—stealing bad love poetry to pass off as his own, wooing me with all the style and grace of a laugh-chasing gnome clown!"

"He came last night?"

"As usual! I had three of the guards throw him from my balcony. He had the brazen gall to try transforming spells on them!"

"You countered them, of course," Amaranthae murmured.

"No," Symrustar said scornfully, "I left them as frogs until morning. No guard worthy of my bedchamber balcony should be unprepared for a simple twice-trying transformation!"

"Oh, Symma!" Amaranthae said reproachfully.

Her cousin's eyes flashed again. "You think me harsh? Coz, you spend a night in my bed, and be pestered by the Love Lord of the Waelvors come calling, and we'll see how charitable you feel to the guards who should have kept him out!"

"Symma, he's a master mage!"

"Then let them be master guards, and *wear* the turnback amulets I gave them. What matter if they must draw blood to work? They'll turn back Elandorr's oh-so-masterful spells on himself! A few scars should be worth that—to say nothing of their professed loyalty to House Auglamyr!"

Symrustar rose and paced restlessly across the little bowl-shaped hollow, the morning sun glinting on the gem-adorned chain that spiraled up her left leg from anklet to garter. "Why, three moons ago," she burst out, waving her arms, "when he got as far as the very curtains of my bed, I found a guard hiding and *watching*, by the Hunt! Watching, to see me swoon in the arms of Elandorr! Oh, he claimed he was there to protect me against the 'last humiliation,' but he was lying atop the very canopy of my bed, clad in black velvet so as not to be seen, and wrapped about with so many amulets that he practically staggered! He got them from my father, he said, but I'd not be surprised to find that some of them came from House Waelvor!"

"What did you do to *him?*" Amaranthae asked, turning her head away to hide a yawn.

Symrustar smiled chillingly. "Showed him what he'd been trying to see, took off every last thing he was wearing, too, and—the fish."

Amaranthae shuddered. "You fed him to—?"

Symrustar nodded. "Umm-hmmm, and sent off all his gear in a bundle to Elandorr the next day, with a love note telling him that such trappings were all that was left from the last dozen lords who thought themselves worthy of wooing Symrustar Auglamyr." She sighed theatrically. "He was baçk trying the next night, of course."

Amaranthae shook her head. "Why don't you just tell your father, and let him go roaring to Lord Waelvor? You know how the old Houses are; Kuskyn Waelvor would be so mortified that a son of his was wooing a lady of such an 'unknown' House as ours—or wooing any high-house lady, without his permission— that Elandorr would find himself in a spell cage for the next decade, before you could draw another breath!"

Symrustar stared at her cousin. "And where,

'Ranthae, would the fun be in that?"

Amaranthae shook her head, smiling. "Of course. Let prudence never get in the way of fun!"

Symrustar smiled. "Of course." She reached for the speaking-chimes. "More dawnberry cordial, coz?"

Amaranthae gave her an answering smile and reclined against the leafy boughs that ringed their bower. "And why not? Hurl all spells behind us, and soar howling into the moon!"

"A fitting sentiment," Symrustar agreed, stretching her magnificent body, "considering my plans for this human, 'Elminster.' Yes, I'll see to it that humans have their uses." Extending her empty cordial glass in her toes, she struck the speaking chimes with it.

As their gentle chord resounded, Amaranthae Auglamyr shuddered at the cold, careless pleasure in her cousin's voice. It sounded somehow *hungry*.

* * * * *

"I'd not be in the boots of this human, no matter how mighty a sorcerer he may be," Taeglyn murmured from below, where he was sorting the gems carefully on velvet with the aid of a magnification spell.

"I care not a whit for this human—a beast of the fields, after all," Delmuth growled, "but it's the boots of the Coronal I'll want to see filled by a new owner, after I do what I must."

" 'Do what you must'? But, Lord, the Lesser Flith is almost complete! It lacks but a ruby for the star Esmel, and two diamonds for the Vraelen!" The servant gestured at the glittering star map filling the domed upper half of the chamber. In response to the star names he uttered, the spell Delmuth had cast earlier awakened two precise points in the empty air into winking life.

They flashed silently, awaiting their gems, but Delmuth Echorn was descending smoothly out of the midst of his life work, the constellations he'd modeled in gems glittering around him. "Yes, do what I must— destroy this human. If we let this go unchallenged, we'll have them in here by the thousands, a sea of rabble around our ankles, begging or threatening us whenever we go out, and despoiling the forest as fast as they so ably know how!" His boots touched the glossy black marble floor. "Why, if they could touch the stars," he snarled, pointing up at his miniature heavens, "we'd have found one or two missing by now!"

Delmuth glared up at the winking points of light, which obediently went out. He handed Taeglyn his gloves, with their long, talonlike metal points, stretched like a great and supple cat of the jungles, and added, still angry, "Yes, our fair and mighty Coronal has gone mad, and none of us seem ready enough to raise our hands and voices against him. Well, I'll take the first step, if no other Cormanthan has the stomach to. The pollution he has allowed to walk right into the very bosom of our fair Cormanthor must be eradicated."

Face set, he strode out of the room, smashing its double doors aside with his enchanted bracers. They boomed, splintered, and shuddered back from where they'd struck the wall, but Delmuth Echorn, striding hard, didn't even hear them.

A few breaths later, he was passing through the high, many-balconied front hall, his best boar sword glowing green in his hands from its many enchantments, when his uncle Neldor leaned down over a stair rail and exclaimed, "By the unseen beard of Corellon, *what* are you about? There's no Hunt called for this even, and it's still morn yet!"

"I'm not going on a Hunt, Uncle," Delmuth replied,

without slowing or looking up. "I'm out to cleanse the realm of a human."

"The one named armathor by our Coronal? Lad, where are thy senses? No trumpet has cried your challenge! No charge has been delivered before the court, or to this man! Duels must be formally declared. 'Tis the law!"

Delmuth stopped at the tall front doors to give a scrambling servant time to swing them open, and looked up and back. "I go to slay one who is vermin, not a person with any right to be treated as one of us, whatever the Coronal may say."

He cast the sword spinning up into the air and followed it outside; just before the doors boomed shut behind him, Neldor saw him catch the blade and set off through the mushroom garden, taking the shortest route to the hawthorn gate.

"You're making a mistake, lad," he said sadly, "and taking our House with you." But there was no one left in the forehall of Castle Echorn to hear him except the frightened servant, whose white face was raised to heed Neldor.

Instead of ignoring him or snapping out a curt order, the eldest living elf of the blood of Echorn sadly spread his empty hands in a gesture of helplessness.

By the doors, the servant began to cry.

* * * * *

The elf in black leathers turned an exultant somersault in the air, crashed through the curtain of evercreeper leaves, and flung the sword in his hand exuberantly into the trunk of a blueleaf tree as he fell past. It struck deep and thrummed, neatly cutting an errant leaf in two on its brief journey.

The pieces were still fluttering down when the elf

sprang up through them and snatched his sword back, crying joyously, "Ho ho, a cat has certainly been set loose among all the sleepy doves at court *this* time!"

"Easy, Athtar; they can probably hear you right down south by the sea." Galan Goadulphyn was carefully arranging small heaps of glass beads on his cloak, spread out atop the stump of a shadowtop that had fallen when Cormanthor was young. Only he knew that they represented the loans paid out to a certain phantom mushroom-growing concern by several too many proud Houses of the realm. Galan was trying to work out how to pay off some of the stiffer-lipped House keymasters by borrowing more from others.

If he couldn't come up with a deft pattern by nightfall, it might be necessary to leave Toril for a lifetime or two. Or however long it took for elves to find spells enough to build completely different, mind- and spell-fooling identities for themselves. A gloomhunter spider wandered onto the cloak, and Galan scowled at it.

"So? Everyone in the realm knows as much!"

"*I* don't," Galan said, staring intently into the eyes of the spider. They looked at each other for a moment, one eye to a thousand. Then the spider decided that prudence wasn't always only for others, and scrambled off the cloak as fast as its spindly legs could carry it. "Enlighten me."

Athtar drew in a deep and delighted breath. "Well, the Coronal has found a human somewhere, and brought him to court, and named him his heir and an armathor of the realm! Our next Coronal's going to be a *man!*"

"What?" Galan shook his head as if to clear it, spun away from his cloak, and snatched at his friend's throat lacings. "Athtar Nlossae," he snarled, shaking the leather-clad elf as if Athtar was a large and floppy doll, "kindly speak sense! Where in the name of all the bastard gods of the dwarves would the Coronal *find* a human? Under a rock? In his vaults? In a discarded slipper?" He let go of Athtar, who staggered back until he found a tree trunk to lean against, and took refuge there.

Galan advanced on him, growling, "I'm engaged in something very *important*, Athtar, and you come to me with wild tales! The Coronal'd never dare name a human armathor even if someone brought him a hundred humans! Why, he'd have all the stiff-necked young lads and old warriors in the realm lining up to spit on their swords and throw them back at him!"

"That's *just* what they're doing," Athtar replied delightedly, "right now! If you stand up on yon stump and listen, Gal—like this!—you'll—"

"Athtar—*nooo!*"

Galan's clutching hands came down just an instant too late. Beads bounced, rolled, and flew. Breathing heavily, the tall, one-eyed elf found his hands locked around Athtar's throat, and the leather-clad elf looking at him rather reproachfully.

"You're very *intense* these days, Gal," Athtar said in hurt tones. "A simple 'I find I feel deeply for you' would've sufficed."

Galan let his hands fall. What was the use? The beads were scattered, now, save for the few that—

There was a crunching sound under Athtar's right boot.

—remained on the cloak, under their feet. Galan sighed, took a deep breath, and then sighed again. When he spoke again, his tone was wearily pleasant. "You came here to tell me that our next Coronal, a thousand years after they kill the both of us for our deeds and forget where our graves lie, will be a human—is that it? I'm supposed to 'feel deeply' about that?"

"No, dolt! They'll never let a human be Coronal! The

realm'll be torn apart first," Athtar said, shaking him by one shoulder. "And with the laws swept away and every House floundering, lowskins like you and me will hold the ready blades at last!" He thrust up his sword in celebration, and laughed again.

Galan shook his head sourly. "It'll never get that far. It never does. Too many mages lurking about to control minds and threaten the high and mighty into obeying whatever they can't force them into supporting. Oh, there'll be an uproar, sure. But the realm torn apart? Over one human? Hah!" He turned away to step down off the stump, trying to shake off Athtar's grip.

Athtar didn't let go. "Even so, Gal," he said urgently, lowering his voice to underscore his excitement. "Even so! This human knows magic, they say, and the folk at court are wild with tales of how he'll shake things up. Whatever happens to him in the end—and it'll happen, never fear; the young blades'll see to *that*—this is the best chance we'll ever see to break the old guard's stranglehold on what's done and not done in Cormanthor! Settle some old scores with the Starym and Echorns, if we don't get trampled in the rush of other Houses trying to do the same thing! Who do you owe the most money to? Who are giving you the hardest time over it? Who can be put down in the forest mud where they belong, forever?"

As the elf in leathers ran out of breath with his last query echoing back from the trees around them, Galan looked at his friend with true enthusiasm for the first time.

"*Now* you're interesting me," he breathed, embracing Athtar. "So settle down, and get yourself some bitterroot ale; it's over by the duskwood that's losing its bark—there. We have to talk."

* * * * *

Elminster, aid me. The mind-cry was faint, but somehow familiar. Could it be, after all this time? It sounded like Shandathe of Hastarl, whom El had carried into the bedroom of a certain baker, to find unintended bliss, and later tested the mind powers Mystra had honed in him by eavesdropping on . . .

Elminster sat up, frowning. Though it was highsun, their work together had been exhausting, and the Srinshee was asleep, floating on air across the chamber, the faint glow of her keep-warm spell eddying around her. Were the Dlardrageth ghosts playing tricks on him?

He closed his eyes and shut out the dark chamber and the weight of his full roster of freshly memorized spells, letting all stray thought and distraction drain away, drifting down into the dark place where mind voices were wont to echo.

Elminster? Elminster, can you hear me?

The voice was faint and distant, yet oddly flat. Strange. He sent a single thought toward it: *Where?*

After a time of echoing emptiness an image came swimming up to him, spinning slowly like a bright coin on edge. He plunged into it, and was suddenly at its glowing heart, staring into a dark, stormy scene: somewhere in Faerûn, with wind trailing across a rocky height, and treetops below. A woman was spread-eagled face down on that rock, wrists and ankles bound apart on saplings, her features hidden by the swirl of her unbound hair. It was a place he'd not seen before. The woman could be Shandathe.

The viewpoint could not be made to move. It was time to decide.

El shrugged; as always, there was only one decision he could make, and still be Elminster. The fool wizard.

Smiling in bleak self-mockery at that last thought, he rose, holding firmly to the image of the peak with the bound woman—a striking trap, he'd grant its weaver that much—and crossed the room to touch the Srinshee's teaching crystal. It could store mind images, and so show her where he'd gone. The stone flashed once, and he turned his back on its light and stepped away, calling up the spell he'd need.

When his foot came down again, he stood on the rocky height with the cool breeze sliding past. He was in the center of a vast forest that looked suspiciously like Cormanthor. The bound woman at his feet was fading and shrinking, her form flowing like pale smoke. Of course. Elminster called up what he hoped was the best spell for the occasion, and waited for the attack he knew would come.

* * * * *

In a dark chamber, a floating figure sat up and frowned at where her human charge had last stood. Some battles must be faced alone, but . . . so soon?

She wondered which elven foe was so swift in calling him to battle. Once news of the Coronal's proclaiming spread across the realm, yes, El would find no shortage of opponents, but . . . now?

The Srinshee sighed, called up the spell she'd cast earlier, and gathered her will around the image of Elminster in her mind. In a few breaths' time she'd be seeing him. Gods grant that it not be to witness his death now, before their friendship—along with the Coronal's dream and the trail that led to the best future for Cormanthor—was truly begun.

Without looking at her crystal, she beckoned it, and touched it when it came. The image of a rocky height amid the Cormanthan forest leaped into her mind. Druindar's Rock, a place none but a Cormanthan was likely to choose for a moot or spell duel. The Srinshee sent her spell sight racing toward it, seeing a familiar young, hawk-nosed man standing above a bound woman, who was no bound woman at all, but a . . .

* * * * *

The woman and the spars she'd been bound to were both flowing and dwindling. Elminster calmly stepped back from the changing magic and glanced over the edge of the rock on which he stood. It was a long, long way down on two flanks, with a prow-like point between. In the third direction rocks rose into broken, tree-cloaked ground. It was from the concealing branches of those trees that cold laughter came as the lady captive shrank at last into a long, wavy-bladed boar sword that flickered and glowed green as it rose smoothly from the ground, turned on edge, and flew toward him point first.

Knowing what is about to kill you doesn't always make it easier to evade the waiting death, as a philosopher—dead now—among the outlaws of Athalantar had once said.

There was little space in which to dodge, and almost no time for El to act. This blade might be only animated by a simple spell, or it might well bear enchantments of its own. If he assumed the former and was wrong, he'd be dead. So . . .

Elminster carried in his mind only one of the mighty spells known as Mystra's unraveling, and disliked casting it so soon when he stood in danger, but—

The blade raced at his throat, turning smoothly as he sidestepped, and following his every move as he bobbed and crouched. At the last moment he hissed the single word of the spell and made the necessary flick of his cupped hand.

The swift-flying sword shivered and fell apart in the

air in front of him. Green radiance sputtered, tumbled away, and was gone as the blade became falling flakes of rust. Dust kissed Elminster's face as it rushed past . . . and then nothing at all.

The laughter in the trees broke off abruptly, into a shout of, "Corellon aid me—human, *what have you done?*"

A finely dressed, youthful elf lord with hair like white silk and eyes like two red and furious flames came leaping out of the trees with the flames of rising magic growing ever-brighter around his wrists.

As the elf came snarling to a halt on the last rock above Elminster, almost weeping in his rage, Elminster looked up at him, used a spell echo to momentarily call up the image of the glowing green sword's destruction, and calmly asked, "Is this elven humor, or some sort of trick question?"

With a wild shriek of rage the elf sprang at El, flames leaping from his hands.

Nine

DUEL BY DAY, REVEL BY NIGHT

Few who've witnessed a spell battle forget the very old saying among humans: "When mages duel, honest folk should seek hiding places far away." Though mantles and araemyths make elven wizardly duels more a matter of anticipation and slowly unfolding complexity than human struggles, 'tis still a good idea to be at a safe distance when sorcerers make war. Out of the realm, for instance.

Antarn the Sage
from **The High History of Faerûnian Archmages Mighty**
published circa The Year of the Staff

"You—you *wretch!*" the elf snarled, hurling fire from his hands in a web of snapping flames. "That blade was a treasure of my House! It was old when humans first learned to speak!"

"My," Elminster replied as his warding spell took effect, sending the flames splashing down around him in a ring, "that's a lot of dead boars. How old did any of them live to be, I wonder?"

"Insolent barbarian *human!*" the elf hissed, dancing around Elminster's ring. His fair hair bounced about his shoulders as he went, flowing in the passing breeze as if it were the flames of a hungry fire.

Elminster turned to keep himself facing this angry foe, and said calmly, "I tend not to be overly pleasant to those who try to slay me, but I have no real quarrel with ye, nameless elf lord. Can we not part in peace?"

"Peace? When you're *dead*, human, perhaps, and the mages of whatever godless grubbing kingdom spawned you have been compelled to replace the sacred sword you destroyed!"

The angry elf drew back, raised both arms above his head with his hands still pointed at Elminster, and spat angry words. El murmured a single word in response and flicked his fingers, altering his warding into a shield that would send hostile magics back whence they'd come.

A trio of racing blue bolts, each with its own nimbus of lightning encircling it, roared out of the elf's hands and came screaming at the last prince of Athalantar. Inside his shield El crouched ready, bringing another spell to mind but not casting it.

The bolts struck, washed over his shield in a soundless fury of white light, and raced back at their source.

The elf's eyes widened in amazement, and he shut his eyes and grimaced as the blue bolts crashed into an invisible shield that surrounded him. Of course, thought El. Every magic-hurling Cormanthan probably wore a conjured mantle of defensive magics when he went to war.

And this was war, El thought, as the elven lord fell back a few paces and snarled out another incantation. With an attacker who'd chosen the ground and had a defensive mantle up and ready on one hand, and the freakish and widely hated human intruder on the other. Oh, joy.

This time the spell that came at Elminster consisted of three disembodied jaws, their long fangs snapping as they swerved and split apart to come at him from three directions. El fell flat on his stomach and raised his left hand, waiting, as the first soundless flash marked the meeting of his shield and the foremost maw.

After the flash, it danced and staggered away, heading back for the elf lord. But the second mouth tore asunder his shield with its collision, both spell effects twisting together into a roiling blast that sent a scorching trail of angry purple flames racing along the rocks.

The returning jaws faded away against the elf lord's mantle at about the same time as the third raced at Elminster, gaping low to be sure of scooping him up off the rocks.

From El's patiently waiting hand flashed a dozen globes of light that spat tiny lightnings behind them as they went. The first blasted the jaws into golden-green nothingness, and the others shot through the spreading fire of that explosion and leapt at the elf beyond in a deadly approaching storm.

The elf lord looked anxious for the first time, and worked a hasty spell as the spinning globes flashed toward him. He fell back a few more steps to gain time to finish his spell—and so tasted Elminster's first trap.

The globes that the elf's stabbing defensive magic did not touch struck the unseen mantle and exploded in harmless, spreading sheets of light. Those the elf did strike burst apart into triple lightning bolts that stabbed rocks, trees, and the nearby elf lord with equal vigor.

With a groan of pain the elf staggered backward, smoke rising from him.

"Not a bad defense for a nameless elf," Elminster observed calmly.

His goading promptly had the effect he'd been hoping for. "No nameless one am I, human," the elf snarled, arms folded around himself in pain, "but Delmuth Echorn, of one of the foremost Houses of Cormanthor! Heir of the Echorns am I, and my rank in your human terms would be 'emperor'! Uncultured *dog!*"

"Ye use 'uncultured dog' as a title?" Elminster asked innocently. "It fits ye, aye, but I must warn ye we humans haven't come to expect such candor from elven folk. Ye may achieve unintended hilarity in thy dealings with my kind!"

Delmuth roared in fresh fury, but then his eyes narrowed and he hissed like a snake. "You hope to overmaster me through my temper! No such fortune will I hand to you—nameless human!"

"Elminster Aumar am I," El replied pleasantly, "Prince of Athalant—ah, but ye won't be interested in the titles of pig-sty human realms, will ye?"

"Yes, precisely!" Delmuth snapped. "Er, that is: *no!*" His arms were acquiring flames again. Circles of firebursts chased each other endlessly about his wrists, betokening risen but unleashed old elven battle magic.

So was the elf lord's mantle gone entirely, or did it survive still? El silently bent his will to spinning another shield of his own as he waited, suspecting Delmuth would try to ruin the next visible spell his human foe cast by hurling his own spell attack into the midst of El's casting.

When El's shield was complete, he acted out the casting of a false spell. Sure enough, emerald lightnings lashed at him in mid-gibberish, clawing at his shield and rebounding. Delmuth laughed triumphantly, and El saw by the rebounding sparks that the elf's mantle had survived, or had been renewed. He shrugged, smiled, and began his own next spell, at the same time as the fiercely smiling elf undertook his own casting.

Unnoticed by either of them, one of the trees struck by Elminster's lightning fell over the edge of the peak, tearing crumbling stone with it, to plunge down, down through the empty air.

* * * * *

"Oh, be careful, Elminster!" the Lady Oluevaera Estelda breathed, as she sat on empty air in a dark and
dusty chamber at the heart of the ghost castle of the
Dlardrageth. Her eyes were seeing a distant peak and
two figures striving against each other there, as their
spells flashed and raged about them. The one just
might be the future of Cormanthor, while the other
was one of the most haughty and headstrong of its oldest, proudest Houses—and its heir to boot.

Some would call it treachery to the People to inter-
vene in any spell duel—but then, this was no proper
duel, but a man lured into a trap by the deceit of an elf.
Many more would deem one who aided any human
against any elf, in any situation, a traitor to the People.
And yet she would do this, if she could. The Srinshee
had seem more summers by far—aye, and winters,
too—than any other elf who breathed the clear air of
Cormanthor today. She was one of those whose judgment would be deferred to, in any high dispute between
Houses. Well, then; her judgment would have to be respected as highly in this more personal matter.

Not that anyone but ghosts were in this shunned
ruin to stop her.

The only swift link she had with Druindar's Rock
was through Elminster himself, and it might well be
fatal to him to create any distraction in his mind at the
wrong moment. However, she could 'ride' through him,
exposing herself to the same magics he faced in the
process, until he happened to let his eyes fall on some
part of the surroundings that wasn't full of erupting
magic or a leaping elf lord—whereupon she could hurl
herself to that spot, and materialize there.

The spell was a powerful but simple one. The Srinshee murmured the words that released it without

taking her eyes off the spell-battle, and felt herself *sliding* into Elminster's mind, as if slipping into warm, tingling waters that carried her swiftly along a dark, narrow tunnel, toward a distant light.

The light grew brighter and larger with terrifying speed, until it became a serenely beautiful face that the Srinshee knew, its long tresses stirring and writhing like restless snakes. A face whose eyes were stern as it loomed up like a vast, endless wall before her, a wall she was going to crash helplessly into . . .

"Oh, Lady Goddess, not *again!*" The Srinshee cried, an instant before she struck those gigantic, pursed lips. "Can't you see I'm trying to help—?"

When the whirling world came back again, Oluevaera was staring at a dark, cobwebbed ceiling inches overheard. She was sprawled on her back on a bed of raging black flames that tickled her bare skin—her bare skin? what had become of her gown?—as if it were a thousand moving feathers, but did not burn.

The flames seemed to be slowly sinking away from the ceiling; had she appeared *through* it? Wonderingly she ran her hands up and down her body. Her gown, with its amulets and spell-gems—yes, even those woven into her hair—were gone, but her body was smooth and full and young again!

Great Corellon, Labelas, and Hanali! What had befalle—but no. Great *Mystra!* The human goddess had wrought this!

She sat up abruptly, amid the descending flames. Why? In payment for aiding the young lad, or as an apology for shutting her out? Was it lasting? Or but a taunting taste of youth? She still had her spells, her memories, the—

"So, old whore, you've traded your loyalty to the realm for some spell of youth the human knows! I *wondered* why you aided him!"

The Srinshee turned her head to stare at the speaker, bringing her hands up to cover her breasts without thinking. She knew that cold voice, but how came it here?

"Cormanthor knows how to treat traitors!" he snarled, and a bolt of ravening lightning crackled across the room.

It sank into the black flames and was sucked in without a sound. The black flames hauled every last spark of the bolt from the hands of the astonished High Court Mage Ilimitar. He stared at the now-youthful sorceress.

She looked back at him with sad reproach in her eyes and spoke softly, using her old pet name for him. "So how is it, Limi, that you rise from being my pupil, and learning love for Cormanthor from my lips, to presuming to speak for all the realm as you try to slay me?"

"Seek not to twist my will with words, witch!" Ilimitar snapped, raising a scepter to menace her. The dark flames touched the stone floor of the chamber and faded, and the Srinshee stood facing him, spreading her hands to show that she was nude and unarmed.

He leveled the scepter without hesitation, saying coldly, "Pray to the gods for forgiveness, traitor!"

Emerald fire raced from it as that last hurtful word left his lips; the Srinshee turned to leap side, stumbled—it had been so long since she'd known a body that could obey swift movements—and then sprawled bruisingly on the stones as the scepter's death roared over her.

Her onetime pupil aimed the scepter lower, but the Srinshee had hissed the words she needed. Its fury splashed in futility along an unseen shield.

Her mantle was up now, and she doubted all the scepters he owned could bring it down. It would be spell to spell, unless she could dissuade him. The High Court Mage *she'd* trained. Earynspieir might attack her, yes, he'd never been her friend. But she'd not thought Ilimitar could be so quick to do this.

Oluevaera rose and faced the furious mage, standing no taller than his shoulder. "Why did you seek me here, Ilimitar?" she asked.

"This tomb of traitors was always your favored spot to bring pupils to try castings, remember?" he spat at her.

Gods, yes, she'd brought Ilimitar here to Castle Dlardrageth, twice. Tears came at the memory, and as the High Court Mage flung down his scepter and wove a spell to bring the roof down on her, he snarled, "Regretting your folly now, eh? Too late, old witch! Your treachery is clear, and you must die!"

In reply the last Lady Estelda merely shook her head and calmly wove the magic that awakened the ancient enchantments the Dlardrageth had used to raise these halls. When Ilimitar's spell smashed and clawed at the ceiling, instants later, his magic turned to fire that rained back down at him.

He staggered back, coughing and shuddering—his mantle must be weak, she thought—and shouted, "Seek not to escape me, Oluevaera! No part of the realm is safe for you now!"

"By whose decree?" she cried, fresh tears on her cheeks. "Have you slain Eltargrim, too?"

"His folly is not yet open treachery to Cormanthor, but something that can be corrected once the human—and *you*, with your lying tongue—are gone. I will hunt you down wherever you flee to!" He muttered an incantation on the heels of that shout.

"I've no intention of fleeing anywhere, Ilimitar!" the Srinshee told him angrily. "This realm is my home!"

The air before her exploded in flames. From each

blossoming ball of fire a beam shot out, to link with the
other fireballs. Oluevaera ducked away from one
whose heat threatened to blister her shoulder and
whispered words that would dissolve a spell into
strengthening her mantle.

"Is that why," the High Court Mage snarled in reply,
"you protected a *human*, keeping him alive and coun-
seling him into flattering the Coronal enough to win
an armathor out of the old fool? He'll just be the first
of a scheming, grasping horde of the hairy ones, if we
let him live! Can you not see that?"

"No!" the Srinshee shouted, over the crash and roar
of his next spell attack. "I fail to see why loving Cormanthor and working to strengthen it must place me
in the situation of having to slay one honorable
human—who came here to keep a promise to a dying
heir, and deliver a kiira to an elder House, Ilimitar!—
or be slain by you, unless I destroy you: a mage in
whom I awakened mastery of magic, and have been
proud of these six centuries!"

"Always you twist folk with clever words!" he
shouted back, and went right on into snarling the incantation of another spell.

The Srinshee found herself weeping again. "Why?"
she sobbed. "Why do you force me to make this choice?"

Her mantle shuddered then, as purple lightnings of
magical force sought to drain its vitality. Through the
tumult, as paving stones cracked underfoot in a
ragged, deafening chorus, her newfound foe cried,
"Your wits are addled by love, old hag, and corrupted
by the Coronals' dreams! Can you not understand that
the security of the realm *must* be paramount over all
other things?"

The Srinshee set her teeth and lashed out with
lightnings of her own; his mantle lit up briefly under
their strike, and she saw him staggering. "And can you

not see," she shouted at him, "that this man *is* the security of our realm, if we but guard him and let him grow into what Eltargrim sees?"

"Bah!" Ilimitar the mage spat derisively. "The Coronal is as corrupt as you are! You and he both stain the good name of our court, and the trust our People have put in you!" The chamber rocked around them as his latest spell clawed its way along every inch of her mantle, but could not break it.

"Ilimitar," the Srinshee asked sadly, "are you mad?"

The chamber fell suddenly silent, with smoke eddying around their feet, as he stared at her in genuine amazement.

"No," he said at last, in almost conversational tones, "but I think I've been mad for years not to see the game you and the Coronal have been playing, moving Cormanthor ever so gently—deftly, like the sly oldlings you both are—toward the day when humans would dwell among us, and outbreed us, and in the end overwhelm us, leaving no Cormanthor at all to serve or be proud of! How much did they offer you? Spells you couldn't find elsewhere? A realm to rule? Or was it this return of your youth, all along?"

"Limi," she said earnestly, "this body you see is not of my doing, and when first you found me here and now, I was but newly aware of it. I know not where it came from—it could be some old joke of the Dlardrageth, for all I know—and the young human certainly didn't give it to me, or promise it; he doesn't even *know* about it!"

Ilimitar waved a dismissive hand. "Words—just words," he said heavily. "Always your sharpest weapons. They don't work with me anymore, witch!" He was panting, now, as he faced her.

"Do you know what this is?" he asked, taking something small from a belt pouch and raising it into view.

"It's from the Vault of Ages," he added mockingly. "You should know!"

"It's the Overmantle of Halgondas," the Srinshee said quietly, her face going pale.

"You fear it, don't you?" he snarled, triumph glinting in his eyes again. "And there's nothing you can do to stop me using it! And then, old witch, you are mine!"

"How so?"

"Our mantles will merge, and become one. Not only will you not ward off my spells, but you won't escape; if you flee, you'll drag me with you!" He laughed, his tones high and wild, and the Srinshee knew then that he was mad, and that she would have to kill him here, or perish.

He broke the Overmantle.

The inexorable surging together of their two mantles began, their ragged ends searching for, and attracted to, each other. The Srinshee sighed and began to walk toward her onetime pupil. It was time to use the spell she hated.

"Surrendering?" Ilimitar asked, almost gleefully. "Or are you foolish enough to think you can fight on—and prevail? I'm a High Court Mage, witch, not the youth you showed castings to! Your magic is all trickery and old sly spells and little magics for scaring younglings!"

The Srinshee drew in a deep breath, and lifted her chin. "Well then, grand and mighty sorcerer—destroy me if you must!"

High Court Mage Ilimitar gave her an disbelieving look, raised his hands, and said gruffly, "I'll make it quick."

A trident of spell spears thrust through her. She stood unmoving, though her eyes rolled up in her head and she bit her lip. After the spell began to fade, her body started to tremble.

Ilimitar watched her. Well, it wasn't his fault she'd

spun so many preservative and guardian enchantments down the centuries, layer upon layer. She'd just have to endure the pain, now, as they kept her alive longer than was necessary.

She brought her head down, eyes closed, and stood breathing heavily. Blood ran down her face from her closed eyelids, and dripped on the shattered stones underfoot. Ilimitar's nostrils flared in distaste. So it was martyr time, was it? He'd make short work of that.

His next spell was a thrust of pure energy that should have left her in ashes. When it faded and he could see again, the stones were melted away in a neat circle, and she stood ankle-deep in rubble, blackened and with all her hair burnt away—but she still stood, and still shuddered.

What foul pact had the sorceress made with human mages? Ilimitar cast the spell she'd once forbid him utterly to use; the one that summoned the Hungry Worm.

The worm materialized coiled about one of her arms, but it slithered straight for her belly, and began burrowing into the cracked and blackened flesh immediately. Ilimitar sighed and hoped it would be quick; he had to be sure that human was dead, and swiftly, so he could be back at court to denounce the Coronal before nightfall. But he was trapped here with the Srinshee, inside the shared Overmantle, until one of them was dead.

It was a pity, really. She'd been a good teacher—if an overly strict one, with little love for pranks and stealing days in high summer to snatch honey and nibble berries and hunt down new owl eggs—and she should never have sunk to this. She'd been old even then, though, and no doubt tempted to take any means to regain youth. But consorting with humans was unforgivable. If she wanted to do that, why hadn't she just quietly left Cormanthor? Why ruin the realm? Why—

The worm was largely done, now. It never touched
the limbs or head when it had a body to feast upon, a
body now little more than rags of skin upon hollowed-
out, empty bones. How was it that she was still standing?

Ilimitar frowned, and hurled a quartet of small
forcebolts into her—the sort one uses to fell woodcut-
ters or running rabbits. Her ravaged body still stood.

He was nearly out of useful battle spells. He
shrugged and picked up the fallen scepter, raking her
with emerald fire until the scepter sputtered and died,
drained away.

The High Court Mage frowned down at it. He hadn't
realized, when bringing it here today, just how little
magic had been left in it. That could have been disas-
trous. As it was, well . . .

The ravaged body of the Srinshee still stood. She
must still be alive—and he knew better than to touch
her directly, even with his dagger. There were tricks
the older casters knew. Best to simply blast her to
nothingness.

He snapped his finger and said a certain word, and
there was suddenly a staff in his hands—long and
black, set with many silver runes. He let it wake
slowly, thrumming in his hands—ah, that delicious
feeling of power—before he poured white-hot death
into his motionless foe.

The staff fell silent after only moments. He frowned,
tried to send it away again, and found it dead—just so
much dark wood, now. In puzzlement he threw it down
and summoned a rod. He had two more scepters he
could call to him after that, if the rod failed. Perhaps
the Overmantle was deadening them. In frantic haste
he called on all of its withering and life-draining
powers.

The body facing him became a withered bag of skin once more, and what skin was left turned gray and rotten. But still the old sorceress stood.

Grunting in exasperated amazement, Ilimitar called first one scepter, and then the other. When it fizzled into crackling, smoking death, the first cold taste of foreboding filled his mouth, for the Srinshee still stood.

Her shattered head hung askew from a broken neck, but those blackened, bleeding eyes opened—to be revealed as two pools of flickering flame—and the mouth beneath them worked its broken jaw for a grinding moment and then croaked, "Are you done, Limi?"

"Corellon preserve me!" the mage shouted, in real horror, as he shrank away from her. Would she start to move toward him?

Yes! Oh, gods, yes!

He screamed as that broken body shuffled forward, out of its pit of melted rubble, and set footless stumps on the paving stones. He fell back, crying, "Stay back!"

"I don't want to do this, Limi," the mutilated thing said sadly, as it thumped slowly and awkwardly toward him. "The choice was yours, I fear, as it was when you began this battle, Limi."

"Speak not my name, foul witch of darkness!" the High Court Mage howled, snatching out his last item of magic with trembling fingers. It was a ring on a fine chain; he slid it onto one of his fingers and pointed at her. The ring-finger swiftly lengthened into a lone, hooklike talon and began to grow scales. "You serve a foe of the realm," he cried, "and must needs be struck down, that Cormanthor endure!"

The ring flashed. A last beam of black, deadly force shot out.

The shuffling body halted, shuddering with fresh violence, and Ilimitar laughed in crazed relief. Yes! It was finally over! She was falling.

The broken thing crashed into his shoulder and slid
down his body, brushing him with its lips as it fell.

There was an instant of crawling magic that made
Oluevaera Estelda retch uncontrollably as the Overmantle surged in through every orifice of her body, and
then out again.

Then it was gone, like mist before a morning sun,
and she was on her knees, whole again, before the body
of Ilimitar—who had just simultaneously received
every spell and magical discharge he'd poured into her.

She *still* hated that spell. It was as cruel as the long
ago elven mage who'd devised it—almost as bad as
Halgondas and his Overmantle. Moreover, its caster
had to feel the pain of all that was done to them—and
Ilimitar had been so enthusiastic in his attempted destruction that the pain would have driven most mages
mad. But not this one. Not the old Srinshee.

She looked down at the heap of blasted, smoldering
bones in front of her, and started to cry again. Her
tears made little hissing sounds as they fell into the
dying fires that flickered within what had been Ilimitar.

* * * * *

"Blood of Corellon, it's raining *trees* now!" Galan
Goadulphyn snarled, springing back and raising his
cloak hastily before his face. The fallen duskwood
bounced deafeningly as it shattered in front of him,
hurling dust and splinters in all directions.

"There's a spell duel going on up there, for sure,"
Athtar said, peering upwards. "Hadn't we better get
out of here? We can come back for your coins later."

"Later?" Galan groaned, as they hastened away together. "If I know bloody yapping mages, they'll split

that mountain apart before they're done, and either leave my cache revealed for every passing sprite to see—or they'll bury it keep-deep under broken rock!"

There was another crash, and Athtar Nlossae looked back in time to see a sheet of rock plunging down the cliff, bouncing and shattering as it struck outcroppings in its fall. "You're right, as usual, Gal—buried it is, or will be!"

As he bent his legs to following the elf in dusty black leathers just as fast as they both could travel, Galan began to sort through his collection of curses. Loudly.

* * * * *

"You can't hope to escape my magics forever, coward!" Delmuth told Elminster, as elven mantle and human shield struck sparks from each other, and yet another mighty old elven spell curled away into harmless smoke.

They stood almost breast to breast, as close as their warring spell-barriers would let them. Elminster went on smiling silently, as the angry elf hurled spell after spell.

Delmuth had discovered that so long as mantle and shield touched, the surging effect of his own spells rebounding on him was minimal; his own defenses didn't crumble away so quickly at each magical onslaught. So he'd advanced, and Elminster hadn't bothered to retreat.

The only place to fall back was over the edge of a cliff, anyway, and the Athalantan mage was weary of running. Let the stand be made here.

The heir of House Echorn hurled another blast— this one past Elminster, avoiding both mage and shield, in hopes that it would rend rock and spray him from behind with stone shards. Instead, it ripped a trench through the rock and spat the stone over the edge of the cliff, away into nothingness below.

El kept his eyes on the elf lord. This had gone on long enough; if Delmuth Echorn wanted to see a death so badly, it'd have to be his own. Safe inside his shield, Elminster carefully made an elaborate casting, and then another that called up his mage-sight, and waited. One advantage to battling elves with human spells was that they largely didn't recognize the castings, and so could be surprised by the final results.

This one was Mruster's Twist, a further modification of Jhalavan's Fond Return. It allowed a mage who could think fast to change spells that were being returned to their caster into different magics. Now if this Delmuth was just foolish enough to try to blast a certain annoying human to dust, and keep close to Elminster as he did it, so he didn't notice that the spreading furies of his spells were left over from their first strikes, and not their rebounds . . .

Delmuth enthusiastically proved he was just foolish enough, hurling a spell El had never seen before that brought into being a tray of acid above the victim's head and let its contents rain down.

The hissings and roilings of El's tormented shield were spectacular. Delmuth never noticed when the rain of acid was twisted into a surging dispel effect that clawed silently at his mantle.

Still angry, and thinking his foe was finally cornered, Delmuth lashed out with a second spell. Elminster put on a scared look this time to distract the elf from noticing that his energy blasts again melted away into something silent, and it worked.

Delmuth raised both hands exultantly and lashed his human foe with bladed tentacles. El reeled and pantomimed pain, as it some part of the fading spell had actually reached him through his shield. And

Delmuth's twisted spell ate away the last strength of his own mantle.

To El's mage-sight, the elf was surrounded now only by flickering, darkening wisps of magic, the failing shell of what had once been an impregnable barrier. "Delmuth," he cried, "I ask ye one last time: can't we end this, and part in peace?"

"Certainly, human," the elf replied with a feral grin. "When you are dead, then there'll be *perfect* peace!"

And his slender fingers shaped a casting El did not know. Force flickered, visible only in its settling outline; it seemed to be the same invisible evocation that human mages wove into what were called walls of force.

Delmuth saw El watching intently, and looked up, gloating, as the last radiances shaped an invisible sword, floating before Delmuth with its point toward Elminster. "Behold a spell you cannot send back at me," the elf lord chuckled, leaning low over it. "We call it a 'deadly seeking blade'—and all of elven blood are immune to it!" He snapped his fingers and broke into open, rolling laughter as the blade leapt forward.

They were standing only a few paces apart, but El already knew what magic he wanted to turn this unseen blade of force into. Delmuth would have been wiser to have wielded it in his hand, and hacked at El's shield as if it were a real blade, giving El no time to twist it in the brief contacts.

But then, Delmuth would have been wiser never to have lured Elminster here at all.

El twisted the blade into something else and flung it back. As it struck the elf, Delmuth's laughter faltered. The last gasp of his mantle, striving vainly to protect him as it scattered into drifting sparks, lifted him up off the ground to kick his heels in empty air.

He stiffened as Elminster's twisted magic struck

him, and then grew still, his hands raised into claws in front of his breast, his legs straining, with the toes of his boots pointed at the ground. The paralysis El had bestowed upon him took firm hold, and all that El could see the elf lord move was his eyes, widening now in terror and rolling around to stare helplessly at the human mage.

Or perhaps not so helplessly. Delmuth could still launch magics that were triggered by act of will alone, like Elminster's shielding spells—and in the elf lord's eyes El saw terror be washed away by fury, and then by cunning.

* * * * *

Delmuth hadn't been so scared for a long time. Fear was like cold iron in his mouth, and his heart raced. That a mere *human* could bring him to this! He could *die* here, floating above some windswept rock in the backwoods of the realm! He—

Yet steady . . . steady, son of Echorn. He had one spell left that no human could anticipate, something more secret and terrible even than the blade. They'd been pressed together mantle-to-mantle; for his own to have failed, the human's must inevitably have collapsed, too. Wasn't that why this Elminster had pleaded for the fight to end? And now the human must think him helpless, and was standing there vainly trying to think of some way of slaying him with a rock or dagger without breaking his paralysis. Yes, if the spell was cast now, the human could not hope to stop it.

The 'call bones' spell had been developed by Napraeleon Echorn seven—or was it eight? he'd never paid all that much attention to his tutors—centuries ago, as a way of reducing giant stags to cartloads of ready meat. It could summon a particular assembly of bones to its caster, so that they tore their way right out of the victim's body. If the caster chose to receive the skull, the victim could not hope but die. Though Delmuth couldn't come up with a use, just this moment, for a blood-dripping human skull, there'd be plenty of time to think of one . . .

Smiling with his eyes, he cast the spell. *Elminster, your skull, please . . .*

He was still gloating—humming to himself, actually—when the world darkened and the brief, incredible pain began. He could not even shriek as red blood bubbled up into his mind and Faerûn went away forever.

* * * * *

Elminster winced as blood fountained. When the grisly, blood-drenched thing came hurtling at him, he used his shield like the warriors' object it was named for, deflecting the bony missile past him and off the peak, into empty air.

The last prince of Athalantar looked at the headless floating body one last time, shook his head sadly, and said the words that would take him back to the room at the heart of the haunted castle, and the Srinshee. He hoped she hadn't wakened and found him gone; he'd no desire to upset her unnecessarily.

The hawk-nosed young man took a step toward the nearest cliff, and vanished into thin air. The buzzards waiting in a tree nearby decided it was safe to dine now, and flapped clumsily aloft. Their long, slow glides would have to be aimed just right; it wasn't every day that the food was floating in midair.

* * * * *

"Gal," Athtar said patiently, as they struggled up the second sheer rockface in a row, "I know you're upset about your cache—gods above, half the *forest* knows it!—but we'll come back for them, really we will, and it isn't serving any useful purpose to—"

Something fast and round and the color of wet blood fell out of the sky and swept Athtar's face away.

The body in black leather, limbs wriggling and twitching, fell past Galan. The thing that had killed Athtar bounced off his chest on the way, rolling to a stop in a tangle of roots beside Galan's face.

He found himself staring into the sockets of an elf skull drowned in fresh blood—for the brief instant before he lost his hold on the crumbling ledge and found himself falling down, down into the darkness that had claimed Athtar.

* * * * *

Elminster took one step into the dark chamber, and saw that something was very wrong. The Srinshee was gone, and a young, naked elven girl was on her knees before a sprawled, ashen skeleton, sobbing uncontrollably. Had his friend caught fire?

The young girl looked up, face streaming, and sobbed, "Oh, Elminster!" As she reached for him, El rushed into her arms, embracing her. Gods look down—*this* was the Srinshee!

"Lady Oluevaera," he asked gently, as he stroked her hair and shoulders, cradling her to his breast, "what befell here?"

She shook her head, and managed to choke out the word, "Later."

El rocked her, murmuring wordless soothings, for some time before her weeping subsided, and she said, "Elminster? Forgive me, but I am exhausted, and in grave danger of failing Cormanthor for the first time in my life."

"Is there anything I can do?"

Oluevaera lifted her youthful face to meet his gaze. She still had those wise, sad old eyes, El noticed. "Yes," she whispered. "Go into danger once more. I cannot ask this; the peril is too great."

"Tell me," Elminster murmured. "I'm beginning to think hurling myself into danger is what Mystra sent me here to do."

The Srinshee tried to smile. Her lips trembled for a moment, and then she said, "You may well be right. I've seen Mystra, while you were gone." She raised a hand to forestall his questions, and said, "So you must stay alive to hear about it later. I've just power enough left to cast a body switch spell."

El's eyes narrowed. "To send me to where someone else stands, and him or her here."

The Srinshee nodded. "The Coronal attends a revel this night, and there is bound to be someone angry enough to try to slay him."

"Cast the spell," El told her firmly. "I'm down a few spells, but I'm ready."

"Will you?" she asked, and shook her head, impatiently brushing away fresh tears. "Oh, El . . . such honor . . ."

She sprang from his lap and ran quickly across the chamber. For the first time Elminster noticed that it was strewn with what looked to be wizards' scepters of power, and even a staff. The Srinshee bent and plucked one up.

"Take this with you," she said. "It has some little power left. One thing it can do is duplicate any spell you see cast by someone else while you are holding it. Handle it, and into your mind it'll whisper its powers."

Elminster took it and nodded. Impulsively she

threw her arms around his neck and kissed him. "Go with my good wishes—and, I know, Mystra's blessing, too."

El raised an eyebrow. Just what *had* happened here?

He was still wondering that as the Srinshee cast her spell, and blue mists whirled the world away again.

Ten

LOVE OFT ASTRAY

The love of an elf is a deep and precious thing. Misused
or spurned, it can be deadly. Realms have fallen and
been sundered for love, and proud elder houses swept
away. Some have said that an elf is the force of his or her
love, and all else just flesh and dross. It is certain that
elves can love humans, and humans love elves—but in
such meetings of the heart, sorrow is never far away.

Shalheira Talandren, High Elven Bard of Summerstar
from **Silver Blades And Summer Nights:**
An Informal But True History of Cormanthor
published in The Year of the Harp

The mists rolled away and Elminster was in a garden he'd never seen before, a place of many tall,
straight shadowtops soaring straight up like huge
black pillars from a manicured lawn of mosses adorned
with small mushroom plantings. High overhead, the
leaves of the trees blotted out the sun completely,
though El could see shafts of sunlight in the distance
where there must be clearings.

Here the only light came from spheres of luminous
air—globes that glowed faint blue, green, ruby-red, or gold
as they drifted softly and aimlessly through the trees.

Elves in ornate silken robes were strolling among
the shadowtops, laughing and chatting, and beneath

each luminous globe floated a tray that held an array of tall, thin bottles, and layered platters of delicacies; at a glance, El recognized oysters, mushrooms, and what looked to be forest grubs in a plum or apricot sauce.

There was also an elf standing very near, and looking very startled. An elf Elminster had seen before— one of the High Court Mages who'd been with the Coronal when Naeryndam had taken him to the palace.

"Well met," Elminster said to him, bowing politely. "Lord Earynspieir, is it not?"

The elven mage looked, if anything, more confused and alarmed than before. He nodded, "Earynspieir I am, human sir. Forgive me if I recall not your name, for I am in some anxiousness: where is the Coronal?"

Elminster spread his hands. "I know not. Was he standing a moment or so ago where I am now?"

The elf nodded, eyes narrowing. "He was."

El nodded. "Then that is as it's supposed to be. I am to attend this revel in his place."

Earynspieir scowled. "You are? And did you decide this yourself, young sir?"

"No," Elminster replied gently. "It was decided for me—for the security of the realm. I agreed to it, aye. By the way, the name's Elminster. Elminster Aumar, Prince of Athalantar . . . and, as ye know, Chosen of Mystra."

The elf mage's mouth tightened. His gaze descended to the scepter thrust through Elminster's belt and tightened still further, but he said nothing.

"Perhaps, Lord Mage, we could set aside thy feelings toward me for a moment or three," Elminster murmured, "while ye tell me where we're standing, and what is customary at an elven revel. I have no wish to give offense."

Earynspieir's eyes slid sideways to meet those of Elminster, and his lips curled in distaste. Then he seemed to come to a decision.

"Very well," he said, as softly. "Perhaps my natural reactions toward your kind have governed me over-much. The Coronal did tell me that 'twould be easier for us all if I regarded you as one of us—one of the People—visiting from a far realm, and wearing a human disguise. I shall assay this, young Elminster. Pray bear with me; I am unsettled just now for other reasons."

"And can ye speak of them to me?" Elminster asked softly.

The elf shot him a sharp glance, and then said shortly, "Let me speak with utter candor—a habit pop-ular with those of your race, I hear. Moreover, I doubt you know any loose-tongued Cormanthans to gossip with, which frees me to speak more plainly than I might otherwise do."

Elminster nodded. The elven mage looked around to make certain no one was within earshot, and then turned to the young prince and said bluntly, "Our Coronal's decision regarding you has not been popular. Many who hold the rank of armathor in the realm have come to the palace to renounce their rank, and break their blades before the Coronal. There has been open talk of deposing and even slaying him, of hunting you down, and of . . . general unpleasantness here this night, and elsewhere until he, ah, comes to his senses. My counterpart, the High Court Mage Ilimitar, has not returned from a visit to several of the elder Houses of the realm, and I know not his fate—or if treason is in-volved. I thought I held the Coronal's closest confi-dence, and yet, without word or warning, he vanishes from my side, and you appear, speaking guardedly of 'the security of the realm,' something I've had good reason to believe was entrusted to *me*. Despite the Coronal's earlier confidence in you, I see you as a human mage of unknown but probably great powers, who has a close relationship with a goddess of your race—and thus, whatever your motives, a great danger to Cormanthor, as you stand here at its heart. Do you see why I am less than gracious to you?"

"I do," Elminster replied, "and bear no ill will toward ye, Lord Mage—how could ye do otherwise, in these straits?"

"Precisely," Earynspieir said in a satisfied voice, almost smiling. "I fear I've misjudged your race, sir, and you with it—I never knew that humans cared about the intrigues and the . . . ah, graces and troubles of others. All we see and hear of you here is axes cutting down trees and swords impatiently settling even the slightest dispute."

" 'Tis true that some among us do favor the most swift and direct form of politics," Elminster agreed with a smile. "Yet I must hasten to remind ye and all others of Cormanthor that to judge humans of all lands as one alike mass is no more correct than to judge moon elves by the habits of the dark elven, or vice versa."

The elf beside him turned away and stiffened, eyes blazing, and then relaxed visibly and managed a short laugh. "Your point is taken, human sir—but I must remind *you* that folk of Cormanthor are unused to such boldly blunt speech, and may like it rather less than I do."

"Understood," El said. "My apologies. Someone approaches. Sorry: a pair of someones."

Earynspieir looked at El, startled by this sudden brevity, and then turned to see the elven couple the young human had indicated. They had glasses in their hands and were walking at a leisurely gait, arms linked, but their surprised expressions left no doubt that they were headed hence because of the unexpected sight of the human armathor there'd been so much talk about.

"Ah," Earynspieir said smoothly, "it lacks some hours yet until dusk, when the dancing and ah, less dignified revelries begin. Those who wish to speak candidly with each other or with the Coronal, or to choose new consorts for an evening, often arrive now, when revelers are few and rather less wine has been consumed than will be the case later; these are some such. Allow me to perform the introductions."

El inclined his head, every inch the polite prince, as the couple swept up to the High Court Mage. The young, handsome elven male stared at Elminster as though a forest boar had put on clothes and come to the revel, but the breathtakingly beautiful, gossamer-gowned elven maiden on his arm smiled charmingly at the elf mage and said, "Fair even, Revered Lord. We—ah, expected to see the Coronal with you. Is he indisposed?"

"Our Coronal Most High was called away on urgent business of the realm only a very short time ago. May I introduce to you instead Prince Elminster of the land of Athalantar, our newest armathor?"

The elven male went on staring at Elminster, and said nothing. His lady giggled uneasily and said, "An unexpected and—dare I say it?—unusual pleasure."

She did not extend her hand.

"Prince Elminster," the High Court Mage purred, "be at ease with Lord Qildor, of the House of Revven, and the Lady Aurae of House Shaeremae. May your meeting and parting be of equal pleasure."

Elminster bowed. "My honor is brightened," he said, recalling a phrase from the memories in the kiira. Three sets of elven eyebrows rose in astonished unison

at those words of ancient elven courtesy as the human
went on, "It is my desire to befriend—yet not alarm or
intrude upon—the folk of fair Cormanthor. To such a
one as myself, both the land and People of this fair
place are so beautiful as to be revered treasures we
honor from a distance."

"Does that mean you're not the first spysword of a
human army?" the Lord Qildor growled, hand going to
the ornate silver hilt of the sword he wore at his hip.

"That and more," Elminster replied mildly. "It is no
desire of my realm or any other land of men that I
know of to invade Cormanthor or intrude our ways
and trade where we are not wanted, and can only do
harm. My presence here is a personal matter, not an
unfolding affair of state or any harbinger of invasion
or prying exploration. No Cormanthan need fear me,
or see me as representing more than a lone human
who stands in just awe of thy People and their
accomplishments."

The Lord Qildor raised his eyebrow again. "Forgive
my forward speech," he said, "but would you permit a
mage to read the truth of your words?"

"I would, and will," El said, meeting his eyes
directly.

"If that is so," the elf said, "I have misjudged you before our meeting, purely on the speculations of others.
Yet, Lord Elminster, you should know that I—as most
of the People—fear and hate humans; to see one in the
heart of our realm is a source of alarm and disgust. I
do not know that any noble thing you can do, or fair
words you can speak, can ever change that. Have a
care for yourself here, sir; others will be less polite
than we. Perhaps it would have been better for us both
if you had never come to Cormanthor."

He fell silent for a moment, looking grave in his yellow silks, and then added slowly, "I wish I could find

fairer words for you, man, but I cannot. It is not in me
. . . and I have seen more humans than most."

He nodded a little sadly, and turned away. Gems
winked here and there among the hair that spilled
down his back, as long and as magnificent as that of
any highborn human woman. His lady, who had listened with eyes downcast, lifted her head proudly,
gave Elminster and the High Court Mage a shared
smile, and said, "It is as my lord says. Fare you well,
lords both."

When they'd drawn a safe distance away, and had
their covert looks back at the elf and the human standing together, Elminster turned to look Lord Earynspieir full in the face. "The folk of Cormanthor are
unused to boldly blunt speech, Lord?" he asked
smoothly, raising his own eyebrows. Earynspieir
winced.

"Please believe that I meant not to lead you astray,
lord sir," he replied. "It seems the sight of a human
awakens a spirit of bluntness in Cormanthans I've not
seen before."

"Fairly spoken," El granted, "and I—but who comes
here?"

Drifting through the trees toward them came two
elven ladies—literally drifting, their high-booted feet
inches off the ground. Both were tall for elves, and
sleekly curved, wearing gowns that showed off every
line of their strikingly beautiful bodies. Heads turned
as they wound their way through the revelers.

"Symrustar and Amaranthae Auglamyr, ladies and
cousins," the High Court Mage murmured smoothly,
and El thought he detected more than a little hunger
in Lord Earynspieir's tone. As well there might be.

The woman who led was stunning even among all
the elven maids El had seen since his arrival in the
city. Hair that was almost royal blue flowed freely over

her shoulders and down her back, only to be gathered in a silken sash that rode low on her right hip, as the tail of a horse is gathered to keep it from trailing along the ground. Her eyes were a bright, almost electric blue, flashing promises to Elminster under dark and archly raised eyebrows as she swept nearer. A black, unadorned ribbon encircled her throat, and her lips were full and slightly pouting; she ran her tongue openly over them as she surveyed the man standing beside the elven mage. The front of her crimson gown was cut away to show the design of a many-headed dragon worked in gems glued to her flat belly, slim waist, and cleavage; frozen flames of fine wire cupped and displayed her high breasts, and gold dust clung to the coyly-displayed tip of one of her ears. She was achingly beautiful—and knew it.

Her cousin wore a rather less revealing gown of dark blue, though one side of it was parted to above her waist to display a fine webwork of golden chains flowing down her bare, almost brown flank. She had flowing honey-blonde hair, startlingly brown eyes, and a far kinder smile than her blue-haired companion, as well as the most tanned skin and lush curves of any elf Elminster had ever seen. But her cousin outshone her beauty as a sun outblazes a night star.

"That is Symrustar in the lead," Earynspieir muttered. "She is heir of her House—and dangerous, sir; her honor consists solely of what she can get away with."

"You deeply prefer the Lady Amaranthae, do you not?" Elminster murmured back.

The High Court Mage turned his head sharply to regard Elminster with eyes that held both respect and a sharp warning. "You see keener than most elven elders, young lord," he hissed, as the ladies came upon them.

"Well met," the Lady Symrustar purred, tossing her hair aside with easy grace as she leaned forward to kiss Lord Earynspieir on the cheek. "You won't mind, wise old Lord, if I take your guest from you? I've— we've—a great hunger to learn more about humans; this is a rare opportunity."

"I . . . no, of course not, Lady." The elven mage put on a broad smile. "Ladies, may I present to you the lord Elminster of Athalantar? He is a prince in his own land, and newly—as I'm sure you've heard—an armathor of Cormanthor."

Earynspieir turned his head to regard El, a clear warning in his eyes, and continued, "Lord Elminster, it is my great pleasure to make known unto you two of the fairest flowers of our land: the Lady Symrustar, Heir of House Auglamyr, and her cousin, the Lady Amaranthae Auglamyr."

El bowed low, kissing the fingertips of the Lady Symrustar—an unaccustomed gesture, it seemed, from the appreciative purr she gave, and the hesitant way Amaranthae then extended her arm.

"The honor, ladies," he said, "is mine. But surely you cannot think to abandon the guardian of the realm just to talk to me? I am the allure of the unknown, 'tis true, but ladies, I confess I am overwhelmed by just one of ye, and have come to deeply appreciate the attentive wisdom of My Lord Earynspieir since our first meeting; he is a finer speaker than me, by far!"

Something leapt in the High Court Mage's eyes as Elminster spoke so earnestly, but he uttered not a sound as the Lady Symrustar laughed easily and said, "But of course Amaranthae will keep the mightiest mage of Cormanthor close and attentive company while we two talk, Lord Elminster. You are quite right in your estimation of his qualities, and one can accomplish far more face-to-face with just two faces thus engaged. You and Amaranthae can enjoy each other later. How splendidly swift-witted of you! Come, let us away!"

As she laced her fingers with his, Elminster turned to nod a polite farewell to the High Court Mage—whose face was unreadable—and to the Lady Amaranthae, who gave the human a look that was both deeply grateful and a mute warning to him about her cousin; El thanked her for both with a second nod and a smile.

"You seem attracted to my cousin, Lord Elminster," the Lady Symrustar purred in his ear, and El turned swiftly back to her, reminding himself that he was going to have to be very careful with this elven maid.

Very careful. As he turned, she did too, extending one slim leg around his so that they came together, breast to breast. Elminster felt the wire-girded points of her bosom low on his chest, and skin as smooth as silk brushing his breeches. She wore a black lace garter around that leg, and knee-high black boots of leather with spiked heels.

"My apologies for thrusting myself so into your path, Lord," she breathed, sounding completely unapologetic. "I fear I am unused to human company, and find myself quite . . . excited."

"No apology is necessary, fair Lady," El replied smoothly, "when no offense is taken." He glanced quickly back at the revel, and saw several curious faces turned in their direction, but no one moving toward them, or nearby.

"You must know how beautiful males of at least two races find you," he added, glancing ahead to ensure that the garden was similarly empty—and knowing that it almost certainly was; this lady planned things carefully—"but I must confess that I find splendid minds more intriguing than splendid bodies."

Lady Symrustar met his eyes. "Would you prefer I dropped the pretense of breathless excitement then,

Lord Elminster?" she asked softly. "Among the People, many males do not believe that their ladies really *have* minds."

Elminster crooked an eyebrow. "With your swift wit gliding through revel after revel to prove them different?"

She laughed, eyes flashing. "Blood to you," she acknowledged. "I think I'm going to enjoy this." She led him on through the garden, walking now, whatever magic had levitated her banished or exhausted. Her hips swayed with every step in a way that left Elminster's mouth dry; he kept his eyes firmly on her eyes and saw a little knowing twinkle growing in them. She knew full well what effect she was having on him.

"I spoke simple truth when first we met," she said, tossing that magnificent hair out of the way again, "I do want to learn all I can about humans. Will you oblige me? My questions may seem witless at times."

"Lady, allow me," El murmured, wondering when her attack would fall on him, and what form it would take. He was mildly surprised, as they walked deeper and deeper into the wild and empty depths of the garden and the last sunlight started to fade, just how thorough her questioning was, and genuine her interest seemed.

They came at last to a pale glow of moonlight in the trees ahead, talking earnestly of how elves dwelt in Cormanthor and humans lived in Athalantar. Symrustar led her exotic human to a stone bench that curved about a circular pool in the center of that clearing. Reflected stars glimmered in its depths as they sat down together in the pleasantly warm night air, and the bright moonlight touched Symrustar's smooth skin with ivory fingers.

Quite naturally and simply, as if this was something elven females always did when sitting on benches in the moonlight, she guided Elminster's hands within the wire breastworks of her gown. She was trembling.

"Tell me more of men," she murmured, her eyes very large now, and seemingly darker. "Tell me . . . how they love."

Elminster almost smiled as a memory flashed through his mind. In the library of a wizard's tomb lost in the High Forest there is a curious book that has no name. It is the diary of a nameless half-elven ranger of long ago, that tells of his thoughts and deeds, and the sorceress Myrjala had made Elminster read it to learn how elves regarded magic. On the subject of giving pleasure to elven maids, it mentioned using one's tongue gently on the palms of the hands and the tips of the ears.

El slipped one of his hands out of where she'd put it, let his fingertips trail down her belly, and then caught hold of her wrist.

"Hungrily," he replied, and bent his tongue to her open palm.

She gasped, trembling in earnest now, and he lifted his head out of long habit to look around.

Moonlight gleamed on a set and furious elven face. A male, there in the trees. El slid his other hand free. There was another, over there. And another. They sat at the heart of a silently closing ring.

"What is it, Lord Elminster?" the Lady Symrustar asked, almost sharply. "Am I—abhorrent in some way?"

"Lady," he replied, "we are about to be attacked." He put his hands on the scepter at his belt, but the elven maid rose and turned with swift, fluid grace, and looked into the trees.

"They'll charge us, now, in silence," she said calmly. "Hold to me, and I'll take us from this place!"

Elminster slipped an arm about her waist and

crouched low, scepter out and ready. She murmured something as the lithe shapes leapt at them out of the trees, and did something behind her that Elminster did not see. An instant later they were gone.

The elven warriors rolled and sprang, snarling in disappointment, blades slashing air that was now empty.

"What's this?" one of them hissed, pausing above the bench where the two figures had been entwined. A small obsidian figurine lay on it, rocking slightly. It was shaped like Symrustar Auglamyr, her hands at her sides, and bindings about her to keep them there. A cautious fingertip prodded it and found it still warm from the heat of someone's body.

"The human!" an elf hissed, raising his blade to smash the thing. "He was using dark magic to ensnare her!"

"Wait—destroy it not! It's clear proof of that!"

"To show to *whom?*" another elf snarled. "The Coronal? *He* brought this human viper into our midst, recall you?"

"True!" the first elf said. Two swords flashed down as one, shattering the tiny piece of obsidian so deftly that neither blade touched the bench beneath.

The explosion that followed tore apart bench, pool, and pave, and sent elven heads and limbs spattering through the trees.

* * * * *

Elminster straightened slowly. The garden they were in now held a circular bed, bathed in the moonlight, and a ring of trees. Far off in the distance lights twinkled through tree branches, but there were no buildings or watchful elves in sight.

"We're quite alone, Elminster," the Lady Symrustar

said softly. "Those jealous males can't follow us here, and my wards keep the inquisitive out of this end of the family gardens. Besides, what I bring to bed is entirely my own affair."

Her eyes flashed as she turned to him again. Somehow her gown had fallen away to her knees, leaving her body bare in the moonlight.

Elminster almost laughed again. Not at her, for she was so beautiful that he could barely control himself, but at his own quirky mind. *She has splendid shoulders*, it was reporting excitedly to him.

That's nice, he told it, and shoved all thought aside.

She stepped forward out of the spreading puddle of silk that had been her gown and came toward him, gems glittering in the moonlight as she moved.

She glided to a stop in front of him. He kissed her eyelids, and then her chin—but at her lips he found his way barred by two raised fingers. "Leave my mouth for last," she said from behind them. "For elves, that's particularly special."

He murmured a wordless assent and reached his head around to her ears. From the way she quivered in his arms, moaned, and stamped her feet, the book had been right.

He licked them gently, teasingly, not hurrying. They had a deliciously spicy taste. Symrustar moaned as El bent to his task, darting his tongue into them. Her fingers raked at his back, drawing blood through his shirt.

"Elminster," she hissed, and then said his name again, rolling it with her tongue as if it was a sacred thing to be chanted. "Prince of a distant land," she added, voice rising in sudden urgency, "show me what it is to know the love of a man."

Her unbound hair swirled around them, its tresses moving at her unspoken bidding, tearing at his clothing like dozens of small, insistent hands. They were circling each other as his shirt was tugged open, moving toward the bed.

Suddenly Symrustar moaned again and said, "I can wait *no longer*. My mouth—Elminster, kiss my mouth!"

Their lips met, and then their tongues. And El faced the attack he'd been expecting.

The bright sparks of a spell seemed to streak through his mind, with her will racing right behind them. Symrustar was seeking to control him, body and mind, to be her puppet, while she raked through his memories to learn all she could . . . especially human magic. El let her race and pierce and rummage while he read what *he* wanted in her bared, open thoughts.

Gods, but she was a ruthless, evil creature. He saw a little obsidian statuette she'd prepared, and how he'd been blamed for what befell. He saw her tresses coiling up to encircle his throat right now, to throttle him if he tried to use any weapon against her. He saw her schemes to entrap any number of elves at court, from the Coronal to a certain rival and suitor, Elandorr Waelvor, to High Court Mage Earynspieir—the other court mage was already hers, ensnared and manipulated, sent to attack someone she dared not go up against: the Srinshee!

Elminster almost struck her then, knowing that with a simple spell he'd have power enough to break her neck like a twig, hair or no hair. Instead he rode the bright flare of his rage into an iron hold on her mind, clamping down until she screamed soundlessly in shock and horror. He cut off her sight into his own memories with brutal haste, leaving her blinded and dazed, and held her that way as he reached out with the power of the scepter her tresses had so deftly plucked away from him, and duplicated the body switch spell the Srinshee had worked on him earlier.

Then he charged back into her mind, overwhelming all semblance of reserve and control she had left, and forcing her mind to stay open and vulnerable, her schemes, memories, and thoughts bared to anyone who touched her. El brought her back to the peak of lust, aching with need. Then he worked the spell, taking himself to where Elandorr Waelvor stood languidly, glass in hand, in the midst of revelry. He whisked the elf back to the hidden bower, thrusting him into Symrustar's arms, his lips to hers, and her mind, with all its treacheries and plans for *him*, bared to him.

El had a last glimpse of her wild eyes staring at Elandorr as she realized who he was and what he was seeing in her mind as she kissed him, nude and two swift paces from her bed. As both elves stiffened and moaned in horror, their mouths and minds mated and open to each other, Elminster broke contact.

He was standing in a softly lit space where Elandorr had been, in the midst of a handful of very startled elves. Others, who wore only bells on their limbs, were dancing in the air overhead, laughing softly. Glasses of wine were soaring up to them like eager wasps, from trays floating in the midst of a group of jaded, bored elves in finery who'd been chatting about the decay of the realm in general—until his sudden appearance.

"You recall Mythanthar's crazy schemes of 'mythals' to shield us all? Why, ther—"

"When *I* was a youth, we didn't indulge in such outrageous displ—"

"Well, what does she expect? Not every young armathor of the realm ca—"

Silence fell as if every throat there had been cut by the same slash of a sword, and all eyes turned to look at one tall figure in their midst.

El faced them, a human male with his clothes in disarray and a scepter in his hand. He was breathing heavily, and there was a trickle of blood at the corner of his mouth where Symrustar had bitten it.

Elves were staring into his eyes in shock and angry recognition. "What did you do to Elandorr?"

"He's slain Elandorr!"

"Blew him to nothingness—just as he did Arandron and Inchel and the others by the pool!"

" 'Ware, all! The human *murderer* is among us!"

"Kill him! Kill him now, before he gets more of us!"

"For the honor of House Waelvor!"

"Slay the human dog!"

Swords were flashing out on all sides, or being magically summoned from distant scabbards and chambers to settle into their owner's hands amid spell glows; El spun around and cried out in a loud, deep voice, "Elandorr lives—I've sent him to confront the murderess who slew everyone by the pool!"

"Hear the human!" sneered one elf, blade glittering in his hand. "He must think us elven folk simple indeed, to believe such a claim!"

"I am innocent," Elminster roared, and triggered the scepter. Bright fire burst forth in a ring around him, striking aside blades and hurling their owners back.

"He has a court scepter! Thief!"

"He must've murdered one of the mages to get it! *Kill the human!*"

El shrugged and used the only spell he could, vanishing an instant before half a dozen hurled blades flashed through the spot where he'd stood.

Into the sudden silence, before the groans of disappointment started, one old elf said clearly, "In *my* time, younglings, we held *trials* before we drew our blades! A simple mindtouch will reveal the truth! If we find him guilty, then will be the time for blades!"

"Fall silent, father," another voice snapped. "We've heard quite enough of how things should be done, or were done in the old dawn days. Cannot you see that the human is guilty?"

"Ivran Selorn," another old voice said in outraged tones, "to think that the day would come when I'd hear you speak to your sire like that! Are you not ashamed?"

"No," Ivran said almost savagely, holding up his sword. Its blade glimmered in the spell light, displaying the scrap of cloth transfixed on it. "We have the human," he said in triumph, holding it high for all present to see. "With this, my magic can trace him. We'll hunt him down before sunrise."

Eleven

TO HUNT A HUMAN

There is no beast more dangerous to hunt than a man forewarned—save one: a human mage forewarned.

Antarn the Sage
from **The High History of Faerûnian Archmages Mighty**
published circa The Year of the Staff

He found himself standing in utter darkness, but it was darkness that *smelled* right. It was dank, and there was open space all around. He did something with his mind, and the scepter in his hand blossomed into a soft green radiance.

The chamber at the heart of Castle Dlardrageth was empty. Only an area of cracked and melted rubble—he'd have to ask the Lady Oluevaera about that when the chance befell—remained to show that he and the Srinshee had been here. She'd taken the Coronal elsewhere.

Something flashed in the gloom above him and moaned softly past, swooping toward the far end of the room. El smiled. Hello, ghosts.

He changed the light of the scepter to the purple-white glow that outlined magic. There! She *had* left it!

Invisible inside three nested spheres of magical concealment, floating in the air just low enough for him to reach, a little way along one wall, hung his spellbook. El smiled, said "Oluevaera" aloud as he touched the outermost sphere, and watched it melt silently away. The second descended to his hand, and he spoke the Srinshee's real name again—and a third time. When the last sphere melted away, the book fell into his hands.

El made the scepter glow green again, thrust it between two stones of the wall as high as he could reach, and sat down under its radiance to study his spells. If he was going to be hunted by every bloodthirsty young blood of Cormanthor, 'twas best to have a full roster of ready magic to call upon.

* * * * *

"Tidings grow worse, Revered Lord." Uldreiyn Starym's voice was grave.

Lord Eltargrim looked up. "And how might they do that?" he asked quietly. "Sixty-three blades were broken before me today." His lips tightened in what might have been the wry beginnings of a smile. "That I know of, thus far."

The burly senior archmage of the Starym family ran a weary hand through his thinning white hair and replied, "Word comes from the Hallows that the human armathor has worked deadly magic there, causing a blast that destroyed the Narnpool and at least a dozen young lords and warriors who were gathered there. Moreover, the Lady Symrustar and the Lord Elandorr have both vanished, and the heir of House Waelvor was snatched by spells out of the midst of folk he was speaking with, to be replaced upon the instant by the human—who protested his innocence but was wielding a court scepter. When menaced by the swords of some of the revelers he teleported away. None know where he is now, but some of the warriors are hunting him with magic."

In the shadows around the table a light-haired head snapped up, eyes catching fire. "My cousin was with the Lord Elminster. They were strolling together when they left us!"

"Gently," the High Court Mage Earynspieir said from beside Amaranthae, putting a soothing hand on her arm. "They could well have parted before these troubles began."

"I know Symma," she said, turning to him, "and she planned to—to . . ." She blushed and looked away, biting her lip.

"To take the human lord to bed, in the private part of the Auglamyr gardens?" the Srinshee asked quietly. Amaranthae stiffened, and the tiny sorceress added gently, "Don't bother to act scandalized, girl: half Cormanthor knows about her career."

"We also know something of the power of Symrustar's magic," Naeryndam Alastrarra said thoughtfully. "In fact, probably far more than she desires we know or suspect. I doubt the human lord has spells enough to do her harm, if they were in her bower, with all the magic she can call to hand there. If the hunt mounted by these young fire brains leads them hence, *they* might be in danger."

Amaranthae turned her head to look at the old mage, white to the lips. "Do you elders know *everything?*"

"Enough to keep ourselves entertained," the Srinshee said dryly, and Uldreiyn Starym nodded.

" 'Tis a common mistake of the young and vigorous," he calmly told the tabletop, "to believe their elders have forgotten to see, or think, or remember things— when what we've really forgotten to do is scare younglings into respecting us, thoroughly and often."

The Lady Amaranthae moaned aloud, anxious and miserable. "Symma could be dead," she whispered, an instant before the High Court Mage gathered her in his arms and said soothingly, "We shall go to the gardens now, to see for ourselves."

"Yet if she's unharmed, she'll be *furious* at our intrusion," Amaranthae protested.

The Coronal looked up. "Tell her the Coronal ordered you to check on her safety, and let her bring her fury to *me*." He smiled a little sadly and added, "Where she's likely to become lost in the crowd of clamoring complainants."

Lord Earynspieir silently thanked the old ruler with his eyes as he rose and led the distraught Lady Auglamyr away.

Lord Starym said heavily, "The murders done by the human in our midst—or perceived by most Cormanthans to be done by him, which at present holds out to us the same trouble—imperils your plan, Revered Lord, to open the city to other races. You know, Lord, as few can, how deeply my sister Ildilyntra felt against this Opening. We of House Starym still oppose it. By all of our gods, I beseech you, don't drive us into doing so with force."

"Lord Uldreiyn, I respect your counsel," the Coronal said softly, "as I have always done. You are the senior archmage of your House, one of the mightiest sorcerers in all Faerûn. Yet does that make you mighty enough to withstand the swarming vigor of the most greed-goaded humans, whose magic grows apace with each passing year? I still believe—and I urge you to think long and hard upon this, to see if you really can seize to, and hold, any other conclusion—that we must deal with humankind on our terms now, or be overwhelmed and slaughtered by men storming our gates in a century or so."

"I shall think upon this," the Starym archmage said, bowing his head, "again. Yet I have done so before, and not reached the same conclusion as you did. Can it not be that a Coronal might be mistaken?"

"Of course I can be wrong," Eltargrim said with a sigh. "I've been wrong many times before. Yet I know more of the world beyond our forest than any other Cormanthan—save this young human lad, of course. I see forces stirring that to most senior Cormyth, as well as to our youth, seem mere fancies. How often in the past few moons have I heard voices at court saying, 'Oh, but humans could never do *that!*' What do they think humans are, lumps of stone? From time to time men hold something they call a magefair—"

"*Selling* magic? Like a sort of bazaar?" The Starym's lips curled in disbelief and distaste.

"More like a House-gathering attended by many mages: humans, gnomes, halfbloods, and even elves from other lands than ours," the Coronal explained, "though I believe some scrolls and rare magical components do change hands. But the burden of my song is this: at the last magefair I saw, in my days as a far-wandering warrior, two human wizards engaged in a duel. The spells they hurled fell far short of our High Magic, 'tis true. But they would also have awed and shamed most sorcerers of Cormanthor! 'Tis *always* a mistake to dismiss humans."

"All those of House Alastrarra would, I believe, support you on that," Naeryndam put in. "The human Elminster wore the kiira more ably than our heir has yet managed to. I mean no slur upon Ornthalas, who will grow to command it, I'm sure, as ably as did Iymbryl before him . . . merely that the human was swiftly capable."

"Too capable, if all these reports of deaths are true," Uldreiyn murmured. "Very well, we shall continue to disagree ami—"

The tabletop glowed with a sudden, sparkling radiance that was laced with the soft, calling notes of a distant horn. Lord Starym stared down at it.

"My herald approaches," the Coronal explained. "When wards are raised, her passage awakens such a warning."

The Starym archmage frowned. " 'Her'?" he asked. "But sur—"

The door of the chamber opened by itself, admitting a cloud of swirling flames of the palest green and white. It rose and thinned as Lord Uldreiyn stared at it, dwindling swiftly into a flickering death to reveal at its heart an elven lady who wore a helm and a mottled gray cloak. "Hail, great Coronal," she said in greeting.

"What news, Lady Herald?"

"The heir of House Echorn has been found dead atop Druindar's Rock—slain in spell-battle, 'tis thought," the herald said gravely. "House Echorn beseeches you to allow them vengeance."

The Coronal's lips thinned. "On whom?"

"The human armathor Elminster of Athalantar, slayer of Delmuth Echorn."

The Coronal slapped the table. "He's a lone human, not an elemental whirlwind! How could he deal death in the backlands and in the Hallows, too?"

"Perhaps," Lord Uldreiyn told the tabletop, "being a human, he's swiftly capable."

As Naeryndam Alastrarra gave him a disgusted look, the Srinshee surprised them all by saying, "Delmuth's own spell slew him. I farscryed the fray; he lured Elminster from his studies and sought to slay the human, who worked a magic that returned Delmuth's attacks upon his own head. Knowing this, the Echorn made the mistake of trusting in his own mantle, and proceeded with his attack. Elminster pleaded with him to make peace, but was rebuffed. There is no fault to avenge; Delmuth died through Delmuth's scheme and Delmuth's hurled spell."

"An unheralded human? Defeat an heir of one of the oldest Houses of the realm?" Uldreiyn Starym was clearly shocked. He stared at the Srinshee in disbelief, but when she merely shrugged, he shook his head and said finally, "All the more reason to stop human intrusions now."

"What answer shall I take back to House Echorn?" the herald asked.

"That Delmuth was responsible for his own death," the Coronal replied, "and that this has been attested to by a senior archmage of the realm, but that I shall investigate further."

The Lady Herald went to one knee, called up her whirling flames about herself once more, and went out.

"When you do catch this Elminster, his brains may run like wax merely from all the truth-scrying," Lord Uldreiyn observed.

"If the young bloods leave us enough of him to do *anything* with," Naeryndam replied.

The Starym smiled and shrugged. "When," he asked the Coronal, "did you acquire a Lady Herald? I thought Mlartlar was herald of Cormanthor."

"He was," the Coronal said grimly, "until he thought himself a better swordsman than his Coronal. Your House is not the only one opposed to my plan of Opening, Lord Starym."

"So where did you find *her?*" Uldreiyn asked quietly. "With all due respect, the office of herald has always been held by one of the senior families of the realm."

"The herald of Cormanthor," the Srinshee told Uldreiyn's favorite spot on the tabletop, "must bear foremost loyalty to the Coronal—a quality unattainable today, it seems, in the three Houses who hold themselves to be senior in the realm."

"I resent that," the Lord Starym said softly, his face going pale.

"Three of the People were approached," the Srinshee told him firmly. "Two declined, one very rudely. The third—Glarald, of your House, Lord—accepted, and was tested. What we found in his mind is a matter between himself and us, but when he knew we'd learned it, he tried to strike down myself and Lord Earynspieir with spells."

"*Glarald?*" Uldreiyn Starym's voice was flat with disbelief.

"Yes, Uldreiyn: Glarald of the easy smiles. Do you know how he hoped to defeat us and deceive us in the first place? He took one of the forbidden enchantments from the tomb of Felaern Starym, and altered it to control not merely wands and scepters from afar—such as your own storm scepter, which I'm afraid was destroyed in our dispute—but minds. The minds of two unicorns and one young sorceress of House Dree."

Lord Starym's face was ashen now. "I—I can scarce believe . . . his beloved, Alais?"

"I doubt his affections for her ran all that deep," the Srinshee told him dryly, "but he did dally with her long enough to work a blood spell—another forbidden magic, of course—and so enthrall her to cast spells at his bidding. The Lady Aubaudameira Dree, or 'Alais,' as you know her, attacked the Lord Earynspieir in the midst of our investigation."

The Starym lord shook his head in dumbfounded disbelief. The Coronal and Naeryndam both nodded silent confirmation of the words of the sorceress.

"Her spells were formidable," the Srinshee continued. "Our High Court Mage owes his life to my magic. As does Glarald, for Alais wasn't pleased with him after I broke his thrall. 'Twas the unicorns that did it; once my spells shook him, he couldn't control their restive natures, and his entire linkage collapsed. So it was that the Coronal gained a new Lady Herald."

"That was Alais?" Lord Uldreiyn breathed, shaking his head and gesturing at the door whence the Herald had departed. "But she was much more—ah . . ."

"Lushly curved than our Lady Herald?" the Srinshee finished his question crisply. "Indeed. You saw her when she was already in thrall, and had been forced to change her body to please Glarald's tastes."

The Starym lord closed his eyes and shook his head again, as if to will away this unwelcome news. "Does Glarald yet live?" he asked slowly.

"He does," the Coronal said gravely. "Though wounded deeply in his wits. The unicorns were not gentle, and he seized upon one of the scepters when his control was already failing, and sought to turn it on them; they hurled its effects back upon him. He is currently in hiding, wrestling with his shame, at Thurdan's Tree at the southern edge of the realm."

"But you've not told me of this!" Lord Uldreiyn snapped. "Wh—"

"Hold!" the Srinshee snapped, just as fiercely. His mouth dropped open in surprise.

"I've had quite enough, Lord," she told him in controlled tones, "of the great Houses of the realm snarling about their rights—in this case, privacy of minds and of the doings of their individuals—whenever Coronal or Court require something of them . . . and then expecting us to break those rights whenever it personally suits them. So we are not to pry into your doings, my lord, or those of your warriors or steeds or cats—but we are to reveal the doings of another of your House to you? He's not your son or heir, and if he chooses not to confide in you himself, that—as you and speakers from House Echorn and House Waelvor have so cuttingly reminded us, on several occasions—is none of *our* affair."

Uldreiyn sat staring at her, stunned.

"You," the Srinshee went on, "have been almost panting to ask me about the disappearance of my wrinkles since first we met this even, and cudgeling your wits for a way to politely slide a query into our converse, so that you don't have to ask me directly. You know it is none of your affair. You respect the rule, and expect us to respect it, too, until our observance inconveniences you, whereupon you demand we break it. And yet you wonder why the Court regards the three senior Houses in particular, and all of the important Houses en masse, as foes."

The Starym lord blinked at her, sighed, and sat back. "I-I cannot discount your words, nor parry them," he said heavily. "In this, we are guilty."

"As for Glarald's schemes—in particular, his ambitious, creative, and wholly forbidden use of magic," the Srinshee went on inexorably, "this is the sort of thing our young bloods are up to, My Lord Uldreiyn, while you and your kith sit around decrying our dreams of Opening, and clinging to false notions of the purity and noble nature of our People."

"Do you want to be toppled from within, great Lord, or stormed from without?" Naeryndam Alastrarra asked mildly, tracing a circle on the part of the tabletop that had listened so attentively to Uldreiyn earlier.

The Lord Starym glared at him, but then sighed and said, "I'm almost convinced, listening to you three, that the elder Houses of the realm are its chief villains and peril. Almost. The fact remains that you, Revered Lord, allowed a human into our midst, here in the very heart of the realm—and since his arrival we have seen death upon death in a wave of violence unmatched since the last orc horde was foolish enough to test our borders. What are you going to do about it before there are *more* deaths?"

"There is almost nothing I can do before more

deaths occur," the Coronal told him sadly. "The fire brains who were at the revel when Elandorr disappeared are hunting the human as we speak. If they find him, *someone* will find death, too."

"And that death will, I fear, be laid at your door," said Uldreiyn Starym. "With the others."

Eltargrim nodded. "That, my lord," he said wearily, "is what it means to be Coronal of Cormanthor. Sometimes I think the elder Houses of the realm forget that."

* * * * *

One of the elves came to a halt so swiftly that his flowing hair swung out in front of him like two tusks. "That's the Ghost Castle of Dlardrageth!"

"And so?" Ivran Selorn asked coolly. "Afraid of ghosts, are we?"

Yet they had stopped, and some of the young bloods were looking at Ivran uneasily.

"My sire told me it bears a terrible curse," Tlannatar Wrathtree said reluctantly, "bringing ill luck—and miscast magics—upon any who enter."

"The ghosts that lurk there," another elf put in, "can claw you no matter what blade or spell you use against them."

"What utter leaf-rotting lies!" Ivran laughed. "Why, Ylyndar Starscatter brought his ladies here for loving six summers running. Who'd do that if the ghosts were a bother?"

"Aye, but Ylyndar's one of the most wild-witted mages in all Cormanthor! He even believes in old Mythanthar's mythals! And didn't one of his ladies try to eat her own hand?"

Ivran made a rude sound. "As if that has anything to do with yon castle!" He laughed again, tossed his blade in the air and caught it, and added, "Well, you weak-knees can please yourselves, but I'm going to cut me a little human into pieces I can present to His High Fool-wits the Coronal, and House Waelvor, and hang up in the Selorn trophy lodge!"

He set off at a run again, waving his sword around his head and hooting. After a few moments of uncertain hesitation, Tlannator followed, and two others trotted off on his heels. Another pair of elves looked at each other, shrugged, and followed more cautiously. That left three. They exchanged looks, shrugged, and followed.

* * * * *

Elminster looked up sharply. A metal sword blade ringing off stone has a particular sound. Distinctive enough to make a hunted human rise, close his spell-book, and stand listening intently. Then he smiled. One elf hissing curses at another has a distinctive sound too.

He tried to remember what the Srinshee had told him about the layout of this place. The castle was . . . nothing, beyond the news that this chamber was 'at its heart.' Hmm. The elves hunting him could be three breaths away, or an hour's hard climbing and peering. That they were hunting him was certain; why else would one of them want another to keep quiet?

El stood there, spellbook under his arm, thinking hard. He could translocate away—once—by calling on the scepter, but he hadn't had a chance to regain his own teleport spell yet. The only place in Cormanthor he could think of to go was the Vault of Ages, and who knew what defenses it would have to prevent thieves just teleporting in and out? To hide would be best. The more blood that ended up on his hands, the harder for his friends here to stay his friends, to let him stay, and to carry out whatever work Mystra had planned for him. Agile, alert elves, however, weren't the easiest folk to hide from. Mystra had given him one slaying spell, not a dozen. He'd have to plunge into the midst of a roused and ready band of human-hunters, to touch one and slay.

A ghostly form swooped past him, trailing a faint echoing sound that might have been wild laughter, and the last prince of Athalantar grinned suddenly. Of course! Take ghost form!

He took two quick steps to see where the ghost disappeared to this time, and was rewarded: high up on one wall was a crevice. Far too small for him, but not too small for a spellbook.

If he cast the spell as Myrjala had shown him, he could shift back and forth between solid and wraithlike form for brief periods—becoming his solid, normal self for no more than nine breaths at a time, or less. Longer would break the spell, and his fourth time becoming solid would also end the magic.

El became a flitting shadow and soared aloft. As he rose to the crevice, there came a scuffing sound from somewhere nearby, as if a boot had slipped on rock. Evidently he hadn't any time to waste.

Something dark but pale-faced rushed out of the gloom at him, seemingly enraged. El almost tumbled and fell in fright, but then ducked aside. The ghost looped once, impressively, then scudded on out of sight around a corner, heading for other rooms. Evidently the Dlardrageth ghosts liked wraithlike intruders even less than solid mortals.

Reaching the crevice, El drifted inside. It opened into a small, cramped room—the remnants of a much larger chamber whose roof had long ago collapsed. There were bones under the rubble here, elven bones,

and El doubted the ghosts would leave him alone if he
took up residence in here for long. Still, he hadn't
much choice. As he peered around, the air seemed to
fill with a faint purplish haze. What was it? Magic,
aye, but what?

Whatever it was, he felt no different, and was still a
weightless flying shadow. He drifted to the other end
of the little room.

Beyond its far wall, through the socket holes that
had once held beams, a ghost could reach another huge
chamber—this one open to the sky, and holding the
first cautious elf, scrambling in over some rubble with
sword raised. Ivran Selorn, if El's memory served him
rightly; a blood-hungry youngling.

There was a jagged hole at one end of the collapsed
room through which he could plunge, if he felt like
dying on broken stones below. Through it, El could
see the route that linked the open chamber where
Ivran was, and the room where he'd been studying.
The hole opened onto a cascade of rubble that spilled
down into a round room once at the base of a now-
fallen tower. A passage ran out of Ivran's room into
an antechamber, and thence through the tower room.
From there a narrow, rubble-choked passage linked
up with the room El's spellbook still lay in. The route
was not a long one, and Ivran—bold and eager—was
moving swiftly.

That left a certain Athalantan boy very little time.
El went to his knees in the room with the bones,
turned solid, and yanked down his breeches.

His one legacy of his thieving days was what he always wore under his clothes: a long, thin waxed black
cord, wound round and round his midriff. He uncoiled
it now and hurled most of it out the crevice, tying its
other end to the splintered end of a ceiling beam in the
little room with the bones. Holding his breeches up

with one hand, El became a wraith again, and returned to his spellbook.

As he became solid and hastily tied the free end of the cord around and around the book, the stealthy sounds coming along the passages told him that Ivran and the other searchers were already entering the tower room: a few paces in the right direction and they'd be able to see him here, feverishly tying a length of cord around a book with his pants around his ankles.

He became a wraith again and almost leapt into the air, soaring up and into the crevice just as fast as he could fly.

Back in the room with the bones, El turned solid once more and hauled on his cord, gasping in his haste. He didn't have long to work before he'd break the magic, so the moment the spellbook was safely up in the crevice, the dust of its passage still drifting out from the wall in a betraying cloud, he had his breeches belted and was a ghostly shadow again, leaving the book and the tangle of cord to deal with later.

As a thing of gray emptiness, he peered out of the crevice. Ivran was just entering the chamber where he'd been studying. The elf had noticed the dust drifting down. El pulled in his shadowy head hastily before any elf might look up and see him, and floated in the darkness, trying to think what to do next. The elves would probably determine that, of course, by what they did.

A moment later, El was spinning in the collapsed room, shaking and chilled, and the ghost that had caused his upset by rushing through him—the *real* ghost—was moaning its way back down into the chamber full of elves.

There were shouts from below, and the flash of a spell. El smiled grimly and set forth from the beam holes into the other chamber, to drift around the castle and learn just what he was facing.

His discoveries were not heartening. The castle was an impressive ruin, but it was still a ruin. The only unblocked well was in the tower room he'd seen already. No less than nine elves, with swords drawn and an unknown number of spells up their sleeves, were prowling through the once-splendid fortress of the Dlardrageth. At least three ghosts were following them like shadowy bats, ducking and diving but unable to do any real harm.

The real problem, however, were the four elven mages sitting together on a hill not far from the ruin, and the mighty glamer they'd cast over the entire area. It was the source of the haze that had appeared when he'd entered the little room, and the castle was now completely surrounded by it.

El drifted back inside, sought the little room, and turned solid again. His shoulder-blades settled into hard rubble, and he sighed as quietly as he could; his ghost form was gone for good now.

Drawing the scepter from his belt, he thrust it up into the air, and cautiously awakened its powers. The tingling that ran along his fingers told him that the elves were using magic that could detect any use of the scepter—something a shout from somewhere below underscored immediately—but the scepter did what he needed it to do. In storing a duplicate of the purplish field enveloping the castle, it told El what the glamer was: a ward field that would twist a teleport spell or any other translocational magic into ravaging fire *inside* the body of the teleport-spell caster.

He was trapped in the castle unless he could slip out on foot or memorize another ghost-shape spell—or *fight* his way out on foot, through all those eager elven swordsmen, to run straight into the waiting spells of those four mages. All of them were ready for the elusive human to appear, eager to destroy him.

El considered what to do next. The scepter was off and in his belt again, and he was lying on his back in near-darkness, amid rubble, crumbling elven bones, and the tangles of a cord tied to his spellbook, with the sagging wreckage of a collapsed ceiling inches from his nose. The exploring elves were back in the room he'd been studying in just below him, now, speculating aloud about where he might be hiding, and stirring around with their blades in the rubble. The use of the scepter had told them he was very near; soon enough they'd think of digging . . . or climbing.

"Mystra," Elminster breathed, closing his eyes, "aid me now. There are too many of them, too much magic; if I seek battle now, many will die. What should I do? Guide me, Great Lady of Mysteries, that I set no foot wrong in this journey to serve ye."

Was it his imagination, or was he floating now, rising an inch or so above the rubble? His prayer seemed to be rolling out into vast, dark distances in his mind— and something black seemed to be coming back to him out of that void, spinning end over end as it approached. Something smooth, glossy, and small, tumbling—the kiira! The lore-gem of House Alastrarra!

Wasn't it firmly on the brow of Ornthalas Alastrarra right now? It raced right at him, growing to impossible size, enveloping him. He was spiraling around its dark interior, now, racing along the inside of its curves. This must be his memory of the kiira, with its sea of memories.

Oh dear Mystra, preserve me! That thought made him see a rushing wave of chaos—ghostly and imperfect, mind-echoes of what he recalled from the gem now torn from him, but plunging at him all the same. He tried to turn and run, but no matter how hard he

struggled, everywhere he ran was *toward* the rushing
wave of memories. It was almost upon him—it broke
over him!

"That babbling—that's human talk! He must be up
there somewhere!" The words were elvish; deep, booming echoes that seemed to come from all around him.

In the shrieking, blinding chaos that followed those
deafening words Elminster Aumar spat blood from
nose and mouth and eyes and ears, and went down,
drifting, into dark oblivion . . .

Twelve

THE STAG AT BAY

The most dangerous moment in the hunt is when the stag turns, at bay, to trade his life for as many hunters as he can. Elven magic customarily turns such moments into mere glimpses of magnificent futility. But what would such moments be, I wonder, if the stag had strong magic, too?

Shalheira Talandren, High Elven Bard of Summerstar
from **Silver Blades And Summer Nights:
An Informal But True History of Cormanthor**
published in The Year of the Harp

"It's coming for me! *Blast* it!"

The voice was elven and terrified; it drew Elminster up out of floating darkness soaked in sweat, to find himself still lying in the little room with the elven bones.

There was a roar of flame off to his right, and a stabbing tongue of fire licked the collapsed ceiling above his nose for one scorching moment. El narrowed his eyes to slits, trying to see; one side of his face felt blistered.

When he trusted his sight again, he looked in that direction. The fire was gone. Three soft globes of radiance were drifting beyond the crevice, high in the air of the room where he'd been studying. By their light he could see the elf who'd cried out. He was standing on empty air, sword in hand, near his crevice. Levitating, not flying freely. Swooping around him, just out of reach of his vainly slashing and stabbing blade, was one of the Dlardrageth ghosts; the fire spell hurled from below had failed to destroy it.

If common or easily crafted spells could fell the ghostly remnants of House Dlardrageth, of course, they'd have all been destroyed long ago, and some ambitious fledgling House would be dwelling in this castle now. There was little chance any of the young elves here today had the power to destroy a Dlardrageth ghost.

On the other hand, the swooping, flitting ghost could probably do little more than frighten living elves—and one of those elves was within easy distance of hurling a deadly spell at Elminster, even if the opening between them was too small to allow any elf to enter.

El reached out and cautiously, quietly picked up his spellbook. He'd just have to drag the tangle of cord attached to it around with him for now, as he crept as far along this room as he could, away from the crevice.

Though he felt like he'd been torn apart and been put back together again, piece by agonizing piece, Mystra had come to his aid. She'd dragged him through a thousand tangled Alastrarran half-memories to what his mage's mind had remembered clearly, at the very depths of his recall: the spells the lore-gem had held.

There'd been one he'd dared not use; its price was too high. Empowering it would strip three of the most powerful spells from his memory and drain something from the scepter as well . . . but now it was needful he do so.

With a sigh, Elminster did what had to be done, shuddering silently as sparks seemed to wash and flow through his mind, stripping spells away. Thankfully, he did not have to awaken the scepter again to drain power from it. When the new spell shone bright and ready within him, El found the deepest niche he could, in a far corner of the collapsed room, and wedged his precious spellbook into it. Taking the cord he'd stripped from his tome, he checked that its other end was still secure about the splintered stub of the ceiling beam, tossed its coils down the cascade of stones into the tower room, and slipped down it as quietly as he could.

Inevitably stones rolled and bounced, but the levitating elf was snarling so much in his battle with the ghost that no one heard the little clatterings. El reached the bottom, rolled up cord until he had a substantial bundle, tied it to itself to keep the mass together, and threw the thing back up the fallen rocks as high and far as he could, hoping it'd not be seen.

Well, not without someone flying, or a very bright light, he judged, studying it. Drawing a deep breath, he started his first casting: a simple shielding, like he'd used against Delmuth. It was time to face Ivran's merry band of blood hunters.

His casting warned the elves that magic was being unleashed, of course, and there was an immediate, excited roar from the room they'd been searching. They'd be coming along the narrow passage soon; it was time to greet them.

Elminster showed himself at the mouth of that passage just long enough to make sure of one thing: the levitating elf wasn't trying to find any ceiling route anywhere, but was descending as fast as he could. Good. El gave the foremost elf a merry wave, and waited.

"He waved at me!" that elf said anxiously, and stopped.

The one behind him—Tlannatar Wrathtree, as it happened—gave him a nudge with the flat of his sword, and snarled, "Go on!"

The elf hesitated. El gave him a grin that must have showed every tooth he possessed, and made an almost amorous beckoning gesture.

The elf stopped, and started to scramble back. "He—"

"I don't *care!*" Ivran barked, from the room behind. "I don't care if he's grown dwarven-dunged gossamer wings! *Move!*"

"Go on!" Tlannatar added, giving another shove with his sword. He did not use the flat this time.

The less-than-brave elf shrieked and stumbled hastily ahead. El took one last glance down that passage—it was *so* tempting to hurl a lightning bolt now, but one of them was sure to have a mantle that would reflect such things—and backed away. He went across the tower room to its other passage, to stand within its opening. Almost none of these noble Cormanthans seemed to have bows; they left that weapon to their common warriors, thank Mystra. Or Corellon. Or Solonor Thelandira, the hunting god. Or whomever.

Still, he'd have to time this perfectly; he'd committed himself now, and would only get one chance. He waited, smiling grimly, for Tlannatar as well as the fearful elf in the lead to scramble out into the tower room and see him before he turned and sprinted down the linking passages, hurrying for the shattered chamber through which the hunters had first entered the castle.

"If this doesn't work, Mystra," he remarked pleasantly, as he ran, "you'll have to send someone else into Cormanthor to be your Chosen. If you want to be gentle on whoever that is, select an elf, hmm?"

Mystra gave no sign that she'd heard, but by then El was out into the shattered chamber, and heading for a rock pile at its center. The elves, running fast, weren't far behind.

El found his spot and spun to face them, assuming an anxious expression and raising his hands as if uncertain which spell to hurl. The blood hunters came racing into the chamber, waving their blades, and howled their way to a halt.

The elf who'd been first in the narrow passage said uncertainly, "This doesn't look right—he wasn't so fearful before. This must be a tr—"

"Silence!" Ivran Selorn snarled, shoving the speaker aside. The fearful elf slipped on fallen stones and almost fell, but Ivran paid no attention. It was his moment of glory; he was swaggering toward Elminster with leisurely grace, almost dancing on the tips of his toes as he came. "So, human rat," he sneered, "cornered at last, are you?"

"You are," Elminster agreed with a smile. The fearful elf raised a fresh cry of alarm, but Ivran hissed, "*Be still!*" at him, and then turned back to favor Elminster with a mirthless smile.

"You hairy barbarians think yourselves clever," he remarked, eyes glittering, "and you are—too clever. Unfortunately, in the half-witted, cleverness breeds insolence. You've certainly shown us ample supplies of that, being insolent enough to think you can slaughter the heirs of no less than *ten* Houses of Cormanthor—eleven, if we count Alastrarra, whose lore-gem you wore when you came trotting into our midst; who's to say you didn't murder Iymbryl to get it?—and pay no price. Some who hold the rank of armathor serve Cormanthor diligently all their lives and slay fewer foes than you have already."

With exaggerated apparent surprise, Ivran Selorn looked around at his companions, and then back to Elminster. "See? There are many more, here. What a splendid opportunity to add to your score! Why do you not attack? Are you scared, perhaps?"

Elminster lifted his lips in a half-smile. "Violence has never been Mystra's way."

"Oh, so?" Ivran said, his voice high and incredulous. "What then was that blast by the pool? A natural occurrence, perhaps?"

With a tight, wolfish smile, he motioned the other elves to encircle Elminster; keeping a safe distance, they did so, silently and smiling. Then the leader of these blood hunters turned back to his quarry and said, "Let me tell you the heirs you've slain, oh most mighty of armathors: Waelvor, and a bloody harvest by the pool: Yeschant, Amarthen, Ibryiil, Gwaelon, Tassarion, Ortauré, Bellas, and, I hear from our mages, Echorn and Auglamyr, too!"

Ivran advanced again, slowly, tossing his long, slim blade into the air and catching it in a fluid, restless juggling that El knew meant he'd throw it soon. "Just one of those heirs—to say nothing of the dozen or so servants and house blades you've felled, along the way—would be more than enough to buy your death, human. Just one! So now we have you at last, and face the difficult problem of how to fittingly slay you ten times over . . . or should it be eleven?"

Ivran came still closer. "Two of the gallants you slew were close friends of mine. And all of us here are saddened by the loss of the Lady Symrustar, whose promise has warmed us all for three seasons now. You took these from us, human worm. Have you anything futile to say on your own behalf? Something to entertain us as we *hack you down?!*"

As he screamed these last words, Ivran charged, hurling his blade in a silvery blur. It was meant to slash El's hand and ruin any spellcasting, before the other elves—leaping in from all sides now—reached him.

Smiling grimly, Elminster worked the spell, and became a rising, roiling column of white sparks. Charging elves crashed through him and into each other, blades biting deep. Elves arched in agony, and screamed, or coughed around the hilts of deeply driven blades, and poured out their blood upon the stones.

The whirling column of sparks began to drift away, heading for the passage El had entered by. Snarling and panting, with two blades that were not his standing out of his body, Ivran cried, "Slay the human! Use the swordpoint spell!"

His last word was choked off by blood bubbling forth, and an elf who streamed blood from a slash on his forehead—the one who'd been so fearful, earlier—hastened to the staggering Ivran, his hands glowing with healing magic.

Tlannatar Wrathtree followed his leader's bidding, shouting, "I have the spell! Throw your blades *up!*"

Obediently those elves who still could hurled swords and daggers into the air above their heads. The spell, which was making blue-white stars of force flare and twinkle around Tlannatar's hands, snared those hurled blades and sent them across the chamber in a deadly stream, point-first.

The whirling white column of sparks and light paused at the entrance to the passage, and the hurled blades swerved in their flight to go around it, picking up speed, and then spray out back across the room like a deadly hail of darts, flung in random directions. Tlannatar cried out as one took him in the ear, and toppled over with his mouth still open; it would gape, now, forever. Ivran, held up by his healer, took one in the throat and spat blood at the ceiling in a last, dying stream, and another elf fell, far across the room, with a sword right through him. He took two staggering steps toward the rock pile he'd been seeking as cover, then collapsed across it, and did not move again.

When the column that had been the human armathor whirled away down the passage and silence fell over the room, the fearful elf looked around. Of them all, only he still stood, though someone was moaning and moving feebly by one wall.

Dazed by grief, he stumbled in that direction, hoping the one healing spell he had left would be enough. By the time he got there, the body was still and silent. He shook it and whispered its name, but life had fled.

"How many of us," he asked the empty room in a trembling voice, "does it take to buy the life of one human? Father Corellon! *How many?*"

* * * * *

Raw power was surging through Elminster—more than he'd ever known outside Mystra's embrace—and he was feeling stronger, warmer, and mightier by the second. As he spun, the purple-hued glamer spun by the mages was being sucked down into him, giving him its energy . . . wild, unleashed, and wonderful!

Laughing uncontrollably, El felt himself growing taller and brighter, as he rose from the shattered base of the fallen tower.

He was conscious of the four mages scrambling up and shouting in fear. He spun in their direction, drunk with power, hungry to slay, and destroy, and—

The mages were casting something in unison. El leaned toward them, trying to get there before they could flee, or do whatever else they were trying to do, but his spinning form couldn't hurry. He tried to bend over, to sweep at them, but couldn't hold the shape, as his spinning whirled him upright again. He was closing on them now, he was—

Too late. The four elves swept their hands down by

their sides—hands that trailed fire—and stood watching him expectantly. They were not fleeing or even looking alarmed.

An instant later, Faerûn exploded, and El felt himself being wrenched apart and hurled in all directions, like dry grass spun away by a gale wind. "Mystra!" he cried, or tried to, but there was nothing but the roaring and the light, and he was falling . . . many of him were falling, onto many treetops . . .

* * * * *

"And then what happened?" High Court Mage Earynspeir's voice was thin with anger and exasperation. *Why, oh Corellon tell me why, did the younger bloods of the realm have to be such bloodthirsty fools?*

The trembling elven mage facing him started to cry, and went to his knees, pleading for his life.

"Oh, get *up*," Lord Earynspeir said disgustedly. "It's done, *now*. You're sure the human is dead?"

"We blasted him to nothing, L-lord," one of the other mages blurted out. "I've been scrying for magic use and invisible creatures since then, and have seen no evidence of either."

Earynspeir nodded almost absently. "Who survived, out of the whole band that went in there?"

"Rotheloe Tyrneladhelu, Lord. He—he bears no wound, but hasn't stopped crying yet. He may not be well in his wits."

"So we have eight dead and a ninth suffering," the High Court Mage said coldly, "and you four unhurt and triumphant." He looked at the ruined castle. "And no body of the foe, to be sure he is dead. Truly, a great victory."

"Well, it *was!*" the fourth mage shouted, erupting in sudden fury. "I didn't see you here, standing boot-to-boot with us, hurling spells at the Heirslayer! He came boiling up out of that castle like some sort of god, a deadly column of fire and sparks a hundred feet high and more, spitting off spells in all directions! Most would've fled, I swear—but we four stood and kept our calm and took him down! And—" he looked around at all of the silent, somber faces around him, court mages and sorceresses and guards, these last all heroes of earlier wars, their aged faces expressionless, and finished lamely, "—and I'm proud of what we did."

"I gathered that," Earynspieir said dryly. "Sylmae? Holone? Truth-scry these four . . . and Tyrneladhelu, to see how much of a wreck his mind is. We need to know the truth, not how windy their boasting can be." He turned away as the sorceresses nodded.

As the sorceresses advanced, one of the mages raised his hands. Red rings of fire encircled them, and he said warningly, "Keep back, wenches."

Sylmae's mouth crooked. "You'll look rather less handsome wearing those flame hoops on your backside, puppy. Dispense with this nonsense, or in the next three paces or so Holone and I'll grow weary of it."

"You *dare* to truth-scry *me?* The heir of a House?"

Sylmae shrugged. "Of course. In this, we act with the Coronal's authority."

"What authority?" the mage sneered as he retreated a step, the flamehoops still blazing about his hands. "The whole realm knows that the Coronal's gone mad!"

The High Court Mage turned around slowly, a slim but menacing figure in his black robe, and said gravely, "After your behind eats those flame hoops you're so fond of, Selgauth Cathdeiryn, and you've been thoroughly truth-scryed, you will be conducted under guard to the Coronal. You will then be free to make that observation to our Revered Lord himself. If you're feeling a trifle more prudent than at present, you *may* be wise enough to do so politely."

* * * * *

Galan Goadulphyn looked at the surface of the pool one last time, and sighed. Had he been less proud, there might have been tears, but he was a warrior of Cormanthor, not one of these weak-knees, the prancing and overperfumed lispers whom the high noble Houses of the realm were pleased to call heirs. He was like stone, or old treeroot. He would endure without complaint and rise again. Someday.

The picture the pool displayed was not inspiring. His face was a mask of old, dried blood, the fine line of his jaw marred where a flap of torn skin had bonded in its dangling state, making his chin square as a human's. The tip of one ear was missing, and his hair was as matted as a dead spider's legs, much of it stuck in the dark scabs that covered the raw furrows the rocks had gouged out of his head.

Galan looked back at the pool. His lips curved in an unlovely smile as he—stiffly—made a formal bow in its direction. Then he turned and booted a stone into its tranquil heart, shattering the smooth surface with muddy ripples.

Feeling much better, he checked the hilts of his sword and dagger to be sure they were loose and ready in their scabbards, and set off through the forest once more. His gut growled at him more than once, reminding him that one can't eat coins.

It was two days' steady travel through the trees to the waymoot of Assamboryl, and a day beyond that to Six Thorns. The hours seemed longer without Athtar's endless inanities. Not that he wasn't enjoying the relative quiet, for once—though he was so stiff, and whatever he'd hurt in his right thigh stabbed with such burning pain, that he was stumping along through the moss and dead leaves like a clumsy human.

Thankfully few folk dwelt hereabouts, because of the stirges. There was one flitting along in the trees right now, keeping well away but following his travel.

Hmmph. It must not be thirsty just now—but if he was heading toward all of its relatives, old Galan the Gallant might be no more than a sack of empty skin before nightfall.

Cheery thought, that.

A mushroom float rose up from behind a ferny bank on his left. His nose twitched. It was piled high with fresh limecaps, their mottled brown stems oozing the white sap that meant they'd just been harvested. His stomach growled again—and without thought he snatched a few and thrust them to his mouth.

"Ho!"

In his weary hunger, he'd forgotten that mushroom floats need someone to pull them. Or push them, as the angry-looking elf at the other end of this float was doing, getting his harvest aboveground in good time for washing and sorting. The elf snatched out a dagger, and swept it up for a throw.

Galan took it out of his fingers for him with his own fast-hurled dagger, and followed it up with a duck under the float and a lunge up the other side, sword point first.

The elf screamed and scrambled backwards, fetching up against a tree. Galan rose up in front of him with slow, silent menace, putting the point of his blade to the farmer's throat.

The terrified elf began to gabble, pleading and wildly unfolding all sorts of friendly information about his name, his lineage, his ownership of this mushroom den, the fine 'shrooms it produced, the finer weather they'd been having lately, and—

Galan gave him an unlovely smile, and raised a hand. The elf misinterpreted the gesture.

"Of course, human lord! Please forgive my tardiness in understanding your needs! I have little, being but a poor farmer, but it is yours—all yours!" With frantic fingers the farmer undid his belt, slid off its pouch, and presented it to Galan in trembling fingers, as his loose, baggy mucking-breeches fell to his ankles.

The belt was heavy with coin—small coin, no doubt, but still probably good thalvers and bedoars and thammarchs of the realm. As Galan hefted it in disbelief, the farmer misinterpreted his expression and gabbled, "But of *course* I have more! I would not dream of trifling with or cheating the great human armathor that Corellon himself has sent to our Coronal to scourge the sinful and decadent from the realm! Here!"

This time his fingers brought out a pouch from a thong around his neck . . . a pouch that swelled with gems. Galan took it in wide-eyed incredulity, and the farmer burst into tears and cried, "Slay me *not*, oh mighty armathor! I've no more to give you but my float of 'shrooms and my lunch!"

Galan growled with approval at that last word— well, after all, what *would* a mighty human armathor speak like?—and extended an insistent, beckoning hand. When the farmer staring at it for a moment, he followed it up with an insistent, beckoning blade.

"Ah- ah- 'shrooms?" the bewildered farmer cried, in a panic. Galan scowled, shook his head, and made the beckoning gesture again.

"Uh . . . lunch?" the farmer said timidly. Galan nodded slowly and emphatically, treating his guest to a crooked smile.

Mushrooms flew as the farmer burrowed into one corner of the float, cursed tearfully, gabbled apologies, and rushed to another corner, where mushrooms flew again.

Galan took the cloth-wrapped bundle, hefted it, and

then slowly held the bag of gems back out to the farmer. Gems were tricky; too many of them, in Cormanthor, bore tracing spells, or even enchantments that could burst forth to do harm when commanded to do so from a safe distance. No, the coins were safer by far.

The farmer burst into tears and went to his knees to loudly thank Corellon, and the volume of his praises was such that Galan was loudly tempted to chop him down where he stood.

Instead, he pointed with his sword, indicating that the farmer should go back down into his mushroom cavern without delay. The tearful farmer neglected to see it, so Galan growled.

In the sudden, total silence that followed he repeated the gesture, swinging his blade grandly—and there was a wet and heavy impact as he was bringing it back down. Galan opened his mouth to emit a startled curse as he saw the slab of stirge fall from one side of his blade, and heard the thump as the rest of it hit the ground somewhere near, but the farmer set up such a deafening storm of fervent praises that the only living Goadulphyn—head of the house, heir, champion, elder, and all—decided he couldn't stand any more of this (it was worse than Athtar), and headed north again. He'd open his bundle and eat when he was well out of whatever territory fervently gullible mushroom farmers dwelt in.

Galan stumped along for quite some time, shaking his head, before he found a tree old enough and large enough to hold Corellon's awareness. He went right up to it and murmured wonderingly, "You do have a sense of humor, Sacred Mother and Father, don't you?"

The tree did not reply—but then, Corellon probably already knew he had a sense of humor. So Galan sat down and devoured the farmer's lunch with gusto. Corellon offered no objections.

* * * * *

"Heirs slaughtered like lajauva birds in spring! Armathors breaking and hurling down their blades in protest! What's Cormanthor coming to?" Lord Ihimbraskar Evendusk was shouting again, face red and eyes redder. A servant who'd frozen into terrified immobility at his sudden and roaring approach found herself uncomfortably in Lord Evendusk's way.

More to the point, so did Lord Evendusk, and he still carried his pegasi goad in his hand. Its leather whip whacked twice, thrice, and then a savage backhand to send the weeping servant pelting down the passage, her platter of pastries fallen and forgotten.

Duilya shuddered. "Oh, gods," she whimpered, "do I really have to go through with this?"

Yes, Duilya—or he'll be carving you up with that goad next!

Duilya sighed.

Don't worry; we're here. Do it just as we agreed.

"It's the Coronal, that's who it is!" Evendusk snarled. "Eltargrim must have got funny ideas into his head while gallivanting off through Faerûn, o'erturning human wenches every night and listening overlong to their sauce . . ."

Lord Evendusk's customary morning rant trailed away into bug-eyed silence. There was his favorite chair, and there on the table beside it—the table that should have held a waiting glass of rubythrymm and a seeing-gem holding scenes of last night's revelry—was a full bottle of his very best tripleshroom sherry.

His wife was sitting in *his* chair, clad in a gown that would have made his pulses race if Duilya had been forty summers younger, twice as slim as she was, and just a bit less familiar. She didn't seem to have noticed him.

As he watched, rocking slightly from side to side and breathing heavily, she picked up an empty glass from the floor beside her, shrugged at it, and set it aside.

Then she calmly unstoppered the sherry bottle, raised it to the morning light and murmured something appreciative—and drank the *whole* thing down, slowly and steadily, eyes closed and throat moving rhythmically.

Lord Evendusk's silently boiling rage slid sideways, as he noticed what a beautiful throat his wife possessed. He didn't think he'd ever noticed it before.

She set the empty—yes, empty; *she'd drunk the whole thing!*—bottle down, face serene, and said aloud, "That was so good, I think I'll have some more."

She was reaching for the bell when Lord Evendusk found his wits and his breath again. Catching firm hold of both, he gave vent to his now-towering rage. "Duilya! Just what by all the pits of the spider-worshipping drow d'you think you're doing?" he bellowed.

As she rang the bell, his wife turned that stupid and customarily yawping face toward his, smiled almost timidly, and said, "Good morn, my lord."

"Well?" he bellowed, striding forward. "Just what is the meaning of this?" He waved at the bottle with his goad, and then glared down at his wife.

She was frowning slightly, and seemed to be listening to something.

Lord Evendusk snatched hold of her shoulder and shook her. "Duilya!" he roared into her face. "Answer me, or I'll—"

Red-faced, he raised his goad, holding it aloft, ready to strike, with a trembling hand. Behind him, the room filled with anxious servants.

Duilya smiled up at him, and tore open the front of her gown. His name was emblazoned in gems across her otherwise bare breasts. "Ihimbraskar" was rising and falling as he stared at it, gaping. Into that stunned silence she said clearly, "Wouldn't you prefer to do that in our bedchamber, lord? Where you've room to take a really good swing?"

She gave him a little smile and added, "Though I must confess I prefer it when you just put on my gowns and let *me* use the goad."

Lord Evendusk, who'd been in the process of turning purple, now turned white instead. One of the servants snorted in suppressed mirth, but when their lord wheeled around, wild-eyed, to glare at them all, they presented him with a row of expressionless faces and said in a ragged chorus, "You rang, great Lady?"

Duilya smiled sweetly. "I did, and my thanks for your swift arrival. Naertho, I'd like another bottle of tripleshroom sherry by my bedside, forthwith. There's no need for glasses. The rest of you, attend please, in case my lord needs something."

"Need something?" Lord Evendusk snarled, turning around again. "Aye, and forthwith—an explanation, wench, of your . . .this . . ." he waved his arms wildly, lost for words, while the servants were still gasping at his insulting use of the word 'wench,' and then finished almost desperately, ". . . behavior!"

"Of course," Duilya said, looking almost scared for a moment. She glanced at the servants, took a deep breath, lifted her chin—almost as though she was following silent instructions—and said crisply, "Night after night you go to revels, leaving your household neglected. Not once have you taken me with you—or any of your servants, if you'd rather not have me witness what you do there. Jhalass, there, and Rubrae—they're much younger and prettier than I am; why don't you show them off and let them enjoy the same fun you do?"

The servants were staring at her as wide-eyed as

Lord Evendusk, now. Duilya lay back in the chair and crossed her legs just as he customarily did, and said, gesturing down at herself, *"This* is all I see of you in the mornings, lord. This and a lot of roaring and groaning. So I decided to try this roistering of yours, to see what attractions it might have."

She wrinkled her nose. "Aside from giving me a powerful urge to relieve myself, I can't see that tripleshroom sherry tastes so wonderful that you need go off all night to plow through a bottle of it. Perhaps another bottle would convince me otherwise? So I've summoned that second one to my bedside—where we're going now, Lord."

Lord Evendusk was purple again, and shaking, but his voice was soft as he asked, "We are? Why?"

"Drinking every night's no excuse for spending every morning stumbling about like an idiot, making a mockery of the honor of the House, and leaving me neglected, night after night, and day after day. We are *partners,* my lord, and it's high time you treated me as one."

Ihimbraskar Evendusk raised his head as a stag does, to draw breath before drinking at a forest pool. When he brought it down again, he looked almost calm. "Could you be more specific about what you want me to do in this regard, Lady?" he asked in silken tones.

"Sit down and talk," she snapped. "Here. Now. About the Coronal, and the deaths, and the tumult over the human."

"And just what do you know of that?" her lord asked, still standing. He slapped the palm of his hand gently with the goad.

Duilya pointed at a vacant chair. Lord Evendusk looked at it, and then slowly back to her. She kept her arm motionless, indicating the chair.

Slowly he went to it, planted one boot in it, and stood leaning on it. "Speak," he said softly. There was something in his eyes, as he looked at her, that hadn't been there before.

"I know, Lord, that you—and other lords like you—are the very backbone of Cormanthor," Duilya said, staring right into his eyes. Her lips quivered for a moment, as if she might cry, but she drew in a deep breath and went on carefully, "On your shoulders the greatness and splendor of us all rests, and is carried. Never think for a moment that I do not revere you for the work you do, and the honor that you have won."

One of the servants stirred, but the room had grown very still.

Lady Evendusk went on. "Ihimbraskar, I do not want to lose that honor. I don't want to lose *you*. Lords and their houses are drawing swords, hurling spells, and defying their Coronal openly over one human. I'm afraid someone will stick their blade through My Lord Evendusk."

Lord and lady were both silent for a moment, their eyes locked, and then Duilya continued, her words ringing in the silent room.

"*Nothing* is worth that. No human is worth feuds and blood spilled and Cormanthor torn apart. Here I sit, day after day, talking with other ladies and seeing the life of the realm unfold. Never do you ask me what I've seen and heard, or talk anything over with me. You *waste* me, Lord. You treat me like a chair—or like a clown, to be laughed at for my fripperies, as you boast to your friends how many coins I've thrown away on my latest jewels and gowns!"

Duilya rose, took off her gown, and held it out to him. "I'm more than this, Ihimbraskar. See?"

His eyes flickered; she stepped swiftly toward him, gown in hand, and said passionately, "I'm your *friend*,

Lord. I'm the one you should come home and confide in and share rude jokes with and argue with. Have you forgotten what it is to share ideas—not kisses or pinches, but *ideas*, spoken of aloud—with an elf maid? Come with me now, and I'll teach you how. We have a realm to save."

She turned away, walking from the room with a determined stride. Lord Evendusk watched her go, bared swinging hips and all, cleared his throat noisily, and then turned and said to the servants, "Ah . . . you heard my lady. Unless we ring, please don't disturb us. We have much to talk about."

He turned toward the door the Lady Duilya had left by, took two swift steps, and then whirled around to face the servants, tossed his goad onto the table, and said, "One more thing. Uh . . . my apologies."

He turned and left the room, running hard. The servants kept very quiet until they were sure he was out of earshot.

Their cheering and excited converse fell silent again when Naertho came into the room. He was carrying the second bottle of tripleshroom sherry in his hand. "The lord and lady said 'twas for us!" he said gruffly.

When the astonished cheer that evoked had died away, he looked out the window and the trees, his eyes very bright, and added, "Thanks to you, Corellon. Bring us humans every moon, if they cause such as this!"

* * * * *

In a pool in a private garden, four ladies collapsed into each others' arms and wept happy tears. Their glasses of tripleshroom sherry floated, untouched and forgotten, around them.

Thirteen

ADRIFT IN CORMANTHOR

*For a time, Elminster became as a ghost, and wandered
unheard and unseen through the very heart of Cormanthor. The elves regarded him not, and he learned much
thereby . . . not that he had much of a life left in which
to make use of what he gained.*

Antarn the Sage
from **The High History of Faerûnian Archmages Mighty**
published circa The Year of the Staff

Faerûn took a very long while to come floating back
again. At first Elminster was only dimly aware of himself as a drifting cloud of thoughts—of awareness—in
a dark, endless void through which booming, distorted
sounds . . . bursts of loudness they were, no more . . .
rumbled and echoed from time to time.

After an infinity of floating, only dimly aware of who
he was or *what* he was, Elminster saw lights appear—
stabbing, momentary flashes of brightness that occurred from time to time as he floated, unwondering,
in their midst.

Later, sounds and lights befell more often, and
memories began to stir, like restless, uncoiling ser-
pents, in the spark of self-awareness that was the
Athalantan prince and Chosen of Mystra. El saw
swords rising and falling, and a gem that held a

whirling chaos of images, the memories of others, raging like a sea that tossed him up into the presence of a female eidolon in the night gardens of a palace . . . the palace of a kindly one, an old elf in white robes, the ruler of pursuivants who rode unicorns and pegasi, the ruler of . . . of . . .

The Coronal. That title blazed like white fire in his memory, like the great and awesome chord of a fanfare of triumphal doom—the march favored by Magelords in the Athalantar of his younger years, that resounded across Hastarl, echoing back from its towers, when wizards were gathering for some decision of import.

The same mages he had defeated in the end, to claim—and then renounce—his throne. He was a prince, the grandson of the Stag King. He was of the royal blood of Athalantar, of the family Aumar, the last of many princes. He was a boy running through the trees of Heldon, an outlaw and a thief of Hastarl, a priest—or was it priestess? Had he not been a woman?—of Mystra. The Lady of Mysteries, the Mother of Magic, Myrjala his teacher who became Mystra his divine ruler and guide, making him her Chosen, making him her—*Elminster!*

He was Elminster! Human armathor of Cormanthor, named so by the Coronal, sent here by Mystra to do something important that remained yet hidden from him—and beset on all sides by the ambitious, ruthless, arrogantly powerful young elves of this realm, chafing under the old ways and unwelcome new decrees of the Coronal and his court . . . *ardavanshee*, the elders called them; or "restless young ones." Ardavanshee who may yet have brought about his death . . . for if Elminster Aumar was not dead, what was he?

Floating here, in dark chaos . . .

He sank back into his thoughts, which were running now like a river. Ardavanshee who defied the will of their elders but stood tall upon the pride of the houses of their birth. Ardavanshee who feared and yet spoke against the power of the High Court Mages and the Coronal and his old advisor the Srinshee.

That title seemed to be another door opening in his mind, letting in a wash of brightness and fresh recollections and a stronger sense of being Elminster. The Lady Oluevaera Estelda, smiling up at him from that noble, wrinkled ruin of a face and then, incongruously, from one that looked like a little elven girl's, yet retained those old and wise eyes . . . the Srinshee, older than trees and deeper rooted, treading the crammed Vault of Ages with reverence for the dead and vanished, holding the whole lore and long lineage of the proud Cormanthan elves in her mind—in the vault behind her eyes that was so much larger than the one she trod with an impatient, hawk-nosed young human . . .

The hated human intruder sought across the realm for the murders he'd done by the ardavanshee—led by the houses of Echorn and Starym and Waelvor . . . Waelvor, whose scion was Elandorr . . . suitor and rival of the Lady Symrustar.

Symrustar! That perfect face, those hungrily tugging blue tresses, that dragon on her belly and breast, the eyes like blue flames of promise, and lips parted in a waiting, knowing smile . . . that ruthless, ambitious sorceress whose mind was as dark a cesspit as any Magelord's, who thought of elves—and men—as mere stupid beasts to be used as she clawed her way up through them, to some as-yet-unrealized goal.

The lady who had almost torn his mind open to make him her plaything and source of spells. The lady he had in turn betrayed into the grasp of her rival, Elandorr, leaving both their fates unknown to him.

Aye. He knew who he was now. Elminster, set upon

by Delmuth Echorn and then by a band of ardavanshee led by Ivran Selorn, who hunted him through
Castle Dlardrageth. Elminster the overconfident, careless Chosen. Elminster, who'd been drunk with power
as he flew right into the waiting spell of the ardavan-
shan mages—a spell that had torn him apart.

Was he whole again? Or was he but a ghost, his mortal life over? Perhaps Mystra had kept him alive—if
this *was* alive—to carry out her purposes, a failure
forced to complete his mission.

Elminster was suddenly aware that he could move
in the void, scudding in this direction or that as he
thought of movement. Yet that meant little when there
was nowhere to move to, dark emptiness on all sides,
lights and noise scattering at seeming random, everywhere and nowhere.

The world around him had once been a series of specific "wheres," an unfolding landscape of different and
often named locations, from the deep forest of Cormanthor to the outlaw wastes beyond Athalantar.

Perhaps this was death, after all. Faerûn, and a
body to walk it in, were what he was lacking. Almost
without thinking he sent himself into a racing flight
through the void, searching the endless for an end, a
boundary, perhaps a rift where the light of Faerûn in
all its familiar glory could shine in . . .

And as this swift but vain movement went on and
on he raised a prayer to Mystra, a silent cry in his
mind: *Mystra, where are ye? Aid me. Be my guide, I beseech thee.*

There was a dark and silent moment as the words
in his mind seemed to roll away into endless distance.
Then there came a bright, almost blinding burst of
light, white and clarioned, with a sennet that echoed
stridently through him, hurling him over and over in
its brassy tumult. When it faded he was racing back

the way he'd come, aimed exactly back upon his former course, though he could not tell how it was he knew that to be so.

At long last, a horizon fell into his void, a line of misty blue with a node of brightness partway along it, like a gem upon the arc of a ring . . . and Elminster of Athalantar was headed for that distant point of brilliance.

It seemed a long way off, but in the end he rushed up to plunge into it with dizzying speed, shedding something as he left the darkness, shooting out into the light. The light of a lowering sun, above the marching treetops of Cormanthor, with the dark ruin of Castle Dlardrageth in the distance, and something urging him in another direction. He followed that urging, unsure even if he could have chosen otherwise, and flew low above shadowtops and duskwoods, roseneedles and beetle palms, rushing as smooth and as swift as if outracing dragons.

Here and there, as he flew, El glimpsed trails and slim wooden bridges that leapt from tree to tree, transforming the forest giants into the living homes of elves. He was crossing Cormanthor in the space of a few breaths. Now he was descending and slowing, as if let fall by a vast and invisible hand.

Thanks to ye, Mystra, he thought, fairly sure whom he should be thanking. He sank past the gardens of the palace, into the many-spired bustle of the central city, Cormanthor itself.

He was slowing greatly now, as if he was but a leaf drifting on a gentle breeze. In truth, he could hear no whistle of wind nor feel any chill or damp as of moving air, at all. Turrets and softly luminous driftglobes rose past him as his plunge ended, and he began to move freely, hither and yon.

He moved from here to there in accordance with

wherever he looked that interested him enough to approach. As he flew, he passed among elves who saw him not, and—as he discovered when he blundered right into the path of several floats piled high with mushrooms, and they slid through him without him feeling a thing—felt him not. He was truly a ghost, it seemed; an invisible, silent, undetected drifting thing.

As he drifted this way and that, peering at the busy lives of Cormanthans, he began to hear things as well. At first there was only a faint, confusing rumble broken by louder irregularities, but it grew to a deafening din of interlaced gabbling. It seemed to be the conversations and noises made by thousands of elves at once, as if he could hear all Cormanthor, without regard for distance and walls and cellar depths, laid all at once upon the ears he no longer seemed to have.

He hovered for a time in a little tangle of shrubs growing between three closely spaced duskwoods, waiting for the din to subside or for his wits to flee entirely. Slowly the noises did die, receding to what normal ears would hear: the sounds nearby, with the gentle, incessant sighing of breeze-stirred leaves drowning out all else. He relaxed, able to *think* again, until thinking begat curiosity, and a desire to know what was befalling in Cormanthor.

So he was invisible, silent, and scentless, even to alert elves. Ideal for prying into their doings. But 'twould be best to make sure of his stealth before seeking to enter any heart of watchful peril hereabout.

El undertook to swoop at elves in the streets and on the bridges, screaming for all he was worth as he did so. He even passed through them whilst clawing at them and crying insults. He could hear himself perfectly, and even shape ghostly limbs to stab and slash with—limbs that he at least could feel, enduring painful scrapings as one limb struck another.

His elven targets, however, noticed him not. They laughed and chatted in a way they'd never have done had they known a human was nearby. El drew himself up in midair after hurling himself through a particularly frosty-looking elven lady of high station and reflected that he might not have all that much time to make use of this state. After all, none of his powers since his awakening had remained unchanged for long. So he'd best be about his spying.

One thing to check on, first.

He remembered these streets dimly: he'd passed along that one, he thought, in his first stagger through the city, trying to search for House Alastrarra without seeming to do more than stroll. A particularly proud mansion, in the heart of walled gardens, should lie in that direction.

His memory was correct. It was the work of an instant to pass through the gates unseen, and seek the great house beyond. He could pass through small items, especially wood, he discovered, but stone and metal hurt or deflected him; he could not burst or even seep through solid walls. A window served him amply, however, and he entered into the tapestried splendor of a lavishly decorated home. Furs lay everywhere underfoot, and polished wood sculpted into lounges and chairs rose in flowing shapes on all sides. Wealthy elven families seemed to love varicolored blown glass and chairs that rose into a variety of little armrests and shelves and curved lounging cavities. El passed among these like a purposeful thread of smoke, seeking a particular thing.

He found it in an ornate bedchamber where a nude elven couple were floating in each other's arms, upright above their bed, earnestly—even angrily—discussing the affairs of the realm. Elminster found the arguments advanced and parried by the aroused tongues of Lord and Lady Evendusk so fascinating that he lingered a long time listening, before a purely personal dispute about moderation and the consumption of tripleshroom sherry sent him swooping to the floor, and a little way across the furs there, to the visibly pulsing enchantments surrounding Duilya Evendusk's gem bower.

It was the Cormanthan custom for elven ladies of means to have a pod-shaped, walk-in portable closet, something like the canopy surrounding a sedan chair. In this closet their jewels were hung or kept in little drawers individually carved to fit into the flowing wooden walls. Gem bowers were equipped with little hanging mirrors, tiny glass light-globes that shone when tapped with a forefinger, and little seats. They also contained powerful enchantments to keep out the wandering fingers of those overwhelmed by the beauty of the gems contained therein; enchantments that in theory could be tuned to keep out all except their lady owner. These "veilings" were so strong that they glowed a rich blue, quite visible to the eye, as they crawled and ebbed around their bowers in a close-clinging sphere of magic.

They were strong enough, El recalled dimly from the Srinshee's comments, to hurl intruders across a room, or stand immobile against the charge of the strongest warrior—even a charge preceded by a spear, or augmented by a second or third warrior, racing shoulder to shoulder. Would they likewise rend a drifting human phantom? Or rebuff him?

Gingerly he drifted closer, moving with infinite patience, extending the thinnest thread of himself cautiously outward to touch the pulsing blue glow.

It rippled unchanged, and he felt nothing. He thrust it in further, reaching with the smokelike finger for three gems hanging on fine chains from the curving ceiling of Duilya Evendusk's bower.

He felt nothing, and the enchantment seemed unchanged. Reluctantly he spread himself out along it, brushing against the blueness. No sensation of pain or disruption, and no change in the enchantment. Drawing himself back across the room from the bower, he swirled around Lord and Lady Evendusk for a moment, as they murmured gentle words to each other with slow but building hunger. Then he raced across the room, charging right at the magical barrier.

He was almost up t—he was through!—bursting through the heart of the bower without disturbing so much as a ring and storming on out its other side, piercing the barrier again and flashing into a silent, unseen turn inches shy of a wall.

Behind him the veiling glowed on, unchanging. El turned and regarded it with some satisfaction. Glancing beyond it, at the langorous midair dance of the amorous elven couple, he smiled—or tried to—and soared away, out an oval window into the mossy gardens beyond, seeking information.

He wanted to find the Coronal, to be sure the bloodthirsty ardavanshee—or worse, the elder mages of the haughty houses to which the reckless younglings belonged—hadn't so lost their senses as to strike at the heart and head of the realm.

Then, assuming the Revered Lord Most High of Cormanthor was unharmed, 'twould be time to seek out the Srinshee and get a certain much-maligned human armathor of the realm his body back, if this condition hadn't passed away by then.

El turned in the direction the palace should be, rose until he was among treetops and spired towers, and sped among them, looking down as he passed at the unfolding beauty of Cormanthor.

There were circular gardens like little green wells, and trees planted in crescentiform arcs to enclose little

moss lawns in their encircling shelter. There were
stone spires around which gigantic trees spiraled in
living helices of leaves and carefully-shaped branches
and little windows opening in the bark, with the forms
of young elves at play dancing and wrestling visible
within. There were banners of translucent silk that
rode the winds as lightly as gossamer threads, and
trees that held those banners on boughs shaped like
the fingers of an open hand, with a domed upper room
squatting like an egg in the palm of that hand. There
were houses that revolved, and sparkled back the sun
from swirling glass ornaments hanging like frozen
raindrops from their balconies and casements.

El looked at it all with fresh wonder. In all his tearing about and fighting, he'd forgotten just how beautiful elven work could be. If the elder elven houses had
their way, of course, humans would never see any of
this—and those few intruders who did, such as one
Elminster Aumar, would not live long enough to tell
anyone of such splendors.

After a time he came out of a knot of tree homes and
spired, many-windowed houses, passing over a wall
that bore several enchantments. Beyond was a garden
of many pools and statues. The garden, El realized as
he drifted onward and onward, was *big*.

And yet it didn't *look* like the Coronal's palace garden. Where were the . . ?

No, that wasn't the palace. It was a grand house,
yes—a mound of greenery pierced by windows and
bristling with slender towers. Its ivy-covered flanks
fell away to the lazy curves of a stream that slid
placidly past islands that looked like huge clumps of
moss linked by little arched bridges.

It was the most beautiful mansion El had ever seen.
He veered toward its nearest large upper window. Like
most such openings it was bereft of glass, and filled

instead by an invisible spell field that prevented the passage of all solid objects, but let breezes blow unchecked. Two well-dressed elves were leaning against the unseen field, goblets in their hands.

"My Lord Maendellyn," someone was saying in thin, superior tones, "you can hardly think it usual for one of my House to so swiftly find common cause with those of younger heritage and lesser concerns; this is truly something that strikes at us all."

"Have we then, Llombaerth, the open support of House Starym?"

"Oh, I don't think that is yet necessary. Those who wish to reshape Cormanthor and stand proud in doing so must occasionally be seen to do things for themselves—and bear the consequences."

"While the Starym watch, smiling, from the sidelines," a third voice said in dry tones, "ready to applaud such bold Houses if they succeed, or decry their foul treachery if they fail. Yes, that would make a House live long and profit much. At the same time, it leaves those of the House in question standing on uneasy ground when presuming to lecture others on tactics, or ethics, or the good of the realm."

"My Lord Yeschant," the thin voice said coldly, "I don't care for the tone of your observations."

"And yet, Lord Speaker of the Starym, you can find it in you to make common cause with us—for you have the most to lose of us all."

"How so?"

"House Starym now holds the proudest rank of all. If this insane plan the Coronal is urging on Cormanthor is allowed to befall, House Starym has more to lose than, say, House Yridnae."

"*Is* there a House Yridnae?" someone asked, in the background, but El, as he drifted nearer, heard no reply.

"My lords," the Lord Maendellyn was saying hastily, "let us set aside this dissension and pursue the stag we've all seen ahead: to whit, the necessity of ending the rule of our current Coronal, and his folly of Opening, for the good of us all."

"Whatever we pursue," a deep voice said despairingly, "won't bring my son back. The human did it; the Coronal brought the human into the realm—so, the human being dead already, the Coronal must die, that my Aerendyl be avenged."

"I lost a son, too, Lord Tassarion," said another new voice, "but it does not follow that the death of my Leayonadas must needs be paid for by the blood of the ruler of Cormanthor. If Eltargrim must die, let it be a reasoned decision made for the future of Cormanthor, and not a blood evening."

"House Starym knows better than many the pain of loss and the weight of blood price," the thin voice of Llombaerth Starym, Lord Speaker of his House, came again. "We have no desire to belittle the pain of a loss felt by others, and we hear the deep—and undeniable—call for justice. Yet we, too, believe that the matter of the Coronal's continued rule must be treated as an affair of state. The misruler must pay for his shocking ideas and his failure to guide Cormanthor capably, regardless of how many or how few brave sons of the realm have died from his mistakes."

"May I propose," a lisping voice put in, "that we resolve and work toward the slaying of the Coronal? With that as a commonly held goal, those of us who see revenge as part of this—myself, Lord Yeschant, Lord Tassarion, and Lord Ortauré—can agree among ourselves who shall have a hand in the actual killing, so that honor may be satisfied. That in turn allows House Starym and others who'd rather not be part of actual bloodshed to work toward our common goal with hands that remain clean of all but the work of loyally defending Cormanthor."

"Well said, My Lord Bellas," Lord Maendellyn agreed. "Are we then agreed that the Coronal must die?"

"We are," came the rough chorus.

"And are we agreed on when, how, and whom shall ascend to the throne of Coronal after Eltargrim?"

There was a little silence, and then everyone started to speak at once. El could see them, now: the five heads of Houses and the Starym envoy, sitting around a polished table with goblets and bottles between them, the slowly revolving flashes of an anti-poison field winking among those vessels.

"Pray silence!" Lord Yeschant said sharply, after a few moments of babble. "It is clear that we are *not* agreed on these things. I suspect that the matter of who shall be our next Coronal is the issue of most contention, and should be dealt with last—though I must stress, lords, that we do Cormanthor a grave disservice if we do not, before striking, choose a new Coronal and support him with the same united resolve we show in removing the old one. None of us benefits from a realm in chaos." He paused, and then asked in a quiet voice, "My Lord Maendellyn?"

"My thanks, Lord Yeschant—and, may I say, how swiftly and ably spoken. Is the 'how' we remove the Coronal easiest to decide among ourselves, as I judge it?"

"It must be some way that lets us strike him down personally," Lord Tassarion said quickly.

"Yet 'twould be best," the lord speaker of the Starym put in, "if it not be a formal audience or other appointment for which a suspicious Coronal could assemble a formidable defensive force, and thereby increase our losses and personal danger as he delays our success and places the realm in jeopardy of the very war and uncertainty we are all so rightly concerned about."

"How then to trick him into meeting with us?"

"Adopt disguises, so as to come to him as his advisors: those six sorceresses he dallies with, for instance?"

Lord Yeschant and Lord Tassarion frowned in unison. "I dislike the thought of involving such extra complications in what we do," said Yeschant. "Should one of them observe us, she'll be sure to attack, and we'll have a spell battle far greater than what we'll face if we can catch Eltargrim alone."

"Bah! As Coronal, he can call and summon a number of things," the Starym envoy said dismissively.

"Aye, but if such aid arrives and finds him dead," Lord Tassarion said thoughtfully, "things are far different than if we draw one or even all six of the lady sorceresses—members of noble houses themselves, remember, with the blood prices their deaths will inevitably carry—into the fray before we are sure that we can slay the Coronal then and there. I do not want to be caught in a drawn-out battle across half the realm with six hostile sorceresses able to teleport into our laps and then out again, if we can't know that we are buying the Coronal's sure and swift death with whatever price we pay."

"I don't think we are ready to slay a Coronal yet," Lord Bellas lisped. "I see us still standing undecided between three alternatives: publicly challenging the Coronal's rule; or openly slaying him; or merely being nearby when an 'unfortunate accident' befalls our beloved ruler."

"Lords all," their host said firmly, " 'tis clear that we'll be some time in reaching agreement on any of these matters. I have engagements ahead this eve, and the longer we six sit gathered here, the greater the chance that someone in the realm will hear or suspect something." The Lord Maendellyn looked around the room and added, "If we part now, and all think on the three matters Lord Yeschant so capably outlined, I trust that when I send word three morns hence, we can meet again armed with what we'll need to strike an agreement."

" 'Strike' is aptly chosen," someone muttered, as the others said, "Agreed" around the table, and they rose swiftly and made for the doors, to depart.

For a moment El was tempted to linger and follow one or more of these conspirators, but their mansions or castles were all easily located in the city, and he had his own needs to attend to. He must see for himself if Cormanthor still had a Coronal to murder, or if someone else had beaten these exalted lords to the deed.

He swooped out of the window and around Castle Maendellyn without delay, racing past its other turrets in the direction he'd originally been heading. The lovely gardens stretched on beneath him as he went. Lovely, and well-guarded; no less than three barriers flashed in front of him as he thrust through them and raced on, seeking the spires he knew.

The gardens ended at last in a high wall cloaked in a thick tangle of trees. A street lay beyond the wall, and a row of houses fronted onto the street. Their back gardens rose through lush plantings and under duskwood trees to another street. On its far side were the walls of the palace gardens.

The watchnorns here might be able to see him, but El had to reach the palace, so he drifted on, cautiously now, for fear that the enchantments that girded the High House of Cormanthor would be more powerful than those he'd encountered thus far.

Perhaps they were, but they saw him not. Nor did any of the ghostly guardians appear. Elminster slipped into the palace by an upper window, and glided up and down its halls, feeling strangely ill at ease. The place was splendid, but its upper floor was almost empty; only a few servants padded about in soft boots, seeing leisurely to the dust with minor spells.

Of the Coronal himself he saw no sign, but in a little outlying turret on the north side of the palace he found a gathering strangely similar to that he'd just witnessed breaking up in Castle Maendellyn: six noble lords sitting around a polished table. This gathering had a seventh grave-faced elf present: the High Court Mage Earynspieir. Elminster did not know any of the others.

Lord Earynspieir was on his feet, pacing. Elminster drifted into the room and took his seat at the table, undetected.

"We know there are plots being hatched even now," an old and rather plump elf down at the end of the table said. "Every gathering, be it revel or formal audience, from now on must be treated as a potential battle."

"More like a series of waiting ambushes," another elf commented.

The High Court Mage turned. "Lord Droth," he said, nodding at the stout elf, "and Lord Bowharp, please believe that we recognize this and are making preparations. We realize we cannot wall away the Coronal behind armathors bristling with weapons, and d—"

"What preparations?" another lord asked bluntly. This one looked every inch a battle commander, from his scars to his ready sword. When he leaned forward to ask that question, his rich voice held the snap of command.

"*Secret* preparations, My Lord Paeral," Earynspieir said meaningfully.

A lord who was sitting beside the head of House

Paeral—a gold elf, and quite the most handsome male Elminster had ever seen, of any species—looked up with startlingly silver eyes and said quietly, "If you can't trust us, Lord High Mage, Cormanthor is doomed. The time is well past for keeping coy secrets. If those who are loyal don't know exactly where and when events are unfolding in the realm, our Coronal could well fall."

Earynspieir grimaced as if in pain for a moment, before assuming a sickly smile. "Well said as always, My Lord Unicorn. Yet as Lord Adorellan pointed out earlier, every word let out of our lips that need not be is another chink in the Coronal's armor. The Lord Most High is in hiding at this time, upon my recommendation, and—"

"Guarded by whom?" Lords Droth and Paeral asked in almost perfect unison.

"Mages of the court," Earynspieir replied, in tones that signaled he preferred to say no more.

" 'The Six Kissing Sisters'?" the sixth lord asked, lifting an eyebrow. "Are they really a match for a determined attack—considering that some of them belong to houses that may be less than heartbroken to see Eltargrim dead?"

"Lord Siirist," the High Court Mage said severely, "I do not appreciate your description of the ladies who serve the realm so capably. Even less do I admire your open misapprehensions about their loyalty. However, others have shared your concerns, and the six ladies have been truth-scryed by the same expert who even now stands with ready spells at the Coronal's side."

"And that is?" Lord Unicorn prompted firmly.

"The Srinshee," Earynspieir said, a trace of exasperation in his voice. "And if we cannot trust her, lords, who in all Cormanthor can we trust?"

It was clear to Elminster as discussions went on

that Lord Earynspieir was going to say as little as possible about whatever preparations he'd made. Instead he was trying to get these lords to agree to muster mages and warriors at various places, under commanders agreeable to obey anyone who gave them certain secret phrases. He wasn't going to say which houses or individuals he knew to be disloyal, and he certainly wasn't going to reveal anything about the current whereabouts of the Coronal and the Srinshee.

Without a means of teleporting, El couldn't even look in the Vault of Ages for himself. It was well underground—and he didn't even know where.

Feeling sudden exasperation himself, he soared up out of that room, hurled himself through the palace like a foe-seeking arrow, and turned north, out of the city. He needed the quiet of the trees again, to drift and think. Probably, in the end, he'd wind up poking and prying into the lives of elves all over the city, just to glean all the useful information he could. He really didn't know how most elves earned coins to spend for things, for inst—

Something moved, under the trees ahead of him. Something that seemed disturbingly familiar.

El slowed swiftly, drifting to one side to circle and thus see it better. He was right out in the woods now, beyond where the regular patrols would pass, on the edge of a region of small, twisting ravines and tangled brambles.

The thing he was looking at was much scratched from those brambles, as it crawled laboriously along, moving aimlessly on hands and knees—or rather, one hand, for the other was bent back into a frozen claw, and the crawling, murmuring thing was leaning on the wrist instead. Sharp sticks or rocks or thorns had long ago torn open that wrist, as well as other places, and the crawler was leaving a trail of blood. Soon something that devoured such helpless things would get wind of it, or happen upon it.

El descended until he was floating chin-down in the dirt, staring through a trailing forest of filthy, matted blue tresses into the tortured, swimming blue eyes of the toast of the ardavanshee: the Lady Symrustar Auglamyr.

Fourteen

ANGER AT COURT

Elves today still say "As splendid as the Coronal's Court itself" when describing luxury or work of exquisite beauty, and the memory of that splendor, now taken from us, will never die. The Court of the Coronal was known for its decorum. Even scions of the mightiest houses were known to pause in admiration and awe at the glittering panoply it presented to the eye; and temper their words and deeds with the most courtly graces; and from the Throne of Cormanthor, floating above them, went out the gravest and most noble judgments of that age.

Shalheira Talandren, High Elven Bard of Summerstar
from **Silver Blades And Summer Nights:
An Informal But True History of Cormanthor**
published in The Year of the Harp

There came a skirling, as of many harp strings struck in unison, and the gentle, magically amplified voice of the Lady Herald rolled across the glassy-smooth floor of the vast Chamber of the Court: "Lord Haladavar; Lord Urddusk; Lord Malgath."

There was a stir among the courtiers; quick conversations rose and then died away into a hush of excitement as the three old elven lords glided in, walking on air, clad in their full robes of honor. Their servants fell away to join the armathors at the doors of the court, and in the tense, hanging silence the three heads of Houses traveled down the long, open hall to the Pool.

A rustling grew in their wake as courtiers along both sides of the room shifted their positions to gain the best possible vantage points. Amid this flurry of movement one short, slim, almost childlike figure drifted behind one of the tapestries that hid exits, and slipped away.

Floating above the glowing, circular Pool of Remembrance was the Throne of the Coronal, and at ease in its high-arched splendor sat the aged Lord Eltargrim in his gleaming white robes. "Approach and be welcome," he said, formally but warmly. "What would you speak of, here before all Cormanthor?"

Lord Haladavar spread his hands. "We would speak of your plan of Opening; we have some misgivings about this matter."

"Plainly said, and in like spirit: proceed," Eltargrim said calmly.

In unison, the three lords held aside the sashes of their robes. Lightning crackled around the hilts of three revealed stormswords. There was a gasp of horror from the courtiers at this breach of etiquette as well as at the danger drawn stormswords could bring, were they wielded in this chamber amid all its thickly laid enchantments.

Armathors started forward grimly from their places by the doors, but the Coronal waved them back and raised his hand, palm up, in the gesture for silence. When it fell, he gestured at the twinkling lights winking excitedly in the pool beneath him, and said calmly, "We were already aware of your weaponry, and have taken the view that it was an error in judgment that you deemed necessary to underscore your solemn resolve."

"Precisely, Revered High Lord," Haladavar replied, and then added what his tone had already made clear: "I am relieved that you see it so."

"I wish I could also take the same view," the Srinshee muttered, settling herself in the ornate ceiling screen high above them all and aiming the Staff of Sundering down through it at the three nobles. "Now that your gesture is made, behave yourselves, lords," she murmured, as if they were children again, and she was their tutor. "Cormanthor will thank you for it."

Glancing up, she saw the row of downward-aimed wands were all in their places, awaiting only her touch to unleash their various perils. "Corellon grant that none of this be needed," the sorceress whispered, and bent her full attention to the events unfolding below.

Unaware of the danger overhead, the three lords ranged themselves in a line facing the Pool, and the head of House Urddusk took up the converse.

"Revered High Lord," he said shortly, "I've not the gift of a sweet or smooth tongue; few and blunt words are my way. I pray ye take no offense at what I say, for it is only right that ye should know: hear us not, or dismiss our concerns out of hand without parley, and we will try to use these swords we have brought against ye. I say this with deep sorrow; I pray it not become necessary. But, Most High, *we shall be heard*. We would fail Cormanthor if we kept silent now."

"I will hear you," the Coronal said mildly. "It is why I am here. Speak."

Lord Urddusk looked to the third lord; Malgath was known as a smooth—some might even have used the word "sly"—speaker. Now, knowing the eyes of all the court were upon him, he couldn't resist striking a pose.

"Most High," he purred, "we fear that the realm as we know it will be swept away if gnomes, halflings, our half-kin, and worse, are let loose to run about Cormanthor, putting trees to the axe and crowding us out. Oh, I've heard that you plan to set all of us lords in steward-ship over the forest, decreeing which tree shall be touched, and which shall stand. But, Lord Eltargrim, think on this: when a tree is cut, and falls dead, the deed is done, and no amount of hand-wringing or apologies for choosing the wrong one will restore it. The proper magics will, yes, but too much of the wis-dom and energy of our best mages, these past twelve winters, has been set to devising new spells to make trees grow from stumps, and trees to become more vital. Those replenishment magics would be unneces-sary if we simply *keep the humans out*. You've said be-fore that the laziness of humans will ensure that most of them will give no trouble. Perhaps that's true, but we see the other sort of humans—the restless, the ad-venturers, the ones who must explore for the sake of spying, and destroy for the sake of dominating—all too often. We also know that humans are greedy . . . almost as greedy as dwarves. And now you plan to let both into the very heart of Cormanthor. The humans will cut the trees down, and the dwarves will snarl for more *to feed the fires of their forges!*"

As Lord Malgath roared these last words some in the court almost shouted in agreement; the Coronal waited almost three breaths for the noise to die down. When things were relatively quiet again he asked, "Is this your only concern, lords? That the realm as we know it today will be swept away if we let other races settle in this our city, and the other areas we patrol and hold dear? For halflings in particular, many half-elven, and even some humans have dwelt for years on the fringes of the realm and yet we are here today, free to argue. I'll have the armathors check, if you'd like, but I'm sure no humans have overrun this hall today."

There was a ripple of laughter, but Lord Haladavar

snarled, "This is not a matter I can find in myself room to laugh about, Revered Lord. Humans and dwarves, in particular, have a way of ignoring or twisting any authority put over them, and of defying our People wherever and whenever they can. If we let them in, they will outbreed us, outtrick us, and outnumber us from the start. Very soon we'll be pushed right out of Cormanthor!"

"Ah, Lord Haladavar," the Coronal said, leaning forward on the throne, "you bring up the very reason I have proposed this Opening: that if we don't allow humans some share of Cormanthor now, under our conditions and rule, they will march in, army after vast army, and overwhelm us before this century, or the next, is done. We'll all be too *dead* to be pushed out of Cormanthor."

"Purest fantasy!" Lord Urddusk protested. "How can you say *humans* can field any army capable of winning even a single skirmish against the pride of Cormanthor?"

"Aye," Lord Haladavar said sternly. "I, too, cannot believe in this peril you threaten us with."

Lord Malgath merely raised a disbelieving eyebrow.

The Coronal matched it, raising his hand for silence, and called, "Lady Herald, stand forth!"

Alais Dree stepped forward from the doors of the Chamber of the Court. Her bright robes of office took wing after three paces, and she floated past the three glowering lords to attend the throne. "Great Lord, what is your need?"

"These lords question the strength of human warfare, and doubt my testimony as being bent to the support of my proposal. Unfold to them what you have seen in the lands of men."

Alais bowed and turned. When she was facing the three lords, she caught the eye of each in turn, and said crisply, "I am no puppet of the throne, lords, nor weak-willed because I am young, or a she. I have seen more of the doings of men than all three of you together."

There was another ripple of alarm in the Court as the lords once again pulled aside their robes to reveal stormswords; Alais shrugged. Seven swords faded into view in the air in front of her, hovering with their points toward the elven lords, and then vanished again. She paid them no attention, and went on, "From what I have seen, the humans have their own feuds, and are much disorganized, as well as being what we might call undisciplined and untutored in the ways of the forest. Yet they outnumber us already twenty to one and more. Far more humans have swung swords in earnest than have our People. They swarm, and fight with more ruthlessness, speed, and ability to adapt and change in battle than we have ever known. If they invade, lords, we shall probably manage two or four victories, perhaps even a decisive slaughter. They will manage the rest, and be hunting us through the streets before two seasons are past. Please believe me now; I don't want the realm to feel the pain of your believing me only as you die, later."

She continued, "To those who, hearing me, then say: 'Then let us fare forth now, and smite all human realms, that they can never raise armies against us,' I say only: no. Humans invaded will unite to slay a common foe; we shall be slain outside our realm, only to leave it undefended when the counterstrike comes. Moreover, anyone who goes to war with humans makes lasting enemies: they remember grudges, lords, as well as we do. To strike at a land now, even to humble it, is to await its next generation, or the one after that, to come riding back at us for revenge—and humans have a score or more generations for each one of ours."

"Will you accept, lords," the Coronal asked mildly, "the testimony of our Lady Herald? Do you grant that she is probably right?"

The three lords shifted uneasily, until Urddusk snapped, "And if we do?"

"If you do, lords," Alais replied, startling everyone save the Coronal by her interjection, "than you and our Coronal stand agreed, both fighting to save Cormanthor. Your shared dispute is only over the means to do so."

She turned again to face the throne, and the Coronal thanked her with a smile and gestured her dismissal. As she floated past the three lords, he spoke again, saying, "Hear my will, lords. The Opening shall proceed—but only after one thing is in place."

The silence, as everyone waited for his next words, was a tense, straining thing.

"My lords, you have all raised just and grave concerns over the safety of our People in an 'open' Cormanthor. Inviting other races in without the elves of Cormanthor having some sort of overarching, pervasive protection is unthinkable. Yet this cannot be a protection of mere law, for we can be swamped and unable to muster blades enough to enforce our law, precisely as if we made war. We do, however, still outstrip humans in one area, for a few more seasons at least: the magic we weave."

The Coronal made a gesture, and suddenly several of the courtiers glowed with golden auras, up and down the hall. They glanced down at themselves in surprise, as their fellows drew back from them. The Coronal pointed at them with a smile, and said, "Elves who have the means to do so, or the skill, have always crafted, or hired others to craft for them, personal mantles of defensive magic. We need a mantle that will encloak all of Cormanthor. We *shall have* such a mantle before the city is laid open to those not of pure elven blood."

Lord Urddusk sputtered, "But such a thing is impossible!"

The Coronal laughed. "That's not a word I ever like to use in Cormanthor, my lord. 'Tis almost always a swift embarrassment to whomever utters it!"

Lord Haladavar leaned his head over to the ear of Lord Urddusk and murmured, "Be at ease! He says this so he can retreat from his plan with dignity! We've won!"

Unfortunately, the Lady Herald seemed to have left some trace of her voice-hurling magic behind, for the whispered words carried to every corner of the chamber. Lord Haladavar flushed a deep, rich red, but the Coronal laughed merrily and said, "No, lords, I mean it! Opening we shall have—but an Opening with the People well protected!"

"I suppose we'll now waste the best efforts of our young mages on *this* now, for the next twoscore seasons or so," Lord Malgath snapped.

The flash of one of the old-fashioned little globes known as "come hither" signals spilled forth among the courtiers then, and everyone looked to see its source. As a buzz of conversation arose and Lord Malgath's comment hung unanswered, the Lady Herald cut through the gaping ranks of well-dressed elves like a wasp seeking to sting, and came at last to an aged elf in dark, plain robes. She smiled, turned to face the Throne, and announced, "Mythanthar would speak."

The three lords frowned in puzzlement as the courtiers burst again into excited whispers, but the Coronal made the gesture for silence. When it had fallen, the Lady Herald touched the old mage with her sleeve, and by her magic his thin, quavering voice rang clear to every corner of that vast hall. "I would remind

Cormanthans of the 'spell fields' I tried to develop from mantles, for use by our war captains, three thousand years agone. Our need passed, and I turned to other things, but I know now what direction to work in, where I was ignorant before. In elder days, our magic weavers could easily alter how magic worked in a given area. I shall craft a spell that does the same, and give Cormanthor its mantle. From end to end of this fair city there shall be a 'mythal.' Give me three seasons to get started, and I shall then be able to give thee a count of how many more I shall need."

There was a momentary silence as everyone waited for him to say more, but Mythanthar waved that he was done, and turned away from the herald; the Court erupted in excited chatter.

"My lord," Lord Malgath snapped, approaching the Throne and raising his arms in his anxiousness to be heard (overhead, the Srinshee aimed two scepters at him, her face set and stern). "please hear me: it is imperative that this 'mythal' deny the working of any magic by all N'Tel'Quess—in fact, by all who are not purebloods of Cormanthor!"

"And it must reveal to all the alignments of folk entering it," Lord Haladavar said excitedly, "to protect us from the shapeshifting beasts and all who dare to impersonate elves, or even specific elven lords!"

"Well said!" Lord Urddusk echoed. "It should also, and for the same reason, make invisible things visible at its boundaries, and prevent teleportation into or out of it, or we'll have invading armies of adventurers in our laps every night!"

Nearly every elf at court was crowding forward now, bobbing their heads, waving their arms, and shouting their own suggestions; as the din mounted, the Coronal finally spread his hands in resignation and pressed one of the buttons set deep in one arm of the Throne.

There was a blinding brilliance as the Coronal's lightshock wave took effect. It kept almost everyone from seeing the dagger hurled at the Coronal from the ranks of courtiers. That blade struck the field created by the scepter in the Srinshee's left hand and was transported to an empty storage cellar deep under the north wing of the palace.

It also had its intended effect: everyone except the Coronal on his throne staggered backward, stunned into silence.

Into the gentle moaning sounds that followed, as folk fought to clear the swirling lights from their eyes, the ruler of all Cormanthor said gently, "No mythal can hope to include every desire expressed by every Cormanthan, but I intend that it act on as many as are possible and tenable. Please make all of your suggestions to the Lady Herald of the court; she will convey them to the senior mages of the court and to myself. Mythanthar, have my deepest thanks—and my hopes that all Cormanthor will soon echo that thanks. It is my will that you craft an initial version of your mythal—no matter how incomplete or crude—as soon as possible, for presentation to the court."

"Revered Lord, I shall do so," Mythanthar replied, bowing low. He turned away again, and high above him, the Srinshee's eyes widened. Had there, or had there not, been a circle of nine sparks around the old mage's head, just for an instant?

Well, there was none to be seen now. Face thoughtful, the Srinshee watched him totter toward one of the tapestries, face thoughtful. Her eyes widened again an instant later—and this time one of the scepters in her hands leapt slightly as it hurled forth magic.

The old mage passed out among the tapestries, and Oluevaera was pleased to note that two of the Coronal's best young armathors fell into place before and behind him, wearing ornamental half-cloaks that her mage-sight could see were generating a metal-warding field between them. Mythanthar's own mantle should take care of any hurled spells, and he should soon stand in his own tower again, unharmed, now that the first opportunistic attack on him had been foiled.

The Srinshee watched grimly as a courtier in a plum-colored tunic, whose name and lineage she did not know, sagged back against a wall, staring down at his hand. His face was white and his mouth was gaping in soundless shock.

Her aim had been good; that hand was now a withered, clawlike thing mottled with age . . . and too weak to hold the deadly triple-bladed dagger that lay on the floor beneath it.

* * * * *

"I must confess I am still gloating about the success Duilya enjoyed," Alaglossa Tornglara confided, the moment they were out of hearing of their servants. The two parties of uniformed retainers carefully set down the purchases made by their lady masters at the side of the street, and stood patient guard over them.

"They'll not all be that easy, I'm afraid," the Lady Ithrythra Mornmist murmured.

"Indeed; have you seen the Lady Auglamyr? Amaranthae, I mean. She was as still and silent as a statue today; I wonder if the wooing of a certain High Court Mage is troubling her."

"No," Ithrythra said slowly, "it's something else. She's worried for someone, but not herself. She barely notices what she's wearing, and sends Auglamyr pages scurrying on dozens of seeking errands, by the hour. She's lost something . . . or someone."

"I wonder what can have befallen?" Lady Tornglara

breathed, a frown drawing down her beautiful features into solemnity. "This must be something serious, I'll be bound."

"Intrigues in the streets, now, is it?" The voice that hailed them was almost exuberantly arrogant; Elandorr Waelvor, flower of the third elder House of the realm, was gleeful about something.

He was resplendent in a jerkin of black velvet trimmed about with white thunderbolts, and a cloak of rich purple with a magenta lining swirled about his shoulders and gleaming black thigh-high boots as he advanced upon them. His slim, elegant fingers bristled with rings, and the jeweled silver scabbard of his sword of honor was so long that it slapped at his ankles with every step. The two ladies watched him strut, their faces expressionless.

Elandorr seemed to sense their unspoken disapproval; he lowered his brows, clasped his hands behind his back, and started to circle them.

"Though 'tis refreshing to see the younger, more vigorous houses of Cormanthor grow into taking an interest in the doings of the realm," he said airily, "I must caution you ladies that overmuch talk about affairs of import would be a bad, nay, a *very* bad thing. It has recently been my painful duty to ah, curb the behavioral excesses of the wayward Lady Symrustar, of the fledgling House of Auglamyr. You may have heard something about it, borne on the lamentable winds of gossip with which our fair city seems so intolerably afflicted . . ?"

The upward, inquisitorial rise of his voice, and his lifted brows, urged a reply; he was momentarily disconcerted when both ladies silently arched scornful eyebrows of their own, locked gazes with him, and said nothing.

His eyes flashed with irritation as he spun away

from the weight of two level stares, swirling his cloak grandly. Then Elandorr put his hand to his breast, sighed theatrically, and turned back toward them. "It would grieve me deeply," he said passionately, "to hear the same tragic sort of news mooted about the city concerning the proud ladies of Mornmist and Tornglara. Yet such misfortunes can all too easily befall any elven she who doesn't know her proper place, and now keep to it—in the new Cormanthor."

"And which 'new Cormanthor' would that be, Lord Waelvor?" Alaglossa asked softly, wide-eyed, two fingers to her chin.

"Why, this realm around us, known and loved by all true Cormanthans. This realm as it will be in a moon or so, renewed and set back on the proper path that was good enough for our ancestors, and theirs before them."

"Renewed? By whom, and how?" Ithrythra joined in the dumbfounded game. "Coyly gloating young lordlings?"

Elandorr scowled at her, and drew his lips back from his teeth in an unlovely smile. "I shan't forget your insolence, 'Lady,' and shall act appropriately—you may assure yourself of that!"

"Lord, I shall await you," she said, dropping her head in deference. As she did so, she rolled her eyes.

With a growl, Elandorr swept past her, deliberately extending his elbow to strike her head as he did so— but somehow, as she swayed out of his reach, he found himself bearing down on the back of a servant who had appeared out of nowhere to attend to the Lady Tornglara. Elandorr cast an angry look around and saw that servants of both ladies were closing in around him, eyes averted from him but with daggers, goads, and carry-yokes in their hands. The scion of the

Waelvors snarled and quickened his pace, striding out of the closing press of bodies.

The servants crowded in around both ladies, who looked at each other and discovered that they were both dark-eyed, quick of breath, and flaring about the nostrils. The tips of their ears were red with anger.

"A dangerous foe, and now one fully aware of you, Ithrythra," Alaglossa said in soft warning.

"Ah, but look how much he blurted out about someone's future plans for the realm, because he lost his temper," Ithrythra replied. Then she looked at the servants all around them both and said, "I thank all of you. 'Twas very brave, walking into our peril when you could—should—have stayed safely away."

"Nay, Lady; 'twas all we could do, and still know any honor in our days," one of the older male stewards muttered.

Ithrythra smiled at him, and replied, "Well, if I ever act so rude as yon lordling, you've my permission to toss me down in the mud and use that goad of yours a time or two on my backside!"

"Best forewarn your lord of his arrival, though," Alaglossa put in with a smile. "This man's one of mine!"

A general roar of mirth erupted, in which all joined—but then died away slowly as, one by one, they turned and looked along the street to discover that Elandorr Waelvor hadn't walked all that far off after all. He obviously thought that their laughter had been at his direct expense, and was standing looking at them all with black murder in his eyes.

* * * * *

Lord Ihimbraskar Evendusk floated at ease several feet above his own bed, naked as his birthing day, smiling at his lady like an admiring young elven lover.

Lady Duilya Evendusk smiled back at him, her chin resting on her hands, and her elbows resting on the same empty air. She wore only fine golden chains studded with gems; they hung down in loops toward the bed below.

"So, my lord, what news today?" she breathed, still delighted that he'd hastened straight home to disrobe after Court emptied—and that he'd reacted with delight, and not irritation, to find her waiting in his bed. The ceremonially ignored bottle of tripleshroom sherry was still on the floor where she'd ordered it set; Duilya doubted her lord had touched a drop since seeing her drain one such bottle. She wondered when—if—she'd ever dare tell him about the magic her lady friends had worked, to enable her to do that drinking.

"Three senior lords," her Ihimbraskar told her, "Haladavar, Urddusk and that serpent Malgath, came to Court and demanded that the Coronal reconsider the Opening. They wore stormswords, and threatened to use them."

"And do they yet live?" Duilya asked dryly.

"They do. Eltargrim chose to view their weapons as 'errors in judgment.' "

Duilya snorted. "The enemy amrathor gasped out blood as my error of judgment took him through the vitals," she declaimed grandly, waving a hand. Her lord chuckled.

"Wait, love, there's more," he told her, rolling over. She shrugged at him to continue; her hair slid down over her shoulder and fell free.

Ihimbraskar watched her tresses spread and swing back and forth as he continued, "The Coronal said their concerns were valid, had his Lady Herald scare us all with tales of the battle-might of humans, and said the Opening will go ahead eventually: *after* the city is cloaked in a huge spellmantle!"

Duilya frowned. "What, old crazed Mythanthar's 'mythal' again? What good will that be, if the realm is open to all?"

"Aye, Mythanthar, and it'll give us control over what these nonelven intruders do, and what magic they work, and what they can hide, by the sounds of it," her lord said.

Duilya drifted closer, and as she reached out to stroke his chest, she added softly, "Elves too, my lord—elves too!"

Lord Evendusk started to shake his head dismissively, then froze, looking very thoughtful, and said in a small voice, "Duilya—however have I kept myself from utter stupidity, all these years I ignored you? Spells can be crafted to work only on creatures of certain races, and to ignore others . . . but will they be? What a weapon in the hand of whoever is Coronal!"

"It seems to me, my lord," Duilya said as she rolled over to rest the side of her face against his and fix him with a very solemn eye, "that we'd better work as hard as we can to see that Eltargrim is still our Coronal, and not one of these ambitious ardavanshee—in particular, not one of the oh-so-noble sons of our three highest houses. They may consider humans and the like no better than snakes and ground-slugs, but they look upon the rest of us elven Cormanthans as no better than cattle. The Opening will make them scared for the security of their lofty positions, and so, ruthlessly desperate in their acts."

"Why aren't *you* a court advisor?" Ihimbraskar sighed.

Duilya rolled over atop him and said sweetly, "I am. I advise the court through you."

Lord Evendusk groaned. "Too true. You make me sound like some sort of lackey you send off into danger every day, to put forth your views."

The Lady Duilya Evendusk smiled and said nothing. Their eyes met, and held steady. There was a twinkle in her eyes as she continued to say nothing.

A slow smile crooked Ihimbraskar's usually hard mouth. "Corellon praise you and damn you, Lady," he said, in the breath before he started to laugh helplessly.

Fifteen

A MYTHAL, MAYBE

It came to pass that Elminster was slain by the elves, or nearly so, and by the grace of Mystra drifted about Cormanthor in the shape of a ghost or phantom, powerless and unseen—akin, some have said, to the lot of scullery maids in service to a highborn lady. Like such wenches, woe would likely befall the last prince of Athalantar if he were to come to the notice of the mighty. The master sorcerers of the elves were powerful in those days, and faster to make war and cast forth reckless magics. They saw the world around them, and all humans in it, as rebellious playthings to be tamed often, swiftly, and harshly. Among certain of the elven, that thinking has changed but little to this day.

Antarn the Sage
from **The High History of Faerûnian Archmages Mighty**
published circa The Year of the Staff

Symrustar was naked, her face a dark mask of dried blood. She stared out of the shadow cast by her overhanging hair, seeing neither Elminster nor anything else in Faerûn. Foam bubbled at the corners of her trembling mouth as she panted and whimpered. If there was still a whole mind behind those eyes, Elminster could see no evidence of it.

Elandorr must be an even more vicious rival than

Symrustar had thought. El felt sick. He had done this, by whisking Elandorr past her defenses and letting him see into her mind. It was his to undo, if he could.

Lady, he said, or tried to. *Symrustar Auglamyr*, he called softly, knowing that he was making no sound. Perhaps if he drifted right into her head . . . or would that do more harm?

She half-fell on her face then, as she blundered into the top of a gully, and El shrugged. How could she be made any worse? The danger of a predator was very real, and would grow worse as darkness came. He drifted in past her eyes, into the confusing darkness beyond, trying to perceive anything around him as he called her name again. Nothing.

El drifted through the tortured elven lady, and looked sadly at her backside as she lurched away from him, drooling and making confused, wordless noises. He could do nothing.

In his present state, he couldn't even stroke her with a soothing touch, or speak to her. He was truly a phantom . . . and she was possibly dying, and probably mad. The Srinshee might be able to help her, but he knew not where the Lady Oluevaera might be found.

Mystra, he cried again, *aid me! Please!*

He waited, drifting, looking anxiously into Symrustar's unseeing eyes from time to time as she waddled onwards, but no matter how long or often he called, there was no apparent reply. Uncertainly El floated along beside the crawling, moaning elven sorceress, as she made her slow and painful way through the forest.

Once she panted, "Elandorr, no!" and El hoped other lucid words would follow, but she growled, made some yipping sounds, and then burst into tears . . . tears that in the end became the murmuring sound again.

Perhaps even Mystra couldn't hear him now. No, that was foolish; it must have been she who restored him after his folly at the ruined castle. It seemed she wanted him to learn a lesson now, though.

If he flew back across the mountains and desert to that temple of Mystra beyond Athalantar, or one of the other holy places of the goddess he'd heard of, perhaps the priests could give him his body back.

If they could even sense him, that is. Who was to say they could, where the spell-hurling elves of Cormanthor could not?

Perhaps he'd be noticed if he passed through an unfolding spell, or blundered into the chambers of a mage trying to craft a new magic. Yet if he left Symrustar . . .

He whirled in the air in exasperation, coming to a wrenching decision. He could do nothing but watch if she got hurt or attacked or killed right now. If he regained his body, surely he could use spells to find her, or at least send someone else to rescue her; the Srinshee, perhaps. He didn't give much for his chances of convincing House Auglamyr that he, the hated human armathor, somehow knew that Elandorr Waelvor had left their dearest daughter and heir crawling through the forest like a mad-witted animal.

No, he could do nothing for Symrustar. If she died out here, it wasn't as though she was an innocent who'd done nothing to bring this on herself. No, gods above, she'd earned it many times over before the blundering human Elminster had happened along and she'd seen him as a good fit for her clutches.

And yet he was almost as guilty of her present state as if he'd broken her mind and body himself.

He had to get back to the city, and hope that he could communicate with someone. At that thought, El hurled himself through the trees, not caring if he went around or through, racing back to the streets and grand homes of Cormanthor. He thrust himself right through the glowing armor of a patrol leader who was

just directing his warriors into the formation he
favored for leaving the city.

Dusk was falling. El swooped through a line of glowing globes of air that hung above the second street he
came upon, illuminating an impromptu party. Though
one of them seemed to bob and flicker after he passed
through it, he could feel nothing.

He turned toward the Coronal's palace once more,
and saw soft light coming from part way up a tower
he'd never noticed before. The last light of day was fading off across the gardens; he slowed near the window
and saw, in the chamber within, the Coronal sitting in
a chair, apparently asleep. The Srinshee was leaning
on one of its arms and speaking to the six court sorceresses, who sat in a ring all around.

If he had any good hope of aid in Cormanthor, it lay
in that room. Elminster rushed excitedly along the
side of the palace, seeking a way in.

He found a slightly open window almost immediately, but it led to a storeroom so securely sealed off
from the rest of the palace that he could go no further.
He boiled up out of it again, frustration rising; every
moment wasted was more of the conversation in that
lighted chamber that he wouldn't hear. He raced along
the wall until he found one of those large windows
whose "glass" was no glass at all, but an invisible field
of magic.

He felt a slight tingling as he darted through it, and
almost whirled to go through again, in hopes that this
heralded a return to solidity, but no. Later. He had a
gathering to eavesdrop on now.

He knew what room he needed to enter, and his
sense of direction was supported by the three tinglings
he felt as he drew near it, and encountered spell after
spell of warding. The Srinshee certainly didn't want
anyone to overhear what was going on in that room.

Its door, however, was old and massive, and therefore worn so much by centuries of swinging that there was a sizable chink around the frame. El darted in excitedly, and raced right through the ring of listening sorceresses to circle the tiny figure at their heart.

The Srinshee gave no sign of feeling or hearing him, as he bellowed her name and waved his hands through her. El sighed, resigned himself to more of this silent ghostliness, and settled down to hover above the empty arm of the Coronal's chair, to listen in earnest. He'd arrived, it seemed—thank Mystra—at the best part.

"Bhuraelea and Mladris," the Srinshee was saying, "must shield Mythanthar's body at all times—and themselves besides, for any foe rebuffed in an initial strike at Emmyth will surely seek out the source of his protection and try to eliminate it. His mantle bests any of ours, and I suggest only one augmentation: Sylmae, you cast the web of watching I gave you so as to mesh with Emmyth's mantle. You and Holone must then take turns observing it. It will lash back at anyone seeking to pierce it with spells by itself, yes, but such attackers may be well protected, and suffer no harm at all. I want you two *not* to strike at them, but simply to identify them and inform us all as soon as possible."

"That leaves us idle again," the sorceress Ajhalanda said a little sadly, her gesture taking in herself and Yathlanae, the elven maid who sat at her elbow.

"Not so," the Srinshee said with a smile. "Your shared task is to lay spells that listen for anyone in the realm who utters the names 'Emmyth' or 'Mythanthar' or even 'Lord Iydril,' though I suspect few of the Cormyth of today recall that title. Identify them, try to follow what they're saying, and report back."

"Anything else?" Holone asked, a little wearily.

"I know what it is to be young, and restless to be doing things," the Srinshree said softly. "Watching and waiting is the hardest work, ladies. I think it best if we meet here four morns hence, and switch tasks."

"What will you be doing?" Sylmae asked, nodding in agreement with the Srinshee's plan.

"Guarding the Coronal, of course," the Lady Oluevaera said with a smile. "*Someone* has to."

Mouths crooked with amusement around the circle. A half smile played about the edges of the Srinshee's mouth as she turned slowly to meet the eyes of each of the six in turn, and receive their slight nods of agreement.

"I know it chafes not to be working unfettered, you six," she added softly, "but I suspect the time for that will come soon enough, when the prouder houses of this realm realize that a mythal is going to curb their own spellhurlings and covert activities. Then our troubles will begin in earnest."

"How far may we go, should things come to open spell battle in these 'troubles'?" Holone asked quietly.

"Oh, they will, spellsister, they assuredly will," the Srinshee replied. "You must all feel free to do what you feel needful; blast any foe at will, to death and beyond. Hesitate not to strike out at any Cormanthan whose intent you are sure of, who works against the Coronal or the creation of a mythal. The future of our realm is at stake; no price is too high to pay."

Heads were nodding in somber silence, all round the circle. The Coronal chose that moment to snore; the Srinshee regarded him affectionately as the six sorceresses smiled and rose.

"Hasten!" she bid them, eyes shining. "You are the guardians of Cormanthor, and its future. Go forth, and win victory!"

"Queen of Spells," Sylmae intoned in a male-sounding roar, striking her chest, "we go!"

This was evidently some sort of quotation; there was a general ripple of mirth, and then the six sorceresses were on the move in a graceful swirling of long hair and robes and longer legs. El cast a brief, sad glance at the Srinshee, who still could not hear his loudest cry of her name, and followed the one called Bhuraelea, making careful note of the face and form of Mladris, in case keeping silent escort to her became necessary instead.

As it happened, the two tall, slender sorceresses kept together, striding down a palace corridor with the haste of a storm wind. "Should we eat something, do you think?" Bhuraelea asked her fellow mage, as they stepped out past the last palace ward-field and turned themselves invisible. El, hovering close by, was relieved to see that they remained clearly visible to him, though their bodies now seemed outlined with a bluish gleam, like strong winter starlight reflected off snow.

"I brought some food earlier," Mladris replied. "I'll summon it before we enter his first ward." She wrinkled her nose. "Wait until you see his tower; some old males embrace the idea of 'home as dump' rather too wholeheartedly."

* * * * *

The two sorceresses were passing a jack of mint water and a cold grouse pie back and forth as they slipped through the glowing wards that surrounded the rather ramshackle tower of Mythanthar the mage. Starfall Turret resembled a long, grassy barrow-hill, pierced along one side with windows, and rising at its north end into a squat, rough-walled stone tower. Its yard was an overgrown tangle of stumps, fallen trees, and forest shrubs and creepers. In the dusk, they looked like a dark chaos of giants' fingers stabbing the darkening sky.

"Ye gods and heroes," Bhuraelea murmured. "Defending this against stealthy foes would take an army."

"That's us," Mladris agreed cheerfully, and then added, "Thank the gods, our foes aren't likely to be any too stealthy. They're more apt to try to crush the wards with realm-shaking spells, and then follow up with more."

"Three wards . . . no, four. That'll take a lot of blasting," Bhuraelea observed, as they finished the pie and licked their fingers. A light flared briefly in one of the high windows of the tower.

"He's at it already," Mladris said.

Bhuraelea grimaced. "He's probably been 'at it' since he stepped out of the Chamber of the Court," she replied. "The Lady Oluevaera told me he's apt to be more than a bit single-minded. We could dance nude around him and sing courting songs in his ear, she said, and he'd probably murmur that it was nice to have such energetic young things around, and could we please fetch yon powders for him?"

"Gods," Mladris said feelingly, rolling her eyes, "grant that I never get old enough to be like that."

Out of the empty air very close by a cold voice said smugly, "Granted."

An instant later, Faerûn exploded into many leaping lightnings, bright arcs that raced hungrily through the air to stab through the gasping, staggering sorceresses and snarl onward. Mladris and Bhuraelea were snatched off their daintily booted feet and hurled back over shrubs and brambles, with smoke streaming from their mouths and flames spitting fitfully from their eyes.

Even Elminster was taken by surprise; how had he missed seeing the cruel-faced elven mage who was now rising, a vengeful column of mist turning solid, above the tangled garden? Clouds of radiance were swirling in from all directions to join the thickening form of the sorcerer. As he grew taller and more solid, he calmly continued to lash the coughing, sobbing sorceresses with crackling streams of lightning, allowing them no moment to recover or escape.

Sparks fell in showers from the elf's hands as he stepped forward, treading on the empty air with a mincing swagger of satisfaction. El felt a stinging pain as they drifted through him and winked out. He swirled around the mage, swooping and shouting in silent futility.

The innermost ward had been no ward at all, but the cloudlike, alert form of the mage, awaiting aid, intentional or otherwise!

"Haemir Waelvor, at your service," the elven sorcerer told the two ladies, when their burned and trembling bodies were so enwrapped with lightnings that they couldn't move. "The Starym seem to be delayed—perhaps wanting me to do the dirty work before they deign to appear. It matters little, now that I have your life-energies to feed my shield-sundering. You're here to protect feeble-witted, doddering old Mythanthar, I take it? A pity; you're going to be the death of him instead."

Bhuraelea managed a groan of protest; little black flames leaped from her mouth. Mladris hung limp and silent, her eyes open, staring, and dark. Only a pulse racing in her throat showed that she yet lived.

El felt rage rising in him like a hungry red tide, demanding release. He turned ponderously, letting the anger build into shaking energy that burst out at last in a long, soundless charge that took him through the lightnings that bound the two sorceresses, and straight at the Waelvor mage.

Halfway there he arched and cried out in silent pain and surprise. He could feel the lightnings! Their caster could see and feel his contact, too; Haemir's eyes narrowed at the sight of his suddenly crackling, spitting, somehow dimmed bolts of lightning. What was *dragging* at them so?

Waelvor's lips thinned. Old Mythanthar, or some other meddler? It mattered little. He snarled something, and moved one hand in a quick spell that spun a dozen slicing blades to clash in the air at the point of the disturbance.

El watched the blades appear and tumble down behind him, and rose up out of the lightnings feeling both pain and exhilaration. Some of their energy was racing around inside him, making him tingle unpleasantly, and scattering sparks from his mouth and eyes.

The Waelvor wizard's eyes widened in surprise as he dimly perceived the lightning-lashed outline of an elven—or was it human?—shape, an instant before it smashed into him.

El struck with all his force, lashing and slashing, trying to overwhelm Haemir Waelvor through sheer ferocity. When he "touched" the mage, he felt no solidity, only a tingling as the lightnings rolled out of him, then searing pain as the interlaced spells of the wizard's mantle tried to tear him apart, phantom that he was.

While Elminster rolled in midair screaming soundlessly in agony, Haemir Waelvor shook his head, roaring, his own lightnings spitting and coiling from his mouth in their rude return. The pupils of his eyes suddenly turned as milky and sparkling as a white opal—a look El had last seen years back, in the eyes of a mage who'd just fallen victim to his own confusion spell.

El shook his head and screamed again, trying to gain control of his own pain-wracked form. So, he could hurt—or at least cause pain and confusion to—folk he rushed through, could he?

Shuddering, he drifted away to a distant vantage

point to watch, knowing he could do nothing to aid the two sorceresses, who lay slumped where the failing lightnings had released them.

He needed to know how long it would take a wizard to recover—and if swooping through one as a spell was being cast would ruin and waste the magic. He'd have to go through this punishment all over again.

Mystra, let this elf be a long time recovering, El said in fervent prayer. But it seemed Mystra was contrary-minded, or at least hard of hearing, this day: Haemir was already staggering about, feeling for his surroundings with an outstretched hand, holding his head, and cursing weakly. El was sorely tempted to gather himself and plunge through the elven mage again right now, but he needed to know what sort of damage his passing through an elf would do. And hadn't this smug Waelvor mage said something about the Starym showing up? It might be best not to be all that clearly visible whenever a group of cruel elven sorcerers arrived, looking for trouble.

Haemir Waelvor was shaking his head gingerly as if to clear it now, and his curses were gathering force.

He seemed on the verge of recovery, while a certain ghostly Elminster certainly still hurt, acutely and all over.

Mystra curse him. He was going to drain these two lady sorceresses to husks while the last prince of Athalantar hovered over him on watch, powerless to stop him!

Of course, Elminster reflected wryly, an instant later, things could get worse—much worse. Right now, for instance.

One after the other, the outer wards were failing, sundering themselves in silent explosions of sparks at a certain point and fading away outwards from there. The center of this disruption was something that looked like a tall black flame, one that promptly split as it glided through the last ward, and died away to reveal three tall, fine-boned elven males in robes whose sashes of flame-hued silk were adorned with twin falling dragons. The Starym had come.

"Hail, Lord Waelvor," one said in tones of velvet softness, as the three figures strode forward together, treading air with a languid air of cold superiority. "What distress finds you here, in the empty night? Did yon ladies seek to defend themselves?"

"A watchghost," Haemir hissed, his eyes glittering with mingled pain and anger. "It awaited, and struck me. I fought it off, but the pain lingers. And how does this fair night find you, my lords?"

"Bored," one of them said bluntly. "Still, perhaps the old fool can provide us with some sport ere we send him to dust. Let us see."

He strode forward, and the other two Starym drew apart to flank him and follow, moving their fingers in the intricate passes and gestures of mighty battle spells. They strode right past the Waelvor wizard and the crumpled bodies of the two fallen sorceresses. El hovered near Haemir, fearing he might take out his rage on the ladies, and watched the Starym strike.

From the cupped palms of one wizard white fire burst forth, rushing upwards in a sinuous column like an eel seeking the stars, only to burst apart into three long, serpentine necks that grew huge, dragonlike maws at their ends. Those heads shook themselves restlessly, and then bent and bit at the old stone tower. Where their teeth touched, stone silently vanished, melting away into nothingness and laying bare the chambers within.

From the fingertips of the second wizard red lances of racing fire then erupted, leaping into the revealed chambers of Mythanthar's tower to smite certain things of magic. Some of those things exploded into bright showers of sparks, or blasts that rocked Starfall Turret and hurled slivers of its stones far away into the gathering darkness, to crash through trees to unseen distant landings. Others burst into rushing red flames, swirling into fiery pinwheels that hung here and there in the tower, pinned in place by the Starym wizard's magic.

From the hands of the third mage a green cloud billowed, grew teeth and many clawed limbs with frightening speed, and flew forth into the tower, hunting Mythanthar.

A breath or two after its dive into Starfall Turret, something flared a vivid purple deep inside those shattered stones, and a bright bolt of that radiance snarled out, spitting aside the dismembered claws of the green monster as it came. Haemir Waelvor watched them spin down to crash into the shrubbery, and cursed in fear.

The three Starym flinched and scrambled away from the tower on the heels of his oath, as the purple radiance burst into three fingers that stabbed out at them, veering to follow each scrambling elf.

Personal mantles flared into visibility as they were tested; one mage stiffened, threw out his arms as his mantle turned to roiling purple and black smoke around him, and then fell hard on his face, and lay still.

The other two mages spun around and cried something to each other that El couldn't catch; their voices were high and distorted in frantic fear. It seemed the old fool was providing them with just a trifle more sport than they'd expected.

The body of the fallen Starym spat sparks and sputtering wisps of dying spells as he expired. His head remained bent at a sickening angle against the old

stump, but the rest of his body slowly melted its way
into the ground.

Waelvor stared down at it in gaping amazement, but
the two surviving Starym paid their relative no heed
as they busily spun magic. Fingers flew and the very
air around the two elves crackled and flowed, like oil
sliding down the inside of a water-filled bowl. Tiny
motes of light flickered here and there as the mages
danced the measures of a long and intricate spell.

As the twin magics unfolded, two glowing clouds of
pale green radiance faded into being above the heads
of the Starym, shedding enough light to show the
sweat glistening on corded necks and working jaws.

Then, with a silent flourish, one cloud coalesced into
a sphere and began to spin. The second followed an instant later, and two globes of force hung in the air
above the busy elven mages.

Haemir swore again, his features as sharp and
white as if they'd been quarried out of milky marble.

A red mist streamed out of the riven turret, reaching for the intruders in a long, inexorable wave, and
they were almost stumbling in haste as they plucked
scepters, wands, gems, and various small and winking
items out of their sashes and hurled them up into the
spheres above their heads. Each item floated there,
drifting lazily around among the other items in the
spheres.

The red mist was only feet away when one of the
Starym snapped out a single ringing word—or perhaps it was a name—and every item of magic in his
sphere went off at once, tearing apart the very air in a
darksome rift of glimmering stars that sucked in the
sphere, the items, the red mist, and much of the gardens and front face of the tower before it vanished
with a high sighing sound.

The other Starym mage laughed in triumph before

he said the word that awakened the items in his sphere.

They rose, like flies disturbed from carrion on a hot day, and spat a deadly volley of bright beams into the tower, which burst apart amid deafening thunders, raining down stones all around and releasing a cloud of crimson dust as some ancient magic or other failed.

The rift in the wake of these beams was small, sucking in only the items themselves and the sphere that had contained them before it vanished; no doubt this was the way the spell was supposed to work.

The two surviving Starym were moving their hands again, weaving unfamiliar—but seemingly strong—magics as they stared into the tower. By their shared manner, Mythanthar must be visible to them, and still very much alive and active.

El made his decision. Scudding low across the darkened garden, he built up speed and smashed through Waelvor. This time the impact was like being hit across the chest by a solidly-swung log; it drove all the breath out of him in a soundless scream. He passed through the body of the mage and plunged into the head of the nearest Starym like a hurled spear.

The blow sent him spinning end over end through the night, shuddering in agony so great that it snatched all his breath away again, and a golden haze of dazedness began to swirl around him.

He had the satisfaction, however, of seeing the Starym he'd struck rolling on the ground, clutching his head and whimpering. The other Starym stared at his fellow in disbelief and so didn't see the blackened figure that trudged out of the tower behind him, trailing smoke. An elf who could only be Mythanthar.

The old elf turned and looked back at the tiny flames that were now leaping from every stone of his shattered tower. He shook his head, leveled one finger at the mage who was still standing, and—as the Starym whirled around belatedly—vanished.

An instant later, a golden sphere erupted out of thin air, cutting the Starym neatly in two at chest level as it englobed his torso.

When the sphere imploded again an instant later, it took the upper body of the proud elven mage with it, leaving only two trembling legs behind. They took one staggering step and then parted company, toppling in different directions to the ground.

"*You!*"

The cry was both furious and frightened. El swirled around, still slowed and mind-mazed by his agonies, and realized that the lone surviving Starym, now staggering up from the ground, meant *him*. The elf could see the human!

Now, if he could only survive to reach the Srinshee, and tell her . . .

The Starym spat something malicious, and raised his hands in a casting Elminster had seen before: a spell humans called a "meteor swarm."

"Mystra, be with me *now*," the last prince of Athalantar murmured, as four balls of roiling flame raced to positions around him, and exploded.

The last thing El saw was the body of Haemir Waelvor turning to ashes as it tumbled helplessly toward him, borne on roaring flames that were bursting forth to consume the world all around. Faerûn turned over, spun crazily, and then whirled away into hungry fire.

Sixteen

MASKED MAGES

*The People looked upon Elminster Aumar, and saw, but
did not understand what they saw. He was the first gust
of the new wind sent by Mystra. And Cormanthor was
like an old and mighty wall, that stands against such
winds of change for century upon century, until even its
builders forget that it was built, and was ever anything
else but an unyielding barrier. There will come a day for
such a wall when it will topple, and be changed by the
unseen, unsolid winds. It always does.*

*That day came for the proud realm when the Coronal
named the human Elminster Aumar a knight of Cormanthor—but the wall knew not that it had been shattered, and waited for its tumbling stones to crash to
earth before it would deign to notice. That fall, when it
came, would be the laying of the Mythal. But the stones
of the wall, being elven stones, lingered in the air for an
astonishingly long while. . . .*

Shalheira Talandren, High Elven Bard of Summerstar
from **Silver Blades And Summer Nights:
An Informal But True History of Cormanthor**
published in The Year of the Harp

Stars swam overhead, and eyeballs gleamed below.
Elminster frowned as he fought his way back to awareness. Eyeballs? He rolled over—or thought he did—for

a better look. The night around him slowly spun itself clear.

Yes, definitely: eyeballs. Scores of blinking and glistening eyeballs, flickering into being and disappearing again in a constant winking cloud as the bored and jaded elves of Cormanthor heard about the latest excitement and hastened to watch from a safe distance.

A few, by the way they drifted up to peer and blink at him, had definitely noticed the motionless, drifting ripple among the stars that was Elminster—a ragged cloud of human-shaped mist, thinned from floating so long, senseless, above the riven stump of Mythanthar's tower.

That still-smoking, charred heap of fallen stones was a sea of the little orbs, flitting here and there like curious fireflies as the eyes of distant elves peered at every last detail of the old mage's revealed magic.

As Elminster watched them dart and peer with mild interest, he slowly became aware of his surroundings—and who he was—again.

Two Starym had died here, but of the third there was no sign. The bodies of the two sorceresses had also vanished; El hoped the Srinshee had whisked them away to safety and healing before less kind observers had spotted them.

Two of the floating eyes in the ruins below suddenly veered to look at the same thing, as if it had done something to interest them. Elminster swooped down to catch a look, startling several other blinking orbs.

The two eyes were staring at nothing. Or rather they stared at something blurred and twisted, rotating in the air and creating nothingness.

It was a cone or spiral of smoky strands that moved purposefully among the ruins, poking at a shelf here, and a pile of tumbled stone blocks there. Where it poked its open end, solid items vanished, whisked away to—elsewhere.

El drifted closer, trying to see what was disappearing. Stone blocks, aye, but only to clear a way through rubble to the space beyond. In that space—magic! An item here, a broken fragment of apparatus there, a stand yonder, a crucible just here . . . the helix of smoke was sucking up and stealing away things that Mythanthar had used to work magic, or that held spells stored within them.

Was this a thing Mythanthar himself was directing, to snatch away what could be salvaged before other Cormanthan hands seized what he was not there to defend? Or did it serve some other master?

It certainly seemed to know where magic might be found. El watched it root through a tangle of fallen spars—ceiling-beams—in one corner, to find whatever had rested on the table beneath, and then . . .

He drifted closer, to peer around the wreckage and see what the helix was after. There was—

Suddenly smoky lines were whirling all around Elminster, and Faerûn was twisting between them, rushing away. The magical gatherer must have been lurking below the lip of the overhanging debris, deliberately waiting for him. Everything was whirling, now, and El sighed aloud. Whither *this* time?

Mystra, he called almost plaintively, as he was whirled down and away into a darkening, sickening elsewhere, *when is my task to begin? And what, by all the watching stars, IS it?*

* * * * *

Long, long, he spiraled, until he almost forgot what stillness was, and could scarce remember light. Panic clutched at Elminster's heart and thoughts, and he tried to scream and sob, but could not.

The whirling continued unabated, through a void that went on and on, heedless of the cries he tried to make. It made no difference to the void whether or not the ghost of a human called Elminster was present, silent or agitated.

He was beneath notice, and powerless.

Yet if he could do nothing, what was there to worry about? He had striven, and known the love of a goddess, and his fate now lay in Mystra's hands. Hands that he knew could be gentle, belonging to one too wise by far to throw away a tool that could still see much use.

As if that thought had been a cue, there came a sudden burst of light around Elminster, and with it an explosion of colors. The smoky cage in which he moved veered into a misty blue area, and raced through it toward a lighter, brighter horizon. Was he rising? It seemed so, as he flashed through clouds of blue mist into—

A chamber he'd not seen before, its floor a glistening sea of black marble, its walls high, its ceiling vaulted. A mage's spellhurling chamber, and in it one elven mage, floating upright, thin, and graceful, pale longfingered hands moving in almost lazy gestures.

A masked mage, whose eyes flashed in surprise at Elminster's sudden appearance.

The vortex of smoky lines was already whirling El across the chamber, to where a sphere of radiant white light floated, trailing mists of its own as if it was weeping.

The mage watched El spin helplessly across the room and plunge into the sphere, the smoky lines vanishing into the stuff of the sphere itself, leaving the human imprisoned. El tried to drift straight on and out through the curving far wall of the sphere, but it was as solid as stone, and his attempt merely took him on a looping journey around the inside of its curves.

He came softly to a stop facing the source of a brightening light outside the sphere: the masked mage was drifting closer, head cocked in obvious curiosity.

"What have we here?" the anonymous elf asked, in a cold, thin voice. "A human undead? Or . . . something more interesting?"

El nodded in grave greeting, as one equal to another, but said nothing.

The mask seemed to cling to the skin around its wearer's eyes, and to move and flex with it. Beneath it, a superior eyebrow rose in amusement. "I require one thing of all thinking beings I encounter: their name," the elf explained flatly. "Those who resist me, I destroy. Choose swiftly, or I shall make the choice for you."

El shrugged. "My name is no precious secret," he said, and his voice seemed to roll out across the chamber. Here, at least, he could be heard perfectly. "I am Elminster Aumar, a prince in the human land of Athalantar, and the Coronal recently named me an armathor of Cormanthor. I work magic. I also seem to have a blundering talent for upsetting elves whom I encounter."

The mage gave Elminster a cold smile and a nod of agreement. "Indeed. Is your present form voluntary? Good for spying out the secrets of elven magic, perhaps?"

"No," said Elminster genially, "and not particularly."

"How is it, then, that you came to be in the ruined home of the noted elven mage Mythanthar? Have you worked with him?"

"No. Nor am I pledged to any sorcerer of Cormanthor." El doubted this masked wizard would consider the Coronal a sorcerer, and the Srinshee was a "sorceress."

"I'm not accustomed to asking questions twice, and

you stand very much within my power." The masked mage drifted a foot or so closer.

El raised an eyebrow of his own. "And whose power would that be? A name for a name is the custom among the People as well as in the affairs of men."

The masked mage seemed to smile—almost. "You may call me The Masked. Speak not again save in answer to my query, or I shall blow you away to nameless dust forever."

El shrugged. "The answer is, I fear, as unrevealing as your name: simple curiosity took me thence, along with half the elves in Cormanthor, it seems, for I fairly swam in peering eyes."

The masked mage did smile this time. "What, then, attracted your curious attention to that locale?"

"The beauty of two sorceresses," El replied. "I wanted to see where they'd go, and perhaps learn their names and where they dwelt."

The Masked acquired a cold smile. "You consider elf-shes fitting mates for human men, do you?"

"I've never considered the matter," Elminster replied easily. "Like most men, I'm attracted to beauty wherever I find it. Like most elves, I see no harm in looking at what I cannot have, or where I dare not venture."

The Masked nodded slightly, and remarked, "Most Cormanthans would deem this chamber around you a place they'd dare not venture into. And rightly so: to intrude here would cost them their lives."

"And have ye come to a decision in the matter of my intrusion?" Elminster asked calmly. "Or was that decision made when ye 'harvested' me in the ruins?"

The elven mage shrugged. "I could easily destroy you. As a visible phantom you have little value other than as a spy or herald—one easily swept away by the right spells. As a whole man, however, you could be of service."

"As a willing agent?" El asked, "Or as a dupe?"

The thin mouth of The Masked tightened still further. "I am not accustomed to overmuch impertinence even from rivals, man—let alone apprentices."

Silence hung between them for a long moment. A very long moment.

Well, Mystra? That silent plea for guidance was instantly rewarded by a glimpse of Elminster nodding in this same room, as the masked elven mage demonstrated something. Well enough.

"Apprentices?" Elminster asked, a breath before his hesitation might become fatally overlong. "Would I be correct in discerning a most gracious offer . . . master?"

The Masked smiled. "You would. I take it you accept?"

"I do. I still have much to learn about magic, and in that learning I should like to be guided by someone I can respect."

The elven mage said nothing, and lost his smile, but something about him seemed to radiate satisfaction as he turned away. "Certain exacting spells are necessary for your return to full and normal physical form," he said over his shoulder, as he strode to a wall, touched it, and watched a stained and battered workbench float into view out of suddenly-revealed darkness behind the wall.

His hands darted here and there among the jars and vessels that littered it. "Remain still and quiet until I bid you stir again," he ordered, turning around again with a mottled purple egg and a silver key in his hand. "The spells I am about to cast will not appear to have any affect; they will take hold about the sphere, and reach you only when I cause the field that now encloses you to vanish."

Elminster nodded, and The Masked began to work magic, laying three small but completely unfamiliar enchantments upon the sphere before embarking on the first magic that El could guess the purpose of. Spheres like the one El was floating in seemed to be the form in which elven mages combined magics to work together upon a single target or focus.

The Masked calmly uttered a single unfamiliar word, and the sphere caught fire.

El wriggled just a little as the heat struck him. The elven sorcerer was already crafting another magic as the flames slowed, faltered, and then abruptly went out, leaving a single rope of smoke climbing into the darkness overhead.

When the Masked turned to face the sphere again, he crooked his finger like a harpist plucking a string, and the smoke abruptly bent toward him. He rotated that hand slowly, as if conducting invisible musicians, and the line of smoke snaked around the sphere, settling into the familiar curves of the helix.

El watched, fascinated, as the masked elf danced and swayed in the working of yet another magic— something that caused a faint music to arise out of nowhere and accompany the tall, graceful body as it swung this way and that.

"Nassabrath," the Masked said suddenly, coming to a halt and kneeling. He drew his left hand, fingers uppermost and palm inwards, vertically down in front of his face as he did so. From the tip of each finger tiny lightnings flared.

They curled and spat toward the sphere with almost aimless sloth; as Elminster watched their slow progress, he called on Mystra once more.

A vision appeared in his mind, as bright and as sudden as if someone had snatched aside a curtain. He was standing naked in the forest, face lined with pain, and covered with scrapes and thorn-scratches. Or rather, he was almost naked: at his wrists and ankles were glowing manacles, attached to chains that rose into the air to fade into invisibility a few feet from his limbs. Their links blazed with the same tiny lightnings as were crawling toward the sphere that held him, right now. The Masked suddenly strode through the background of the scene, making an impatient beckoning gesture almost absently as he hurried on his way.

Elminster was jerked around by the chains and forced to follow his master. They went through the trees for quite some distance, stumbling and scraping along, until El fetched up against a jutting rock with bruising force. The elf left him there as he bent down to examine a certain plant, and the vision swept in to show Elminster laying his hand flat on the stone, whispering Mystra's name, and concentrating on a particular symbol—an unfamiliar and complex character of shining golden curves that hung in El's mind and caught fire, as if it was was being branded into his memory.

In the scene, Elminster's bare body changed, arching away from the rock as it flowed into the smooth, full curves of a woman, a form he'd worn before in Mystra's service. 'Elmara,' he'd been then, and it was Elmara who stepped away from the stone, chains gone, and began a swift casting even as The Masked straightened up and spun around, his face sharp with astonishment and fear. That face that promptly vanished in the bolt of emerald fire Elmara flung through it. The green flames flowed and splashed through his head, and the scene was gone.

El found himself shaking his head to clear his dazed vision. Through the sudden glimmer of tears, he saw the lightnings, back in the here and now, touch the sphere around him at last, and awaken it to fresh fire.

He tried to recall the symbol he'd seen, and it swept back into his mind in all its intricate glory. Well enough; touch stone and think of that while calling aloud of

Mystra, and he would wear a woman's shape again—a changing that would be enough to break the bindings this treacherous elven sorcerer was going to lay upon him now. The Masked—a proud elf with a thin, cold voice that he'd heard before, he was sure . . . but where?

El shrugged. Even if he learned who wore the mask, what then? Learning a face and a name meant little when you knew little or nothing of the character behind them. To a Cormanthan born and bred the identity of The Masked might well be a secret as valuable as it was deadly; to Elminster, it was simply something he didn't know yet.

He suspected his very unfamiliarity with the realm was his chief value to this elven mage, and he resolved to reveal as little as possible of his own true powers and nature, belittling even his experience with the kiira. Who was to say what an overwhelmed human mind could even comprehend of its stored memories, let alone retain after the gem was gone?

"Look into my eyes," The Masked commanded crisply. El looked up in time to see one long-fingered hand make an imperious gesture. There was a flash of light from all around, and a high singing sound, as the sphere burst into a sheet of golden sparks.

For an instant El felt as if he was falling—and then there was a sickening surging feeling, as if eels were wriggling through his innards, as the sparks streamed into the midst of his misty form.

Fire followed, and the wracking pain of being caught squarely in the raging, blistering heat of hot flame. Elminster threw back his head and shouted—a sound that echoed back off the high vaulting above as he fell in earnest this time, dropping several feet before he was rudely caught up in a tangle of webs.

The webs were spells spinning themselves down and around him from the smoky helix. He was caught in their coils, their substance melting into his skin and pouring into his nose and mouth, choking him.

He gagged, writhed, and tried to vomit, throat shuddering spasmodically. Then it was over, and he was on his knees on cold flagstones, the masked elven sorcerer standing on air not far away, looking down at him with a superior smile.

"Arise," the Masked said coldly. El decided to test things right now. Acting dazed, he hid his face in his hands and groaned, but did not try to get up.

"Elminster!" the elf snapped, but El shook his head, murmuring something wordless. Abruptly he felt a burning sensation in his head, like heat flowing down his neck and shoulders, and an irresistable tugging began, making all of his limbs leap and tremble. He could fight this, El thought, and resist for some time, but it was best to seem entirely in thrall, so he hastened to his feet, to stand as The Masked posed him: upright but with both arms extended, offering his wrists as if for binding.

The elven sorcerer met Elminster's gaze with eyes that were very level and very dark, and El suddenly found his limbs being pulled again. He surrendered utterly this time, and the elf made him wave his arms wide, point downwards, and then slap himself across the face, hard, once with each hand.

It hurt, and as El shook his numbed hands and felt his lips with his tongue where his teeth had rattled under the blows, The Masked smiled again. "Your body seems to work well. Come."

El's limbs were suddenly free to move as he willed. He set aside any urge to strike back, and followed humbly, head bent. A heavy feeling of being watched rode his shoulders, but he didn't bother to look up and back to find the floating eye he knew would be there.

The Masked touched the featureless wall of the spell

chamber and an oval doorway suddenly opened in it.
The elf turned on its threshold to look his new apprentice up and down and allowed himself a slow, cold
smile of triumph.

El decided to act as if it was a smile of welcome, and
tremulously matched it. The elven mage shook his
head wryly at that and turned away, crooking one
hand in a beckoning gesture.

Rolling his eyes inwardly but careful to keep his
face looking both dazed and eager, Elminster hastened
to follow. Thanks be to Mystra, this was going to be a
long apprenticeship.

* * * * *

Moonlight touched the trees of Cormanthor, and in
the remote distance, somewhere off to the north, a wolf
howled.

There was an answering bark from the trees very
nearby, but the naked, shivering elf who was crawling
aimlessly down a tangled slope did not seem to hear it.
She slipped partway down, and plunged most of the
rest of the way on her face. Her hair was a muddy
mass, and her limbs glistened darkly in a dozen places
in the pale blue light, where they were wet with blood.

The wolf padded out onto the mossy rocks at the top
of the slope and stood looking down, eyes agleam. Such
easy prey. He trotted down the incline by the easiest
way, not bothering to hurry; the panting, mumbling
woman at the bottom wasn't going anywhere.

As he loped nearer she even rolled over to present
her breast and throat to his jaws, and lay back bathed
in moonlight, gasping out something wordless. The
wolf paused, momentarily suspicious of such fearlessness, and then gathered himself to spring. There'd be
plenty of time to sniff around warily for others of her

kind after her throat was torn out.

A forest spider who'd been creeping cautiously along above the sobbing elf for some time drew back at the sight of the wolf. Perhaps it could gain two blood-meals this night, rather than just one.

The wolf sprang.

Symrustar Auglamyr never saw the single blue-white star that blazed into being above her parted lips. Nor did she hear the startled, chopped-off yelp as it emptied into the jaws of the wolf, nor the silent disintegration that followed.

A few hairs from the wolf's tail were all that was left of it; they drifted down to settle across her thighs as something unseen said, "Poor proud one. By magic bent. Let you be by magic restored."

A circle of stars spun up from the ground then to flash around Symrustar in a blue-white ring. The spider recoiled from their light and waited. Light meant fire, and sure, sizzling death.

When the whirling ring had faded and only the moonlight remained, the spider moved down the tree again, creeping swiftly now, in little runs and jumps and dodges. Its hunger was exceeded only by its rage when it reached the flattened leaves where the elf-she had rolled, and found her gone. Gone without a trace, and the wolf too. The bewildered spider searched the area for some time and then wandered off into the woods by moonlight, sighing as loudly and gustily as any lost elf—or human.

Humans, now; humans were fat, and full of blood and juices. Long-dimmed memories stirred in the spider, and it climbed a tree in eager haste. Humans dwelt in *that* direction, a long way off, and—

The head of the giant snake shot forward, its jaws snapped once, and the spider was gone. It never even had time to worry about choosing the wrong tree.

PART III

MYTHAL

Seventeen

APPRENTICED AGAIN

For some years Elminster served the elf known only as
The Masked as apprentice. Despite the cruel nature of the
high sorcerer, and the spell chains that bound the human
in servitude, a respect grew between master and man. It
was respect that ignored the differences between them,
and the betrayal and battle that both knew lay ahead.

Antarn the Sage
from **The High History of Faerûnian Archmages Mighty**
published circa The Year of the Staff

There came a spring day twenty years after the first
greening season Elminster had known in service to
The Masked, when a golden, shining symbol surfaced
in the Athalantan's mind, a symbol he'd almost forgotten. It troubled him; as it revolved slowly inside his
head, other long-buried memories stirred. *Mystra*, he
heard his own voice calling, and a gaze fell upon him—
her gaze. He could not see her, but he could feel the
awesome weight of her regard: deep and warm and
terrible, more mighty than the most furious glare of
the Master, and more loving than . . . than . . .

Nacacia.

He looked down at Nacacia from where he hung in
the great glowing spell web they'd spent all morning
crafting together, and their gazes met. Her eyes were

dark and liquid and very large, and there was longing
in them as she looked up at him. Soundlessly, trembling, her lips shaped his name.

It was all she dared do. El fought down a sudden
urge to lash out at the masked sorcerer, who was floating with his back to them not far away, weaving spells
of his own, and gave her a wink before he quickly
turned his head away. The Master delved too much
into both their minds to hide their mutual fondness
from him. Already the mysterious elven mage had
taken to making Nacacia slap his human apprentice,
otherwise keep well away from Elminster, and speak
harshly when she spoke to the Athalantan at all.

The Masked seldom compelled Elminster to do anything. He seemed to be watching El and waiting for
something. One of the things he watched for was any act
of defiance, and he took open delight in punishing his
human apprentice for all of them. Remembering some
of those punishments, El shuddered involuntarily.

He risked another glance at Nacacia, and found that
she was doing the same thing. Their eyes met almost
guiltily, and they both hurriedly looked away. El set his
teeth and started to climb the spell web away from
her—anything to be moving, *doing* something.

Mystra, he thought silently, seeking to thrust away
his vivid memory of Nacacia's smiling face. Oh, Mystra, I need guidance . . . are all these passing years of
my servitude part of your plan?

The world around him seemed to shimmer, and he
was suddenly standing in a rocky meadow. It was the
field in which he'd watched sheep, above Heldon, as a
boy!

A breeze was blowing across it, and he was cold.
Small wonder—he was also naked.

Lifting his head, he found himself staring at the
sorceress he'd trained under for so long, years ago:

Myrjala, she known as 'Darkeyes.' The great dark eyes for which she was named seemed deeper and more alluring than ever as she reclined on the empty air above the blown grasses, regarding him. The winds did not touch her dark satin gown.

Myrjala had been Mystra. Elminster stretched out a hand to her, tentatively.

"Great Lady," he almost whispered, "is it ye in truth—after all these years?"

"Of course," the goddess said, her eyes dark pools of promise. "How is it that you doubt me?"

El almost shuddered under the sudden wash of shame that he felt. He went to his knees, dropping his eyes. "I—I am wrong to do so, and . . . well, it's just that it's been so *long*, and . . ."

"Not long to an elf," Mystra said gently. "Are you beginning to learn patience at last, or are you truly desperate?"

Elminster looked up at her, eyes bright, as he found himself suddenly hovering on the edge of tears. "No!" he cried. "All I needed was this, to see ye, and know I'm doing what ye intend. I—I need guidance still."

Mystra smiled at him. "At least you know you need it. Some never do, and crash happily through life, laying waste to all they can reach in Faerûn around them, whether they realize it or not." She raised a hand, and her smile changed.

"Yet think on this, dearest of my Chosen: most folk of Faerûn never have such guidance, and still learn to stand on their own feet unaided, and follow their own ideas as their lives run, and make their own mistakes. You've certainly mastered that last talent."

Elminster looked away, fighting back tears again, and Mystra laughed and touched his cheek. Warm fire seemed to race through him.

"Be not downhearted," she murmured, as a mother

does to a crying son, "for you *are* learning patience, and your shame is unfounded. Much though you fear you've forgotten me and strayed from the task I set you, I am well pleased."

Her face changed, then, as Heldon darkened and faded around it, and became the face of Nacacia.

Elminster blinked at it, as it winked at him. He was back in the spell web, staring down at the real Nacacia once more. He drew in a deep, tremulous breath, smiled at her, and climbed on through the web. No matter what he did, however, his thoughts stayed on his fellow apprentice. He could see her face as clearly in his mind as his eyes had beheld it, moments ago. Sometimes he wondered how much of such mind-scenes the master could see, and what the elven sorcerer truly thought of his two apprentices.

Nacacia. Ah, leave my thoughts for a moment, leave me in peace! But no . . .

She was a half-elf, brought into the tower as a bright-eyed waif one night, huddled in the arms of The Masked. Elminster suspected he'd raided the village where she lived.

Bright and bubbly, possessed of a pranksome nature that The Masked harshly beat out of her with spanking spells and transformations into toads or earthworms, and a merry nature it seemed nothing he did could crush, Nacacia had swiftly grown into a beauty.

She had auburn hair that flowed down to the backs of her knees in a thick fall, and a surprisingly muscular back and shoulders; from where he'd been standing in the web above her, El had admired the deep, curving line of her spine. Her large eyes, smile and cheekbones bore the classic beauty of her elven blood, and her waist was so slim as to seem almost toylike.

Her master allowed her the black breeches and vest of a thief, and let her grow her hair long. He even taught her the spells to animate it so as to stroke him, when he took her into his chamber of nights and left Elminster floating furiously outside.

She never spoke to him of what went on in the spell-locked bedchamber, save to say that their master never took off his mask. Once, when awakening from a shrieking nightmare, she babbled something about "soft and terrible tentacles."

The Masked not only never removed his mask; he never slept. As far as El could tell, he had no friends or kin, and no Cormanthan ever called on him, for any reason. His days were spent crafting magic, working magic, and teaching magic to his two apprentices. Sometimes he treated them almost as friends, though he never revealed anything about himself. At other times, they were clearly his slaves. Most of the time they worked as drudges, together. In fact, it seemed that the masked mage almost taunted his two apprentices with each other's company, thrusting them into messy, slippery jobs half-naked to help each other lift, sort, or clean. But whenever they reached for each other, even to give innocent aid or comfort, he struck out with punishments.

These visitations of pain were many and varied, but the Master's favorite punishment for apprentices was to paralyze the bared body of the miscreant with spells and set acid leeches on it to feed. The slow, glistening creatures excreted a burning slime as they slid over skin, or bored almost lazily in. The Masked was always careful to use his spells in time to keep his apprentices alive, but Elminster could attest that there are few things in Faerûn as painful as having a sluglike beast eating its way very slowly into your lungs, or stomach, or guts.

Yet El had learned true respect for The Masked during twenty years of learning deep-woven, complex elven magics. The elf was a meticulous crafter of spells and a stylish caster, who left nothing to chance, always thought ahead, and seemed never to be surprised. He had an instinctive understanding of magic, and could modify, combine, or improvise spells with almost effortless ease and no hesitation. He also never forgot where he'd put anything, no matter how trivial, and always kept himself under iron control, never showing weariness, loneliness, or a need to confide in anyone. Even his losses of temper seemed almost planned and scripted.

Moreover, after twenty years of intense contact, Elminster still did not know who the mage was. A male of one of the old, proud families, to be sure, and—judging by the views he evidently held—probably not among the eldest Cormanthans. The Masked spun and projected a false body for himself often, directing it in activities elsewhere with part of his mind, while he devoted some part of the rest to instructing Elminster.

At first, the last prince of Athalantar had been astonished by what powerful spells the anonymous elven mage had let him learn. But then, why should The Masked worry, when he could compel instant obedience from the body he'd given to his human apprentice? Elminster suspected he and Nacacia were among the very few Cormanthan apprentices who never left their master's abode, and they were probably the only apprentices who weren't pureblood elves, and who were never taught how to create their own defensive mantles.

Sometimes El thought about his tumultuous early days in Cormanthor. He wondered if the Srinshee and the Coronal thought him dead, or if they cared about his fate at all. More often he wondered what had become of the elven lady Symrustar, whom he'd left crawling in the woods, when he'd been unable to defend her or even to make her notice him. And what had become of Mythanthar, and his dream of a mythal? Surely they'd have heard from the Master if such a spectacular giant mantle had been spun, and the city opened to other races. But then, why would he tell news of the world outside his tower to two apprentices whom he kept as virtual prisoners?

Recently, even the attentive teaching of magic had stopped. The Masked was absent from his tower more often, or shut away in spell-sealed chambers scrying events elsewhere. Day after day during this most recent winter his apprentices had been left alone to feed themselves and follow a bald list of tasks that appeared written in letters of fire on a certain wall: drudge-work, and the spinning of small spells to keep the Master's tower clean, well-ordered, and strong in its fabric. Yet he kept a watch over them; unauthorized explorations of the tower, or overmuch intimacy between them, brought swift and sharp retributive spells out of the empty air. Only two tendays ago, when Nacacia had dropped a kiss on Elminster's shoulder as she brushed past him, an unseen whip had lashed her lips and face to bloody ribbons, defying El's frantic attempts to dispel it as she staggered back, screaming. She'd awakened the next morning wholly healed. But a row of barbed thorns grew all around her mouth, making kissing impossible. It was more than a tenday before they faded away.

These days, when the masked mage put in one of his rare appearances in the rooms where they dwelt, it was to call on them for magical aid, usually either to drain some of their vital energies in an arcane—and unexplained—spell he was experimenting with, or to help him create a spell web.

Like the one they were working on now. Incredible constructions these were, glowing nets or interwoven cages of glowing force-lines that one could walk along as if striding along a broad wooden beam, regardless of whether one was upside down, or walking tilted sharply sideways. Multiple spells could be cast into the glowing fabric of these cages, placed in particular spots and for specific reasons, so that triggering the collapse of the web would unleash spell after spell at preset targets, in a particular order.

The Master rarely revealed all of the magics he'd placed in a web before its triggering displayed their true natures, and had never shown either apprentice how to start such a web. El and Nacacia didn't even know the primary purpose—or target—of most of the webs they worked on; El suspected The Masked often used the aid of his two largely ignorant apprentices purely to remain hidden, so that the spells striking down a distant rival would bear no hint of who was behind them.

Now the elf turned, his eyes flashing beneath the mask that never left his face. "Elminster, come here," he said coldly, indicating a particular spot in the web with one finger. "We have death to weave, together."

Eighteen

IN THE WEB

There comes a day at last when even the most patient and exacting of scheming traitors grows impatient, and breaks forth into open treachery. Henceforth, he must deal with the world as it is, reacting around him, and not as he sees or desires it to be in his plots and dreams. This is the point at which many treacheries go awry.

The sorcerer known as The Masked was, however, no ordinary traitor—if one may think of an "ordinary traitor." The historian of Cormanthor, reaching back far enough, can do so, finding many ordinary treacheries, but this was not one of them. This was the stuff of which wailing doom-ballads are made.

Shalheira Talandren, High Elven Bard of Summerstar
from **Silver Blades And Summer Nights:
An Informal But True History of Cormanthor**
published in The Year of the Harp

Elminster shook his head to try to banish mind-weariness; he'd been spinning spells with another, colder mind for too long, and almost staggered in the patiently humming web.

"Get clear now," the thin, cold voice of the Master said into his ear then, though the elven mage was standing in the air at the other side of the spell chamber.

"Nacacia, hie you to the couch in the corner. Elminster, here to stand with me."

Knowing his impatience was apt to flare at such times, both apprentices hastened to obey, dropping lightly out of the webwork as soon as they were low enough to do so without disrupting anything.

El had scarce reached the spot The Masked was pointing at when the elf hissed something and used one finger to bridge the gap between two protruding points at the end of the glowing lines. That set the web to working; its magic snarled forth, trailing sparks as the web dissolved itself, discharging spell after spell. The elven sorcerer looked up expectantly, and El followed his gaze to a spot in the air high above them, where the air, encircled by an arching strand of the web, was flickering into sudden life. A scene appeared there, floating in the emptiness like a bright hanging tapestry, and growing steadily brighter.

It was a view of a house El had never seen before, one of the sprawling country mansions made by elves. A house that lived, growing slowly larger as the centuries passed. This one had been standing for more than a thousand summers, by the looks of it, at the heart of a grove of old and mighty shadowtops, somewhere in the forest deeps. An old house; a proud house.

A house that would be standing only a few moments more.

El watched grimly as the unleashed magics of the spell web shattered its magical shields, set off its attack spells and forced their discharges back inwards to strike at the heart of the old house, and snatched guardian creatures and steeds from their posts and stables, only to dash them back against the walls, right through the full fury of the awakened spells, reducing them to raglike, bloody tatters.

It took only a few minutes to alter the proud, soaring

house of mighty branches and lush leaves to a smoking crater flanked by two splintered, precariously wavering fragments of blackened and splintered trunk. Misshapen things that might have been bodies were still raining down around the wreckage when the spell web drank its own scene, and the air went dark again.

Elminster was still blinking at the empty air where the scene had been when sudden mists snatched at him. Before he could even cry out, he was somewhere else. Soft soil and dead leaves were under his boots, and the smells of trees all around.

He was standing in a clearing deep in the forest with The Masked reclining at ease on empty air nearby, and no sign of Nacacia or of any elven habitation. They were somewhere deep in the wild forest.

El blinked at the change in light, drew in a deep breath of the damp air, and looked all around, delighting in being out of the tower at last, and yet filled with foreboding. Had his master espied his meeting with Mystra, or seen it in his mind since? She'd reclined in almost the same way.

The clearing they were standing in was odd. It was a semicircular bare patch perhaps a hundred paces across—completely bare, just earth and rock, with not a stump or lichen or pecking woodbird to enliven its barren lifelessness.

El looked at The Masked and raised inquiring eyebrows in silence.

His master pointed down. "This is what is left behind by a casting of the spell I'm going to teach you now."

El looked at the devastation once more, and then back at the Master, stonefaced. "Aye. Something potent, is it?"

"Something very useful. Properly used, it can make its caster nigh-invincible." The Masked showed his teeth in a mirthless grin and added, "Like myself, for instance." He uncoiled himself from his reclining position and said, "Lie down just here, where the waste ends and the living forest begins. Nose to the ground, hands spread out. Move not."

When the Master spoke like that, one didn't hesitate or argue. Elminster scrambled down onto his face in the dirt.

Once he was there, he felt the icy touch of the Master's fingertips on the back of his head. They only felt so cold when a spell was being slipped into his mind, stealing in without need for studying or instruction or . . .

Gods! This magic would fuel any spell you already possessed, doubling its effects or making a twin of it. To do so, it drained life-force—from a tree.

Or a sentient being.

And it was so *simple*. Powerful, aye, one had to be a very capable mage to wield it, but the actual doing was so hideously easy. It left utter lifelessness in its wake. And *elves* had wrought this?

"When," El asked the moss under his nose, "would I ever dare to use this?"

"In an emergency," the Master said calmly, "when your life—or the realm or holding you were defending—was in the most dire peril. When all else is lost, the only immoral act is to avoid doing something you know can aid your cause. This is such a spell."

El almost turned his head to glance up at the masked elf. His voice, for the first time in twenty years, had sounded eager, almost hungry.

Mystra, El thought, *he loves the thought of utterly smashing a foe, regardless of the cost!*

"I can't think, Master, that I'll ever trust my own judgment enough to be comfortable using this spell," El said slowly.

"Comfortable, no; not one thinking, caring being would be, knowing what this magic can do. Yet capable you can become. That's why we're here. Up, now."

El rose. "I'm going to practice?"

"In a manner of speaking, yes. You'll be unleashing the spell in earnest against an enemy of Cormanthor. By decree of the Coronal, this spell is only to be used in direct defense of the realm or of an imperiled elven elder."

El stared at the ever-present enchanted mask his master wore, wondering for perhaps the ten thousandth time what its true powers were—and just what he'd find beneath it, if he ever dared snatch it away.

As if that thought had crossed the elf's mind, the masked mage stepped back hastily and said, "You've just seen our spell web destroy a high house. It was an abode used by certain conspirators in the realm who desire that we trade with the drow. They are so hungry for the wealth and importance the dark ones have promised will flow to them personally that they'll betray us all into becoming vassals of some matron of Down Below."

"But surely—" Elminster began, and then fell silent. Nothing was sure about this tale beyond the fact that his masked Master was lying. That much Mystra had given him in the meadow. He could now tell when the thin, cold voice of the elven sorcerer was straying from the truth.

It was doing so with almost every word.

"Soon," the Masked went on, "I'll transport us to a place that is specifically warded against me. It is a place I can enter only by blasting my way through its shields, alerting everyone within to my arrival and wasting much magic besides."

The elven sorcerer's pointing finger shot out to indicate El. "You, however, can step right in. My magic will bring a chained orc to your side—a vicious despoiler of human and elven villages whom we captured while he was roasting elven babies on spits for his evening meal. You'll drain him to power your spell, and then hurl your antimagic shell—augmented by this magic in both area and efficacy, of course—into the house you'll be facing. I can then summon a few loyal armathors with ready swords, and the deed will be done. The traitors will lie dead, and Cormanthor will stand safe for a while longer. With that deed under your belt, you should be ready for presentation to the Coronal at last."

"The Coronal?" Elminster felt almost as much excitement as he put into that gasp. 'Twould be good, indeed, to see old Lord Eltargrim again. Still, that did nothing to drive away the uneasy feeling he had about this whole arrangement. Who would he really be slaying?

The Masked saw his dislike in his face. "There is a mage in the house you'll be striking at," he added slowly, "and a capable one at that. Yet I hope that any apprentice of mine will go up against true foes with the same bravery as we transform toadstools and conjure light in dark places. The true mage never allows himself to be awed by magic when he's using it."

The wise mage, Elminster thought silently, recalling the words of Mystra, pretends to know nothing about magic at all.

Then he wryly added the corollary: When he gains true wisdom, he'll know that he wasn't pretending.

"Are you ready, Elminster?" his master asked then, very quietly. "Are you ready to undertake a mission of importance at last?"

Mystra? El asked inwardly. Instantly a vision appeared in his mind: The Masked pointing at him, just as he'd done a moment ago. This time, in the vision, El smiled and nodded enthusiastically. Well, that was clear enough.

"I am," Elminster said, smiling and nodding enthusiastically.

The mask did not hide the slow smile that grew across the face of his master.

The Masked raised his hands and murmured, "Let us be about it, then." He made a single gesture toward El, and the world vanished in swirling smoke.

When the smoke curled away to let the human mage see clearly again, they stood together in a wooded valley. It was probably somewhere in Cormanthor, by the looks of the trees and the sun above them. They stood on a little knoll with a well beside them, and across a small dip that held a garden stood a low, rambling house of trees joined by low-roofed wooden chambers. Except for the oval windows visible in the tree trunks, it might have been a human home rather than an abode of elves.

"Strike swiftly," the Masked murmured beside Elminster's ear, and vanished. The air where he'd been standing promptly spun and shimmered. Then an orc was standing beside him, wrapped in a heavy yoke of chains. It stared at him, pleading with its eyes, trying frantically to say something around the thick gag clamped into and over its jaws. All it managed was a soft, high whimpering.

A babe-devourer and raider, eh? El set his lips in distaste over what he had to do, and reached out to touch the orc without hesitation. The Masked was sure to be watching.

He worked the spell, turning to thrust one spread hand at the house, and settle his antimagic over every part of it, willing it to seek down into even the deepest cellar, and blanket even the mightiest of realms-shaking magics. Let that building be dead to all magic, so long as his power lasted.

The orc's keening became a despairing moan; the

light in its eyes flickered and went out, and it buckled slowly at the knees and crashed to the ground; El had to step aside hastily as the chained bulk of its corpse rolled under his feet.

The air shimmered again, nearby; he looked up in time to see elven warriors in gleaming, high-collared plate armor rushing out of a rent in the air. None of them wore helms, but they all waved naked long swords—enchanted blades that flickered with ready, reaving magic—in their hands. They spared no glances for El or the surroundings, but charged at the house, hacking at shutters and doors. As the blades breached those barriers and the elves plunged inside, the radiances dancing on their blades and armor winked out. From inside, the muffled shouting and the ringing of striking steel began.

Feeling suddenly sick, El looked down at the orc again and gasped in horror.

As he flung himself to his knees and reached out to touch and make sure, he felt as if Faerûn was opening up into a dark chasm around him. The chains were lying limp and loose around a small and slender form.

An all-too-familiar form, lolling lifelessly in his hands as he rolled it over. The eyes of Nacacia, still wide in sad and vain pleading, stared up at him, dark and empty. They'd be so forever, now.

Shaking, El touched the cruel gag that still filled her gentle mouth, and then he could hold back the tears no longer. He never noticed when the swirling smoke came again to take him.

Nineteen

MORE ANGER AT COURT

*Among the tales and accounts of men, the Court of Cor-
manthor is portrayed as a glittering, gigantic hall of enchanted wonders, in which richly robed elves drifted
quietly to and fro in the ultimate hauteur and decorum.
It was so, most of the time, but a certain day in the Year
of Soaring Stars was a decidedly noticeable—and no-
table—exception.*

Antarn the Sage
from **The High History of Faerûnian Archmages Mighty**
published circa The Year of the Staff

"Hold!" The Masked cried, and there was a hubbub
of shocked voices from all around. "I bring a criminal
to justice!"

"Really," someone said, severely, "is there any—"

"Peace, Lady Aelieyeeva," broke in a grave but stern
voice that El knew. "We shall resume our business
later. The human is one I named armathor of the
realm; this affair demands my justice."

El blinked up at the throne of the Coronal, where it
floated above the glowing Pool of Remembrance. Lord
Eltargrim was leaning forward in its high-arched
splendor in interest, and elves in splendid robes were
hurriedly gliding aside to clear the glassy-smooth floor
between El and the ruler of Cormanthor.

"Do you recognize the human, Revered Lord?" The Masked asked, his cold voice echoing to every corner of the vast Chamber of the Court in the sudden stillness.

"I do," the Coronal said slowly, a trace of sadness in his tone. He turned his head from Elminster to regard the masked elf, and added, "but I do not recognize you."

The Masked reached up, slowly and deliberately, and removed the mask from his face. He did not have to untie it or slip off any browband, but merely peeled it off as if it was a skin. El stared up at him, seeing that coldly handsome face for the first time in over twenty years . . . a face he'd seen once before.

"Llombaerth Starym am I, Lord Speaker of my house," the elf who'd been Elminster's master said. "I charge this human—my apprentice, Elminster Aumar, named armathor of the realm by yourself here in this chamber, twenty years ago—murderer and traitor."

"How so?"

"Revered Lord, I thought to teach him the life-quench spell, to make him capable of defending Cormanthor, so he could be presented to you as a full mage of the realm. Having learned it, he made use of it without delay both to slay my other apprentice—the half-blood who lies beside him now, still in the chains in which he trapped her—and to doom one of the foremost mages of the realm: Mythanthar, whom he cloaked in a death-of-magic, so that our wise old sorcerer could not avoid the swords of the drow this human is in league with."

"*Drow?*" Among the courtiers who lined both sides of the long, glassy-smooth floor of the hall that cry was almost a shriek.

Llombaerth Starym nodded sadly. "They fear the creation of a mythal will hamper their plans to storm us from Below. Later this summer, I suspect."

There was a moment of shocked silence, and then

excited voices rose everywhere; through the tears he was fighting to master, El saw the Coronal look down the hall and make a certain gesture.

There came a skirling, as of many harpstrings struck in unison, and the insistent, magically amplified voice of the Lady Herald rolled down the long, open Chamber of the Court. "Peace and order, lords and ladies all. Let us have silence once more."

The hush was slow in coming, but as armathors left the doors of the court and started purposefully down the ranks of the courtiers, silence returned. A tense, hanging silence.

The Starym mage put on his mask again; it clung to his face as he raised it into place.

The Coronal rose from his throne, his white robes gleaming, and stood on empty air, looking down at Elminster. "Justice has been demanded; the realm will have it. Yet in matters between mages there has always been much strife, and I would know the truth before I pass judgment. Does the half-elven yet live?"

El opened his mouth to speak, but the Masked said, "No."

"Then I must call upon the Srinshee, who can speak with the departed," Lord Eltargrim said heavily. "Until her arr—"

"Hold!" The Masked said quickly. "Revered Lord, that is less than wise! This human could not have made contact with the drow without the aid of citizens of Cormanthor, and all here know of the long series of reverses Mythanthar suffered in his work to craft a mythal. One of the traitors powerful enough to work against that wise old mage undetected, and to traffic with the dark ones and survive, is the Lady Oluevaera Estelda!"

His voice rose dramatically. "If you summon her here, not only will her testimony be tainted, but she

could well strike out at you and other loyal Cormanthans, seeking to bring the realm down!"

The Coronal's face was pale, and his eyes glittered with anger at the masked mage's accusation,
but his voice was level and almost gentle as he
asked, "Who, then, Lord Speaker, would you trust to
examine the minds of the dead? And of the one you
have accused?"

Llombaerth Starym frowned. "Now that the Great
Lady, Ildilyntra Starym, is no longer with us," he said
slowly, carefully not watching the Coronal's face turn
utterly white as all blood drained out of it, "I find myself at a loss to find a mage to turn to; any or all of
them could be tainted, you see."

He turned, walking on air, to stride thoughtfully
along the edge of the courtiers. Many of them drew
back from him, as if he bore a disease. He paid them
no heed.

"How, Lord Speaker, would you view the testimony
of the mage Mythanthar?" The rolling tones of the
Lady Herald, who still stood by the doors at the end of
the chamber, startled everyone. The heads of both the
Coronal and The Masked jerked up to stare down the
long, open Chamber at Aubaudameira Dree.

"He's *dead*, Lady," The Masked said severely, "and
anyone who questions him can by their spells conjure
up false answers. Do you not see the problem we face?"

"Ah, Starym stripling," said a slight figure, placing
his hand on the shoulder of the Lady Herald to gain
the use of her voice-throwing magic, "behold your problem solved: I live. No thanks to you."

The Masked stiffened and gaped, just for a moment.
Then his voice rang out in anger. "What imposture is
this? I saw the human cast the lifequench. I saw the
drow, hastening into the house of Mythanthar! He
could not have lived!"

"So you planned," said the old mage, striding forward on the silent air, the Lady Herald at his side. "So you hoped. The problem with you younglings is that you're all so lazy, so impatient. You neglect to check every last detail of your spells, and so earn nasty surprises from their side effects. You don't bother to ensure that your victims—even foolish old mages—are truly dead. Like all Starym, young Llombaerth, you *assume* too much."

As he'd spoken, the old elf mage had been walking the length of the Chamber of the Court. He came to a stop beside Elminster, and reached out with his foot toward the body of Nacacia.

"You would blame *me* for the murder of my apprentice?" The Masked shouted, sudden lightnings crawling up and down his arms. "You accuse *me* of trying to work your death? You *dare?*"

"I do," the old mage replied, as he touched the body of the half-elven lady in its chains.

The Lady Herald said formally, "Lord Starym, you stand in violation of the rules of the Court. Stand down your magic. We duel with words and ideas here, not spells."

As she spoke those words, and the Coronal stirred, as if to add something more, the body in the chains vanished. In its place, a moment later, another form melted into view: a half-elven girl with long auburn hair who stood straight, angry, and very much alive.

The Masked recoiled, his face going white. Mythanthar said in dry tones, "A lifequench spell is a potent thing, Starym, but no antimagic shell, however strengthened, can prevail against a spell shear. You need more schooling before you can call yourself any sort of wizard, whether you wear Andrathath's Mask or not."

"Peace, all!" the Coronal thundered. As heads snapped around to him, and the armathors began to gather by the Pool, he turned his head to regard Nacacia, who was embracing a sobbing Elminster, and asked, "Child, who is to blame for all of this?"

Nacacia pointed at the masked Starym mage and said crisply, "He is. It is all his plotting, and the one he truly seeks to slay, Revered Lord, is *you!*"

"Lies!" the Masked shouted, and two bolts of flame burst from his eyes, snarling across the Chamber of the Court at Nacacia. She shrank back, but Mythanthar smiled and lifted his hand. The streaming fire struck something unseen and faded away.

"You'll have to do better than that, Starym," he said calmly, "and I don't think you know how. You didn't even recognize a seeming when it lay before you here, in chains, an—"

"*Starym!*" The Masked bellowed, raising his arms. "Let it be *NOW!*"

Among the courtiers, all over the chamber, bright magic erupted. There were screams, and sudden explosions, and suddenly elves were running everywhere in the hall, swords flashing out.

"*Die*, false ruler!" Llombaerth Starym shouted, wheeling to face the Coronal. "Let the Starym rule at last!"

The roaring white bolt of rending magic that he hurled then was only one of many that lashed out at the old elf standing before his throne, as Starym mages hurled death from many places in the hall.

The Coronal vanished in a blinding white conflagration of meeting, warring spells. The very air roiled and split apart in dark, starry rifts; the Lady Herald screamed and collapsed to the gleaming floor as the shield she'd spun around her ruler was overwhelmed. The hall rocked, and many of the shrieking courtiers were hurled from their feet. A tapestry fell.

Then the bright, roiling radiance above the Pool was

thrust back, to reveal Lord Eltargrim standing atop the floating Throne of the Coronal, his drawn sword in his hand. Light flickered down the awakened runes on the flanks of that blade as he growled, "Death take all who practice treachery against fair Cormanthor! Starym, your life is forfeit!"

The old warrior sprang down from his throne and waded forward, swinging his sword like a farmer scything grain, using the enchantments that smoked and streamed along its edges to cleave the magic trained upon him. The swirling flames and lightnings faded in tatters before the bright edges of that blade.

Someone shouted in triumph among the courtiers, and the ghostly outlines of a great green dragon began to take shape in the air above their heads, its wings spread, its jaws open and poised to bite down on the slowly advancing Coronal. As the Starym who'd summoned it wrestled against the wards of the chamber to bring the wyrm wholly into solidity, and its outlines flickered and darkened, El and Nacacia could see the neck of the dragon arching and straining, trying to reach the lone old elf in white robes who stood beneath it.

Mythanthar said two strange words, calmly and distinctly, and the flickering lightnings and smokes of magic the Coronal was hacking his way through suddenly flowed up and over Eltargrim's head, straight into the straining maw of the dragon.

The blast that followed smashed the roof of the chamber apart, and toppled one of its mighty pillars. Dust swirled and drifted, as elves screamed on all sides, and Elminster and Nacacia, still in each other's arms, were hurled to the floor as the magical radiances that gave light to the vast Chamber of the Court winked out.

In the sudden darkness, as they coughed and blinked, only one source of light remained steady: the empty throne of the Coronal, floating serenely above the glowing Pool of Remembrance.

Lightnings clawed and crashed around it, and the body of a hapless elven lady was dashed to bloody ruin against it. She fell like a rag doll into the Pool below, and its radiance went suddenly scarlet.

The Chamber of the Court shook again, as another explosion smashed aside tapestries along the east wall, and sent more broken bodies flying.

"Stop," snapped a voice in the darkness. "This has gone *quite* far enough."

The Srinshee had come at last.

Twenty

SPELLSTORM AT COURT

And so it was that a spellstorm was unleashed in the Court of Cormanthor that day. A true spellstorm is a fearful thing, one of the most terrible dooms one can behold, even if one lives to remember it. Yet some among our People hold far more hatred and fear in their hearts for what happened after the spellstorm blew apart.

Shalheira Talandren, High Elven Bard of Summerstar
from **Silver Blades And Summer Nights:
An Informal But True History of Cormanthor**
published in The Year of the Harp

Sudden light kindled in the darkness and the dust. Golden motes of light, drifting up from the open hand of a sorceress who seemed no more than an elf-child. Suddenly the Chamber of the Court was no longer lit only by the flashes of spells, the flickering steel of the Coronal's sweeping blade, and the leaping flames of small fires blazing up tapestries here and there.

Like a sunrise in the morning, light returned to the battlefield.

And battlefield the grand Chamber of the Court had become. Bodies lay strewn everywhere, and amid the risen dust, the sky could be seen faintly through the rent in the vaulted roof of the hall. Huge fragments of the toppled pillar lay tumbled behind the floating throne, with dark rivers of blood creeping out from beneath some of them.

Elves still battled each other all over the Court. Armathors struggled with courtiers and Starym mages here, there, and everywhere, in a tangle of flashing blades, curses, winking rings, and small bursting spells.

The Srinshee was floating in front of the throne, conjured light still streaming up from her tiny body. Lightnings played along the fingertips of her other hand, and stabbed out to intercept spells she deemed too deadly, as they howled and snarled above the littered floor of the Court.

As Nacacia and El found their feet and staggered back into each other's arms, they saw something flicker in the hands of their former master. Suddenly The Masked was holding a stormsword conjured from elsewhere, purple lightnings of its own playing up and down its blade. His face no longer looked so desperate as he watched the Coronal hewing slowly through the Starym retainers gathered in front of their lord speaker.

Llombaerth Starym looked over at the human and the half-elf standing in each other's arms then, and his eyes narrowed.

He crooked a hand, and El felt a sudden stirring in his muscles. "No!" he cried desperately, as The Masked jerked him out of Nacacia's grasp, and lifted his hands to work a spell.

As his eyes were dragged up to focus on the Srinshee, El cried out, "Nacacia! Help me! *Stop* me!"

His mind was flashing through magics as The Masked rummaged his spell roster, seeking one particular spell and, with a warm surge of satisfaction, found it.

It was the spell that snatched blades from elsewhere and transported them, flashing in point-first, to where one desired.

Where the Masked desired the points to go was the eyes and the throat and breast and belly of the Srinshee, as she stood on emptiness deflecting the worst magics of the warring elves.

All over the hall fresh spells flared. Elves who'd hated rivals for years took advantage of the fray to settle old scores. One elf so old that the skin of his ears was nearly transparent clubbed another of like age to the ground with a footstool.

The falling elder's body spread its brains over the slippers of a haughty lady in a blue gown, who didn't even notice. She was too busy struggling against another proud lady in an amber dress. The two swayed back and forth, pulling hair, scratching, and spitting. There was blood on their nails as they slapped, kicked, and flailed at each other in panting fury. The lady in amber slashed open one cheek of the lady in blue; her foe responded by trying to throttle her.

As similar battles raged in front of him, El raised his hands and set his gaze upon the Srinshee.

Nacacia screamed as she realized what was happening, and El felt the thudding blows of her small fists. She jostled him, shoved him, and beat at his head, trying to ruin his spell but not hurt him.

Slowly, fighting his own body but unmoved by the pain she was causing, El gathered his will, took out the tiny sword replicas he needed from the pouch at his belt, lifted his hands to make the gesture that would melt them and unleash the spell, opened his lips, and snarled desperately, "Knock me down! Push me against the floor! I need—*do it!*"

Nacacia launched herself into a desperate, clumsy tackle, and they struck the floor hard, bouncing and driving the wind out of El. He convulsed, arching his body on the smooth, bruising stone as he sought to find air, and she fought to keep on top of him, riding him as a farmer tries to hold down a struggling pig.

He shook himself, dragging her this way and that, and tried to lash out at her, but fell hard on that shoulder, needing his arm for support.

Something was spinning in his mind, rising up out of the depths as he struggled. Something golden.

Ah! Aye! The golden symbol Mystra had put in his mind so long ago gleamed, wavering like a coin seen underwater. Then it shone steadily as he bent his will to capturing it.

The image of the Srinshee overlaid its spinning splendor as The Masked struggled to master El's will, but the golden symbol burst through it.

As Nacacia shoved El's head back down against the stone, he held to that blazing image and gasped, "Mystra!"

His body shuddered, squirmed, and . . . *flowed*. Nacacia tried to slap a hand over his mouth, clinging to him desperately, and El gasped, "Enough! Nacacia, let be! I'm free of him!"

They broke apart, and Nacacia rolled over and up again to find herself staring into the eyes of a human woman!

"Well met," El gasped with a weak grin. "Call me El-mara, please!"

The half-elf stared at him—her—in utter disbelief. "Are you truly . . . yourself?"

"Sometimes I think so," El said with a crooked smile, and Nacacia flung her arms around her long-time companion with a shout of relieved laughter.

It was drowned out, an instant later, by shouts of, "For the Starym! Starym risen!"

The two former apprentices clambered to their feet, stumbling over the motionless body of the Lady Herald, and saw elves crowding into the east side of the hall from behind a tapestry. The last armathors of the court were dying under their swords—and their slayers were a swarm of elves whose maroon breastplates bore the twin falling dragons of House Starym, blazoned in silver.

"Make a stand," someone snapped, near at hand. "Here. Guard the Herald, and keep *them* out from under the Srinshee."

It was Mythanthar, and the sudden hard grip of his bony hands on their shoulders made it clear he was speaking to Elmara and Nacacia. Barely turning to acknowledge him, they nodded dutifully and raised their hands to weave spells.

As the Starym warriors burst across the hall, carving a bloody path through the fighting courtiers with complete disregard for whoever they might be slaying, El unleashed the bladecall spell into the throats and faces of the foremost.

Nacacia sent lashing lightnings over the falling, dying first rank of Starym warriors, to stab into the second. Elves in maroon armor staggered and danced to death amid the hungry bolts.

Then the Srinshee sent a spell down to aid them, a wall of ghostly elven warriors who hacked and thrust in complete harmlessness, but blocked the living elves from advancing until they'd been hewn down, one by one. El and Nacacia used the time that took to pour magic missiles into specific warriors, slaying many.

New faces peered in at the doors of the great chamber, as the heads of mighty Houses came to see for themselves what new madness was ruling the Coronal this day. Almost all of them gaped, turned pale, and hastily retreated. Some few swallowed, drew blades that were more ceremonial than practical, and picked their way cautiously forward through the blood and dust and tumult.

Across the great chamber, the ruler of Cormanthor was fighting for his life, slaughtering Starym courtiers like an angry lion. He was one against many, as they stood in a desperate, struggling wall against him. His blade sang and flashed around him, and only two thrusts had managed to slip past it to stain his white robes red. He was back in battle, where he belonged.

Lord Eltargrim was happy. At last, after twenty long years of whisperings and elf-slaying 'accidents' and rumors of the Coronal's corruption and setbacks in the mythal-work, at last he could find and see a foe. The spells in his blade and shielding the court were both beginning to fail, but if they kept off the worst of the magics these Starym were hurling just a few breaths longer . . .

"Hold him, you fools!" Llombaerth Starym snarled, striking angrily at the backs and shoulders of the retainers who were being driven back against him. The stormsword in his hand whistled as he plied it, using its flat to slap and spank elves who were failing him.

And when the time came, he had one magic no Cormanthan could stop, a dark secret he'd held for years now. He shook it down into his free hand and waited. One clear throw at Eltargrim's face, and the realm would belong to the House of Starym at last.

Then something slapped across his mind, as brutally as he was striking his retainers. The surging scene of the battling Coronal in front of his eyes was blotted out by a scene in his mind—two dark, arresting stars that swam and flowed into the bleak, merciless old face of the mage Mythanthar, wrinkled and spotted with age, but with eyes that held his like two dark flames.

Going somewhere, young traitor?

The mocking words rang louder in his head than the clangor of the Coronal's blade, and Llombaerth Starym found that he could not move, could not look away from the grim old mage who stood facing him in the heart of the chamber, with Starym warriors raging all around and elven blood staining the once-gleaming pave under the old sorcerer's boots.

"Get . . . *out* . . . of my *head!*" The Masked snarled, thrusting desperately with his will.

He might as well have been trying to push an old duskwood tree aside. Mythanthar held him in an unyielding grip, and gave a smile that promised death.

Go down and feed the worms, worthless Starym. Go down to your doom, and trouble fair Cormanthor no more.

That grim curse was still ringing through Llombaerth Starym's head as Eltargrim Irithyl, Coronal of Cormanthor, burst past the last reeling Starym warrior and thrust his glowing blade over the snarling stormsword. The two blades were outlined in fire as they struck the mantle of The Masked together, and breached it. With a sudden wet fire more terrible than anything he had ever felt before, the Lord Speaker of the Starym felt the blade of the Coronal slide into his left side, and up through his heart, and on through to strike his right arm upwards as it burst out of his body. The last thing he felt, as darkness reached up claws to spin him down into its cold and waiting grip, was an irritating itching washing out from where the hilt of the Fang of Cormanthor was nudging against his ribs.

He had to scratch it, he had to . . . the damned old mage was still watching and smiling . . . take him away, sweep him off, let him be . . .

And then Llombaerth Starym left Faerûn without even time for a proper farewell.

* * * * *

"He's dead," Flardryn said bitterly, watching the masked elf slump down out of sight. He turned away from the scrying sphere, not even bothering to watch

as a spell of bright streaking stars rained down from
the Srinshee to fell the Starym army, where they
struggled to win past the human and the half-elf—too
few, too feeble, and too late to win the day, whatever
befell now.

Other Starym stared in white-faced, trembling disbelief at the glowing sphere, where it hovered above
the pool of enchanted water. Tears ran down some of
their chins, but they were older than Flardryn, and so
did not think of turning away. The least one could do
for those who wore the Starym dragons was watch
them until the end, and mark what happened, to
avenge them in time to come. It was simple duty.

"Killed—the Lord Speaker *killed* by the Coronal in
his own court! The throne of the realm slapping the
face of all Starym, that's what it is!" one of the elder
Starym hissed, nose and ears quivering in rage.

The eyes of another senior Starym, this one a lady
so old that her hair had almost all fallen out, and was
mounted now in a jeweled tiara, flickered across to her
outraged kins-elf. She sighed and said sadly, "I never
thought to see the day when a Starym elf—even an arrogant and foolish youngling, overblown by a rank we
should never have given him—would stand in the
Court of Cormanthor and denounce its ruler. And then
to attack him openly, with spells, and plunge the folk
of the court into all this bloodshed!"

"Easy, sister," another Starym murmured, his own
lips trembling with holding back the tears.

"*Have you seen?*" a sudden bellow rang off the rafters
above them, as a distant door banged open against the
wall with booming force. "This means *war!* To spells,
Solonor damn you for witless old weak-knees, to spells! We
must to court before the murderous Irithyl can escape!"

"Have done, Maeraddyth," the broad-shouldered elf
seated closest to the sphere said quietly.

The young elf didn't hear him as he stormed up to the gathered Starym. *"Move*, you gutless elders! Where've you lost your pride, all of you?! Our Lord Speaker *cut down* in his blood, and you all stand around *watching!* What—"

"I said: have done, Maeraddyth," the seated elf said again, just as quietly as before. The raging young male stiffened in mid-growl, and stared down past all the silent faces, each wearing its own shock and sorrow.

The senior archmage of House Starym looked back up at him with mild eyes. "There is a time for throwing lives away," Uldreiyn Starym told his trembling young relative, "and Llombaerth has used it—more than used it—this day. We shall be fortunate if House Starym is not hunted down and slain, to every last trace-blood. Hold your anger, Maeraddyth; if you hurl your life after all those lost in yon chamber—" he inclined his head toward the sphere, where scenes of battle still flickered and flowed, "—you will be a fool, and no hero."

"But Elder Lord, how can you *say* that?" Maeraddyth protested, waving at the sphere. "Are you as craven as the rest of these—"

"You are speaking," Uldreiyn said in a voice of sudden steel, "of your elders; Starym who were revered and celebrated for their deeds when your sire's sire was still a babe. Even when he puled and wailed, he never disgusted me by his childishness as you are doing, here and now."

The young warrior stared at him in genuine astonishment. The archmage's eyes thrust into his like twin spears, keen and merciless. Uldreiyn gestured to the floor, and Maeraddyth, swallowing in disbelief, found himself going to his knees.

The mightiest archmage of House Starym looked down at him. "Yes, it is right to be aghast and angry that one of our own has perished. But your fury should be sent to him, wherever what remains of Llombaerth is wandering now, for daring to drag down all of House Starym into his treachery. To work against a misguided Coronal is one thing; to attack and denounce the ruler of all Cormanthor before all his court is quite another. I am ashamed. All of these kin you deem 'craven' are sad, and shocked, and shamed. They are also thrice your quality, for they know above all that a Cormanthan elf—a noble Cormanthan elf—a *Starym* Cormanthan elf—keeps himself under control at all times, and never betrays the honor and pride of this great family. To do so is to spit upon the family name you are so hot to uphold, and besmirch the names and memories of all your ancestors."

Maeraddyth was white, now, and tears glimmered in his eyes.

"If I was cruel," Uldreiyn told him, "I would share with you some of the memories of Starym you've never known, drowning you in their prides and schemes and sorrows. These kin you ridicule carry such weights, when you are too young and stupid to know true duties. Speak to me not of war, and going 'to spells,' Maeraddyth."

The young Starym burst into tears, and the old mage was suddenly out of his chair and kneeling knee-to-knee with the weeping Maeraddyth, enfolding his shaking arms in a grip like old iron. "Yet I know your rage, and grief, and restlessness, youngling," he said into the young warrior's ear. "Your need to do something, your ache to defend the Starym name. I need that ache to be in you. I need that rage to burn in you. I need that grief to make you never forget the foolishness Llombaerth wrought. You are the future of House Starym, and it is my task to make of you a blade that does not fail, a pride that never tarnishes, and an honor that never, *never* forgets."

Maeraddyth drew back in astonishment, and Uldreiyn smiled at him. The shocked young warrior saw tears to match his own glimmering in the giant elf's eyes. "Now heed, young Maeraddyth, and make me proud of you," the archmage growled.

"You—all of us—" The warrior on his knees was suddenly aware that he knelt in the center of a ring of watching faces, and that tears were falling around him like raindrops in a storm. "—must put this dark day behind us. Never speak of it, save in the innermost rooms of this abode, when no servants are about. We must work to rebuild the family honor, pledge our fealty anew to the Coronal as soon as is safely possible, and swallow whatever punishments he deems fitting. If we are to pay wealth, or give up our young to the Coronal's raising, or see retainers who fought today put to death, so be it. We must distance our House from the actions of those Starym who have defied the Coronal's wishes. We must show shame, not proud defiance . . . or there may soon be no House Starym, to rise to greatness again."

He rose, his firm grip dragging Maeraddyth to his feet also, and looked around at the ring of silent faces. "Do we have understanding?"

There were silent nods.

"Do we have disagreement? I would know now, so that I can slay or mind-meld as necessary." He looked around, eyes hard, but no one, not even the trembling Maeraddyth, said him nay.

"Good. Disturb me not, but dress in your best and wait my return. The Starym who flees this abode is no longer one of us."

Without another word Uldreiyn Starym, senior archmage of the House, strode out from them and marched across the room, face set.

Servants fled at the sight of his face, on the long

walk through the halls to his own spell tower. When its
door closed quietly behind them, he laid a hand on it
and said the word that released the two ghost dragons
from the splendid wyrms of the Starym arms emblazoned on the outer surface of the door.

They prowled up and down the last little stretch of
corridor all night, ready to keep even those of House
Starym out, but no one came to try to win a way past
them. Which was just as well, for ghost dragons are always hungry.

* * * * *

The Pool of Remembrance shone white again, and
the Coronal, looking weary, raised his hand to the
Srinshee where she stood on air beside the throne.
"None of them understand," he said quietly. He
touched the gleaming blade that hung at his side. "For
twenty years and more the foolish younglings of the
great houses struggled to seize the throne. But even
had they triumphed, the victor would have gained no
more than the opportunity to submit to the blade-right
ritual." He looked at Elmara, now Elminster again,
standing with Nacacia and the Lady Herald. "Many
may try that ritual, but only one will be chosen, surviving tests of talent, head, and heart." He sighed.
"They are so young, so foolish." Mythanthar stood listening, a little smile on his face, and said nothing. His
eyes were on the elves busily cleaning the Chamber of
the Court of blood and bodies.

The Coronal said quietly to the Srinshee, "Do it now.
Please."

Above them, the aged child-sorceress touched the
floating Throne of Cormanthor, cast a spell, and then
stood trembling, her eyes closed, as the great sound of
the Calling rolled out through her.

Light lanced from every part of her body. From where those beams touched its walls and ceiling and pillars, the whole vast chamber hummed into a great rising chord.

It built to a soaring height, and then died away as slowly. When it was done, the leaders of all the Houses of Cormanthor stood before the throne, and lesser elves were crowding in the doors.

Eltargrim sheathed his sword and rose slowly through the air until he stood before the throne. When the Srinshee reeled in the aftermath of the mighty magic she'd awakened, he put an arm around her shoulders to support her, and said, "People of Cormanthor, great evil has been done—and undone—here today. Mythanthar declares that he is ready, and I will not wait longer, lest those who seek to control the realm as their private plaything find time to make another attempt, and cost us more Cormanthan lives. Before dusk, this day, the promised Mythal shall be laid, stretching over all the city from the Northpost to Shammath's Pool. When it is deemed stable—which should befall by highsun on the morrow—the gates of the city shall be thrown open to folk of all races who embrace not evil. Envoys shall go out to the known kingdoms of men, and gnomes, and halflings—and yes, dwarves. Henceforth, though our realm shall remain Cormanthor, this city shall be known as Myth Drannor, in honor of the Mythal Mythanthar shall craft for us, and for Drannor, the first elf of Cormanthor known to have married a dwarven lass, long ago though that be."

He looked down and the Lady Herald caught his eye, stepped forward, and announced grandly, "The wizards have been summoned. Let all who abide here keep peace and watch. Let the laying of the Mythal begin!"

EPILOGUE

The Mythal that rose over the city of Cormanthor was not the most powerful ever spun, but elves still judge it the most important. With love, and out of strife, it was wrought, and was given many rich and strange powers by the many who wove it. Elves still sing of them, and vow their names will live forever, despite the fall of Myth Drannor: the Coronal Eltargrim Irithyl; the Lady Herald Aubaudameira Dree, known to minstrels as 'Alais;' the human armathor Elminster, Chosen of Mystra; the Lady Oluevaera Estelda, the legendary Srinshee; the human mage known only as Mentor; the half-elven Arguth of Ambral Isle; High Court Mage Lord Earynspieir Ongluth; the Lords Aulauthar Orbryn and Ondabrar Maendellyn; and the Ladies Ahrendue Echorn, Dathlue Mistwinter, known to bards as 'Lady Steel,' and High Lady Alea Dahast. These were not all. Many of Cormanthor joined in the Song that day, and by the grace of Corellon, Sehanine, and Mystra some of their wants and skills found mysterious ways into the Mythal. Some did not, for treachery never died in Cormanthor, whether it was called Myth Drannor or not . . .

Antarn the Sage
from **The High History of Faerûnian Archmages Mighty**
published circa The Year of the Staff

Armathors who had run from their guardposts at the Coronal's palace hastened into the Chamber of the Court, led by the six court sorceresses. Grim-faced, they drew their blades and made a ring, shoulder to shoulder and facing outwards, on the pave before the throne.

Into that ring stepped the Coronal, his Lady Herald, Elminster, Nacacia, Mythanthar, and the Srinshee. The warriors drew their ranks closed.

Their swords lifted in readiness almost immediately, as a mage hesitantly approached, looking to the Coronal. "Revered Lord?" he asked cautiously, trying not to let his eyes stray to the bloodstains on Eltargrim's white robes. "Have you need of me?"

The Coronal looked to the Srinshee, who said gently, "Aye, Beldroth. But not yet. Those of us here in the ring must die a little, that the Mythal live. Here is not for you."

The elf lord withdrew, looking a little ashamed, and a little relieved. "Join in when the web is spun, and shines out over us," the little sorceress added, and he froze to hear her every word.

"If dying's involved," an ancient and wrinkled elven lady husked then, stepping out of the crowd with a slow hitch to her step, leaning on her cane, "then I might as well go down at last doing some good for the land."

"Be welcome within, Ahrendue," the Srinshee said warmly. But the guards did not move to clear a way into the ring until the Lady Herald said crisply into their ears, "Make way for the Lady Ahrendue Echorn."

Their swords came up, and a murmur rippled across the court, when an elf standing by a far pillar stepped forth and said, "The time for deception is done, I think." An instant later, his slim form rose a head taller, and grew bulkier around the shoulders. Many in the Court gasped. Another human—and this one hidden in their midst!

His face was cloaked in conjured darkness; the tense Cormanthan guards saw only two keen eyes peering at them out of its shadow, but the Srinshee said firmly, "Mentor, you are welcome within our ring."

"Move, stalwarts," the Lady Herald murmured, and this time the warriors were quick to obey.

There was another stir in the crowded hall then, as a line of folk pushed through the assembled Cormanthans. The High Court Mage strode along at the head of this procession, and behind him walked Lord Aulauthar Orbryn, Lord Ondabrar Maendellyn, and a half-elven lord whose cloaked shoulders were surrounded by a whirling ring of glowing gemstones, whom the Srinshee identified in a whisper as "the sorcerer Arguth of Ambral Isle." Bringing up the rear was the High Lady of Art Alea Dahast, slim, smiling, and sharp-eyed.

It was becoming crowded in the ring, and as the Coronal embraced the last of these arrivals, he asked the Srinshee, "Is this all Mythanthar needs, do you think?"

"We await one more," the little sorceress told him, peering over the shoulders of the guards, and finally rising so as to stand on air above them. Playfully Mythanthar began to tap her toes, until she commenced to kick.

"Ah," she said then, beckoning at a face among the gathered citizens. "Our last. Come *on*, Dathlue!"

Looking surprised, the slender warrior stepped forth in her armor, unbuckling the slim long sword that swayed at her hip. Surrendering it to the guards, she slipped into the ring, kissed the Coronal full on the mouth, clapped the Srinshee on the arm, and then stood waiting.

They all looked at each other. The Srinshee looked at Mythanthar, who nodded.

"Widen the ring," the little sorceress commanded crisply. "A long way, now, we need as much space again. Sylmae, did you get all the bows brought in here?"

"No," the sorceress in the ring replied, without turning. "I got the arrows. Holone got the bows."

"And I got some *nasty* wands," Yathlanae put in, from her place along the ring. "Some of these ladies were wearing *four* garters just to carry them all!"

The Srinshee sighed theatrically, and said to Mythanthar, "*Don't* say anything—whatever you're thinking, just don't say it."

The old mage assumed a look of exaggerated innocence, and spread his hands.

The little sorceress shook her head and started taking folk in the ring by the elbows and leading them to where she wanted them to stand, until they stood widely spaced in a ring around Mythanthar, facing inward.

Elminster was surprised to find himself trembling. He shot a look at Nacacia, caught her reassuring smile, and answered it. Then he cast a long look all around the hall, from its floating throne to the gap in the ceiling to the huge, rough sections of toppled, broken pillar and, revealed behind it, the statue of a crouching elven hero who was menacing the Court with his outthrust sword. He stared hard at it for a long moment, but it was just that: a statue, complete with a thin mantle of dust.

He drew in a deep breath, and tried to relax. *Mystra, be with us all now,* he thought. *Shape and oversee this great magic, I pray, that it be what ye saw so long ago, to send me here.*

The Srinshee drew in a deep breath then, looked around at them all, and whispered, "Let it begin."

In the excitement, no one in all that vast hall noticed something small and dark and dusty crawling among them, humping and slithering like some sort of inchworm as it made its slow way out across the bloodstained floor of the chamber—heading steadily for the ring.

Within the ring, Mythanthar spread his hands again, eyes closed, and from his fingers thin beams of light forged out, silent and slow, to link with each person in the ring. He murmured something, and the watching Cormanthans gasped in awe and alarm as his body exploded into a roiling cloud of blood and bones.

Elminster gasped, and almost moved from his place, but the Srinshee caught his eye with a stern look. He could tell from the tear that rolled down her cheek that she'd not known Mythanthar's spell required the sacrifice of his own life.

The cloud that had been the old mage rose like smoke from a fire, and became white, then blinding. The white strands still linking it to the others in the ring glowed with fire of their own.

White flames like tongues of snow soared up to the riven ceiling of the Chamber of the Court, as the bodies of all in the ring suddenly burst into white fire.

The Cormanthans crowded into the hall gasped in unison.

"What is it? Are they dying?" the Lady Duilya Evendusk cried, wringing her hands. Her lord put his own hands on her shoulders in silent reassurance, as Beldroth leaned toward her and said, "Mythanthar is dead—or his body is. *He* will become our Mythal, when 'tis done."

"What?" Elves were crowding forward on all sides to hear.

Beldroth lifted his head and his voice to tell them

all, "The others should live, though the spell is stealing something of the force of life from all of them now. They'll begin to weave special powers—one chosen by each—into it soon, and we'll start to hear a sort of drone, or singing."

He looked back up at the rising, arching web of white fire, and discovered that tears were streaming down his face. A small hand crept into his, and squeezed reassuringly. He looked down into the eyes of an elf-child he did not know. Her face was very solemn, even when she was smiling back up at him. He squeezed her hand back in thanks, and went on holding it.

* * * * *

In a little glade where a fountain laughed endlessly down into a pool of dancing fish, Ithrythra Mornmist straightened suddenly and looked at her lord.

His scrying-globe and papers tumbled from his lap, forgotten, as he stood up. No, he was rising off the ground, his eyes fixed on something far away!

"What is it, Nelaer?" Ithrythra cried, running over to him. "Are you . . . well?"

"Oh, yes," Lord Mornmist gasped, his eyes still fixed on nothingness. "Oh, gods, yes. It's beautiful . . . it's wonderful!"

"What is it?" Ithrythra cried. "What's happening?"

"The Mythal," Nelaeryn Mornmist said, his voice sounding as if he wanted to cry. "Oh, how could we all have been so *blind?* We should have done this centuries ago!"

And then he started to sing—an endless, wordless song.

His lady stared at him for some minutes, her face white with worry. He drifted a little higher, his bare feet rising past her chin, and in sudden fright she clutched at his ankles, and clung.

The song washed through her, and with it all that he was feeling. And so it was that Ithrythra Mornmist was the first non-mage in Cormanthor to feel what a mythal was. When a servant found them a few minutes later, Lady Mornmist was wrapped around her lord's feet, trembling, her face bright with awe.

* * * * *

Alaglossa Tornglara stiffened and sat up in Satyrdance Pool, water streaming from her every curve. She said to the servant who knelt beside her with scents and brushes, "Something's happening. Can you feel it?"

The servant did not reply. Tingling to her very fingertips now, the Lady Tornglara turned to speak sharply to her maid, and stared instead.

The lass was floating in the air, still bent forward with a scent-bottle in her hand, and her eyes were staring. Tiny lightnings flickered and played about them, and darted in and out of her open mouth. She started to moan, then, as if aroused, and the sound changed to a low, wordless, endless song.

Alaglossa started to scream, and then, as the servant—Nlaea was her name, yes, that was it—started to drift higher, she reached out to take hold of the Nlaea's arm.

The servant who heard the scream and sprinted all the long way through the gardens fetched up panting at the pool, and stared at them both: the floating servant and the noble lady who was staring up at her, eyes wide and fixed on something else. They were both nude, and moaning a chant. He looked at them in some detail, swallowed, and then hastened away again. He'd be in trouble if they came back from that humming and saw him staring.

He shook his head more than once, on his way back to his watering. Pleasure spells were certainly becoming powerful things these days . . .

* * * * *

Galan Goadulphyn cursed and felt for his daggers. Just his luck—within sight of the city with all the dwarven gems his boots could hold, and now a patrol was bearing down on him! He looked back at the trees, knowing there was nowhere he could hide, even if he'd been swift enough to outrun them. Gleaming-armored bastards. With weary grace he straightened out of his footsore shuffle and affected a grand manner.

"Ho, guardians! What news?"

"Hold, human," the foremost armathor said sternly. "The city will be open to you at highsun tomorrow, if all goes well. Until then, this is as far as you go."

Galan raised an incredulous eyebrow, and then doffed his dirty head scarf. The strips of false, straggly haired sideburns he was wearing came off with it—rather painfully.

"See these?" he said, flicking one of his ears back and forth with a grubby finger. "I'm no human."

"By the looks of you, you're no elf, either," the armathor said, his eyes hard. "We've seen dopplegangers before."

"No wife jokes, now," Galan told him, waggling a finger. That got him a dirty look (from the armathor) and some chuckles (from the rest of the patrol). "You mean they've *finally* got that mythal thing working? After all these years?"

The guards exchanged looks. "He must be a citizen," one of them said. "None else know about it, after all."

Reluctantly the patrol leader snapped, "Right—you can pass. I suggest you go somewhere you can bathe."

Galan drew himself up. "Why? If you're going to let *humans* in, what does it matter? Hmmph. You'll be telling me dwarves have the run of the city, next!"

"They do," the armathor said, grinding out every word from between clenched teeth. "Now get going."

Galan gave him a cheery wave. "Thank you, 'my *man*,' " he said airily, and flicked a ruby as big as a good grape out of the top of his right boot, to the startled guard. "That's for your trouble."

As he walked on into the city, Galan whistled happily. The gesture—gods above, the looks on their *faces!*—had been worth one ruby. Well, half a ruby. Well . . . was it too late to go and steal it back?

* * * * *

The essence that was Uldreiyn Starym rose up the thin line of flame his careful spell had birthed, touched the web of white fire, and allowed himself to be swept into the growing web of magic. Power surged through him. Yesss . . .

As he flashed along its strands, he deftly spun himself a cloak of fire from a gout of flame here, a strand shaved there, and a node robbed of a flicker of force as he flashed past.

He was just possibly the most powerful worker of magic in all Cormanthor—and if doddering Mythanthar could weave this, then the senior Lord Starym could ride it, and cloak himself in it, and conceal who he was as he rode the glistening white strands across the city and down, down to the gaping hole in the roof of the Court.

His body was still slumped in his chair, at the heart of his dragon-guarded speculum in the tallest tower of

House Starym, the one that stood a little apart. Leaving it behind made him vulnerable—not that these rapture-mazed weavers would notice him until he did something drastic. Which, of course, is what he was here for.

A child could ride a spun spell, once shown how, but he wanted to do more than just ride. Much more. In a world where such as Ildilyntra Starym died and foolish puppies like Maeraddyth had to be kept alive, one had to make one's own justice.

He was plunging down, now, moving as fast as he dared. They were all standing together, and he had to strike the right one without any delay, or risk being sensed by that little shrew the Srinshee or perhaps one of the others he did not know.

Ride the white flames—an exhilarating sensation, he admitted—down, down to . . . *yes!* Farewell, Aulauthar!

His passing saddens us greatly, Uldreiyn thought savagely, as he hurled the full force of his will, bolstered by a burst of the white fire, against the timid, carefully perfectionist mind of his chosen victim. It crumbled in an instant, bathing him in chaotic memories as he wallowed and thrust ruthlessly in all directions.

The watchers in the Court saw one of the living pillars of white flame waver for a moment, but witnessed no other sign of the savage spell attack that burned the brain and innards of Lord Aulauthar Orbryn to ashes, leaving his body a mindless shell.

Now he was part of the weave at last, part of the eager flow and growth of new powers. Orbryn had been crafting the part of the future Mythal that identified creatures by their races. Dragons were to be shut out, were they? Dopplegangers, of course, and orcs, too.

Well, why not expand on Aulauthar's excellent work, and make the Mythal deadly to all non-pureblood elves? Deadly by, say, highsun tomorrow. Dearly though he'd have loved to slay that pollution Elminster, awakening the power now would smite down two more of the weavers of the Mythal—Mentor and the halfblood—and would mean his own certain detection. And after Uldreiyn Starym was dust, they'd simply spin another Mythal to replace the one he'd shattered.

Oh, no, best to bide a bit; he had much grander plans than that.

* * * * *

This outstrips everything but knowing the love of a goddess, Elminster thought, as he soared along pathways of white fire, feeling power surge through him. With every passing instant the grandeur grew, as the Mythal expanded in size and scope. Half a hundred minds were at work, now, smoothing and shaping and making it all larger and more intricate; crossconnected here and augmented there, and . . .

Elminster stiffened, where he was floating in the web, and then whirled through an intricate junction and turned back. There had been sharp, very brief pain and a flash of intolerable heat, followed by a whiff of confusion. A death? Something had gone wrong, something now concealed. Treachery, if that's what it was, could doom the Mythal before it was even born.

It had been a long way back, down and deep. Gods, were they under attack, back in the court? As he descended, his mind flashed out to touch that of Beldroth, part of the expanding web now, humming as he floated just clear of the ground, a wide-eyed child floating with him. People all around were murmuring and drawing back from him warily, but there was more wonder than hostility. No, the guards stood watchfully, but peace held in the Chamber of the Court.

So *where*, then . . . ?

He sank down warily, to where the web was anchored, heading for the elves. The High Court Mage was fine, as was Alea Dahast, an—*no!* There! An awareness that did not belong to Lord Aulauthar Orbryn had peered at him along the white fire, just for a moment; a sentience whose regard had been anything but kindly.

The work the false Orbryn was doing on the Mythal was tainted to destroy all non-elven! This must be why he was here, what he'd spent twenty years working toward! To stop this treachery! *Be with me now, Mystra,* El thought, *for now I strike for thee.*

And riding a plume of white fire, Elminster arrowed down into what had once been Lord Aulauthar Orbryn, and lashed out at who he found there.

The wave of white fire rolled through the ruins of what had once been Orbryn's mind, and El drew back from it a little. The mental bolt that would have impaled him flashed out and missed. The body around them shuddered under its searing impact.

Snarling silently, Elminster struck back.

His bolt was rebuffed by a mind as strong and as deep as his own. An elven elder with whom he'd never brushed minds. A Starym? El sped sideways along the lines of fire, so that the next strike—and his counterstroke—both tore through the construct the false Orbryn had woven, wrecking it beyond repair. The Mythal would not now slay non-elves, whatever else befell.

That left nothing to shield Elminster Aumar. The next thrust from the mighty mind he faced pierced and held him no matter how hard he thrashed, bearing down with mindfire.

Red pain erupted, and with it memories began to flow as they were lost, crashing over him one after another in a racing, confusing flood. Elminster tried to scream and break away, but succeeded only in spinning

himself around, still transfixed on the shearing probe
that was boring deeper and deeper into him.

He saw his attacker for the first time. Uldreiyn
Starym, senior lord and archmage of that House, sneer-
ing at him in serene triumph as he yielded that identi-
fication to the tortured mind he was sundering . . .

Mystra! Elminster cried, writhing in agony. *Mystra,
aid me! For Cormanthor, come to me now!*

The human worm was dying, thrashing, weeping for
his god. Now was the time; the others would sense
something amiss soon enough. Uldreiyn Starym
lashed out at Elminster one more time, and then drew
back long enough to work the magic that would call his
body to himself, to cloak the weakness of his disembodied mind and give him the means to really strike
out, if he had to leave this web under the weight of
many aroused attackers. There! Done. Exultantly, he
surged back to the attack, stabbing again at the shuddering, tumbling human.

* * * * *

There was a stir of fresh excitement in the Court
when the large, burly, grandly robed form of Lord Uldreiyn Starym appeared suddenly within the ring,
standing near the human Elminster. His boots were
firmly on the pave, only inches from something small,
dark, and dusty, that was crawling slowly toward the
young human mage. It stopped for a moment, and wavered, reaching toward the Starym sorcerer's boot, but
then seemed to come to some sort of decision, and resumed its humping, inching progress toward the last
prince of Athalantar.

Holone was not a Sorceress of the Court for nothing.
Something was happening behind her, something
wrong. She spun around. Gods! A Starym!

He was standing still, though, his eyes as vacant as all the rest, and from his mouth and raised hands white fire was streaming, back and forth . . . he was as much a part of the building Mythal as any of them. Starym could never be trusted, but . . . was he a foe?

Holone bit her lip. She was still standing watching, ruled by indecision, when a tapestry and the window behind it burst inward with a crash. Out of the dust and falling rubble a slim figure flew, hands outstretched to spit fire—real fire!

Holone's gasp was echoed by many of the watching Cormanthans. Symrustar Auglamyr—*alive?* Where had she been these twenty years? Holone swallowed and raised her hands to weave a barrier, knowing there was no time.

That gout of flame was already snarling ahead of the flying lady, headed straight for the unseeing Starym. There were shouts and screams and oaths in the Chamber of the Court once more as fire struck Lord Uldreiyn Starym, and spun him around. He staggered, went to one knee, and his eyes flamed in dark fury. He looked at his foe.

The Lady Symrustar Auglamyr was only a few feet away from him, still plunging down on him at full speed, her lips pulled back from her white teeth in a snarl of anger, her eyes aflame. She was shouting something.

"*For Mystra!* A gift for thee, sorcerer, from Mystra!"

The senior Starym sneered in reply as he activated the full force of his mantle.

Elves had swords in their hands, now, and were uncertainly approaching the ring—while armathors and the court sorceresses warned them to stay *back*, for the love of Cormanthor!

They watched, aghast, as the flying lady smashed into something unseen that splintered her arms like

dry branches, flung her head back, and then broke her
legs and spine almost casually as it spun her around
in the air, in a tangle of unbound hair, and flung her
back whence she'd come.

Many of the watching elves groaned as they saw
that twisting, arching, shuddering body aimed firmly
sideways, toward the statue of the elven hero. Steered,
and turned about with cold, exacting precision, to face
them in the last moments before it was thrust onto the
hero's stone sword.

Symrustar Auglamyr threw back her head to cry out
in hoarse agony as the sword burst forth under her
breast, dark and wet with her own blood. Lightnings
sang and played around her as her magics began to
fail.

Uldreiyn Starym put his hands on his hips and
laughed. "So perish all who dare to strike a Starym!"
he told the Court, and lifted his hands. "Who shall be
next? *You*, Holone?"

The court sorceress blanched and fell back, but did
not flee from her place in the ring. She drew in a deep
breath, tossed her head, and said, voice trembling only
a little, "If need be, traitor."

                              * * * * *

He had called, and Mystra had sent Symrustar, and
she was dying for him! Writhing in agony, El could find
no time for grief. *Mystra!* he shouted, as a warrior bel-
lows in battle. *Send me something to aid her! The
Starym prevails! Mystra!*

Something golden shone in his tattered mind—a
thread, a ribbon, moving and turning. His eyes could
not help but follow it, and the image of his unleashing
it that overlaid it briefly. It twisted, to form a shape
thus, and so! Set that upon the foe!

Thanks be, Mystra, El thought with all his heart, and seized on the shape firmly as he lashed out with another bolt, straight at Uldreiyn Starym. This would hurt.

The Starym arch-sorcerer stiffened, turned with slow menace, and smilingly dealt a counterblow, sending a mocking message with it.

Not crazed yet, human? You will be. Oh, you will be.

Oh? Eat this, arrogant elf! Elminster replied in Uldreiyn's mind—and unspun Mystra's weaving.

* * * * *

The watching Cormanthans saw Beldroth shriek first, snatching his hand away from the child to clutch at his head with both hands, clawing at his ears and howling in raw pain.

* * * * *

Lord Nelaeryn Mornmist spasmed and kicked out. His lady was hurled back, bowling over two anxiously watching servants. One of the others rushed forward to aid his convulsing lord, who was shrieking like nothing the servant had ever heard before. Droplets of blood were gouting from his mouth, his eyes, and from under his fingernails. He thrashed in midair like a struggling fish, then slumped, crashing to the ground and smashing the servant senseless beneath him.

Ithrythra Mornmist struggled to her feet. "Nelaer!" she cried, tears streaming down her face. "Oh, Nelaer, *speak to me!*" With frantic fingers she rolled him over, staring at the working face of her lord.

"Get a mage!" she snarled at the servants who were still standing. "All of you *go!* Get *twenty* mages! And *hurry!*"

* * * * *

There was a splashing, and a heavy weight tumbling on top of her. Alaglossa Tornglara came back to awareness with a shock as the waters of Satyrdance Pool closed over her head. She kicked out and thrust herself up to the air again, tumbling a stiff body off of her—Nlaea! Gods, what had happened?

"Help!"

The gardener looked up from his watering. That was the lady's voice!

"Help!"

He hastened, kicking over the waterspout he'd just set carefully down in his haste. It was a long run to Satyrdance Pool, Corellon curse it! He got up onto the path and put some leg into it, only to come to a halt, staring.

The Lady Alaglossa Tornglara, naked as the day she was born, staggered along the path toward him, her feet cut open on the flagstones, leaving a trail of blood behind her as she came. She was cradling her maid Nlaea in her arms, her eyes wild. "Help me!" she roared. "We must get her to the house! Move, Corellon curse you!"

The gardener swallowed and scooped Nlaea out of his lady's arms. Corellon, he reflected wryly, as he turned around to run, was going to have a busy day.

* * * * *

Uldreiyn Starym opened his mouth in surprise—the first time it had worn that expression in earnest in some centuries.

And the last. White fire surged through him and stripped him bare just as he had burned out Lord Orbryn earlier, leaving nothing behind his eyes but a

rushing nothingness. A new potency raced through the
Mythal, crashing through the heads of mages all over
Cormanthor, as the hungry white fire drank the life
and wits and power of the Starym archmage.

The elves standing uncertainly in the Court, not
knowing where or how to strike, saw the tall, broad
body of the great Starym lord blaze forth yellow
flames, for all the world as if he were a tree struck by
lightning.

He burned like a torch before their shocked faces,
while the web of white fire hummed on serenely overhead and profound silence reigned in the Chamber of
the Court. Hundreds of elves held their breaths, until
the blackened body of the archmage toppled, collaps-
ing into swirling ashes.

* * * * *

The backlash spun Elminster away, whirling him
like a leaf in a gale, the golden symbol around him like
a protective hand. When the whirling stopped at last,
the symbol faded, the light leaving him at last in darkness.

He was floating in a void, a sentience without body.
Again.

Mystra? His first call was little more than a whisper.
It seemed he'd done a lot of demanding of the goddess
recently, managing nothing without her aid or guidance.

Think you so? Her voice, in his mind, was warm, and
gentle, and utterly overwhelming. He felt loved and utterly safe, and found himself basking silently in the
warmth coiling around him, floating in timeless, endless joy. It might have been hours before Mystra spoke
again, or only moments.

You have done well, Chosen One. A brave beginning,

but only that: you must abide in Myth Drannor—the new Cormanthor—for a time, to nurture and protect. While you do so, you will also be learning as much as you can of the wielding of magic from those who will come to this bright new fellowship. I am pleased with you, Elminster. Be whole once more.

* * * * *

Abruptly he was elsewhere, floating upright amid many strands of humming white fire, with the shattered stone of a fallen pillar below him and the bloody, pain-etched face of Symrustar Auglamyr in front of him.

There was a chorus of excited whisperings from the elves crowded into the Chamber of the Court, but El scarcely heard it. Mystra had left extra spell energy tingling in his hands, far too much for him to carry for long, and he thought he knew why.

She was a broken thing, her body slumped atop the stone sword that impaled it. Only the failing magics around her had kept her alive this long. With infinite care Elminster lifted the dying elven lady in his arms and drew her off the bloody blade.

She gasped and opened her eyes at his touch, and then sagged against him, her ravaged body quivering once when she slid entirely free of the stone. El thrust a hand against the terrible hole through her ribs and let healing power flow out of him.

She caught her breath and shuddered then, daring to hope—and breathe—for the first time in a long while.

El turned her in the air until he was cradling her in his arms, and drifted very slowly down to the floor. As his knees touched the pave, he could feel the regard of many elven eyes, but he bent his head forward and kissed Symrustar's bloody mouth as if they'd been ardent lovers for years. Holding her lips with his, he thrust life into her, letting all the power Mystra had given him flow into her shattered body. Then he gave of his own vitality, holding his mouth on hers, until trembling weakness made him rise to breathe at last.

She spoke for the first time then, a ragged whisper. "'Tis you, isn't it, Elminster? I certainly had to wait long enough for that kiss."

El chuckled and held her against him as the light in her eyes came back.

Almost lazily her eyes found Faerûn again, and the shattered ceiling of the Court, and then him. Slowly, wincing and working her mouth, she managed a smile. "I thank you for making my passing easier . . . but I am dying; you cannot stay that. Mystra snatched me from death that night in the woods—the death Elandorr planned for me—for a task. I have served her, and . . . 'tis done. I can die."

Elminster shook his head slowly, aware of the anxious faces and raised hands of the sorceresses Sylmae and Holone waiting above him—waiting to blast Symrustar with spells should she try any last treachery.

"Mystra does not treat folk so," El told her gently.

Symrustar grimaced as a fresh ripple of pain ran through her. A rivulet of bright blood ran from the corner of her mouth. "So you say, Chosen One. I am an elf, and one who misused magic, at that. I tried to enslave you—I would have stolen your magic and slain you. Why should she have a care about my fate?"

"For the same reason I care," El said gently.

Those pain-ridden eyes flickered. "Love? Lust? I know not, man. I cannot tarry to think on it . . . life slips away. . . ."

"One life," Elminster told her urgently, as he realized Mystra's plan at last. "But not all that is Symrustar."

He pulled open the bloodsoaked ruin of her bodice, and upon the ravaged flesh beneath traced the first golden symbol Mystra had put in his mind; the one that would shine there forever.

Her breath caught, and she sat up, eyes shining. "I—I see at last. Oh, human, I have wronged you from the start. I have—"

She wasted no more time on words, as blue-white fire stole out of her skin to claim her, but turned into his embrace to kiss him tenderly.

Her lips were still on his as she faded away. A few motes of blue-white light swirled where she'd been, and then flickered and were gone.

El looked up, and saw four of the weavers, their limbs still ablaze with white fire and linked to the web above, standing above him, looking down with love and concern.

He looked up and told the Srinshee, Lady Steel, the Herald Alais, and the Coronal, "Mystra has claimed her. She will serve the Lady of Mysteries now."

Something crawled up his arm, then, and he snatched at it and held it up, bewildered. A scrap of something dusty, bloodstained, and moving—the mask that Llombaerth Starym had worn for so long. It tingled in his grasp, warm and somehow welcoming.

As he stared at it, there was a sudden flare of rainbow-hued light from overhead, and all the gathered elves gasped in awe. The Mythal was born!

Elminster felt a stirring in his throat, and rose with all the others, to join in what he could already hear echoing through the streets. All over Cormanthor, every elf and half-elf and human was breaking into song. The same swelling, involuntary song of the Mythal's birth—high, radiant, beautiful, and unearthly. And as the singers turned to embrace each other in wonder, every face was wet with tears.

* * * * *

"Yes," Lord Mornmist whispered, his eyes on something far away. The servants looked from his vacant face to that of their lady. Tears ran in floods down her face, dripping from her chin, as she bent over her lord.

"Why?" she whimpered frantically. "*Why* do the mages not come?"

The servants shot anxious looks at each other, not daring to answer. Then Nelaeryn Mornmist rose up out of their gentle hands as if torn aloft by some invisible hand. Ithrythra screamed, but her shrieks turned to sobs of joy an instant later, as her lord opened his eyes and cried out, "Yes! At last! The glory is come to Cormanthor!"

His voice rang like a trumpet as he hung in the air above them, and blue flames spurted from his eyes. He looked down.

"Oh, Ithrythra," he called, "come and share this with me. All of you, come!" He held out his hand, and there were gasps as the Mornmist servants below felt themselves lifted with infinite gentleness, and awesome power, up into the air to join the man whose laughter rang out, then, like triumphal horns.

* * * * *

Nlaea moved in the gardener's arms, and made a small, satisfied sound. He looked down, slipped on the path, and almost dropped her.

"Careful!" the Lady Alaglossa Tornglara snapped at his elbow, her strong arms steadying both him and his burden.

Nlaea moved again, stretching almost luxuriously, and her weight was suddenly gone. The gardener stumbled, overbalanced by its sudden disappearance, and slid into a galamathra bush.

"Nlaea?" Alaglossa cried in terror. "Nlaea!"

Her maid turned in the air and smiled down at her. "Be at peace, Lady," she said softly, and blue flames seemed to blaze in her eyes as she spoke. "Cormanthor is crowned at last."

And as her maid hovered over her, the Lady Alaglossa went to her knees on the path and started to pray through happy floods of tears.

* * * * *

Galan Goadulphyn looked around in disbelief. On all sides, elven bodies were floating up into the air, and there was much laughter, and weeping—happy weeping. Here and there shouts of exultation rose. Had all Cormanthor gone mad at once?

He hastened toward a richly appointed house whose door stood open. Well, if everyone was going to be lost in celebration, perhaps they'd not notice the loss of a few baubles.

He was almost inside when firm fingers took hold of his left ear. He wrenched himself free and spun around, hand snatching out a dagger. "Who—?" he snarled—and then fell silent, gaping.

The lady some had known as the most beautiful and deadly in all Cormanthor smiled almost dreamily at him as she floated in the doorway, blue fire playing about her limbs. "Why, Galan," Symrustar Auglamyr said delightedly, "you please me greatly. To think that at long last you've put thieving behind you, and have come to the houses of Myth Drannans to repay them in gems for all that you've stolen!"

Galan's face twisted in utter incredulity. "What? Repay? 'Myth Drannans'?"

Those were the last words he uttered before lips that blazed came down on his—and gems started to fly out of his boots like angry wasps leaving a nest, away into the bright air of Myth Drannor.

* * * * *

Moonrise over Myth Drannor that first night was a time of joy. Horns blew and harps were struck in a delighted cacophony, as if a year's festivals and revels had been rolled into one frantic celebration. Thanks to the silent, invisible wonderwork that overlaid the city like a domed shield, those who'd never been able to fly before could do so now, without need of spell or item. The air was full of laughing, embracing elves. Wine flowed freely, and troths were plighted with eager abandon. The moon was full and bright, and spilled down through the riven roof of the Chamber of the Court in a bright flood.

An elven lady glided alone into the empty room, her jeweled slippers treading air above the bloodstained pave. The hems of her low-cut gown glittered with a breathtaking fall of gems, and on her breast diamonds sparkled in the shape of twin falling dragons. Only streaks of white and gray at her temples betrayed her age as she moved sinuously through the stillness, coming at last to where a small pile of ashes lay in the bright pool of moonlight.

She looked down at them in silence for a long time, the quickening rise and fall of her breast the only difference between her and a statue. A tattered song floated in through the rent in the roof above as joyous elves soared past, and the silent lady clenched her fists so tightly that blood dripped from where her long nails pierced her palms.

Lady Sharaera Starym raised her beautiful head to look at the moon riding high above, drew in a deep breath, looked down at what little was left of her

Uldreiyn, and hissed fiercely, "The Mythal must fall, and Elminster must be *destroyed!*"

Only the ghosts were there to hear her.

At the time of the laying of the Mythal, some of the elves of Cormanthor thought opening their realm to other races was a mistake. I'm sure some still do.

There was some small dispute and bother at the time, as there is at the birthing of any new thing that is not a living babe, but nothing that minstrels or sages need be overly concerned about. A matter of a few swords, a handful of spells, and some hasty words, followed by a party. In short, it was very like most of what human heroes are wont to call "adventures."

Elminster the Sage
from a speech to an assembly of Harpers in Twilight Hall,
Berdusk
The Year of the Harp

Starlight & Shadows

New York Times best-selling author Elaine
Cunningham finally completes this stirring trilogy
of dark elf Liriel Baenre's travels across Faerûn!
All three titles feature stunning art from award-
winning fantasy artist Todd Lockwood.

New paperback editions!

DAUGHTER OF THE DROW
Book 1

Liriel Baenre, a free-spirited drow princess, ventures beyond the dark halls
of Menzoberranzan into the upper world. There, in the world of light, she
finds friendship, magic, and battles that will test her body and soul.

TANGLED WEBS
Book 2

Liriel and Fyodor, her barbarian companion, walk the twisting streets of
Skullport in search of adventure. But the dark hands of Liriel's past still
reach out to clutch her and drag her back to the Underdark.

New in hardcover – the long-awaited finale!

WINDWALKER
Book 3

Their quest complete, Liriel and Fyodor set out for the barbarian's homeland
to return the magical Windwalker amulet. Amid the witches of Rashemen,
Liriel learns of new magic and love and finds danger everywhere.

The Avatar Series

New editions of the event that changed all Faerûn...and the gods that ruled it.

SHADOWDALE
Book 1 • Scott Ciencin

The gods have been banished to the surface of Faerûn,
and magic runs mad throughout the land.

TANTRAS
Book 2 • Scott Ciencin

Bane and his ally Myrkul, god of Death, set in motion a plot to seize
Midnight and the Tablets of Fate for themselves.

The New York Times best-seller!

WATERDEEP
Book 3 • Troy Denning

Midnight and her companions must complete their quest by traveling
to Waterdeep. But Cyric and Myrkul are hot on their trail.

PRINCE OF LIES
Book 4 • James Lowder

Cyric, now god of Strife, wants revenge on Mystra, goddess of Magic.

September 2003

CRUCIBLE: THE TRIAL OF CYRIC THE MAD
Book 5 • Troy Denning

The other gods have witnessed Cyric's madness
and are determined to overthrow him.

October 2003